MELANIE BLAKE

Guilty Women

HarperCollins*Publishers*

HarperCollins*Publishers*
1 London Bridge Street,
London SE1 9GF

www.harpercollins.co.uk

HarperCollins*Publishers*
1st Floor, Watermarque Building, Ringsend Road
Dublin 4, Ireland

Published by HarperCollins*Publishers* Ltd 2022
1

A catalogue copy of this book is available from the British Library.

ISBN: 978-0-00-850560-8 (HB)
ISBN: 978-0-00-850561-5 (TPB)

This novel is entirely a work of fiction.
The names, characters and incidents portrayed in it are
the work of the author's imagination. Any resemblance to
actual persons, living or dead, events or localities is
entirely coincidental.

Typeset in Meridien by Palimpsest Book Production Limited,
Falkirk, Stirlingshire

Printed and bound in the UK using 100% Renewable Electricity
at CPI Group (UK) Ltd

MIX
Paper from
responsible sources
FSC
www.fsc.org   **FSC™ C007454**

GUILTY WOMEN

Melanie Blake is the bestselling author of *Ruthless Women*, which became a Number 4 *Sunday Times* hardback bestseller and an ebook bestseller in 2021, selling over 150,000 copies and translated into several foreign languages, captivating readers around the world. *Guilty Women* is her second novel about the 'fictitious' cast of 'Falcon Bay', and her first with HarperCollins. Melanie previously built up a hugely successful acting agency from scratch where she managed clients from some of the biggest internationally syndicated shows in the world.

In 2018, Melanie decided to concentrate on her other passion, writing. They say write about what you know, and *Ruthless Women* and *Guilty Women* are tales that only a true television insider could create . . .

www.melanieblakeonline.com
@MelanieBlakeUK
/MelanieBlakeUK

Also by Melanie Blake

Ruthless Women
The Thunder Girls

This book is dedicated to *you*, my
wonderful readers.
I'm eternally grateful for your love of my
'twisted tales'.
Hold on tight and fasten your seatbelts,
it's going to be another *bumpy ride* . . .

Falcon Bay's on- and off-screen players . . . The Living, the Dead and the Missing

Amanda King – 50-year-old kind-hearted, truly decent woman, a real rarity in show business. Recently promoted to sole runner and executive producer of global smash hit drama *Falcon Bay*. A talented, caring woman and devoted mother with a good heart who is now enjoying being loved by her new partner, production accountant Dan, after years in a loveless marriage with her estranged husband, Jake Monroe.

Jake Monroe – Former Head of Drama and showrunner of *Falcon Bay*, ousted by his wife Amanda and her all-female associates at CITV, the production company which makes the long-running soap. Bitter, angry, vengeful and determined to regain control of the network and the island. Well preserved mid-sixties, but whilst attractive on the outside, he's ugly on the inside.

1

Melanie Blake

Catherine Belle – Falcon Bay's leading actress. 71 years old and fabulous with it. She's won every award all over the globe for her portrayal of the lovable 'Lucy Dean' – Falcon Bay's famous beach bar owner. This show is her life, so much so that she's gone to shockingly great lengths to stay in it, and in the home it provides her on the beautiful island of St Augustine's Cove.

Sheena McQueen – Fifty something strong alpha female. Agent to Catherine Belle and CEO of the McQueen Agency. The toughest agent out there, who has every network by the balls. Once a child star on a globally syndicated drama called *Second Chances,* and herself a victim of dead sexual predator Jeff Nichols. She's sexy, ballsy and most importantly, she takes no shit from anyone. Do not mess with Sheena McQueen . . .

Chad Kane – Forties. Mourning widower husband of Madeline. Six foot five with shoulders like a tank. Rugged, deeply likeable, son of an extreme Southern Baptist evangelical preacher from the Deep South. Adored his wife and won't rest until he gets to the bottom of her suspicious death.

Helen Gold – Head of Casting on *Falcon Bay* and has been at the network since day one. A determined, sensual woman in her early sixties who has always had a thing for younger men, but has recently had her eye turned by a mature man, which has confused her. Helen despises Jake Monroe . . .

Farrah Adams – Late forties. Former child actress turned writer and only female director on *Falcon Bay* – close friend to Helen, Sheena, Catherine and Amanda. Has spent her whole

2

life fighting the sexist studio system that pitches men higher than women.

Ross Owen – Ruthless showbiz hack in his fifties, editor of tabloid newspaper *The Herald*, toxic blogger and would-be author – a true low-life. If it's bad and online or in the papers, then he's usually behind it . . .

Mickey Taylor – 70. Owner of Fonda Books, home of the tell-all celebrity biography. Dripping in money and lacking in taste, subtlety is not Mickey's thing and he can spot a battered celebrity with a juicy tale to tell a mile off. Publisher and agent of missing star Honey Hunter.

Candy Dace – Australian, mid-twenties, ruthlessly ambitious assistant producer with ambitions as high as the splits in her revealing dresses. Will do whatever it takes to climb the career ladder, preferably in six-inch heels.

Tabitha Tate – Reporter on tabloid newspaper *The Herald* and podcast host. Late twenties, from New York, came to London to further her credentials before heading to Hollywood where she wants to 'make it big'. Sassy, determined and dangerously ambitious.

Dead

Madeline Kane – Former owner of CITV and stunningly beautiful wife of billionaire Chad. He inherited the network that makes *Falcon Bay* following her on-screen death during the broadcast of the now infamous Christmas Day live episode two months ago.

Missing

Honey Hunter – 50. Oscar-winning actress and former lover of Jake Monroe. She was due to take a leading role in *Falcon Bay* during its Christmas Day live episode, but disappeared out of the public eye on the eve of her big comeback and hasn't been seen since.

Part 1

Chapter 1

<u>February</u>

Every brightly decorated street, building, bar or restaurant – and even all the houses the cab from Louis Armstrong International Airport passed on the way to their hotel – looked exactly how Sheena McQueen had always imagined they would during New Orleans' world-famous Mardi Gras celebrations.

Even when she'd backpacked around the globe in her twenties before setting up the now world-famous McQueen Agency in London, Sheena had never been to the Deep South. It truly looked magnificent. The quaint wooden houses that popped out of the landscape reminded her of George Rodrigue's famous Cajun paintings. She had an original of his 'Blue Dog' at home and had always loved the vibrancy of it, the way his work seemed to come alive. It was the only pet she'd ever allow in her pristine home, although there'd certainly been some animals passing through her doors. She was just making a mental note to try to visit his studios to pick up something to add to her collection, when she reminded herself why she

5

was here and refocused on what was going to be an incredibly difficult day ahead.

In defence of finding herself distracted, she reasoned that the decision to hold Madeline Kane's funeral in the midst of a carnival was bizarre, rather like a plot from one of the soap operas her renowned clients appeared in. She really hadn't wanted to come, but her number-one client Catherine Belle was attending, and despite Sheena's best efforts, nothing, not even getting *Falcon Bay* executives to deny Catherine official leave, could stop her. Even though *Falcon Bay* was the show that had made her a star, Catherine didn't always play by its rules. She had been determined to attend and as it certainly wasn't safe to let her go alone, Sheena had extended her role as agent into that of chaperone.

They'd barely spoken a word on their two-hour boat journey from St Augustine's, where *Falcon Bay* was filmed, to Paris to catch their thirteen-hour flight to America, but Sheena had been glad of the pods in First Class that kept them apart, helping to ease the awkwardness of how tense Catherine clearly was. The morning after checking into their suites at the Maison de la Luz, a stunning boutique guest house close to the French Quarter of the city, they were picked up by a limousine to join the Kane family on the infamous *Delta Queen* steamboat.

Since Catherine had officially been cleared by the police of any involvement in her co-star Madeline's death, Sheena hoped her continued silence, although uncomfortable to endure, could ultimately work in their favour. The last thing she needed was for Catherine to say something she shouldn't when the case had been finally been closed. But with the way she was acting, which was unnervingly unpredictable for a woman she'd known for thirty years, Sheena intended to stick to her side all day. Once on board the mourning vessel, she'd only left her alone once, when she'd needed the bathroom, which was, annoyingly, below decks.

Now, as the ornate three-tiered steamboat chugged along the waters of the Mississippi, Sheena quickly started making her way across the crowded deck back towards Catherine. It was so packed that it was going to take some time before she could take up her guardswoman position once more.

Sheena had googled the *Delta Queen* before they'd arrived, as she was certain it had been famously retired and was no longer in service. Sure enough, she'd been right; clearly, the Kane family had serious clout in this part of the world to get an old girl like this back on the water. If Wikipedia was right, the vessel was known to be haunted by the wife of the man who'd owned the company that had made it, and when it had been in service, her spirit was said to be heard often around its vast interiors late at night. She wasn't usually bothered by that sort of thing but considering why they were here, Sheena hoped old Mary Becker Greene's ghost would be the only one on board today.

Taking her third glass of wine from a passing waiter's tray, Catherine Belle, a woman who usually sipped any alcohol with the same delicacy a newly married princess may demonstrate at her first state gala, took several large gulps until it was empty. She reached out to take another glass and did the same. How could it have only been eight weeks since *that day*? she mused, almost haze-like as the alcohol washed over her system. She hadn't eaten in days, so an empty stomach combined with the heat had given the wine extra power.

Feeling slightly unsteady on her feet, she moved closer towards the boat's edge and out of the protective shadow of its canopy. The sun's rays beat down on her. Due to all the chemical peels she'd had to keep her looking years younger than the seventh decade she was in, she usually avoided even the merest hint of the sun, like a vampire hiding in a turret. Today, she didn't care. She could feel the fabric of her dress clinging to her skin, but as uncomfortable as she was, the heat was the least of her problems. Her mind ambled away from the noise of the steamboat and its teary-eyed passengers, back to the terrible night when she'd gone into battle with Madeline Kane on the set of *Falcon Bay* – a battle only one of them had survived.

Just feet away was Madeline's widower, Chad Kane, who was sobbing violently, flanked by his father, Chad Senior, and his sister Melissa. He looked about as broken a man as she'd ever seen in her life – and she'd seen a lot of broken men, off screen as well as on. She knew a performance, and this wasn't one: this was horribly, gut-wrenchingly real, and *she* was responsible.

The guilt she felt was all-consuming; it clawed its way up the back of throat and into her mouth. Keeping silent was almost choking her. She knew coming to the funeral had been a risk, but like a moth to a proverbial flame, she'd *had* to be here. As Chad let out another wail, suddenly, Catherine could take it no more. Overcome with the desperate need to unburden her terrible secret and let Chad's tears turn to anger, she took an unsteady step towards the family in her six-inch black stilettos, bracing herself to finally speak her truth, but found herself in the shadow of Sheena, who had returned from below the deck and was deliberately blocking her way.

'Turn around now,' Sheena mouthed silently, and the two women moved away from the family and back towards the boat's edge. Even dressed in the thinnest of the linen suits she owned, Sheena was finding the heat unbearable. The humidity in the air was making her sweat, something she rarely did. 'And wipe your eyes,' Sheena said quietly to Catherine, who had mascara streaking out from under her square Prada sunglasses.

Sheena knew Catherine well enough to recognise when she was about to lose it, and that would never do – not now they'd come this far. Sheena enjoyed watching lesbian prison porn from the comfort of her silk-covered queen-size bed, but that was as close to visiting an incarceration centre as she ever wanted to get, and she most certainly did not want to see her most bankable client behind bars either.

Slipping an arm around Catherine's shoulders, Sheena pulled her in closer. To anyone watching, they looked just like any of the other guests – overcome with emotion. Silently, the women scanned what looked like hundreds or possibly thousands of mourners who'd lined the banks of the Mississippi to pay tribute to the dead wife of the city's favourite son as the boat slowly came to a stop on the Tchefuncte River, next to a docking bay with a huge sign above it, almost billboard size, showing the late Madeline Kane in all her glossy-haired, full-lipped glory. The words above her beautiful face read *we will never forget you*.

Sheena couldn't wait for the day when they all could.

As the vessel docked, more waiters passed amongst the crowd, offering long-stemmed white roses to throw into the water. Sheena winced as she felt one prick her finger, causing it to bleed. The thorns were still on the stems, which seemed strange considering they were being placed in people's hands. As she reached into her handbag to look for a tissue to stem the blood, a faint smile crossed her lips – perhaps leaving them on was actually rather appropriate, considering who they were for.

Catherine hadn't taken a rose; her eyes had stayed firmly on Chad as he walked slowly and sombrely, carrying a golden urn in his manly hands. When he reached the boardwalk, which stretched about twelve feet in length over the water, he hovered underneath Madeline's image and began hugging the urn close to his chest as the tears once again ran down his handsome face. He howled like an injured animal. His broad shoulders were shaking, and his sister Melissa rushed towards him, placing her arm around his waist.

Unable to watch any longer, Catherine closed her eyes behind her sunglasses and tried to block the sound out with an actor's rhyme she often used before filming a scene. Sheena, who was still holding a tissue to her injured finger, was transfixed by Chad. With Melissa's support, he had finally got his sobbing under control. Slowly, he turned away from his wife's image and back towards the passengers and onlookers on the riverbank.

'There are so many things I need to say, but I do not know if I will get through them,' he started, his usually velvety deep Southern accent strained and almost high-pitched with the pain and anguish in his words. 'It was right here, where we are now, that Madeline agreed to be my wife,' he managed, before taking a breath, which evened his voice out enough for him to continue. 'It may have seemed like I was the giant one,' he said, clearly in reference to his six foot five height and his impressive body, which had even Sheena, who hadn't slept with a man in twenty- five years, wondering what he looked like under his funeral suit. 'But it was my wife who was the true strength of us. She was my backbone, my everything, *my princess.*'

Catherine's rhyme wasn't working, and Chad's words were infiltrating her ears. There was nothing else for it; she was going to have to let Chad's pain in. Linking arms with Sheena, she allowed her gaze to fall on him.

'I know how much you all loved Madeline,' he continued.

In the far corner, Sheena noticed that Chad Snr didn't look as moved by his son or daughter's grief, which was interesting. 'And you know how much she loved our city,' Chad continued. 'She once told me she felt born again in New Orleans and her life here with me. To think she was so close to coming home when she was taken away from us is too much to bear.' He looked up again at Madeline's face, which shone out like that of a movie star at a premiere, then raised the urn up in a gesture to her. 'You'll always be a part of all of us,' he said, turning to the crowds on the riverbank, who began a round of applause that was soon deafening, and starting to unscrew the lid of the urn.

'You will live on in our ever-flowing river, my darlin'.' Chad spoke softly as he stepped to the end of the walkway and poured Madeline's ashes over hundreds of lily pads, which had been placed in a heart shape and were floating on the water. Melissa once again walked over to his side, looking worried he was going to follow the ashes over the edge, but Chad stepped back and composed himself. 'Tomorrow our festival will be in full swing, and you know how much my wife loved our special traditions, so as much as my heart is broken, I urge you all to celebrate this year more than ever before. Do it in honour of the finest woman I was lucky enough to ever know – our Mardi Gras Queen.'

The crowds clapped again. Sheena squeezed Catherine's arm as the two of them silently watched Chad pick up a glass of champagne and raise it up to his wife's effigy.

'Ladies and gentlemen, raise your glasses and salute the first lady of your city, my baby doll,' he said, tipping the flute towards her image. 'I'm counting the days until we can be together again. I will love you forever.' With that, his voice faltered, and Melissa took over.

'To Madeline,' she toasted. All the mourners on the boat

11

chanted her name as another round of applause rang out from the crowds. Chad Snr raised his glass ever so slightly lower than everyone else.

'Right, time to go,' Sheena said, with the skill of a ventriloquist, her lips barely moving as she discreetly guided Catherine across the packed deck and towards the mooring ramp.

Silently they strode up the gantry and were just feet away from the exit when Chad's father appeared before them.

'Ladies,' he said, in a Louisiana drawl that sounded straight out of *A Streetcar Named Desire*. 'Since you've come all this way, I'd like you to come for dinner at the house tonight. Despite the circumstances, it would be improper of me not to extend our hospitality.'

'That is so kind of you, Mr Kane,' Sheena said, as calmly as she could muster. She was still surprised at how he had managed to move along the boat to the exit at the exact moment she would have expected him to be by his grieving son's side. She also noted the passengers' attention was now on him and not his son; clearly, his role as preacher and pastor for New Orleans' biggest evangelical church had made him quite the name around these parts.

'But sadly, we have an early flight to catch as Catherine is filming,' she said. She gestured towards Chad, who was crying again, and lowered her voice. 'We wouldn't want to intrude. I'm sure you need some private time as a family to grieve. We just came to pay our respects.'

Catherine nodded in agreement.

'Nonsense,' Chad Snr continued, ignoring Sheena's attempt to reference the state his son was in. He reached out a hand and touched Catherine's.

'The Kane Foundation, which of course now owns Madeline's shares in the production company where your divine Ms Belle here does her finest work, officially insists.' He cast his eyes over Catherine's beauty with obvious appreciation, then came eye-to-eye with Sheena, a little less admiringly.

'A car will pick you up at eight this evening; my people will rebook your flights for later in the day, at the Foundation's cost of course.' He leaned in a little closer to Catherine as Sheena tried not to bristle.

'Being well-known myself, I understand that a great star like you will want to avoid the official wake, so as not to be pestered,' he continued, moving even nearer. 'So I can assure you that at the house there will just be our family, and of course, the Good Lord above who is ever present. I'm sure He is impressed with your kindness to come all this way, just as we all are.' He finished by squeezing her hand gently, then stepped back as the women began to exit.

'See y'all tonight,' he called out as Sheena and Catherine's heels clicked on the boardwalk and into the sunshine.

'Oh my god. I can't go,' Catherine hissed as they made their way towards a fleet of waiting limousines, where a driver was holding the door open for them. 'If he starts with the religion, I'll crack, I know I will. I don't know how much more I can take.'

As soon as they entered the car, Catherine began to sob almost as loudly as Chad had. The handsome young driver looked into his mirror at her with concern.

'It's been an emotional day,' Sheena said calmly. 'Maison de la Luz, please.' Then, looking as though she was comforting her friend, she leaned closer to Catherine and whispered in her ear.

'Don't say another word until we're back at the hotel.'

The car drove off as fireworks were released from the boat behind them, turning the dusky sky the colour of a rainbow. After a few hours' sleep, aided by the Xanax Sheena had scored from Peyton – the hot hotel receptionist who'd made it very clear whilst checking them in that she was happy to accommodate 'any special requests' – Catherine was feeling a bit more composed. She'd swept her hair into an updo, which not only showed off her fine jawline but would help keep her cool in the heat. She finished doing her make-up – not too heavily; humidity was a killer for foundation. She'd just used the lightest BB cream she had, added extra lashes to give her Bardot eyes, then completed the look with some nude lip gloss. Happy with what she saw in the mirror, she popped another Xanax, downed her glass of wine, then slipped on the vintage Zandra Rhodes she'd had since the eighties. The white sleeveless maxi dress was not only simple and elegant, but more importantly, unlined, meaning she was less likely to feel the heat.

As she felt the drugs mellow her mood out even further, Catherine sprayed Opium perfume across her shoulders and pondered how much she'd changed since what had happened on Christmas Day. Her whole life, she'd avoided taking most prescription drugs, a true believer in herbal remedies and rest as the best way to deal with life's ups and downs. But she was plagued with nightmares of the moment she'd pulled her hand away from her co-star thrashing about in the water, reaching for her help. Every night since, Madeline's screams, the same ones which had been broadcast live into millions of homes all over the world as her on-and off-screen enemy had met her demise, had filled her every sleeping moment. No amount of Rescue Remedy or soothing bath salts could wash away that guilt, and so this daily cocktail mix had become her coping mechanism.

She was just closing the clasp on her morganite pendant, which hung low around her neck, when Sheena's familiar knock on the door drew her mind out of that dreadful day in the past and back into what she was sure was going to be a dreadful night in her present.

'Come in,' she called out, and Sheena entered. She was wearing a white trouser suit with a matching fedora hat that made her look a bit like a seventies-style mafia boss. Sensing Catherine's reaction to her outfit, Sheena raised an eyebrow.

'I'm dressed for the mood of the evening; I feel I'll need to be on protection duty around old Chad Senior. He looked like a man with lust in his eyes to me,' she said with a smirk, as she gestured for Catherine to grab her bag and follow her out. Catherine slipped her lip gloss, phone and foundation brush into her peach calfskin YSL clutch. Sheena noticed her slide in what was left of the strip of Xanax she'd scored for her after she'd already got through her own stash.

'I'll look after those,' she said, walking over, taking them from Catherine's bag and slipping them into her pocket. 'You know you're not supposed to mix them with booze. We don't want any confessional outbursts over the amuse-bouches, do we?' she said dryly.

The Kane mansion was set high in New Orleans' Garden District. Although it was only a four-mile drive from where they were staying in the Vieux Carré, it might as well have been on a totally different continent – the two areas couldn't have been more opposite. As their car took them past the Grecian-style mansions, many flanked by huge grand pillars with beautiful gardens, it was clear to the women that the Kanes lived in the very finest part of town.

'Being a spokesman for God clearly pays well,' Sheena said as their car entered a massive drive bordered by oak trees, which looked hundreds of years old. They're all corrupt, these preacher types, you know; you don't get an estate like this without some sort of game going on, do you?'

Catherine wasn't listening; she had the window open and

was taking in the scent of the magnolias and sweet olive trees dotted around the huge courtyard. The car finally stopped. It was only when they exited that they could take in the sheer grandeur of the Kane family estate.

'It's like something from a film set,' Catherine breathed in awe, for a moment forgetting her dread, impressed with the sheer magnificence of the building.

'Yes, a horror movie,' Sheena replied dryly. 'Let's just hope we can get through dinner with everyone still alive.'

Catherine shot her a look, which Sheena took as a sign to stop her jokes as the huge, ornate double-doored entrance doors swung open and Chad Snr appeared.

'Ladies,' he drawled. 'Come in, come in.' Two male servants were holding the doors open as he gestured for Sheena and Catherine to follow him into a big hallway. It had the highest ceilings Catherine had ever seen. Above them were portraits of the family, with dust marks where it looked like some pictures had been recently removed, creating gaps in the wall. Sheena noticed that none of them featured Madeline.

'As everything has been so emotional today, I've stripped this evening down to a skeleton staff. But rest assured, dinner is ready for your consumption and Nellie, our much-loved cook, has prepared for you our city's finest fare.'

They reached another set of huge doors, which Chad Snr pushed open to reveal an ornate dining room with a huge, lavishly laid table – it looked like it could easily seat thirty people. At the far end sat Chad and Melissa. Either side of them stood two waiters holding wine. If this was what they called a skeleton staff, Sheena couldn't imagine what it was like around here with the full service.

The waiters pulled out their chairs, seating the women directly opposite the solemn and silent Chad, still dressed in his black morning suit from the funeral, and Melissa, who was also still in the same clothes she'd worn to the ceremony. She wore a black Gucci two-piece suit with a huge pearl on a chain that looked to Catherine like the one Madeline used to wear. Melissa, aware of her gaze on it, touched the pearl and offered a smile that didn't quite reach her eyes.

Finally, Chad Snr took his seat at the head of the table. They were all gathered quite tightly for such a vast space, and certainly a little too close for comfort for Catherine's liking.

'I'm so glad you could join us tonight. Let the first course commence,' Chad Snr said, gesturing for the waiters to wheel huge silver trolleys towards them. Freshly opened oysters were placed in front of everyone. Sheena, who hated oysters, couldn't believe that even the food was living up to the dread of them being here.

'You will never have tasted anything like these, ladies. Nellie gets them from the St Roch Market herself. Try them, they slide down your throat like Jesus's nectar,' Chad Snr said, then raised one to his lips, sticking out his tongue in a way that looked almost sexual before sucking the oyster into his mouth and heaving a contented sigh. Catherine ate one, but as Sheena tentatively reached out for hers, Chad pushed his plate away and stood up abruptly.

'Ladies,' he said, with a slight bow towards Catherine and Sheena, 'you will have to forgive me, I just cannot do this right now. I am sure you understand.' His voice was broken, and tears were welling up in his eyes. Catherine's heart felt like it was being trampled on by the same stampeding herd of cows that had been used for the on-screen death of Lydia Chambers, an actress from one of Falcon Bay's rival shows.

Melissa went to speak, but was cut off by Chad Snr, whose demeanour and tone went from eccentric jovial host to menacing in just moments.

'You will sit down and be respectful to our guests who have come all this way for *your wife*,' he shouted, his voice echoing around the huge hall. The waiters didn't flinch; clearly, this was one evangelist who was anything but saintly behind closed doors.

'She has a name, Father,' Chad said, his voice still faltering.

Melissa looked down at her plate between the pair, aware a storm was about to blow in the Kane mansion. Sheena slipped her hand under the table and squeezed Catherine's leg in an effort to ensure she didn't try to intervene.

'*Had*,' Chad Snr sneered as he gestured for one of the unflinching waiters to fill his glass with red wine, which he proceeded to slug aggressively.

There was something about the way he had put emphasis on his one-word retort that told Sheena and Catherine that Madeline's secret past may not have been buried with her after all.

'Show my wife some respect!' Chad shouted, his voice now bellowing out at a tone to match that of his impressive frame.

Chad Snr rose up from his chair faster than a man of his years would usually have been able to.

'Don't you see child, Jesus has shown his respect for our family, by stepping in to give you a chance to start again,' he said, gesturing with his wine towards a huge portrait of Christ on the cross. It was hung on one wall, surrounded by lit candles. 'Now you can find a *real* wife, one who can carry on the family name.'

Chad stared at him, his eyes burning like black coals. Melissa looked at her father with an expression that made clear that she was desperate for him to stop his attack, but it just seemed to anger him more.

'Save your weepy eyes, Melissa, you're as much use as him! Neither of you have created grandbabies to carry on my bloodline. Why, if I were to die right now, what would be my legacy? The people of this city need someone to believe in, to be guided by – who would they have left? You two? One living here alone as a lonely spinster getting older and less desirable by the day . . .' He spat in Melissa's direction, spilling his wine, then darted past her so that he was facing his son. Although vastly different in height, Chad Snr's temper appeared to have risen him up to almost be level with his son, who stood his ground behind Melissa's chair with a comforting hand on her shoulder. 'Or you, with your taste for circus freaks!' Chard Snr shouted, spilling what was left of the wine, which was immediately topped up by another silent, emotionless waiter.

Chad's face turned to full-on rage, and the veins in his neck pumped. Catherine and Sheena, now holding hands, geared up to witness a showdown of such epic proportions it would outdo anything either of them had ever seen on any of the scripted dramas they'd spent their lives working on.

'Madeline was worth a hundred of you,' Chad raged at his father. 'I'd have left here years ago if it hadn't been for Melissa. You're the circus act. It's you who is the freak show, the holy hypocrite. If your church could see who you really are, they'd abandon you just like our mother did.'

Chad was in full flow; Melissa was sobbing. Chad Snr raised his hand in his son's direction, attempting to strike a blow to his face when Catherine, who couldn't take any more, bolted out of her seat and made a dash for the exit, quickly followed by Chad who stormed out of the room. A torn looking Melissia paused for a moment, but then also fled after him, leaving just Chad Snr and Sheena at the table. The sudden silence felt deafening. Chad Snr broke it by gesturing for the waiters still hovering nearby to fill their glasses. Sheena put her hand over hers.

19

'I'll better go after her,' Sheena said, rising from her seat, determined to catch Catherine before she could spend any time alone with Chad or Melissa.

Chad Snr shook his head dismissively. 'Do not be perturbed by my children's behaviour, this is what families do, Ms McQueen; perhaps the one bonus of your sinful way of life is that you won't have to deal with this sort of disappointment,' he said with a smirk.

Not quite sure she'd heard him correctly, Sheena challenged him, her hand on the back of her seat as she prepared to leave.

'I'm sorry?' she said.

'And so you should be, but be sorry to the Lord, not me. I'm just his conduit. As I was saying, perhaps the one blessing of the curse of gayness is that you won't have children failing to live up to your expectations like mine have.'

As the vile words sank into Sheena's head, she felt like she'd been shot. She'd dealt with snide remarks about her sexuality years ago, in less civilised decades, but never in a situation where she felt unable to assert herself like this. There was something so hate-filled about the words he'd used, and she felt deeply wrongfooted, a position the unflappable Sheena McQueen was not used to being in.

Her need to locate Catherine, however, was more urgent than the time it would take her to hit back at his disgusting slur.

'I must go and find Catherine; she hates conflict,' she said, with all the composure she could muster, then left the table, absolutely fuming.

After following the flames of the gothic torches that lit the estate's grounds, Catherine had managed to find the terrace and was standing by the stone balustrade, overlooking a huge ornate pond, being sick. Her body shook with each convulsion as every ounce of the wine she'd drunk and every morsel of oyster came out of her.

Sheena suddenly appeared behind her and fished inside her purse for a tissue, then, like a mother might with her child, gently dabbed Catherine's mouth. For a moment they stood in silence. When Catherine had stopped retching, Sheena spoke.

'Catherine, you've got to pull yourself together,' she said softly.

'That's easy for you to say – don't you think I want to?' Catherine snapped, her tone harsh. Considering all the drama Sheena had had to deal with this evening, this immediately got her back up. She placed her hands on Catherine's shoulders and roughly spun her around to face her.

'Well, stop fucking *wanting* to and start fucking *doing* it,' she hissed. 'I've just about had enough of this. I'm your agent and your *friend,* Catherine, but I'm not supposed to be your bloody guardian. I'm exhausted with constantly trying to defuse this *truth bomb* you seem intent on setting off, and what the hell for? You heard what Chad's loony father said – well, most of it, you were spared the personal attack he launched at me after you left. It's clear this family is insane and even in this madhouse, no one wanted Madeline, so start remembering that she just was a stone-cold bitch with a vendetta, so twisted she wanted you dead – *it was you or her, remember*. You just did what you had to do – the drama kicking off in there *wasn't* focused on us, our involvement with her is over, so let's keep it that way. Even Farrah couldn't have scripted something as vile as the show Chad Snr put on. Madeline was clearly in good company here, so stop acting like you killed Joan of fucking Arc – she was no saint. Get a fucking grip before you finally say something that even I can't save you from.'

Tears welled up again in Catherine's eyes; she'd never rowed with Sheena before. They'd been close for over thirty years, but she just didn't seem to understand what Catherine was battling with.

'But Chad wanted her; look at how he was at the funeral, he loved her so much and it was clear from the way he responded to his father's remarks about Madeline that they obviously were aware of her past after all, though she didn't know it.' Catherine surprised herself by finding she was now shouting. Sheena gestured for her to lower her voice, but it was too late; words were tumbling out of Catherine's mouth fast and loud, and she was powerless to rein herself in.

'And we threatened to tell them her secret, didn't we?' she screeched. 'And she was so terrified that he wouldn't love her if he knew. She let us control her. And now she'll never know that he *did* know about her past, but that he loved her anyway. We were so cruel!'

Sheena looked around, worried that someone might be nearby to hear. Seeing no one, she stepped back and let Catherine unload. It was clear this was the conversation that'd been brooding behind the silence she'd endured on the flight over.

'When you say *we*, you really mean *me,* don't you?' Sheena snapped, spitting like a cobra.

Catherine said nothing, which riled Sheena further.

'Well, if you remember, back in the world of reality rather than this grim fairy tale you seem to be recounting, I was protecting you and your life on *Falcon Bay* by using that information about her past, Catherine. That's my job, and I did it bloody well. Let's not forget that she bought the network with one mission only, to ruin your career, and if that wasn't enough, she even cast herself in the show to be the one to humiliate you in front of millions! This is not Snow White we're talking about.'

Catherine softened. 'I know, I know. I'm not blaming you.'
Sheena eyed her suspiciously. 'Well, it sounds like you are.'

Catherine ran her hands up her neck, something she always
did when she was stressed. 'I'm not. It's just . . . to think how
scared she was about Chad's reaction when we blackmailed
her, she was so scared that he would reject her that she let
us derail her plans, as wrong as they were, which led to *that
day*.' She paused.

'If we could go back in time, I'd never have taken part in
any of it. I'd have let her drive me out of *Falcon Bay* and
keep it all. Nothing is worth the amount of guilt I feel. I can't
go on like this; I need to tell him what I did.' Her voice
descended into a part sob, part screech again as she attempted
to dart back towards the main house. 'Whatever happens, I'll
bear the consequences,' she said as she went to leave the
terrace, but before she could get any further, Sheena grabbed
her firmly, her face full of anger.

'But the *consequences* are not just for you, are they, Catherine?'
she snapped, her last nerve well and truly shattered.

'What do you mean?' Catherine said, staring at Sheena,
looking like she was going to burst into tears. 'It was only
she and I on the dock. I was the one who did what I did. I
was the one who had the chance to save Madeline, and in
that split second, I chose not to reach out and pull her from
the water. I left her to the shark.'

'That may be true, but the fact that Amanda and I covered
up for you by burying the video footage implicates all three
of us, then us explaining to Helen why she had to keep the
press off our scent makes four, and although Farrah hasn't
actually said anything to me, as she was directing that scene,
she'll have seen everything that happened on those underwater
cameras, so if you think you feel bad now, how will you feel
if you take down the four women who've had your back for

decades? Because we'll all pay the price together, just for trying to help you.'

They stood in silence for a moment. Sheena, sensing that this meant her harsh words were sinking in, barrelled on in the same tone. Perhaps direction was what Catherine needed; she was an actress after all.

'The police and everyone in the whole world think that Madeline's death was nothing more than a horrendously tragic accident, and after tonight we are out of this mess once and for all. So if you say one word that contradicts what we've all been saying for months, we'll all go to prison. It's nearly over, so if you can just keep your mouth shut for a few more hours, then we'll never have to see any of them again and we can finally forget about Madeline fucking Kane once and for all.'

Sheena's words rang out loudly around the vast empty space and into the star-filled sky above them.

Catherine was still. As the words percolated in her brain, now clear of the effects of the drink and drugs she'd expelled from her body whilst vomiting, she began to see reason. Hearing it out loud, she knew Sheena was right. If she did tell the truth, the Kanes and the police would work out that she couldn't have hidden her tracks alone, and she truly didn't want anyone else to lose their freedom for a decision she'd made. The very thought of her friend Amanda King being prised away from her young baby daughter for trying to help was enough to finally bring her to her senses. She wiped her eyes and turned back to fully face Sheena.

'I'm sorry.'

Sheena's contorted face softened as she gestured for her to continue.

Quietly, slowly regaining her composure, Catherine started to speak. 'I do appreciate everything you've all done to help me, Sheena, I just lost it tonight. You were right; I should never have come. I understand now that it's me who has to learn to live with what I've done, and I will, somehow. I promise never to speak about it again after tonight.'

Sheena looked at her intensely, then held out her hand.

'Do you pinky promise?' she said, referencing the phrase Madeline Kane used to use. It should have felt distasteful to copy their dead enemy, but somehow it felt like putting the lid back on the exhumed coffin of a secret that they could now leave well buried, never to be dug up again.

'Yes, I pinky promise,' Catherine said solemnly. The two women twisted fingers, then kissed each other on both cheeks. Catherine straightened her dress and adjusted her pendant, which had become twisted when she'd leant over the balcony. With a tinge of sadness, she noticed the huge morganite stone that hung from the end of it was missing and must have fallen over the side. Perhaps it was for the best, she thought – gemstones were known for carrying their wearer's energy with them. Tonight's memory was one she didn't want to bring home with her.

'So are you OK now, and are *we* OK now?' Sheena asked, her tone restored to that of loving friend.

'Yes, and of course – yes,' Catherine said, squeezing Sheena's hand. 'But we need to leave New Orleans immediately if I'm to hold it together. I'll go back to the hotel and pack our things. Just make some excuse for me; I can't go back in there. Like you said, the past ends tonight. We'll go straight to the airport and get on the first flight out. I don't even care if it's economy.'

Sheena nodded, pleased that the reasonable and sensible Catherine she knew and admired had finally come back to life. She'd deal with the mention of 'flying economy' later. The suggestion terrified her as much as a prison sentence.

'Take the chauffeur, and I'll blame the oysters for making

25

you ill and see you back at the hotel as fast as I can.' The women hugged, and Catherine made her way up the stone terrace that led back to the villa's walkway. Sheena waved her off, then lit a cigarette and turned back to the balcony. She readied herself to pull off an Emmy-award-winning performance straight from her previous life as an actress – before she'd moved behind the scenes in showbiz – that would convince the vile Kane Snr that Catherine's emotional outburst and subsequent exit were no more than sisterhood grief for the loss of a dear colleague and a bad reaction to that evening's dinner. She decided she wouldn't be picking him up on his homophobic slurs to her; he wasn't worth her energy. She just wanted this nightmare to be over.

Fucking Madeline, Sheena raged internally. Even dead she was still causing trouble. She hadn't ever really said it to anyone in their group, as there had been so much pressure on keeping Catherine level, but as far as she was concerned, Madeline had got what she deserved.

Hoping tonight was the night they'd finally be able to draw a line under this horrendous saga, Sheena felt relief wash over her as she looked into the night sky and thought about how the remnants of the woman who'd turned their lives upside down were now floating in the Mississippi river. She quickly glanced around to double check she was alone, then spoke aloud: 'You'll get no tears from me; I'm glad you're dead, bitch. You brought it all on yourself anyway. I hope the alligators ingest you and shit you out in the swamps where you deserve to be.'

Then she flicked her cigarette over the balcony towards the ornate pond, where it bounced against a huge fountain with a statue of Jesus on it.

'Sorry about that, God,' she said, mocking the absurdity of this being a holy house when the man of it was clearly nothing but a deranged religious charlatan. 'I doubt you'll be seeing Madeline at your pearly gates anytime soon,' she said in a perfect Deep South accent. Even now, decades since she'd abandoned performing, she still had skills most actresses would envy. 'I feel sure she's gone to that other place, where your rival lives, *down below*.'

She laughed at the idea of Madeline being whipped by the Devil in some sort of horror movie fantasy that, not being in the slightest bit religious, she didn't really believe in. Just the imaginary vision caused a huge smirk to cross her crimson lips as she headed back towards the house, her Jimmy Choos clacking on the stone slabs.

It was gone 1 a.m. when Sheena finally arrived back at their hotel, where she was surprised to find Catherine standing in the lobby with all their cases and their bill already paid.

'At last,' Catherine said with visible relief. 'I've packed for us, now we just need to order a cab.' She signalled to the receptionist, miming a steering wheel. Sheena thought this was an odd gesture considering everyone spoke English, but decided against correcting Catherine's manners. She'd probably topped up her depleted Xanax.

Sheena had wanted to check out of her own room to make sure Catherine hadn't left anything behind in a hazy stupor, but decided that it was more drama than it was worth to insist on going back up to her suite. She'd check her cases at the airport lounge, then if anything was missing, she could call the hotel and get it biked over before they boarded their flight. At this time of night, they'd no doubt be in for a few hours' wait. The sooner they were in the air, the quicker they could close this chapter and get on with their lives.

'On the plane, we'll write your speech for when you pick up that best actress award when we get home,' Sheena said with a wink, wanting to leave on a high note.

Catherine looked genuinely surprised. 'Oh God, I forgot about the awards ceremony, my mind has been all over the place. When is it?'

'*Tomorrow*!' Sheena said, tapping her rose-gold, diamond-encrusted Theo Fennell watch, loving the way it sparkled on her wrist. 'Well, technically it's tonight. With the time differ-ence, it starts eight hours after we were due to fly back on our original plane. But since we got delayed at Hell Manor, you've even less time to prepare now.'

Catherine's face looked panicked as she fished around in her Lady Dior handbag for her mobile. Turning it on for the first time in days, her inbox flashed up with emails containing the results of the Google alert settings she had pre-set. Sure enough, hundreds of emails swamped her inbox, all with her name and pictures of her face next to the other nominees she was up against from competing dramas. Her stomach flipped as she realised Sheena was indeed correct. Even if they caught the first commercial flight out, *and* it was on time, *and* they made their connections back to the island, she'd still only have an hour max to get back to her condo on St Augustine's.

Sheena could see she was beginning to panic.

'I can't think about that now. I won't win anyway, and we'll never make it in time,' Catherine said, scanning the empty road for the cab she was so desperate to arrive.

Sheena looked her deeply in the eyes. 'Well, you better start thinking about it, because you *will* win and I will make sure we make it in time. We're going to fly into London instead of Paris, where I'm going to charter a helicopter direct to Jersey, which will take us less than an hour.'

Catherine's eyes looked tearful once more, but this time with gratitude and what looked like just the faintest glint of excitement.

'We made a pinky promise: we are returning to our old lives,' Sheena said firmly. 'And this is what we do. We fly A-List, so forget about economy!' She held up her own phone, showing Catherine that she'd found an option for them to start their long-haul return as they'd arrived – in First Class. Then they'd be picked up at Heathrow and whisked into the sky once more on a private helicopter called the *Bullet*.

'We'll email the glam squad from the airport and make sure Brad and everyone down at the Bay has your dressing room ready. They'll buff and polish the memories of this trip out of you so you're sparkling when you pick up that statue and pose for all you're worth in that press room. I'll work the room and bash the phones. This is *who we are*, Catherine. Let's return with a bang! I'll be using this win to get you on all the front covers you've been splattered over since Christmas – but for the *right* reasons.'

Catherine felt a hint of a smile reach her lips; Sheena was the most inspirational woman she knew. She wasn't just a glass-half-full person, she could spin the merest drop into a full pint. Perhaps she *could* carry on with her life as she had before.

Sensing that the old Catherine she knew well was starting to rise to the surface, Sheena barrelled on enthusiastically. 'We're going to use this moment of victory to celebrate a fresh start, for all of us,' she said with a grin.

Catherine nodded softly. Before Sheena could continue her pep talk, a car horn beeped in the distance and Catherine's eyes lit up at the sound of it. They were about to begin their return home to St Augustine's.

'OK, you're on, let's get back to being us,' Catherine said, with the first real smile she'd managed in months as the two women walked arm in arm out of the lobby. She understood now that as she couldn't change the past, she must give her all to her future. The receptionist pushed their trolley behind them, and with the slam of a cab door, they were gone.

Down by the river, Madeline's photo was now illuminated by hundreds of fairy lights that had been sprinkled all around the billboard's edges, in keeping with Mardi Gras, due to start in a few hours' time. Chad made his way down to the moorside decking, and looked up at his dead wife's beautiful effigy. With tears streaming down his face, he continued to stare deep into her feline eyes. In a scene from one of the *Sinbad* movies he'd loved in the seventies, a beautiful female figurehead which had been carved into the front of the boat for luck on their voyage into the unknown suddenly came to life. He prayed Madeline's billboard would do the same and she would speak to him.

But no matter how long he stared, nothing happened. His beautiful wife was dead and his longing for her was agony; he needed so badly to be close to her, to feel her touch, to have her pressed against his body. No woman had ever reached him the way that Madeline had. When his father had uncovered her *history* and used it to try to stop him from marrying her, not once had Chad's feelings wavered. He'd never cared about her life before they'd met, and he had vowed to protect her from being humiliated by telling his father that if he ever tried to hurt her or reveal to her that he knew her past, he'd leave the country and never speak to him again.

His father's vanity as a New Orleans man of God was too strong for a public rejection of his only son, so that had kept his silence as they were married in a lavish ceremony celebrated by the whole of New Orleans. Chad knew that if Madeline had wanted him to know what she'd been through she'd have told him. He'd hoped that maybe one day, she'd have felt able to share what had happened to her, but if and when that conversation ever happened, it would always have been up to her. Now he knew that day could never come.

From the moment they'd said 'I do' just feet from where he now stood, inches away from where the remnants of her body had been sprinkled into the floating lilies, he'd vowed to love, honour and defend her. Death may have parted them, but he was determined to keep those promises alive. First, though, he had to have one last moment with his beloved wife.

Moments later, he'd taken off his suit, stripped fully naked, and begun walking into the middle of the lily pond. The flashing lights of the bulbs highlighted his ripped physique. He waded into the water until his thick thighs were out of sight, then picked up an ash-soaked lily and pulled it up to his face. He kissed it, then rubbed it along his chest, imagining it was the silky touch of his wife's caress. Chad submerged himself in the water, praying Madeline's DNA would soak into his skin and become part of him. Even in the depth of his grief, the very thought of her presence was arousing; he imagined his wife's lean, perfect body was wrapped around him. Every lily that brushed past his skin felt like the tips of her perfect fingernails.

Overcome with heartache, emotion and desire, as his body throbbed for her, he felt his legs buckle as he sank under the water. Knowing this was the last time he'd ever be anywhere near her, he lay there, his blood pumping as his lungs desperately signalled that they needed air, but he didn't want to leave her. For a moment he considered letting the water enter his throat, so that he'd drown right there. Perhaps beyond the corruption of his father's fakery, the true God would reunite them again. He was just about to let go when his eyes focused under the water on Madeline's face once more. As their eyes connected, he was sure he saw a glint appear in

31

her eye, the one he used to see when she was determined to get what she wanted. Arising from the water with a huge gasp of breath, he stood up and walked towards her image, his beautiful naked body highlighted by the moon. When he reached the bank, he pushed his wet hair off his face, then looked deep into her eyes. He knew his job of protecting her was far from over; in fact, it was about to begin all over again.

Chapter 2

Fourteen hours later, Amanda King, executive producer and showrunner of *Falcon Bay*, watched Catherine Belle and Sheena McQueen land on the helipad on one of CITV's giant production building roofs. She let out a sigh of relief.

Safe in the knowledge that their biggest star was back where she belonged, and just in time, she turned her gaze towards the vast ocean that surrounded the studio complex. The sea looked more beautiful than ever. Amanda was up on the luxury balcony of the office, and the view was spectacular. Even after all the years she'd spent living on the island, Amanda never tired of watching the sun set over the tiny private piece of nature's heaven where they filmed the show. The primetime soap opera had kept audiences glued to their TV screens all over the world and had been dubbed in a dozen foreign languages for nearly forty-one years. Her hazel eyes scanned the shore, which was decorated with a red carpet today and could easily have made the Oscars or even the Met Gala look dull. *Falcon Bay* had been nominated in several categories for the international drama awards, one of the most prestigious events of the television industry's annual calendar. Knowing the eyes of the world would be on them in just hours, Amanda had made sure St Augustine's looked even more beautiful than usual. Due to the eight-week hiatus they'd had to take to show respect for the fatal sequence of events of their Christmas Day live episode, they were now playing serious catch-up – with a schedule of five episodes a week to return to.

The industry rumour mill was in full force, with the social media sites ablaze with predictions that they were going to win big tonight. As much as she'd have loved the cast and crew to fly to America where the awards were taking place, there was the production backlog, and *Falcon Bay*'s leading lady Catherine Belle had put their schedule even further behind by taking time off to attend Madeline Kane's funeral. Amanda had had no choice but to make the executive decision that they would only attend via video link. To make up for the disappointment she knew everyone was feeling, she'd thrown a quarter of a million out of their annual marketing budget to make sure that when the cameras cut to them, the press party CITV was hosting would make all those attending the actual awards in person jealous that they were not in St Augustine's Cove themselves.

All the island's palm trees were covered in sparkling lights and rigged with speakers blasting their theme tune out, and *Falcon Bay* branded bunting ran between them, giving the effect of a huge late-night street party. All around the bay, ornate, Hollywood-style and size-projection screens with authentic retro seating had been erected, with huge lights projecting the show's logo into the darkening night sky and far out into the ocean. Several of the pop-up viewing areas filled the sandy boardwalk set, giving the effect of a 1950s drive-in cinema. The biggest screen had been bolted high up on the rockface above the cove, where the candy-coloured cottages used for filming exterior scenes were. They also had a huge platform with an illuminated

Falcon Bay sign, brightly shining out, and each of the fake housefronts had pre-set pyrotechnics, ready to be detonated in celebration should they win.

Amanda hadn't told anyone about the fireworks; she wanted it to be a surprise. Although never one to tempt fate, not allowing herself to believe the bookies' odds that they were due to sweep the board, she had allowed herself to be cautiously optimistic that at least some of them could well be setting the sky ablaze with glory if they picked up even one prestigious gong. She smoothed down her ivory jumpsuit and adjusted the gold locket her boyfriend Dan had bought her to celebrate the nominations so that it nestled just above her discreetly displayed hint of cleavage. Inside it was a photo of them both holding her daughter, Olivia. Dan may not have been her biological father, but in less than a year he'd proved that blood meant nothing when it came to parental love. He made both of them feel like they were the most important people in the world to him – everything that Olivia's father and Amanda's estranged husband Jake had revelled in failing to do.

The thought of Jake having to watch them celebrating made her smile. Just a few months ago, he'd have had total control over what was happening at CITV, but now she was in charge and she could imagine how jealous he must be feeling. He'd kept an uncharacteristically low profile since his axing from the show. She'd expected him to pop up at one of their rivals to launch an attack on their ratings, especially when they'd been off-air, which would have given him the perfect head start, but he'd totally gone off-radar. He hadn't even contested the application for sole custody of Olivia she'd applied for via their divorce lawyers. Not that that had been a surprise either, as he'd shown zero interest in their daughter when they were together, but it still brought tears to her eyes, wondering what she'd tell their baby when she was old enough to ask why he'd never wanted to be part of her life.

Determined to bury her sad feelings about Jake and concentrate on the big night ahead, Amanda grabbed the bottle of champagne chilling on the balcony bar and poured herself a glass, reminding herself that tonight was all about celebrating the future, not mourning the past. Every moment since she'd regained control of *Falcon Bay* had been special, but tonight's buzz in the air was off the scale. As she downed her drink, the bubbles tickled her nose and Amanda's eyes followed glammed-up cast members emerging from their trailers, all having taken advantage of the show's extensive wardrobe to dress up for the evening. Even actors who usually played the more dowdy, comedic characters on the show had undergone almost unrecognisable transformations. She could feel their happiness rising up and mixing with the sea air wafting through her softly curled hair.

CITV had been started in the sixties by the most adorable couple – Harry and Tina Pearson – who'd stayed on the island crafting the show they loved until both passed away. Since Amanda had returned to power, she'd been determined to turn CITV back into the happy ship she knew they'd be proud of.

Tina and Harry had started the network off as Channel Islands Television, having bought the cove of St Augustine's, just off the Jersey coast. Their whole ethos was about happy programming making for happy people. Looking at their photos on the in-memoriam wall by the main production office, it was hard to imagine that such a kind and unassuming couple had created one of the world's most glamorous, longest-running, and ultimately dangerous on-screen and off-screen soap operas. But they had.

Amanda had only got to work with them for a few years

before they passed and their sons took over, who were nowhere near as committed to their parents' vision. She'd never forgotten their passion and belief in the show. It was something that was sorely lacking in the multiple owners who took over after the boys had moved on, much more interested in the dollar than the drama.

Things had been slowly on the wane with the change in television habits, and *Falcon Bay*'s ratings had been dropping so fast that Amanda had feared they'd never make their fortieth anniversary. It wasn't until Madeline Kane arrived – with her twisted vision of how they'd regain the show's long-lost number-one slot in the ratings war – that Amanda had begun to believe the show still had a future. How terribly Madeline's reign had ended. Madeline would turn out to be its last owner and although her revenge-filled plans had worked, she hadn't been alive long enough to see the show thrive.

But that was karma for you, Amanda thought as she took another sip of her drink. She was determined not to let the memory of the freakshow of how badly they'd hit the rocks at Christmas derail her positivity; it was the beginning of what was going to be a brand new era. Now she was firmly in charge of the rudder, it was going to be plain sailing from here on in, with no icebergs or sharks ahead.

In the distance, *Falcon Bay*'s head of casting, Helen Gold, popped into her vision. She looked stunning in a bright red Bardot minidress with matching sky-high heels. In amongst hundreds of waiters, caterers, and crew milling around, setting up bars and food stations, she certainly stood out from the crowd. Amanda watched Helen as she authoritatively held court on the boatyard set in front of the show's world-famous beach bar, The Cove. She was giving the press pack a run-through of how the night ahead would go. Helen wasn't meant to be doubling up for CITV as press officer, but since the chaos at Christmas, and given the importance of ensuring that the true events behind the lurid headlines remained secret, she'd been juggling both jobs admirably.

Over the last few months, she'd grown her hair out from her previously severe, although still trademark, sexy bob cut, and now her blonde tresses were almost shoulder length, gently caressing her perfect frame, which the cut of her dress showed off to full effect.

She may have been in her sixties but there wasn't a man, or possibly a woman, in that row of hacks who wasn't salivating at or captivated by the presence and sexuality she exuded – apart from one. The nosiest and noisiest of hacks, Ross Owen, formerly of the biggest newspaper to constantly document *Falcon Bay*'s ups and downs: *The Herald*.

Amanda was some distance away, but even from up on the office balcony, she could hear Ross's braying drunken tones as he interrupted nearly every update Helen was giving them on what to expect that evening. Amanda rolled her eyes. The office she was in was actually the same one from which she'd had her estranged husband turfed out during the power struggle they'd fought – and she'd won – with Madeline on the eve of her death last year. The world was full of men like Ross and Jake who were desperate for power. Amanda popped in the earpiece she'd be wearing once she was down on set, which would allow her to hear the gallery telling her in which order the awards were being announced as she mingled. She tuned it to the press pit frequency so she could hear exactly what Ross was saying.

The show had rarely been out of the headlines since the Christmas Day live tragedy, but his stories, which were now all featured on his own blog, had been never-ending and had always been the worst. CITV had had an OK relationship with him until he'd left *The Herald* and signed a mega-bucks book deal with the legendary sleazy publisher Fonda Books, supposedly to write a tell-all about their show, which according to the press release was entitled *The Curse of Falcon Bay*. Its Amazon press blurb stated that it would give readers 'a fascinating in-depth look into the suspicious death of Madeline Kane'. It would be exploring 'the conspiracy theories surrounding the supposed curse which had befallen the cast and crew of the island', and 'the disappearance of Oscar-winning actress Honey Hunter, who'd been due to join the cast for their now infamous Christmas Day live episode but never showed up, and has been missing ever since'.

Appearing in the show was meant to be a huge comeback for Honey, who hadn't worked in decades, but thanks to her previous career as a Hollywood child star cum rock star's wife, cum habitual rehab resident, she was actually a brilliant signing who had been due to be a huge boost for the show's ratings.

Honey had been clean and sober for years, and the press and fans were desperately looking forward to seeing her return to the spotlight. There was definite fascination in her story, and as Amanda listened to Ross interrupt Helen for the fifth time, she did wonder if perhaps his sordid little book could solve the mystery of what had happened to poor Honey.

She heard him ask Helen if there would be any more statements on Madeline Kane if they won any awards tonight, and Amanda knew, no matter how hard he'd been digging, that the truth of what led to Madeline's death was clearly nowhere near close to being revealed within the pages of his book. It would take a severe break in the chain for him to get anywhere near that, and after chatting to Sheena via text as she was escorting Catherine Belle back to the island for her big moment, Amanda felt confident that there was no longer a weak link in their sisterhood. They were united in silence, and Amanda was starting to believe that tonight could be the start of the whole world recognising *Falcon Bay* as the best drama out there. She felt sure she could keep the show high in the ratings – for all the right reasons this time.

Amanda smiled to herself, allowing the sound of waves lapping at the shore and gulls soaring past to soak into her soul. She finally understood what being happy meant. Yes, having Olivia had been the best moment of her life, but it was marred by all the years of failed IVF and the babies she'd lost along the way. When her dream of being a mother finally did come true, she wasn't able to fully enjoy it because that's when her husband Jake had chosen to show his true colours. She looked down at her bare wedding ring finger and smiled once more. *Free*. That was the word she was looking for; she felt *free*. She had both her babies.

In the few short months she'd been in charge at Falcon Bay, she'd already greenlit several female-written and directed pilots with an aim to replace the toxic male-dominated culture Jake had not only allowed but actively encouraged to fester. She'd turned the once dreaded Meeting Room 6 into a happy, creative space, where the writers, producers, and storyliners of *Falcon Bay* felt safe to share and discuss the show's future without fear of Jake throwing one of his legendary tantrums, or furniture, or sacking someone on the spot because he didn't like what they were wearing. After years of turmoil, the future finally felt possible.

Yes, this is what it's all about, Amanda thought. For the first time, her whole life was perfect; she'd never been happier, so if they did win anything tonight, it was simply going to be the cherry on top. She already had the cake.

After closing the balcony doors, she went over to the mirror and touched up her lipstick, ready to make her way down to the awards ceremony. Taking her phone from her clutch bag, she quickly read a text from Dan whilst heading to the lift that would take her down to the studio floor.

So proud, I'll be watching online, I love you xxx

Amanda replied with a smiley face emoji with the words

I love you too, see you later xxx

Just the thought of Dan waiting at home for her, holding Olivia in his strong arms, made her smile broadly. As much as she was looking forward to the party, she couldn't wait to get home and lie in his arms once more, but first, she had business to do. As the lift doors pinged open, she shook her hair out, allowing the smile on her face to turn into a full showbiz beam, as she began to mingle with the guests.

In Catherine's dressing room, Brad was just putting the finishing touches to her hair, which was an elaborate mass of curls with gold leaf frosted over them to match her full-length Moschino ballgown. Catherine was staring into the mirror.

'Do you think it's too much?' she said to Sheena, who was sat on a chair in the corner, smoking a cigarette and scrolling through her phone. She eyed Catherine's ensemble from head to toe, then looked over at Brad, the head of *Falcon Bay*'s make-up and wardrobe department, who looked equally desperate for her approval.

'Well?' Catherine urged.

Sheena, dressed in a skin-tight leather trouser suit, with the hint of a lace cami bra showing, got out of her chair and walked in her spiked-heeled boots closer to the two of them to get a better look. Brad looked more nervous than Catherine, so she decided to put them out of their misery.

'Too much?' Sheena said dryly. 'If anything, it's not enough!'

Catherine and Brad both broke into massive smiles.

'Stick some more lashes on her, Brad, really make her eyes

pop. She's going to be photographed a lot when she's holding those statues tonight, and this dress is the perfect colour to go with the latest one and to add to the collection.' Sheena winked as she gestured to the huge display cabinet on the far wall in Catherine's dressing room, which was full of all the awards she'd won during her years on the show. In truth, the last one she'd picked up was nearly a decade old, so tonight's new editions were really going to bring that trophy collection up to date.

Catherine let out a squeal of excitement as Brad finished her eyes and gestured to say he was done. She wasn't usually a fan of helicopters, but after dropping a couple of her trusty Xanax and sharing a drink that Sheena had smuggled in her bag, much to the pilot's horror, she'd found their dash to St Augustine's all rather exciting. She was so grateful that it had given her the time to get ready properly and not feel rushed.

As they'd landed on the helipad situated on the highest of CITV's studio buildings, Brad had met her on the roof carrying the dress she'd be wearing that night, which billowed under the helicopter's wings as if it were floating. From her vantage spot, Catherine had been able to see every inch of the place that had been her whole world for years, and all thoughts of what she'd been through had dissipated. She felt like a Bond girl, a part she'd always wished she could have played. Now, feeling as golden as her outfit, she was determined to shine.

Sheena pulled the door open for her and signalled it was time to make their way down.

All three beamed as they entered the corridor and headed for the giant studio doors located at the end on Catherine's floor, which slid open at the push of a big green button and opened straight onto the beach bar set of Lucy Dean, Catherine's long-running *Falcon Bay* character. As the most important character on the show, Catherine had recently had her dressing room relocated to be moments away from where she filmed the majority of her scenes, away from the hustle and bustle of the main corridors where the other actors shared dressing rooms. It allowed her to spend as much time preparing as possible but was also another sign of her status on the show. The remodelling of her new dressing room alone had cost the price of a small house.

As the doors flew open, what felt like a million flash bulbs immediately went off. Catherine seemed to grow even taller than the mega high gold heels that already elevated her. Sheena put her arm across Brad's chest to hold him back and keep him in the lift, making sure Catherine's arrival photos were not photobombed by him milling around in the background. This was her moment and Sheena felt proud watching her embrace it.

'You did an amazing job,' she said to Brad, who was also looking on with pride as Catherine posed up a storm.

'It was easy. She seems like her old self,' he said.

'She is,' Sheena replied. The two of them smiled as they watched Catherine finish on the red carpet and make her way across the sand dunes, towards the main stage, where Helen Gold was waiting by the steps, ready to hand her a microphone.

'Here she is, ladies and gentlemen of the press! I use the word gentlemen lightly,' Helen said. She nodded towards *The Herald*'s Ross Owen, who had pushed himself right to the front of the twenty or so reporters from stations all over the world. They were ready to watch the results live with the cast and crew on one of the cinema screens. Ross raised his glass, which was his fifth of the evening so far, and toasted Helen with a sarcastic look on his face as the rest of the crowd gave Catherine a rapturous round of applause.

'You look sensational,' Helen whispered in her ear as the women hugged.

Catherine took the microphone. Looking out at the crowds and all the activity on the island suddenly made the whole night seem real. She'd rehearsed what she was going to say in her dressing room earlier, after Amanda had asked her to do the official opening, but now she was overwhelmed with pure excitement at what seemed to be a magical night ahead. All plans went out of her head and she decided to freestyle it.

'Hello, hello, hello!' she said coquettishly, the velvety tone of her voice booming out of the speakers. 'Well, I guess I don't need to ask if you can hear me at the back!' She laughed and signalled to the director's box above her to turn down the volume.

Farrah Adams, her long-time friend and *Falcon Bay*'s main director and scriptwriter, gave her a thumbs-up through the widow. A technician next to her adjusted the sound. Sheena entered the box and hugged Farrah before taking a place next to her and looking at a close-up of Catherine on one of the monitors.

'I don't know how you've managed it, but I see our girl is glowing again, literally,' Farrah said with a smile, looking at Catherine. All the lights on the stage were hitting Catherine's dress and hair, and she was sparkling as though she'd been sprinkled in fairy dust. Sheena spotted a bottle of champagne on the side and poured them both a glass, handing one to Farrah. Priding herself on being totally professional, Farrah pushed it away.

Sheena thrust it towards her again with a raised eyebrow. 'C'mon, you're not directing a *real show* tonight, darling. Let's have some fun.'

Farrah looked stunning in a lime-green, one-shouldered

minidress that clung to her beautiful black skin and exposed her long lithe legs. She took the glass and clinked it with Sheena's.

'I hate to admit this – and I'll leave the story for another day,' Sheena said, 'but as hideous as it was, she needed to go to that funeral to put it all behind her. That vision of a leading lady we can see below is nothing like the hysterical wreck I flew out with. And that alone deserves a drink or ten.'

'Amen to that,' Farrah said with a laugh, taking another sip from her glass. 'Our belle of the Bay is back!' She smiled, then made her own toast. 'To all of us. A new era begins; let's celebrate!'

They both downed their drinks. Farrah signalled to Dustin, one of the assistant directors, who was sat inside a separate booth further down the galley, to turn his microphone on so he could hear them.

'Dustin, come take over and let someone else do those crowd shots for the VT,' she said. She grabbed her Prada bag off the back of her chair and followed Sheena towards the exit.

'You mean, you're not coming back in for the awards links?' he called after them.

He sounded part hopeful that she would confirm she wasn't, and part nervous that if that was the case, the responsibility of making sure there were no fluffed cues was suddenly down to him – it was no easy feat with a time-delayed link from a live ceremony happening in America.

'Yep, that's right, this one's over to you.' Farrah smiled.

She knew manning the box alone would help his confidence, and Sheena was right, it wasn't like she was responsible for the whole show. They were only nominated in several of the fifty categories, and they'd done a full rehearsal earlier in the day. She'd noted Dustin watching it intently, so now was as good a time as ever to see if he was up to the bigger challenges. Farrah was all about championing the rise of others, and if it meant that she got to go down to the party and hang out with her friends, then that was just a bonus.

She reached the door, then, after checking that Sheena had already left and was out of earshot, she turned and said to him, 'I'll keep my earpiece in, so if you need me don't worry, I can come back.'

Dustin's face went from worried to excited, and as soon as the door closed behind Farrah, he sat in her chair and spoke down the microphone which connected him to the crew.

'OK, people. Twenty minutes till the opening ceremony,' he said confidently. 'The first category we're up for is Best Actress, so can someone make sure Ms Belle is in the screening bay in front of the rockside? If she wins, we can let off what I hope will be the first of tonight's celebratory fireworks. Then I'll count you in. Have a great night, everyone, and good luck!'

With that, he put his feet up on the desk and tweeted a picture of himself in the control room with the hashtag #BossingIt.

*

After Catherine finished her speech, which went down a storm – bar some drunken heckling from *The Herald*'s Ross Owen, who was being even more annoying than usual – Helen left the journalists to take advantage of the free bar that Ross had certainly been enjoying. She handed a still sparkling Catherine over to Sheena, Amanda and Farrah, who were also in fine spirits. Helen promised she'd meet them all at The Cove Bar to watch the opening of the ceremony on the live link from Los Angeles, after she'd taken care of something urgent that couldn't wait.

She looked at her phone, which she'd set to stopwatch. That had given her exactly fifteen minutes, meaning she was currently nine minutes away from having to put her clothes back on, fix her make-up, and dash from the wardrobe trailer. She'd arranged to meet her lover Detective Matt Rutland for a pre-awards bonk.

The moment the door opened he was on her, pulling her dress up and going down on her within seconds. So expert was the lapping of his tongue that her knees were already trembling as she struggled to push the lock on the door so she could allow herself to fall onto his naked body. In one swift move, Matt's powerful arms took her weight and they rolled to the floor of the make-up Winnebago. Only hours earlier, it had been the site of a totally different set of touch-ups.

'God, you look so beautiful, Helen,' Matt breathed in her ear.

His tongue slid down her neck and he kissed her all the way down to her pink nipples, which he'd been cupping in his firm grip. As her body met his, she could feel his hardness pushing between her legs. She pulled her dress off over her head, for fear that it would get covered in what she could already feel was the wet release her body was gearing up for. She'd had hundreds of lovers, not that she'd admit that number to anyone, not even the girls, although it was no secret amongst them that she was definitely the most sexually active of the bunch. Not a single one was a patch on the way Matt seemed to be able to make her body explode in record time. That was handy, since the stopwatch on her phone said she was down to seven minutes before she'd have to run back to the set.

'Fuck me,' she said.

She put her hands between her thighs and slid his thick shaft deep inside herself. He rolled them over so Helen was on her back and began to drive himself into her. She used one hand to claw at his perfect arse and the other to stroke herself faster and faster until she knew she was getting close. She'd always been able to climax fast; loads of her friends struggled to achieve an orgasm with their partners, having to resort to faking it, then to toys when they were alone, but not Helen. She knew her body expertly and had a knack for choosing lovers who could take her to the mountain's edge quickly.

'Deeper, faster,' she breathed. She clawed at him again as their tongues explored each other's mouths. As her nipples stiffened, she knew it was a sign she was close.

'Are you ready?' he breathed, licking her neck once more in a way he'd learnt drove her crazy.

'Yes,' she managed.

He pushed himself deeper and deeper and she moved her hands across her clitoris faster and faster until they both came in unison. Wave after wave of that special sensation some women only dreamt of travelled up and down her body as she felt Matt flood her with every drop of lust he'd been saving up for her. In a sweaty mess, they collapsed as one on the floor together and lay still.

What was it about Matt that had Helen, a woman who had sworn never to stay with one man ever again, suddenly not want to ever be touched by anyone else? As if reading her mind, he whispered in her ear the one thing that in the eight months they'd been seeing each other, neither of them had dared to say: 'You know I love you, don't you?'

Just as the words made her heart swell, the alarm on her phone went off.

'Shit!' she squealed, sliding herself out from under him. She ran naked over to the mirrors in the make-up area of the trailer as he lay on the floor, watching her.

'Well, that's not the response I was hoping for,' Matt said, with a hurt look on his face.

'Sorry! I've got four minutes to get on set,' Helen said.

She frantically repaired her make-up and mussed-up hair in the mirror whilst expertly running a steamer over her dress at the same time. Luckily, she'd kept her shoes and jewellery on so within ninety seconds she was fully dressed and, with a quick slick of Dior Spice lip gloss, she looked like she had when she'd arrived. Grabbing her bag and radio mic, which she had turned off to make sure no one had heard them, she stepped over his still naked body, towards the door. She turned back and touched his handsome face.

'You know I've got to go,' Helen said, touching his cheek affectionately. Clearly feeling exposed, Matt pulled a towel over his body as she began to open the door. 'Lock this behind me and I'll see you at the afterparty,' she said, making her exit.

Once outside, she looked up to the night sky where the *Falcon Bay* logo was beaming, thanks to the light display Amanda had organised. It was so high they must be able to see it across the Channel in Paris, she thought, as she jumped into a beach buggy and sped over the dunes towards where she'd arranged to meet the girls. As she got closer, she mulled over what Matt had said to her and why she hadn't been able to say it back. She certainly *felt* it, but saying it, well, that was a whole new level and one she just wasn't ready to open herself up to. Not yet anyway.

*

In the director's box, Dustin had called in Candy, his co-assistant producer, to deal with the crowd cutaways he'd been doing before Farrah handed him the main links control. The atmosphere was as frosty between them as it had always been. Although they'd been at the network roughly the same amount of time, and power wise had been promoted evenly and equally over the last few years, they were like oil and water. Dustin was a true studio geek, with shaggy curly hair and thick-rimmed glasses, usually paired with a variety of vintage sci-fi movie T-shirts and trainers. He was happiest working on the technical side of the output of their show. Candy, with her killer figure, closely cropped peroxide-blonde hair, and piercing green feline eyes, looked much more *industry*.

It wasn't just their looks that set them apart. Candy's ambition was as bold as her outfits, even though her position behind the scenes meant she should essentially pass by unnoticed. She'd obviously borrowed her sparkling silver dress, with a huge slit down the side, from wardrobe – Dustin recognised it from a previous episode, where a now dead villainess had made a grand entrance into a ballroom scene. Candy looked like she should be on the monitors, not in charge of them.

Both choosing to avoid small talk, they took their positions and began to train the cameras on the key players in tonight's game. As Dustin zoomed in on Catherine, who'd taken her position next to the other cast members in the main seating area in front of the cliffside, Candy fine-tuned the cutaways of the senior crew members for reaction shots. As she focused on where Farrah and Amanda were sitting, joined by Catherine's agent Sheena, a flustered-looking Helen Gold glided into their aisle. She was in a last-minute dash to get to her seat as the opening credits of the awards show rolled, and all the countries who were joining virtually were invited by the host to wave in the opening montage. Candy smiled wickedly as she tightened the frame just enough to make sure Helen was no longer in shot.

*

Down in the screening area, Sheena was sitting through the usual boring woke-filled gags that seemed to go on forever, and none of them were funny. Sheena had even wished Ricky Gervais was hosting, as at least it would have been edgy. Although, if he'd been the compere for the night he would have pulled no punches on the season *Falcon Bay* had gone through to get here, she thought. Relaxing slightly, Sheena found herself getting into the rhythm of the old-fashioned and traditional format of the night.

A waiter brought another round of drinks to their row. Amanda and Farrah signalled to hide them under their seats as the first award they were up for was just about to be announced. For Catherine, this was the most important one of the night.

'And now we come to Best Actress in a long-running drama,' announced the host – Catherine had already forgotten her name.

A montage of the four women she was up against played out on the big screen. She and the others, some in Hollywood, one on a live link like she was, were projected into boxes on the huge screen. They were filmed watching the sections of their acting that had been submitted for the committees to choose a winner from.

Catherine usually hated watching herself, and had rarely looked at herself onscreen in decades. She didn't mind mirrors, but there was something about the camera that did something to one's face. She'd avoided any episodes of the show since 2010 – the year she'd turned sixty. Tonight though, there was nowhere to hide from the 100-foot screen right opposite her. It was showing a scene where her character Lucy Dean was sobbing on the beach, lamenting the mistakes she'd made in her life and asking God above for another chance. Even Catherine, after a moment or two, was able to distance herself and believe in her character's plight; it was a powerful scene written and directed by Farrah, and Catherine leaned over and squeezed Farrah's hand.

'If by any miracle I do win this, it'll be down to you, not me,' she said.

Farrah, who prided herself on having a badass attitude, began to feel a little emotional. She'd worked her arse off to write and direct the scene, and had struggled to reach the top of a very much male-dominated world. She smiled as she felt herself blush.

'Shhh!' Sheena said.

The clips ended and the host pulled out the envelope that would reveal who was going to land the much coveted trophy. All the women held hands and Amanda touched her locket for luck as Dustin zoomed in on Catherine's face, waiting for the verdict.

'And the award goes to . . . and I shouldn't say it, but after what she went through at Christmas, I don't think there's a more worthy winner – Ms Catherine Belle, for her role as Lucy Dean in *Falcon Bay*!'

'Oh my god!' They were the only words Catherine could manage as the girls jumped out of their seats, squealing, and began to hug her. Brad, who was on the row behind, leaned forward and into the shot, but not to get a moment of glory – he just wanted to warn the women they were in danger of creasing Catherine's dress.

'Be careful with her, it's delicate,' he whispered.

Catherine got out of her seat in a total daze and walked

up to the podium they'd had made for the occasion. The host threw the link to CITV, explaining that she couldn't be here in person, but they were about to speak to her live from the set of *Falcon Bay* on St Augustine's Cove. As Catherine reached the top of the steps, a replica of the award was handed to her by a runner and she looked at it lovingly, then turned to the camera as she readied herself to address the world.

'To say I'm speechless would be an understatement,' she said. The fireworks that had been built into the rockside to celebrate any wins exploded and lit the night sky behind her. Catherine jumped with surprise at the sound and the audience laughed. Then she regained her composure.

'I think that just summed it up for me! This is mind-blowing,' she said, trying to deliver the speech she and Sheena had worked on should this wonderful moment come their way. 'I know I don't have long, but I want to start off by saying that I share this award with all the other actresses nominated tonight.'

Candy laughed in the box as the expressions of the rivals showed that no one bought that line for a moment; there was only one winner, and that was Catherine.

'It's been a tough year down on the Bay,' Catherine continued, looking at the statue in disbelief. Sheena had been right; she had won after all. 'This time last year, I didn't even know if I was still going to be here, let alone be holding this!' She beamed.

'I want to thank all the members of the foreign press for voting for me. I can't say I've had the best coverage but I guess you have all kept me *out there*,' she continued, dryly referring to the mauling she'd had before the police investigation into Madeline's death had cleared her of any wrongdoing. 'Most importantly, though, I want to thank you, the people at home, all of you, all over the globe, for allowing me and us the privilege of being in your homes week after week for all these years. This means the world,' she kissed the statue, 'but your loyalty means more. Without you, our audience, we are nothing.'

The music began to start, meaning she was nearly out of time, and she could see a hostess coming to take her off the stage. Catherine managed a last few words. 'Thank you, thank you, and Madeline, wherever you are – this one's for you too!'

A round of applause broke out at home and away and the music rolled. The live link was severed, and knowing they were off camera, Sheena, Helen, and Amanda all pulled a still shaking Catherine into a group hug, then took her towards the beach bar.

'I told you you'd win, but why the hell did you mention her name?' Sheena said smugly.

'It just felt right,' Catherine said earnestly.

Amanda, wanting to keep the moment jolly, jumped in. 'Well bloody done,' she said with a huge smile as Farrah gestured for a waiter to pass them more drinks.

'Well, you really deserved that award,' Farrah said, passing Catherine a glass. 'To Catherine,' Farrah toasted.

They all raised their glasses to the dummy award Catherine was holding and clinked them against the side of it. Before Catherine could say any more, a runner arrived to take her to the press pit where she would be photographed with her award so the images of her could be syndicated on the world's wires. Sheena went to grab her bag, but Catherine gestured for her to stay.

'Stay and enjoy the awards. Best Drama is up soon, we might get the double! I'll be back in ten minutes max. I know how to do a press room fast,' she said with a wink, feeling emboldened.

The time for hand-holding had come to an end; she felt back to her old confident self. Sure, the Xanax she'd dropped earlier had kept the nerves at bay, but winning the award had made her feel she was back where she belonged. She was a star again for the right reason: her acting ability. She made her way to the press room, holding her dress up so that she didn't trip. Even though the six-inch heels she'd been wearing all night had been killing her just moments earlier, she suddenly felt like she was walking on air.

Two hours and five award wins later, the ceremony was finally coming to an end. All in all, *Falcon Bay* had scooped Best Drama, Best Episode, Best Director, Best Actress, Best Storyline, and the Best Multimedia Award. Amanda had not known what to say when she found herself on the podium for the fourth time; all she knew was that every win they had that night set her up for a strong future of keeping the show alive and burning brightly. It wasn't lost on her that her ex Jake would be livid from wherever he was watching. They hadn't won a haul like this in years, and although victory and vindication were already sweet, knowing how bitter he would be feeling was the extra sugar dusting on top.

After they'd gone off-air, they'd all made their way down to the press party, which was being held in Lucy Dean's beach bar. It was rammed with journalists as well as cast and crew. Amanda didn't believe in segregation or hierarchy, unlike Jake, who would have roped off a VIP section for himself and a few of his cronies. No doubt he would have been sneaking off doing lines of coke and then slipping away to the trailers to bang any of the show's minor players who were desperate for bigger roles. Just the mere image of him was enough to wipe the smile off her face, so she shook all thoughts of him out of her head. This was a celebration he had no place in.

As she pushed through the crowded bar towards Farrah, Catherine, Helen, and Sheena, she looked down at her phone and saw a text from Dan congratulating her. It was then that she realised she didn't need to stay out partying with the girls to celebrate; her biggest prize was waiting for her to snuggle up to at home alongside her sleeping baby. The thought that if she hurried, she could be across the dunes and wrapped up with them within fifteen minutes made the decision for her. She would sneak off before anyone noticed. With one quick wave to the girls, who all knew exactly what she was like, she fled down the beach steps and looked for the lantern-lit boardwalk that would lead her to her condo. As her foot hit the last step, a shadow blocked her presence. Looking up, she saw a swaying and clearly stinking drunk Ross Owen.

'Why are you leaving so soon?' he slurred. 'I thought you and the bitches would be doing some sort of voodoo celebration considering what you've done to Jake.'

'What are you talking about?' she said, surprised at the mention of her ex's name. Jake had always hated Ross. In fact, he used to refer to him as Lurch for his distinctive way of walking, which tonight, combined with a ton of booze and sandy ground, was really exaggerated.

'I've been interviewing him for my book. He's told me all about you and what you all did to get control.' Ross paused for maximum effect before continuing. 'He says you had something over Madeline to get her to oust him and he's going to tell me *all* about it when I see him for our next session.'

Amanda knew he was bluffing. Jake was clueless as to how they'd gained control from Madeline. If he had had even the slightest inkling, he'd have already used it to cause them no end of trouble. Knowing he was bluffing, she decided the best thing she could do was ignore him.

'Go home, Ross, and sober up,' she said, pushing past him, but as she drew level with him he grabbed her arm. The bracelet she was wearing, which had gold spikes on it in a gladiatorial style, cut into his hand.

'Ow,' he moaned loudly. And she brushed past and carried on walking.

'*I know things*, Amanda, just you wait and see,' he shouted after her, whilst dramatically holding the cut on his hand. Amanda continued walking. She could see the lights of the condo from where she was now; only a few hundred yards and she'd be away from his drunken ramblings.

As she reached the set of steps that would take her upwards to her home, and out of his line of vision, she noticed his blood had stained her cream jumpsuit.

Annoyed, she turned round and shouted down the beach. 'I'll be sending you the bill for this, you bloody idiot. And when you wake up, *if* you don't remember what a prick you've been tonight, look forward to an email confirming you are now barred from ever setting foot on this island again, Ross. Without access to anyone who works here, let's see how you write a book from the other side of the ocean. *Goodnight*,' she said sarcastically.

She disappeared into her condo. She was going to take off her ruined outfit, jump in the shower and wash the stain of him touching her off her skin, then climb into the fresh crisp sheets where she knew Dan's gorgeous body would be waiting for her.

Farrah, who'd been watching the exchange intently, turned to the others with raised eyes.

'We get rid of one loony and another pops up,' she said, as Sheena also honed in on Ross, who was now making an unsteady return towards where they were all seated, surrounded by their awards.

'Oh god,' Catherine said. 'It's been such a lovely evening, I really don't want it spoiling by *him*. Ross shouted out some really inappropriate and weird stuff when I was in the press tent. Can't someone get him removed?' She eyed him worriedly, looking for security, who were nowhere to be seen as Ross got closer and closer.

'He'd love that,' Helen said, narrowing her eyes. 'He's been trolling us, calling us *power mad bitches*, and stoking his conspiracy theory clickbait for months. "Man booted out of *Falcon Bay*'s awards ceremony" is exactly what he wants, and I'm not going to give it to him, as a quote from me will make it authentic.'

Sheena stood up to head him off. 'Well, I'm *not* an official spokeswoman, so a quote from me means nothing. I'll deal with him,' she said, slicking her ponytail back and raising her shoulders in a 'bring it on' manner. She got out of her seat to head him off at the entrance just in front of where they were sitting, which he'd now reached.

'It's a private party here, Ross. Get back down to the press pit, please.'

'Oh fuck off, Sheena, you don't even work here, although you probably wish you did. What is it they say? Those that can *do* and all that,' he slurred, referring to her previous life as an actress, and getting in her face aggressively.

Helen had had enough and walked over to join Sheena, blocking Ross's way. 'I have the authority to have you removed, so you can go quietly or I can have you dragged out in front of everyone, Ross. I know what I'd choose if I were you, so just leave now before you do something else you'll regret in the morning,' she said firmly. She stood next to Sheena, the pair of them looking like Bond girls turned bodyguards. Still undeterred, Ross pushed past them roughly, knocking them aside, and headed up to where Catherine was sitting behind Farrah.

'Give me an exclusive with your golden girl here and I'll go,' he said, directing his words at Catherine, who was now shaking.

Sheena came after him and blocked his way; in her six-inch heels she towered above Ross. 'Listen up and listen good. Get the fuck away from us right now, before I kick your sorry ass down these stairs and you end up on the floor with everyone looking down on you more than usual. Have you got that? And feel free to quote me, just remember to add award-winning actress and multi-millionairess CEO of the most successful talent agency in the world when you do,' she sneered, raising her heel and resting it on his leg so hard he winced.

'Fuck you, McQueen,' he shouted, then stuck a finger in Helen's direction. 'The show bike here doesn't need you to speak for her, although I guess that could come in handy for when her mouth is full of random cock. Which is pretty often, isn't it, Helen?' he said, laughing.

Helen, humiliated by this, her face now almost as red as her dress, lashed out, slapping him hard across the face. Her emerald and diamond cocktail ring left a large graze on his jowly cheek. An enraged Farrah was next out of her seat and in Ross's face as Catherine continued to tremble.

'How dare you speak to her like that, you disgusting piece of shit! Get the fuck out of here before I come at you. And it won't just be a slap, I'll knock your yellow teeth out,' she said, raising a fist towards him.

Ross dramatically held a hand to his now bleeding cheek and let out a drunken laugh. 'What are you hiding back there for, Catherine? Come and join the party. This will make a great exclusive tomorrow. I'd hate you to be left out, especially seeing how much you've been enjoying all the attention again tonight.' He pointed to where she was, all alone in the seating area, clearly stressed out by what was going on.

He went to take another step towards her, but all three women stood united and pushed him back. Undeterred, he shouted insults at her over them as she gathered her bag and award and fled the nook, making her way along the waterside terrace in a desperate attempt to flee the dream night that he'd turned into a nightmare. As she disappeared out of sight, he shouted after her, 'Come back! I think I can see a shark coming, don't you want to try and pretend to save me from it for a nice picture to go with the story?'

That was the last straw for Farrah, who in one fell swoop punched Ross straight in the face, sending him flying down the step and into the sand.

Holding his face, he looked up, dazed but undeterred, from the ground. 'I've got witnesses to that, you crazy bitch,' he shouted. He looked around for others in the press area to back him up, but it was clear that everyone in the close vicinity of where he'd landed had turned their backs, not wanting to get involved. Helen grabbed a walkie talkie and called security, telling them to get over here now.

'Oh, save them the trip!' he said, standing up and dusting off the sand. 'I'm leaving, now I've got what I needed from you. You do realise you played right into my hands?' The women looked at each other, confused, as he pointed to his top pocket and pulled a camera out from it. 'I've got all this on film. I'll edit my bits out – you'll be trending on Twitter by morning and be front-page news for the second edition of *The Herald*. Let's see what the Hollywood press think of you *ladies* then, shall we? I bet they'll have those awards off you before we come off print!' He staggered off, half laughing, half wincing as the women had whacked him with all their might.

Sheena turned to look for Catherine. 'Shit, she's gone,' she said, sounding devastated. 'I so wanted this to be such a special night for her.' She was genuinely upset.

Helen pulled Sheena and Farrah towards her and back down into their seats. 'He's always been a pain but I've never seen him so vile. That was hideous,' she said, clearly shaken, scanning the crowd to see if Matt had been anywhere in earshot to hear Ross calling her a slut. She knew he couldn't have been, or he'd have intervened, but she still panicked at the idea of him thinking of her like that, so not seeing him was a relief.

Feeling tired, Farrah had had enough. 'I'll go and check on her; her condo is closest to mine. I'm sure she'll have gone home. Leave it to me. I'll text you when I know she's OK. Let's not let that idiot ruin our night. We won big tonight, ladies, and no one cares what a washed-up boozy old hack thinks. Sheena, I know you'll sort it with your contacts and discredit whatever he says or what that video shows.'

Sheena nodded that she intended to do just that.

'So please let's keep all those wins as our memory – not that prick.' Farrah hugged them both, before Sheena placed a hand on her arm.

'Don't go yet. You are right, we should be celebrating, especially your Best Director Award for the special live episode,' she said, gesturing to the statue, which in her haste to try to leave, Farrah had left on the table. 'Have one more with us and then go after her. She probably wants to be alone. Let's stay a bit longer and end tonight on a high.'

Farrah's tired face livened up when she looked at her award again and then back to Sheena's cheerful face. Helen waved a champagne bottle with a pleading expression.

'Oh, go on then.' Farrah laughed, gesturing to her glass. 'Fill it up!'

*

Up on the rockside, where the fireworks display had gone off when she'd won her award, Catherine was crying. Her dress

61

had torn as she'd climbed the temporary stairs to the rigging deck. Behind her was the giant illuminated *Falcon Bay* logo Amanda had designed to look as impressive as the Hollywood sign itself. Mascara-filled tears streamed down her face as she looked way down on the party below her, then out to the sea, wishing tonight had ended as it had begun. When she'd flown back from the funeral last night, she'd hoped Sheena was right, that she could have her old life back. When she'd won the award, which she still held in her perfectly manicured hand, she really had started to believe it was possible to start again. The night had been so wonderful and for the first time since that terrible day she'd actually not thought about the moment when she and Madeline locked eyes as she'd disappeared into the shark's razor-sharp tooth-filled mouth. The guilt that had consumed her night and day had finally started to subside and she'd found herself having fun tonight, something she thought would never happen again.

'Well, you didn't bring me much luck for long, did you?' she said softly to the statue, which glinted in the light of the bulbs illuminating the sign.

She wiped her eyes and tried to block out the music from the dance floor down in the dunes and tune into the sounds of the sea. The waves crashing had always been a source of solace for her. In her forty-one years on the island, every time something bad happened, she'd come to the shoreline and allow its waters to calm her. Even when storms were raging and waves were crashing, somehow, she always found its vastness soothing.

She fished in her clutch bag for the strip of Xanax she'd brought with her for an emergency situation. She'd wanted to take it out and pop a few during the altercation in the press pit, but was terrified she'd be papped pill-popping and then, instead of her win tonight, all the bad headlines would start again, ripping her life apart just like before. Looking at the pills, she knew it was time to face the harshness of the future, and step out of the marshmallow-soft version of reality they coated her days in.

With her spare hand, she threw the pills out into the sea, vowing that every day from now on was going to be real. She was going to allow herself to feel it, the good, the bad, the guilt, or the glory, for however many years she had left in the job or on this earth. She was going to pull herself together and make the best of it. If nothing else, tonight's disastrous ending had somehow made her realise nothing would ever be perfect again, so she was just going to have to make the best of it.

For a moment longer she listened to the sea, and then started the affirmations she'd found on Google, which she'd. been using to get her through her darker days.

'I am strong. I am a survivor. I am a good person. I will be forgiven.'

'Forgiven for what?' a voice rang out behind her.

Startled, she spun round to see Ross had climbed the stairs and was also on the rockside platform. The shock of seeing him made her grab the safety railing and step backwards towards the edge.

'What are you doing up here?' she said, panicked, looking down towards the party again to see if anyone was watching that she could wave at to attract attention. The way Ross was swaying, he looked even more drunk than he had down at the party. As her eyes darted around desperately, hoping someone had seen them, he got closer.

'I said, what do you need to be forgiven for?' he said again, this time stumbling further forwards so they were now just feet apart.

Aware no one was going to come to her rescue, she took a deep breath and channelled her Lucy Dean voice to show her authority. She still had her heels on – she'd been too flustered to take them off in her desperation to climb up to the platform and away from the madness – meaning that she was eye to eye with him.

'Ross, I'm going to walk past you now and leave. I will not engage in this,' she said, striding to the side of him, aiming for the staircase. As she reached him, he stepped back and let her pass. Surprised, she hurried her steps, and was just feet away from him when suddenly she felt his hands on her shoulders, pulling her back.

'What are you doing?' she shouted, genuinely scared.

'Don't tell me you don't want it,' Ross leered as he tried to kiss her. She was disgusted as his body odour wafted under her nose. Despite pulling her head away from him as hard as she could, his tongue touched the side of her mouth and she felt him slobber on her cheek.

'Get off me!' she screamed as loudly as she could.

She no longer feared the headlines of whatever any paparazzi would spin out of shots of her looking dishevelled and tearful on what was supposed to be her big night. There was no way she was going to allow herself to be sexually assaulted to protect her image. To silence her, he placed a fat clammy hand over her mouth as he slid the other down her dress and felt her breast.

'You old ones always want it,' he said, squeezing her skin so hard it hurt.

Suddenly she was scared for her life. The weight of him on her was beginning to make her feel like she was going topple over in her heels, and if he got her on the floor, the very thought of what he could do to her out of sight made her stomach lurch. With all her might, she threw her arm backwards, and with the hand that was still clutching her award she hit him in the face as hard as she could. The shock of it made him lose his grip, and as she stumbled forward towards freedom, he stumbled backwards towards the barrier. As she ran towards the stairs, she heard the sound of breaking metal and a scream. Everything in her told her to keep going but she found herself turning round to see that Ross had smashed backwards through the barrier and gone over the cliffside.

In shock, she dropped the award and tentatively stepped towards the edge of the platform. There was now a gap in the guard rail and she looked down to see Ross about 100 feet below her. On the last few rocks that separated them from the sea, she could make out his crumpled body, and with the glow of the lights bouncing off the water, she could see a massive flow of blood coming from his battered head.

Catherine held onto what was left of the safety rail, fearing she was going to faint and follow him over, then looked out for people who would be coming to help her. Their screams alone must have caught people's attention even over the loud music, she was sure, but as she scanned the island, she saw there was no one near the rockside apart from her above and now Ross below. Her hands were shaking as she got down on the floor of the platform to look for her bag, which she'd lost as she'd tried to fight him off. She was praying it hadn't gone over the edge and into the water when she spotted it. With trembling hands, she pulled her phone out and dialled Sheena's number and she answered immediately.

'I'm up on the rockside sign, help me,' was all she managed before collapsing to the floor in floods of tears and wondering how the fuck she was going to get out of this mess.

After driving one of the beach buggies at top speed along the coast, less than five minutes later, Sheena, Farrah and Helen pulled up under the rockside platform to find Catherine standing by the ladders that led up to it. As the women rushed towards her, the sheer look of panic on her face sobered them up immediately. Sheena gestured for the others to stay back as she spoke gently.

'Catherine, don't be silly, going up there is dangerous,' she said, as Catherine turned her back to them and started crying loudly.

'It's too late,' she sobbed.

Farrah looked up and, spotting the broken barrier above, was suddenly terrified that if she fled up the steps and they couldn't stop her in time, she might fall off. Farrah took another step towards her. 'We're here now, Catherine, come away from the stairs. It was just a bad night, everything's going to be OK.'

Helen nodded and took a step too. Now all three of them were just feet from her.

'But it's *not* going to be OK!' Catherine screamed, letting go of the rail of the staircase and turning to face them.

Sheena took in her torn dress and the bloodied statue in her hand.

'What do you mean?' she said.

'Follow me,' Catherine said quietly, then led them around the base of the rockside towards the side of the cliffs. It led into the hidden cove where they would often meet for lunch to get away from the hustle and bustle of the busy production hub on the island.

The women followed her. Farrah and Helen held their dresses as the rough waters splashed them; Sheena took her heels off and carried them to get a better footing. Although it was dark in the cove, the lights from the *Falcon Bay* sign above were throwing a glow on the waters and the jagged rocks around them. Catherine's golden dress, now all tattered and torn, was catching the light. Helen was just about to ask her what had happened to it when Sheena, who was the closest behind Catherine, broke the silence.

'Oh my god,' she gasped, as she took in the broken body at the bottom of the cove being lashed by the waves. 'It's Ross.'

'Not again,' Farrah raged, rushing forward in anger and almost slipping on the rocks in her spiked heels. Helen wasn't far behind. 'What the fuck is he doing now?' she added furiously, but before they could reach Sheena, she stepped aside to show them what Catherine had led her to.

'He's dead,' she said solemnly.

All three women stared at each other in shock, then at Catherine, who was shaking, her dress now soaked by the waters. In one hand she still held her Best Actress statue, which was streaked with blood.

'He attacked me,' she said through chattering teeth as the cold, combined with her sobs, made her words almost illegible.

Sheena pulled her close and turned away from the sight of Ross, whose head had split badly on the rocks, which was so gruesome it made her want to vomit.

'Do you mean he . . .?' Farrah began, gently looking at Catherine's torn dress, now with different eyes as she took in what Catherine was trying to say.

Catherine, still shaking, nodded. 'I was up on the sign and he followed me up. I had to fight him off, and he went over the edge,' she managed, before breaking into large sobs once more.

Helen's eyes widened. 'That fucking bastard.'

'We need to call the police,' Farrah said in fury, rushing

over to put an arm around Catherine, who was now sandwiched between herself and Sheena. 'It's clearly self-defence.'

'*It was*!' Catherine cried. 'I only hit him with this to get him off me, then he fell through the barrier! I didn't push him, I swear,' she sobbed.

Helen grabbed her phone from her bag. 'Matt's still here, I'll call him,' she said, dialling his number, but Sheena let go of Catherine and leaned forward, grabbing Helen's phone.

'*Don't*,' she said firmly.

'Why?' Helen and Farrah said in unison.

'Look at her, it's obvious what happened,' Helen added, still holding her finger over the dial button on her phone.

Sheena looked around the cove to see if any party stragglers had made their way towards its location, but was relieved to see they were still alone.

'Everyone in that party saw *us* fighting with him earlier,' she said in a matter-of-fact tone that she might have used during one of her network negotiations. '*All of us* attacked and publicly threatened him. The whole of the press tent saw it. He also grabbed hold of Amanda on the beach. He'll be covered in all our DNA.'

'I slapped him, I didn't bash his head in and push him over a cliff,' Helen snapped.

'I told you I *didn't* push him!' Catherine cried.

Farrah, who was still holding Catherine, turned towards Sheena. 'He tried to rape her, that overrides what happened earlier.'

'Try telling the police that,' Sheena said bluntly.

'That's what I'm suggesting we do,' Helen spat, still annoyed at what Sheena was saying.

'Listen to me,' Sheena continued, stepping towards Ross's battered body and pulling the hem of her jumpsuit up higher as the waves crashed against them. 'It will be her word alone and after what happened at Christmas, are they really going to believe her – twice?'

The women looked at each other as Sheena continued.

'There are so many witnesses who can all say what we did to him *and* how we felt about him. We'll all be pulled in over this. We've only got one chance to walk away from this unscathed.'

'What exactly are you saying?' Farrah said quietly, now overwhelmed by everything and starting to feel the cold.

'Everyone saw how drunk he was, and that he staggered off away from the party way before we left, so let's just push him into the water, and let it wash away any association with us. Everyone will just assume he climbed the cliff and fell off the barrier on his own.'

'I'm *not* touching that body,' Helen said furiously.

Catherine stood up straight and faced them all. 'She's right. I want to tell the truth. I'll tell them what happened. I was protecting myself. I can't live another lie.'

Sheena gestured for her to keep her voice down. 'And that's the problem, isn't it? If you tell them what happened tonight and they start grilling you over Madeline again, then you'll confess everything then, won't you, which will drop us all in the shit.'

Catherine didn't answer. Her silence confirmed the accusation was true.

Seeing her reaction, the other women began to realise what Sheena was trying to say. Once she could see they got her point, she began to drive it home.

'Farrah, take Catherine back to yours. Helen, you and I will return to the party.'

Helen looked at her, aghast. 'I can't do that. Matt is waiting for me, how will I think straight?'

'You'll think a lot straighter back at that party than you will in a prison cell if she tells them everything about last year whilst they are questioning her about this piece of shit,' Sheena said, gesturing towards Ross's body. With the tide rising, it was starting to bob up and down and bash against the rocks with the power of the waves. 'We'll go back with Farrah and Catherine and change outfits. Everyone's so pissed no one will notice as long as we stick to the same colours.'

'*Matt* will notice,' Helen said, her anger rising at finding herself dragged into another situation not of her making.

'Then tell him you've changed into something new you thought he'd like,' Sheena continued. 'Get with the programme, Helen. We've got to head back there now so we don't look like we've been gone long enough to be involved.'

As the realisation of what they were dealing with sank in, Farrah led Catherine, who was still shaking, back to the buggy. Helen began to follow them with a face like thunder. Once all three were inside, she called out to Sheena, who was still on the rocks by Ross's body.

'Let's go then,' she said aggressively.

'Hang on,' Sheena said, searching Ross's pockets for the camera he'd shown them he had on him during the press pit bust-up – but it wasn't there.

'Shit,' she said, scanning the rocks where he'd landed, looking for it.

'*Are we leaving or what?*' Helen snapped.

Unable to see anything, and aware they were running out of time, Sheena waded into the freezing ocean and used all her strength to drag Ross off the rock that his clothes had snagged on. Once he was free, she gave the corpse a hard push, making it float out to sea.

I wish that bloody shark was here now, she thought.

Soaking wet, she climbed back over the rocks. Once on the

coveside, she put her shoes back on and joined the others in the buggy. In the driving seat, she pushed her heel down hard on the accelerator and they sped away from the cove in total silence.

Chapter 3

In her office, Helen controlled the CCTV. It covered the entrance to St Augustine's, and she was using it to scan the crowd of journalists and reporters who had been camped outside since Ross Owen's body had been found washed up on a nearby shore a week earlier. Spotting Tabitha Tate, she zoomed in. With her perfect black skin showcased by a fitted two-piece white skirt and polka-dot top combo, Helen was surprised to see she wasn't shivering in the freezing cold as she delivered yet another viral media report on CITV for *The Herald*'s blog. Scanning the camera down her body, she took in her killer heels and the board she'd had placed under the sand to stop herself sinking whilst a cameraman filmed her.

'Clever little witch,' Helen said to herself, then flicked her eyes over to her computer and onto *The Herald*'s Instagram page, where Tabitha was broadcasting live.

Helen turned the volume up as Tabitha's perfectly made-up face, framed by her long dark hair, filled the screen. Her irritatingly upbeat American tone delivered yet another sensationalist set of questions for the viewers to bombard the studio with. It was her opinion, apparently, that CITV were not 'doing their all to help the media retrace her beloved late colleague Ross's final moments', which she once again emphasised that her newspaper felt was suspicious.

It was well known that Tabitha and Ross were arch enemies at *The Herald*. Her ambition for a scoop, plus her being half his age, had made him block her at every turn, so much so that she wasn't even at the fateful press party he'd lost his life at. But following his death, Tabitha had certainly picked up his *Falcon Bay*-bashing baton, and they'd been under almost constant scrutiny since Ross's body had been found. That level of attention wasn't abnormal after what happened at Christmas, but it had certainly intensified since the awards night.

Helen had felt a bit better about everything when her boyfriend Detective Matt Rutland had told her, off the record, that although the coroner's report on Ross was yet to be announced, the police saw Ross's death as that of an intoxicated man's poor judgement call on climbing the rockside before falling. His body, bloated and battered by the rocks, according to Matt, had been in the sea for five days before being found, so there was little evidence to work with. He'd told Helen this when they were in bed together. She'd felt guilty, tricking the information out of him, but she really was the only one of the group that had access to that sort of useful pillow talk. If she hadn't had Matt's reassurance, she wouldn't have been able to calm Catherine, Farrah, and the usually cool Sheena. Thanks to Tabitha's constant conspiracy theories, even she'd started to wonder if perhaps the knock was coming.

She switched off the CCTV and got out of her huge chair, the one she'd been sitting in for the last three decades in her casting director's office. This was the place where she had the power to turn an unknown nobody into the nation's sweet-heart, or the most desirable hunk, with her decision alone.

She made her way over to the cast wall. She scanned the pictures and let her gaze fall on Catherine's angelic headshot. She hadn't cast Catherine in the role that had made her famous worldwide; that had been before her time on the show. But she had been the one to convince Catherine that Farrah was the right actress to play her daughter. It seemed a lifetime ago that both Farrah Adams and Sheena McQueen had been actresses. Sheena's downfall and spiral into drink and drugs had made her the Lindsay Lohan of her day, and seeing Sheena unable to handle the fame being on a syndicated drama gave you had been a warning sign to Farrah. Both left the screens, but not the business. When Sheena returned to the industry some years later, she'd reinvented herself as the true Queen of Soaps, one of the most powerful soap agents in the industry.

Out of the three actresses – Sheena, Farrah and Catherine – it was only Catherine Belle who'd had the sheer determina-tion to remain a 'star'. She was so desperate to continue soaring around the celebrity sun, it had caused burns to all those around her. Unlike the others, Catherine *lived* for her role as Lucy Dean. Helen knew that after so many years, an actress's character could become so undistinguishable from their own persona that they felt they couldn't let go. Helen just wished Catherine would stop killing people to retain her crown, albeit accidentally.

Her eyes turned to a photo of all five of them that was sitting on her desk, and she looked at it fondly, thinking of the memories of their girls' trip to Monaco where it had been taken.

Even including Amanda, who joined them ten years into their thirty-year-old union, these were the longest relationships she'd ever had. The many men had come and gone, but their friendship had stayed true. Which was why, despite her better judgement over not wanting to follow Sheena's plans on the night of Ross's death, and going along with Amanda's cover-up over what really happened to Madeline King, she had decided she was going to continue to choose loyalty to her friends over anything else, even if it did leave a niggle of worry in her perfectly toned tummy.

She was just about to turn her out-of-office on and meet Matt down by the set when her phone rang. Her mind had already clocked out of work mode and she was enjoying imagining having his naked body on every inch of the island. She knew the press were flying drones overhead, trying to get exclusives pictures to go with their sensational stories. That should have made her play things safe and keep him confined to the safety of a soundproofed room, and have him on her sturdy leather desk, which in its heyday had held the weight of many a threesome. But Matt's gorgeous thick thighs and the way he went down on her made her want to christen every area of St Augustine's all over again.

In a way, she saw it as cleansing the past. If she made love to Matt in every area she'd ever banged someone on this island, it would be like a fresh start, because ever since he'd told her he loved her, she'd been choking back the urge to say it back. But after the events of last week, she'd decided that life could literally be too short. Tonight, as she was lying in his manly arms somewhere they shouldn't be, she was going to say the three little words back to him that she'd never, in her whole sixty-something years, said to any man before.

She finally picked up her ringing phone. Suddenly the smile that had spread across her face at what she was planning to do was gone.

*

Half a mile down the rugged coastline, Farrah lay in her queen-size bed in the condo she'd lived in since arriving in St Augustine's Cove in the early nineties. Not once in all those years had she missed a day on set.

The stars of *Falcon Bay* were well known to throw a sickie or two, but never Farrah Adams. She'd played Lucy Dean's daughter to great acclaim before tiring of the spotlight and stepping behind the cameras. Her love of the show and the drama world had never been in doubt though. She just wanted to get away from the glare of its harshest light before it burnt her, as it had done so many teenage stars before.

Falcon Bay's amazing location and the lifelong sisterhood she'd built with Catherine, Helen, and Amanda meant she hadn't even travelled far to fulfil her next ambition, writing. Thanks to her agent, the indomitable Sheena McQueen, her profile had thrived. And recently, thanks to the entertainment industry finally realising that women like her in positions of power were as rare as unicorns, she'd become one of the few black women at her level in entertainment to win multiple awards for her work. But seeing her name in lists like 'top ten female trailblazers' and in various media power lists wasn't what Farah was in the business for. She didn't care for accolades that related to her skin colour, didn't want to be judged on her appearance or heritage. She prided herself on being recognised for her work alone, which in her opinion was worth the awards she was given. This included the one she'd won when she was on a high the week before Ross Owen's death had turned her beloved haven of St Augustine's Cove into a media circus once more.

The last year should have been the best of her career. She'd finally made the move she'd really been working towards all along, infiltrating the male-dominated roster of male directors on the show. They hated her, of course, for daring to unbalance their testosterone-fuelled band of brothers, but Farrah didn't care. Sure, she'd had to play dirty to get the Christmas live episode that the whole world was still talking about, sadly for the wrong reasons, but she'd barely thought twice about the levels she'd sunk to to sabotage *Falcon Bay*'s number-one director, Aiden Anderson.

He'd only been number one because he was best friends with their former network controller, Amanda's uber prick of an estranged husband, Jake Monroe. If there were two men who she despised more on this earth, she wasn't sure she could name them. She hadn't been able to step onto the set since what happened on the rockside after the awards. At first, she thought she must be having some sort of physical reaction to what had happened, but now she began to contemplate that, if possible, the reason she'd been unable to show up was even worse.

She heard the sound of the waves crashing on the rocks outside. With her balcony doors open, she could smell the sea breeze. Normally it soothed her, made her feel calm. On other days its roughness mirrored the attitude and authority she felt she needed to show on a set that was filled with middle-aged, vanity-filled actors, who behaved as if they were in a kindergarten session rather than on the world's most watched soap opera.

Suddenly she felt the urge to vomit again. She crawled from under her Egyptian cotton sheets. Her lace Valentino kimono dropped from her defined shoulders and she made it to the en-suite just in time to be sick for the third time that morning. After the last of the peppermint tea she'd drunk to calm her stomach earlier hit the porcelain base, and the dry heaves that followed finally eased, she lay flat. She let the cool of the tiled floor chill her skin, which felt like it was burning.

'Fuck, fuck, fuck,' she said, looking down at what was definitely the beginnings of a swollen stomach protruding from her otherwise perfectly athletic and lean body. On the floor next to her were several used pregnancy tests, all with clear lines confirming, without doubt, that she was not alone in her bathroom.

'This *can't* be happening,' she mumbled as the dry heaves began again. Then, as she started to shake from the coldness of the porcelain tiles, which had taken the heat from her naked body, she burst into tears.

Chapter 4

Suddenly, without a knock, the door swung open and Helen Gold appeared, taking Amanda by surprise. It was well known that Helen rarely worked past 4 p.m. Hanging around the set to watch the sun go down was not the kind of thing she did. Considering the amount of noise the reporters had been making at the studio's security gates all day, Amanda assumed perhaps Helen had come for a drink on her balcony.

'Rosé or white?' Amanda asked, gesturing to the bottles chilling by the window.

'Neither,' Helen said, closing the door firmly behind her. Dressed in a lime-green silk suit, she appeared to float as she moved, as if a wind machine was aimed at her. She strode across the vast room to reach Amanda's side of the office and took a seat in one of the armchairs that faced the sea view. Sensing all was definitely not OK, Amanda steeled herself for yet more bad news, placed her bag back down, and sat in the seat next to her.

'It's going to be a late one here for us again, I'm afraid,' she said, looking out towards the calm sea and not directly at her friend, which instantly made a knot appear in Amanda's stomach. Knowing Helen would usually be swinging from a chandelier at this time of the early evening and not in her office avoiding eye contact told her it must indeed be serious.

As Amanda geared herself up to hear whatever she was about to hear, Helen turned her face towards her and their eyes locked.

'Now, try not to panic, but the Kane Foundation called just as I was about to leave.'

Amanda's tummy did another flip. The tension released somewhat as she was relieved Helen hadn't said the police were at the building again. The grilling they'd had over what they'd seen of Ross before he fell to his death had been exhausting enough.

'Chad wants a video conference with us here at 6 p.m. *his time* today,' Helen said, and gave a slight grimace that showed her perfectly veneered teeth against her blood-red YSL lip gloss.

Amanda did a quick calculation in her brain, trying to work out the time difference. Helen, who'd already googled it, decided to save her the bother.

'That's our midnight, *tonight*.'

Before Amanda could react, Helen barrelled on. 'And yes, I've already asked what it's about, as casually as I could, but it was Melissa, his sister, the one Sheena texted us about from the funeral. She must be acting as his PA.'

Amanda poured herself a glass of wine as Helen continued.

'She wouldn't say what it was about, just that we were both to be on it. It's a real pain in the ass as I've got Matt downstairs and I've been trying to give him one of my *private* island tours, which was going to end in us staying over in one of the cabanas. He's on nights from tomorrow, meaning he won't be able to stay over till the weekend.' She looked uncharacteristically disappointed.

As Helen continued to wax lyrical about her plans with Matt, Amanda couldn't believe Helen seemed unbothered about 'the problem' she'd announced as she arrived.

Amanda looked pale as Helen then slapped her own wrist in recognition of Amanda's worried expression. Helen decided she would join her in a glass of wine after all.

'Sorry! I know I'm going on, but take that as a good sign that I'm not too freaked out about tonight. Let's not be alarmist until we hear what he has to say. We knew we'd hear from him at some point. Without Madeline, he's effectively our boss. He's got loads of businesses in the States, maybe tonight's just the only time he was free to speak to us.' She said all of this unconvincingly.

'Whilst we're right in the middle of yet another media shitstorm, Helen, a coincidence? Really?' Amanda said, with a slight tremor in her voice.

Helen went to top up Amanda's wine glass but she pulled it away.

'He'll know the time differences, and that I've got a young baby, so to make it midnight is one thing, but to say it has to be *here* and for us both to be on . . . Come on, Helen, we both know this can't be good.' She looked out of the balcony at the precious bay that just moments before Helen's arrival had seemed calm, peaceful, and serene. Suddenly the weather had turned; it was as if the waves on their famous beach had ingested the poisoned news Helen had brought and was now frothing. The sea began to crash against the rocks and seagulls passed by the balcony, making what now sounded like warning siren sounds.

Placing her hand gently on Amanda's shoulder, Helen tried to pull her out from what was an obvious spiral. 'Look, I like to think I'm important to the show, but we both know no one higher than you ever thinks I am. The fact that he's asked me to be on the call probably means he wants some changes.'

Amanda's eyes stayed on the sea. 'Hmm. God, I'm dreading seeing his face – Sheena said she'd never seen anyone cry so much as he did at Madeline's funeral,' she murmured.

They both looked at each other in a moment's recognition of the fact that Chad was a victim in all this, then, wanting to move the mood on, Helen stood up. 'Look, let's not assume the worst – it might just be about the network. Maybe he's selling it? The show wasn't his baby, was it? It was Madeline's.'

Helen's words fizzed into Amanda's brain, pulling her from the mesmerising sea. If Helen was right, a new network owner could come in and ruin everything she had.

Suddenly, remembering Dan was downstairs holding Olivia, she was disgusted with herself. This was exactly the way Jake would think.

Had she been with him so long that some of his toxicity had become embedded in her, so that all she could think about was losing control of the show? During the IVF they'd gone through to get Olivia, had some of his self-centred seeds entered her body at the same time? She'd certainly never believed she'd have done what she did on Christmas Day, nor covered up for the others again in the middle of the night after Catherine and Ross had fought on the platform. All this deceit was very Jake.

Feeling a migraine coming on with the stress, she rubbed her temples then turned to Helen, who had taken advantage of Amanda's lack of participation in their talk to get her phone. Only Helen Gold, the most single woman on the Bay, would choose a member of the police to shack up with at the exact time that the police were the very last people they needed around. By the look on her face, she was probably in the middle of sexting him right now. If it wasn't so bloody scary, she'd have laughed at the absurdity of it all.

Getting out of her seat, she smoothed her auburn hair and finished her wine.

'You get back down to Matt,' Amanda said, 'but please be careful of *where* you give him your tour – remember where the cameras are. A sex tape leaking is the last thing we need right now on top of everything else.'

'Oh, I'll stay on top of him, and I promise no leakage.' Helen winked with a wry smile.

Amanda rolled her eyes.

'Right, I'll go home with Dan and put Olivia to bed. Shall we meet back here at eleven p.m.? That gives us an hour to prepare. Let's cross our fingers for the best; see you later.'

She forced a smile as she pulled her pink and grey Louis Vuitton shawl off her chair and threw it around her shoulders, picked up her bag and phone, then headed for the exit. Helen was already on her phone again, probably texting Matt to come up to Amanda's office so they could do it on her balcony, which had the best view of the island.

Chapter 5

When Tabitha Tate had contacted Fonda Books MD Mickey Dean's secretary for an appointment, she'd expected to wait weeks, maybe months, to get in to see him. For years he'd been the publisher everyone looked down on, always seen as the runt of the literary world, despite several (critically slaughtered) bestsellers under his brand's belt.

The publication of Honey Hunter's autobiography, selling over ten million copies so far, and reviewed with universal acclaim, had finally made his once sneered at central London office *the* place everyone who had a book to sell wanted to be.

The success for Mickey, though, was bittersweet. The very reason he was an outsider was because he specialised in bringing fallen stars back into the public eye. He didn't follow the zeitgeist and sign up the latest Instagram influencer or some teenager off TikTok. He loved *real* stars and had a theory that if the world knew about you before the rise of social media, then the core audience would always be interested in you because back then there were only a handful of channels. So if you'd been in a soap opera or a successful movie, sometimes half the country that it had been shown in had invested in your life – the good, the bad, and the ugly.

The world might have moved on, with everyone able to be 'famous' at the click of an Instagram button, but there was a whole era of stars that had been left by the wayside during the reality star revolution. And that's where Mickey had cleaned up. He'd tracked down reclusive former child star, wild child, and Oscar winner Honey Hunter. He'd persuaded her to let him take her back into the spotlight with a starring role on *Falcon Bay*, as well as with an international bestselling autobiography.

What he hadn't accounted for – what no one had, not even the most imaginative mind in the world of PR spin – was that his star act could disappear off the face of the earth.

Jake Monroe had called him on the eve of the day she was due to make her acting comeback – to an audience of hundreds of millions around the world as *Falcon Bay*'s new bitch, in their now infamous Christmas Day live episode. Honey had confided in Mickey that she'd been having an affair with Jake, who had called to say she'd fled the villa they'd been staying in near the set. Since then, no one had seen or heard from her.

At first, he'd hoped she'd got 'the fear', which wasn't unusual for a former star to get on the night before the gaze and expectancy of so many millions of viewers. But as weeks turned to months, Mickey tried every hack and contact he had, and he knew everyone. He turned up nothing, apart from learning that she'd booked a one-way flight from France to Los Angeles. According to border control, she'd arrived at LAX, but there was no trace of her beyond that.

In desperation, he'd even flown over to her home in Switzerland, but her maid was adamant she had not been in contact. After the success of her book – and before filming was due to start – he'd advised Honey to transfer her assets to his accountants, who knew how to help keep her earnings safely tucked away in a tax haven. They'd confirmed that not one of her accounts had been touched since Christmas Day. For a woman as high maintenance as Honey, it just made no sense that she'd not needed any resources to air her low profile. He would have understood if she'd suddenly felt she couldn't cope with the pressure of being propelled back into the public's consciousness.

She'd hidden before, having gone through three bitter divorces, a breakdown, public sackings and some tawdry affairs. So she knew how to keep a low profile if she wanted to. Years ago, at the age of thirty-five, when she felt as though her career was flatlining, she'd holed herself up in Switzerland. Ashamed of her past and not ready to embrace the future, she'd escaped the tabloid hell and stayed there for twenty years. Mickey felt an incredible amount of guilt, an unusual emotion for him, that he had not persuaded her to come back at the time. If he'd been able to, perhaps she would now be safe and sound in her snowy haven rather than nowhere on God's earth.

The prize of reintroducing her to the world as the fabulous actress she was had been too tempting for both of them: a starring role on TV's hottest show, in a storyline that would see her replace Catherine Belle as *Falcon Bay*'s new leading lady. But now the world's media was obsessed with the mystery surrounding her disappearance, which coincided with the tragic death of Madeline Kane, owner of CITV, the production company that made the show.

When Honey had failed to turn up to film the live episode, Madeline had inexplicably taken her place. She'd stepped into Honey's role on the very fateful night the show had aired its first live episode to celebrate its fortieth anniversary.

Since then, there'd been much speculation about exactly what had happened on the Cursed Island of St Augustine's, as the press were now calling it, and no one speculated more than the young and feisty reporter and blogger Tabitha Tate. There wasn't a day that went by when she wasn't presenting some new take on what might have happened. Mickey was so impressed by her tenacity, considering her young age, that he'd abandoned his recent protocol of making people wait weeks for a meeting with him and arranged for her to come in on the same day she'd made the call.

Mickey was deep in thought when, after a brief rap of her knuckles on the solid oak door, and without waiting for an answer, Tabitha entered his office. She immediately took a seat opposite Mickey's marble desk. It was filled with photos of him standing next to his favourite stars. A photo of him and Honey cutting the ribbon in front of a queue of hundreds waiting to get their books signed was in pride of place.

'Thank you for seeing me,' Tabitha said, in her distinct New York twang. 'I know you like it straight, so I won't beat around the bush,' she continued matter-of-factly. She pulled a separate cushion from the opposite chair to put behind her back on the one she sat on.

Mickey's office, and the whole of Fonda Books, was definitely style over substance. The cage chair Tabitha was doing her best to not only sit upright in, but also keep steady in by balancing her zebra-print boots' spiked heels on the floor, was already killing her back. That was part of why she came straight to the point. The other reason was that both she and Mickey spoke the same showbiz shorthand. They both came from tabloid backgrounds, and from what she knew of him, she felt she could ditch the usual ass-kissing airs and graces she'd noticed the Brits seem to go in for, and cut straight to the chase.

87

'Just because Ross Owen is dead doesn't mean the book deal you had in place with him has to be,' she said firmly.

If he'd thought she was direct on TV, that was nothing compared to what she was like in the flesh.

'Go on,' he said, intrigued.

'I've got a pitch for you. I know you'll want it. It's a new and much better take on what Ross was going to do – no offence to the dead intended,' she said, her feet slipping on the floor so much she had no choice but to roll with it and lean back in the chair, trying to style out the swinging motion as chilled-out confidence.

Mickey peered curiously at her from behind the vast desk. He leaned over to where he always kept a bottle of Cristal in an ice bucket, next to some ornate Baccarat flutes, picked up it up and eyed Tabitha with interest.

'Continue,' he said, expertly popping the bottle's cork. He filled a glass for himself but didn't offer one to his guest.

Irritated by the chair's swinging, as well as the lack of hospitality, Tabitha expertly pulled herself from the chair and sat on the edge of his desk.

'I know he was going down the *Falcon Bay, the unauthorised biography* route, but with recent events going the way they have, I think it's deeper than that. Think *The Curse of Falcon Bay, heartbreak, tragedy, and death,*' she said dramatically. She crossed one perfect leg – encased in a bright pink Stella McCartney trouser suit – over the other.

Mickey drank from his glass and gestured for her to continue.

'*Falcon Bay* has world-wide fan attention thanks to the media's obsession with the show since it became a bloodbath. That Christmas Day live episode went down in history as the most watched episode of anything in modern-day viewing, so the reach for this book is now on a whole new global level.

That means we've got a multilanguage translation rights proposition here. Footage of the moment Madeline was eaten by the shark reached a billion YouTube views before the Kane family had it removed. And it still surfaces every day as mobile phone footage people filmed of their TVs, racking up a few hundred thousand shares before being taken down again. Combine that with Ross Owen's death last week, on the night of the awards ceremony. It was held just feet from where Madeline met her maker. We're not just topical, we're shit hot in the middle of a firestorm, and the flames are only just getting started.'

Mickey still eyed her with interest, a sign she took to continue.

'The world's obsessed, not just with what happened surrounding those *terrible* deaths.' She emphasised the word *terrible* as if to make herself sound compassionate. 'They want to know the truth about everyone associated with that show, on screen and off. The mysterious way Jake Monroe was replaced by his wife on the eve of that episode. How a real shark was brought in for that stunt, when sources tell me they had a perfect CGI version that would have kept everyone safe. The truth behind the rumours of the cast affairs, of which there are many. The blackmail, the backstabbing, and so much more.

'We can go into Sheena McQueen's past as an actress, her drink and drug years, re-examine that dead rock star found in her bath years ago. There'd be an expert opinion on just how much surgery Catherine Belle has had to look the way she does *at her age*. And of course, we need to investigate what happened to your client, Honey. The whole world was waiting for her to appear, and then when she didn't, why exactly did Madeline take over her role? This is a soap within a soap. We'll have a Netflix documentary special ready before we even hit the shelves. It's going to be *huge*.'

At the mention of Honey, Mickey finally offered Tabitha a glass, which she accepted. She felt she'd hit a home run, as they'd say back in the States.

As Mickey poured the champagne into her glass, he reminded himself not to show Tabitha his personal feelings for Honey. He noted that despite the fresh young looks she had, her tender age didn't match the hardened nose she'd developed for stories. Her blog reports on *Falcon Bay* certainly pulled no punches; press types like her had a code of practice, and caring wasn't in it. He paused to hold back his personal feelings of relief that someone so obviously cut-throat was showing an interest in what might have become of his star client.

Tabitha decided to take the gap in conversation to reiterate her passion for the project. 'Mickey – I hope I can call you that,' she said, leaning towards him.

He nodded.

'I left my whole life behind my in New York to follow this story – and a role at *Variety*, one of the biggest publications in the States. I wouldn't be here if I didn't know I was onto a winner. This book will make us a fortune. It'll solve some mysteries that will help bring closure to a lot of people, one of which, if you'll forgive me for saying so, I know will be you. You saved Honey once – now's your chance to save her again. This book will put so much heat on where she is that any maid, busboy or even hairdresser, no matter how well tipped, will ring our hotlines offering info on wherever she's hiding. Let me help you bring her home, and bring down whoever it is on that island who is behind this never-ending spiral of death and deceit. Let's be honest, as an American, I want commercial success, but beyond that, there's a truth here that needs to be uncovered. I'm the woman to do it.'

She leaned back, confident she'd given him her absolute

A-game. She wished her dad, James Tate, the late renowned ABC News anchor, was still alive to hear her smash it. He'd died of cancer the year before. He'd have loved her passion, as he taught her all she knew about killer stories. This had his name written all over it. She'd already decided to dedicate the book to him.

Mickey took a couple more sips of his drink. He needed to cool his composure after the emotions he'd felt at the hopes of finding Honey. Mickey was ready to talk business.

'So, how do you propose to write this tell-all book around your role at *The Herald* newspaper and hosting their online blog?' he said, as flatly as he could, like a poker player determined not to show his hand.

Tabitha smiled. She'd already expected this question and had the answer ready to go.

'We all know traditional newspapers are on the way out,' she said. 'The digital gossip sites that syndicate what I do for *The Herald* online make me way more money than my actual role there. I make more for a sponsored post on Instagram or Twitter. They've already allowed me to reduce my work to just one column a week. It's a money-saving exercise for them, which works for all of us. It means I can do projects I'm passionate about, like this, but gives me the kudos of having a national tabloid behind me. I can access all their best resources in return.

'The deal is that they get first dibs on the headlines and the scandal from any books I write. If they give our book a week's worth of front-cover headlines, combined with my streamed content, which is hitting two million views, it guarantees us a bestseller in Europe alone. I'd estimate that we'd have a global audience of at least 150 million consumers who are interested in *Falcon Bay*. If only 20 per cent of that audience bought it, which, by the way, I feel is a grossly low estimate, we're still talking tens of millions of sales. Everyone's a winner.'

She finished her speech, then, with a toast, knocked back the rest of her glass. Feeling confident, she leaned it towards Mickey, gesturing for a top up.

Mickey slid the bottle over the desk towards Tabitha, for her to do it herself. He got up and walked over to the bookcase that held all his bestsellers; only Honey's had been sold all over the world. He stared at the front cover, which featured her beautiful face in extreme close-up, then turned back to face Tabitha.

'How much?'

'I want a quarter of a million advance, 25 per cent royalties, and I want 50 per cent of all tabloid serialisations. Plus I get to keep the dramatic rights, but we'll split the documentary ones as they will essentially be PR for book sales.' Tabitha was enjoying the Cristal, which had started going to her head, as she hadn't eaten all day. She hoped if they agreed the deal Mickey might open another.

After a brief pause, Mickey turned to look her in her hazel eyes.

'Royalties of 20 per cent, a 150,000k advance, and yes to the serial and drama rights,' Mickey countered. 'But I can tell you now, that is the most that I've ever paid anyone, ever, so think carefully before rejecting it.'

Tabitha paused for a moment. He hadn't said no to the tabloid deal; that alone could be worth a few hundred grand if she uncovered something really juicy. Whilst she knew Mickey could well afford to pay what she'd asked for, she reasoned that, added up, it wasn't a bad offer at all. Plus, she knew he could move quickly, rather than some book publishers, where you'd wait months to hear from 'the board' about whether your proposal was accepted. Mickey being the actual boss meant his word was a lot more powerful than if she started doing the rounds pitching, especially if the story turned cold. Only Ross's death had brought the interest back up in a world where headlines were never hard to find.

'OK, it's a deal,' she said, 'but I want a hundred grand upfront as I need to pull in quite a few spies on this and they don't come cheap.' She downed her drink and gestured for a refill.

Mickey smiled. He liked Tabitha, could feel her hunger, but that didn't mean she was going to have it all her own way.

'There's no problem with that, but I have one condition,' Mickey said firmly, as he topped her glass up. He reached back towards the bookshelf, took Honey's autobiography off it, and placed it right in front of where Tabitha was sitting on the edge of his desk. 'Call it *The Curse of Falcon Bay*, or whatever you think viewers are going to want to buy. You can lead on the deaths of Madeline Kane and Ross Owen, dig into the truth of cast scandals and all the rest of that shit they get up to behind the scenes. But first, you have to put all of your efforts into finding Honey Hunter. That is non-negotiable. No Honey, no money.'

Tabitha was about to object, on the grounds that Honey, although clearly an interesting part of the story, was not as hot or topical as the mysterious deaths of Madeline and Ross. But Mickey's resolute face told her to bite her tongue.

'If you can find her,' he continued, 'you can have the full 250,000 advance you wanted, and I'll even double the royalties. If she's back with me, that's chicken feed compared to the future I had laid out for her. I've done everything I can to find her, so if I give you this contract, hunting her down has to be your number-one priority beyond the rest of the twisted shit that's going on.'

Both were looking at each other from opposite ends of the desk.

'If that's clear, then we have a deal,' Mickey said, leaning back into his seat.

Tabitha took a moment to let his words sink in. Madeline Kane and Ross Owen's deaths were much more interesting to her from a journalistic perspective, but fuck it, for double the deal and exactly what she'd wanted, she was sure she could make finding out what had happened to Honey part of her mission, if not her openly primary one. How hard could it be? she mused. She thought of all the high-profile has-beens that had disappeared from public view, only to be tracked down in some off-the-track hellhole, hiding from the public's gaze because they were back on the very vices they'd sworn to the world they were clean of.

'OK,' she said, with a glint in her eye. She got off the desk and leaned her glass towards his to gesture another toast. 'We have a deal.'

Chapter 6

Sheena's marble bath was so deep she had to use a special neck pillow to stop her delicate frame from slipping to the bottom and her hair, which was twisted in a high ponytail, from getting wet. She inhaled the scent from the natural lavender-infused candles lit all around her. They were from Harrods and the packaging declared they were 'guaranteed to soothe'. Despite their hefty price tag, they were definitely not working.

Reaching over to the side, she grabbed a spliff she'd rolled earlier and lit it using one of the candles. At least they were good for that, she thought, as she inhaled deeply on it and let its effect sink in. The smoke filled her lungs and gave her the sense she was now floating in the vastness of the water.

Even as a recovering drug addict, twenty years and counting without a single slip-up, Sheena had never counted marijuana, or 'puff' as the kids called it, as a real drug. It had been the harder drugs that had been her downfall: coke, speed and ecstasy. Booze and dope had never been her Achilles heel, so luckily, she had been able to hang on to a few vices, like this

95

and a few glasses of a fine wine, without slipping back into her old ways.

As the smoke mellowed her mood, she allowed herself to think back to what had set her nerves on edge earlier that day.

Helen had phoned to say Chad was video-conferencing them later that evening and that she and Amanda were guessing it was to break the news that he was selling CITV. Her feelings were torn. If he sold the network, at least she'd finally be able to stop worrying about Catherine, who, two bodies down, was like a walking truth bomb that might pull its own pin and blow everyone up who'd tried to help her. But on the other hand, *Falcon Bay* was her living. If she got rid of half of the stars she repped at the McQueen Agency, on screen and off, she could happily live on just the commission Catherine Belle's royalties brought in alone.

As she looked around at her opulent bathroom, which took over a whole floor of her Knightsbridge townhouse, the idea of not earning such hefty weekly pay cheques made her feel more uneasy than having to wade into the water to push Ross Owen's body far out into the sea.

She hadn't even lost a night's sleep over his death. Madeline Kane's death, however, had given her countless sleepless nights. She didn't want to let her mind wander down that particularly dark passage, so she took another drag on the roll-up and cast her eyes around her lavish bathroom, with its Swarovski-covered tiles, chandeliers, and dramatic wall hangings.

She wasn't ready to scale back her lifestyle just yet. If Helen was right, she'd just hope that whoever bought the network would keep the show on air, and she'd work her usual magic and not only keep Catherine as its top earner but maybe slip a few new faces in there too. She was definitely feeling more relaxed now. She stretched her legs out and raised one in the air to take in its shape. *Still looking good*, she thought to herself, especially as the big sixty was heading her way in just a couple of years' time.

She'd decided not to tell Catherine about the meeting until it was over and there was a proper update. Why bother, when she was already so on edge over all the Ross Owen press headlines? It might all be for nothing anyway, she'd reasoned.

As she moved into the centre of the bath and gently started to lather her body up with her favourite mandarin-infused body wash, she surprised herself with just how calm she now felt about the possibility of a new boss coming onto *Falcon Bay*. Yes, they could end her reign, but that could happen at any network. All actresses were only safe as long as the new owners or producers liked them. It didn't matter how popular you were with the audience; if you didn't fit someone's bill, you were out.

'That's showbiz, kid,' she said quietly to herself.

She took one last toke on the roll-up, then wet the end to put it out. Nothing could be as bad as the battle they'd found themselves in with Madeline when she'd reappeared, reincarnated, last year. Even covering up Catherine knocking Ross to his death had been a breeze compared to the battle with that bitch.

As the drug made its way to her toes, which felt like they were little marshmallows floating in the water, she decided she was just the right side of mellow. Sheena pulled the plug on the bath and stepped out, wrapping a zebra-print Biba towel around her slim frame. She made her way towards the bedroom.

After drying herself and applying a generous amount of body cream all the way up to her neck, she quickly switched products, dabbing moisturiser on her face. She pulled back the white silk sheets on the queen-size bed and slipped between them. As she massaged the cream in a circular motion, she mused once again on what the outcome of tonight's video-conference call with Chad would be.

Despite everything Catherine had been through, she'd received a global profile boost after surviving the Christmas Day live episode. Last week's Best Actress award against stiff competition showed she was more in demand than ever. So if the axe did fall, Sheena had absolutely no doubt that Catherine Belle would never be out of work, and therefore Sheena would never be out of commission. It didn't matter that Catherine was seventy-one, which in TV years for a woman usually meant you were more than ready for the slaughter yard.

A faint smile crossed her lips as she reached out for her pink silk eye mask from the pillow next to her. She popped her ear plugs in, then flicked a switch on the control by the bed, which sent the aircon into a gentle whirring mode and blew a soft cool breeze in her direction. She'd always been the lightest sleeper, but after the menopause, without her routine of temperature, darkness and silence, not even the strongest spliff on the block would send her to sleep.

As she adjusted the soft pink fabric of the sleep mask over her head, she peeped down at her phone, which was always by her side, even when it was on silent. There were no texts from Helen or Amanda. *No news is good news*, she told herself, as she switched it to aeroplane mode, then flicked the lights off.

In the dark, her mind slowly wandered back to what news Chad would be delivering. She'd felt so sorry for him in Louisiana, married to a bitch from hell, even if he didn't know it, and born into the craziest family she'd ever witnessed – and my god she had seen a few. She hoped that maybe he was going to say the Kane family's reign on the show was over, and he would start a new life away from all this pain. *Falcon Bay* had had several owners before Madeline returned to dig her claws back into it, and by his own admission, Chad knew nothing about television, had innocently been just the bankroller behind his wife's twisted desires.

Yes, she decided, *that must be it. He'll be announcing he wants to sell up and leave the bad memories behind.* A man as decent and kind as Chad would want to do it face to face, albeit by video call. He was a man of respect; you could tell that just by crossing paths with him. *Someone new will come in. I'll win them over and it'll be for the best.* She smiled as sleep began to overcome her . . .

Chapter 7

After several more glasses of champagne at Fonda Books to celebrate her new deal, Tabitha Tate was on a high and definitely not ready to go to sleep. Looking down at the signed contract, which Mickey had created right there and then, she knew she was about to embark on a life-changing journey.

New York was fun, and although all New Yorkers liked to pretend that was where it was at, Los Angeles – and more specifically Hollywood – was where anyone in the creative business really wanted to gain power. She knew she had a mega-hit book on her hands, but rather than go out and celebrate, she decided to channel the buzz of her energy straight into working late into the night at the newspaper office.

She looked out at the vast views that only the highest buildings in London's Canary Wharf, legendary press central, had access to. She saw a helicopter's lights pass by in the dark night sky. She imagined it coming to pick her up, whisking her away to a waiting private jet, where she'd travel the world to promote the book, sitting on talk show after talk show, maybe even being introduced by Oprah Winfrey as 'bestselling author Tabitha Tate'. Her dad would love that.

The sign above her workstation still had Ross Owen's name on. HR hadn't removed it, supposedly out of respect, but Ross had been as hated inside these walls as he was out of them. The day he'd gone from missing to dead, she'd marched upstairs to the top brass and stated that she alone was the only person in the building with the balls to take over his senior position, and that she didn't even want a pay rise. Then, later, she'd spun that into the line she'd given Mickey about them allowing her to lessen her workload. 'Say whatever it takes' was Tabitha's motto. After speaking with top brass, she'd swanned back down and thrown Ross's possessions into a box, making the space her own, even though she'd got a few stares from his former colleagues. She didn't care how unpopular she was in the company. Popularity didn't bring you a Pulitzer, and besides, if things went according to plan, she wouldn't be here much longer anyway.

She cast a glance across all the work bays taking up the huge editorial floor, then placed a high heel on the edge of the desk and rummaged around in the drawers. Ross had been a notorious boozer; there was bound to be something in here she'd missed when she did her impromptu clear-out. She spotted a bottle of bourbon in the bottom drawer and smiled.

The idea that her life was about to change thrilled her. There'd be no more sitting at press junkets waiting to interview some faded star, or having to toe the line with some irritating press officer for scraps to make some dead-behind-the-eyes soap star seem interesting. With a book like this behind her, she'd be the star. People would know her name.

She thought back to Andrew Morton, who'd famously written Princess Diana's exposé, which had made him mega millions. *Yes.* She smiled. *It's my turn now.* All she had to do to create a spine for the tome that would set her career alight was find exactly what the witches of *Falcon Bay*, as Ross had named them, had been hiding. They'd been hiding something since they'd somehow managed to get Madeline Kane under their thumb enough to oust Jake Monroe on Christmas Eve, just hours before Madeline herself had died on the set. Even for soap operas, nothing on screen, bar Madeline's death by shark bite, was ever this dramatic.

In a series of interviews with Ross, Jake had tried to bluff his way out of the sacking by stating he wanted to try some new projects. But she'd listened to the tapes on Ross's Dictaphone and, off the record, in a rare moment of truth, Jake had confided in Ross that not even Madeline had explained why she'd turfed him out at the eleventh hour. Apparently, she'd backed him all the way to the Christmas live episode. She'd relished them joining forces to try to make Amanda, Farrah, and Helen quit the show after Madeleine's decision to axe Catherine Belle's character. So how, in just the space of a few hours, had they managed to not only reverse her decisions, but persuade her to axe Jake? It was like a soap plot itself. One that Ross had been determined to unravel.

As she looked down at all his notes, Tabitha gave Ross a bit more credit than she'd previously considered him worthy of. He might have been a bitter old soak, but he'd done some great groundwork for her. She pulled out the bourbon bottle and raised it up to his name sign, which she made a mental note to insist was replaced with her own tomorrow. She already had the perfect outfit in mind to wear whilst standing under it for a photo, to share across all her social media platforms with news of her promotion. She wanted that, alongside her book deal, announced on the press wires. That would get the Hollywood jungle drums beating.

'Cheers,' she said, and toasted Ross. 'I won't be drinking as much of this as you would though.'

She laughed, then poured herself a shot and placed it on the desk next to her keyboard. Tabitha began logging in to *The Herald*'s crown jewel, its digital vault. Every tabloid had a vault so sacred that only a few of the key staff had access to it. Tabitha had never been cleared for that until today, but she knew that inside the vault there would be everything from photographs of a celebrity sex tape for blackmail, paparazzi shots of a politician's drug use, or secret sex orgy pics, which were always handy when negotiations were not going the way the publication wanted and they needed other leverage to make sure they kept the exclusive.

The vault was also home to some of the most unspeakable crime scene photos, which would shock even the hardest journalist's well-scorched eyes to the core. If crime scene photos were in the vault, deals had often been done with the wealthy families of the deceased, who wanted to keep their late loved one's dignity intact or stop the reproduction of death-scene photography.

This was exactly what had happened in the case of the press photos of Madeline Kane's remains. The world had witnessed her death live onscreen before the live feed was cut, so grainy screenshots of the moment the shark opened its massive jaws were out there – most of which had been bought up by the Kane family. But the actual press photographers who were on set had taken photos of what was supposed to be the moment the now missing actress Honey Hunter was set to make her triumphant return to television. Why Madeline, the network owner who was not even an actress, had taken her place on screen in the first place was yet another weird twist Tabitha mused over as she entered the seventh password needed to access the deepest level of the vault.

Her password was accepted, and she scrolled through the file list, surprised to see that *The Herald* had even bought the photos of Ross Owen's bloated washed-up corpse. She briefly considered opening them to see what hadn't made it onto their front pages, but was determined to concentrate on the task at hand. She went past them, and even ignored the temptation to peek inside the infamous 'Red Rooms' files. Those held the stuff of press legend, but she kept scrolling until she found the file marked 'Madeline Kane'.

Lifting her shot of whisky to her mouth, she downed it in one and prepared to look over the grisly images.

Chapter 8

Helen was feeling relaxed as she made her way down the central studio corridor of CITV, heading towards the dedicated Zoom offices they'd had built during the first Covid outbreak. It felt strange being in the office so late and not being naked. A steamy sex session was usually the only reason she'd ever still be at *Falcon Bay* at this hour.

She smiled to herself at some of the memories of her late-night shenanigans, but all that was now BM – before Matt – as the girls had started calling it. It was true that before she'd met him, she'd never imagined that she could ever be satisfied with just one lover, let alone one that was nearly the same age as her. She was fifty-eight. There were three years between them; with other men, it was usually at least thirty, and that was pushing it. Yet they were celebrating six months of being together.

On Valentine's Day a few weeks back, he'd written her a card saying that he loved her. The same words he'd whispered in her ear after their quickie during the awards ceremony, and after she'd returned from Hell Island – as she was referring to The Cove section of St Augustine's – where they'd rescued the dishevelled Catherine Belle from her altercation with Ross Owen.

She and Sheena had established their alibis by rejoining the party. As soon as she felt she'd been 'seen' enough, she'd led Matt into one of the internal location layouts, which only VIP staff had access to, taking him up to Lucy Dean's bedroom, the most glamorous set. There, they'd truly, from her point of view anyway, really made love.

As she'd felt every thrust of his perfectly thick length being buried between her legs, each stroke felt like a wave of ecstasy was building from her clitoris, so glorious it made her want to sing. It was like a heat was unleashed in her heart with every entry of him into her body. Her mouth was getting further and further unlocked, and words were tumbling up her throat, dancing round. His tongue was gently touching hers as he kissed her deeply, and words were now dangerously close to being expelled out of her soul and loudly into the elaborate setting.

Catherine's character Lucy Dean must have filmed a dozen love scenes over the years, but nothing was on the scale of what the cameras would have captured if they were rolling as Helen and Matt held each other, naked, after their session reached its triumphant climax.

As she'd come, a little sob had slipped out of her mouth. Concerned, he placed his strong hand to her gentle face and turned it towards him. She tried to look away; she felt so exposed. The night had been so emotional, filled with such extreme highs and horror. She so desperately wanted to tell him everything that had happened that night and unburden herself, but she knew that was not an option. In love with her or not, he was a detective for the very police office that had the power to change the women's lives forever. So instead she did the second most unthinkable thing she could think of: she told him that she loved him too.

His eyes lit up when she said it, and soon they were rolling in passion once again, both repeating the same three little words some people spent their whole lives waiting to hear but never did.

Afterwards, as she lay in his warm arms, she tried to blank out all the fear she felt and believe that maybe he could be the one to save her. Younger men were simple creatures, easy to control, great in bed. She'd had no regrets about the number of notches on her bedpost, but now she was with Matt, it was very different.

As she rounded the final bend of the corridor to reach the video conference room, her mind was wandering back to just moments earlier when she'd waved him off to his night shift, thinking about how much she couldn't wait to see him again. She opened the door to reveal an agitated Amanda, pacing the room, waiting for her.

'We said eleven. It's ten to twelve. He'll be on the link in a few minutes. I thought we were going to prepare,' Amanda said, closing the door behind Helen.

They both took seats opposite the huge screen, which filled one end of the room, flanked by full-size cameras and lights set up either side to film the UK side of the call.

Helen winced at the brightness of the lights and looked for the control panel to turn them down. 'There's nothing to prepare for,' she said, and shrugged her shoulders. She dimmed the lights to a much more flattering tone and turned the Zoom link on to test how they looked on camera. 'You really need to learn how to operate this, Amanda – we'd have looked like ghosts the way you had it set up.'

Helen flicked the autotune feature on the camera, which made them both look ten years younger on the screen.

'Ghosts is not an appropriate reference considering everything that's been going on round here, Helen,' Amanda sniped, clearly unimpressed. 'The way we look is the least of our problems,' she continued, running her fingers through her hair. 'I've not been able to relax all evening. What do you think he's going to say?' Her throat was as tight as the feeling in her chest.

Helen was about to reply with some words she'd usually give to an actor or actress she was about to film to help relax them for an audition if she was casting a new role on the show. Before she could speak, the incoming video call bell began to ring, and the words *Chad Kane calling* appeared on screen.

Amanda looked panicked. Helen grabbed her hand and spoke slowly. 'Stay calm. Let him do the talking. Let's hear what he's got to say before we react to anything, and if it starts to go horribly wrong, I'll click the off button and we'll pretend we've lost connection. That will buy us a few moments of privacy if we need it – OK?'

Amanda nodded.

'Just remember, we are not linked to Ross Owen in any way, shape or form, so do not let your own knowledge interfere with anything he has to say, right?'

Amanda nodded once more. Helen gave her hand one last squeeze, checked her hair in the video screen, then clicked connect. The handsome face of Chad Kane filled the screen as the call went live.

'Hello, ladies,' he said, in his distinctive Southern tone. He was obviously at home. It immediately irked Helen that he'd requested they log in from the conference room when they too could have joined remotely.

'Nice to see you, Chad,' Amanda said as confidently as she could. Helen just smiled and gave a gentle wave with one hand.

108

'I'm sorry to have disturbed your evening like this, but I'm afraid the matter I need to discuss with you couldn't wait.'

Amanda pushed her leg against Helen's under the table, to stop it from trembling.

There was a pause, and the women took in the background of Chad's home. It looked large – behind him was a huge photo of himself and Madeline, obviously taken on their wedding day. It was hard not to let their eyes focus on it, as Madeline radiated happiness as a years-younger Chad held her in his arms. Chad noticed them looking at the photo and turned to look at it too.

Another pause.

Then Amanda broke the silence.

'I know it's a silly question, but how have you been?' she said softly.

As Chad turned back towards them, it looked like a tear was welling up in his eye.

'Apologies, ladies. I am not comfortable talking about how I am feeling, only business,' he said, his tone faltering, clearly emotional. He coughed gently, cleared his throat and continued. 'Tonight, we have some serious matters to attend to,' he said solemnly.

Now it was Helen's turn to push her leg against Amanda's under the desk. For all her bluster and bravado, deep down, the real reason she'd been late was because she was desperately trying to enjoy every last moment she could with Matt, just in case – despite what she was trying to convince Amanda of – the next words out of Chad's mouth changed their lives forever. The irony of the fact that it might even be Matt who was sent to arrest her wasn't lost on her.

After clearing his throat again, Chad continued with regained composure.

'As you know, the purchase of CITV and the reboot of

109

Falcon Bay was my late wife's doing – the show was her baby, her only baby.' He paused for a moment and took another look at bridal-clad Madeline's picture, then looked back into the lens. 'She was only on the island a short time, but her passion to save the show, to redeem it, and restoring it to success as she did, was outstanding. Just like she was.'

If Helen wasn't so nervous about what was coming next, she would have been struggling not to roll her eyes at Chad's deluded opinion of the woman he was married to. She and Amanda clearly knew her way better than he did.

'She loved the show,' Amanda offered, desperate to keep the conversation on track, 'and we've been honouring her commitment by putting out storylines we know she would have been proud to champion.'

'I have not called you ladies here to discuss what is on screen, Ms King. I will confess that after the horror of Christmas Day, I have not and do not think I will ever be able to view the show again. Melissa, my sister, watches it and reports directly to the board. I am of course still the owner of the network, I just don't wish to watch its output.' He picked up a glass of water and took a sip. 'In truth, right now the last thing I even want to think about is *Falcon Bay*, but in honour of Madeline, I am trying to see if I can honour *her* love for it, even if I can't do it myself.'

Helen and Amanda stayed silent; Chad continued.

'This will be the last direct contact you have from me for the foreseeable future. From next week, Melissa will be the contact at the Kane organization for general overseeing of the running of CITV from a legal perspective. I need to take a step back whilst I grieve, which I'm sure you understand.'

A huge knot released in Amanda's stomach. Clearly he was about to announce some changes, but it didn't seem like they were major, and more importantly, there was no sign that he wanted to discuss Christmas Day. Maybe Helen had been right; there was nothing to worry about after all. Her legs stopped shaking and she sat upright in her white leather-backed chair, ready to hear what she assumed was now some basic explanation of how they would deal with Melissa. Considering that she was going to be their new contact, she was surprised Melissa wasn't actually on this call.

Helen, also feeling more relaxed, poured a glass of water from one of the bottles on the table and readied herself to hear the new rules coming their way.

'As it's late, I'll get straight to the point of why I have called you here. The death of the reporter Ross Owen has thrown our production company back into the headlines, once again for all the wrong reasons.'

Helen cut in. 'Yes, it's a tragedy, but we have it on good authority that the police will soon be revealing his death was just a drunken accident. We all saw him at the awards ceremony before he made the decision to climb the rockface. We as a whole here at CITV feel for his family, but our insurers have confirmed we are liable for nothing. As awful as it is, it truly has no link to or impact on our production, which as you know we are now finally back up to date with.'

Amanda was so impressed with Helen's tone and sense of purpose, she almost believed her version of events herself. Chad, however, looked unmoved.

'That is as may be, but it has brought all types of scrutiny on CITV and our lawyers confirm there is now a tell-all book being written about our show. Its tone is not positive.'

The women looked at each other in surprise. Ross had mentioned the book, but they'd assumed it had died with him. Chad continued before they could reply.

'A reporter by the name of Tabitha Tate has been bombarding us with requests for private memos from the company files under the freedom of information act, which applies to the islands you film in. Amongst her many questions, one sticks out. Even I, with my little knowledge of what had been going on since my wife's arrival, know nothing about it. That is, why was Jake Monroe sacked on Christmas Eve?' Chad picked up a document from his desk. It showed a slew of email correspondence from Tabitha to him. He picked up another document, which looked more formal. 'I also have a lawsuit here from his lawyers, claiming unlawful dismissal, and there is nothing in Madeline's files that justifies the termination of his contract. In fact, from everything she said to me, he was her top man on the island. I am sorry Farrah is not at this meeting.'

'She's been off sick for two weeks, or she'd have been here,' Helen replied.

Amanda nodded, not liking where this was going. She wasn't even sure of how to answer what was obviously coming next.

'And he cites you three as the reason for his departure, so if we are to fight this, I need to know exactly what happened and why.'

'Well, what happened was—' Helen began confidently, as Amanda's tremoring leg pushed against her once more. As Helen spoke, she clicked the off button on the remote that controlled the video call, disconnecting them.

'Shit!' Amanda said, as the screen went blank.

Helen swung round in her chair and grabbed her by the shoulders. 'Right, we've got about sixty seconds before that line reconnects, so we need to decide what to say, and quick.'

'This is why I said to meet at eleven, so we could plan,' Amanda replied breathlessly.

'We couldn't have planned for this – we both know we were expecting him to say he was selling the network, or something about Ross, not asking about how we got rid of Jake. He was the last thing on my mind in this,' Helen finished.

The video call began to ring out, and *Chad Kane calling* appeared on the screen once more.

'We'll have to answer it.' Amanda's face showed Helen she was in no state to be able to give Chad a decent enough story to cover up the truth of how they had blackmailed Madeline into firing Jake.

Helen decided to take the lead. 'Just agree with everything I say and stay calm.'

She clicked answer on the video and once again Chad's face reappeared.

'So sorry, Chad, it's because it's so late here. The network hub usually uploads all our digital episodes overnight and it's heavy on the connection, so it must have cut us off,' she said, as casually as if she was ordering from a restaurant menu.

All those years of rehearsing with the show's aspiring actors had obviously paid off, Amanda thought, as Helen barrelled on with her cool delivery.

'As I was saying, and I have to be honest with you here . . .'

She paused, and Chad's deep brown eyes looked patiently down the lens. Amanda geared herself up to hear whatever Helen had managed to script in her head.

Helen leaned forward. 'Madeline was a wonderful leader,' she said softly. Chad's face was moved by the praise for his wife. Amanda stayed silent. 'And as you know, she made a lot of changes here on the show. Occasionally, as is the way with brilliant creatives, she sometimes changed her mind again, and because we trusted her instinct – and that's what it was, she had a gut instinct for *Falcon Bay* – we followed her lead. It wasn't just Jake's promotion then dismissal. She reversed some of her on-screen plans, including the decision she took not to axe Lucy Dean from the show and instead to put it in the hands of the public with the audience vote. This includes the tragic decision to take over Honey Hunter's role herself when she failed to show up.'

Chad listened in silence.

'So, I guess what I'm saying is, even though, yes, as you initially said, she pushed Jake to the front, making him our showrunner, on Christmas Eve she simply changed her mind, decided she wanted him out and brought Amanda back.' Helen nudged Amanda under the table in an attempt to get her to co-operate.

'It was a surprise to all of us, but I can't say I was unhappy about it, Chad,' Amanda said. This part was easier to chip in on as it was actually true. 'I was so thrilled to be back here that I didn't question her reasons. I was just grateful, and there's no point in me lying and saying I was disappointed to see Jake go, because everyone knows we're divorced. Of course I was glad. I can't tell you why she chose to do what she did, but having been married to him for as many years as I was, all I can say is that she will have had a good reason.' She was on a roll now, feeling empowered that she and Helen were steering this conversation back into a safe place and off the cliff edge it had felt they were perched on when it began.

'I see,' Chad said, and took another look at the paperwork he had in front of him. 'Well, marital feelings aside, Ms King, nothing new has been unearthed, so without a real reason for his dismissal, we have no choice but to reinstate Jake – and the Bay's former lead director, Aiden Anderson – with immediate effect.'

As both of the women tried to hide their shock at the news, neither of them spoke. Helen eventually nodded, with Amanda following suit.

'So please call a meeting with the team tomorrow telling them that Jake will be returning to the show. Amanda,' Chad continued, 'I do understand this will be difficult for you, but with all due respect, nothing is as difficult as what I am going through right now, so I expect you to behave professionally.'

Amanda was still taking the news in.

'Is that understood?' Chad concluded.

Amanda nodded. Helen, realising there was no way out of this, decided to do what she did best and try a last-minute negotiation.

'Chad, we totally respect the situation you've found yourself in here regarding CITV's HR department. It goes without saying that not only do we feel deeply for you and your loss, but we are also grateful that you are keeping the network, which must currently be the last thing—'

'Thank you, Helen, I appreciate that,' Chad said, cutting her off mid-flow. 'I must be honest with you though and say, if the show does not live up to the values I know my wife wanted it to have, to be joyful and create escapism in a world full of pain and sorrow, then I will authorise the sale of it to a new owner. No doubt they would be better suited to it than any of us here, without Madeline's guiding light.'

Helen took the opportunity to try to steer him back into safer territory than the potential sale of their beloved network.

'Chad, before you go, I would like to say that whilst I may not have worked with your wife for long, she left a great impression on me – well, on all of us. Having her as the boss was so empowering for so many of our female staff. Can I ask you one thing, something I feel Madeline would have approved of, being the *woman's woman* she was? If Jake is to return, could you at least place him on equal footing with Amanda? It's the role he had before his original promotion – which Madeline definitely regretted, or she wouldn't have fired him. It would create a much better gender balance on the show if they were joint showrunners. I know Madeline would not want this show to lose its female touch.'

Chad watched the two women, and Amanda sat quietly whilst Helen was in full flow.

'I feel sure the team would feel more balanced knowing Madeline's essence of female empowerment were to reign on, rather than giving a man sole control.'

Chad paused, taking in Helen's words, then cast his eyes over his wife's portrait again.

Amanda took a slow, deep breath, which she hoped was not visible on camera as she waited for his reply. The very thought of Jake being back on the Bay was enough to make her want to scream and cry all at once, but she was determined to hold it together until the end of this call at the very least. If Helen's even-power pitch worked, it might be just about possible for her to stay on the show. She ruminated in her brain, before she wondered if, away from the work they'd have to do together, she truly could cope working alongside Jake if Chad agreed.

Eventually Chad's deep voice broke Amanda's musings.

'I'm sorry, Ms Gold. Whilst I appreciate the kind words about Madeline's effect on the women of the network, I am not a TV man. CITV has shareholders and they quite frankly do not want the hassle or expense of a public and costly battle with Mr Monroe when there is no proof of the reason for the demotion or sacking. So later today we will approve Jake's return to the role Madeline originally promoted him to, as *Falcon Bay*'s showrunner. Meaning everyone will report to him.'

A silence fell over the room. Helen, who had been sure that using Madeline in her pitch for Amanda to retain her power would work, didn't have anything left to say. Amanda also stayed silent.

Chad looked at his watch, then back to the camera.

'I've kept you ladies for far too long already, for which I deeply apologise. Please go home and sleep on the news I've just given you. I also want to be honest with you on one last issue before we conclude tonight's meeting. I do not have to repeat to you how difficult a time for me this has been. My instinct, if I am truly honest, is to sell the network and cut all ties with the memory of the events that led up to the loss of my wife.'

He paused – clearly emotional – then resumed.

'But I know how much Madeline's wish was for *Falcon Bay* to stay in the number-one slot and be the fine example to the world she had recrafted it to be, up until that dreadful day. I admittedly have no idea how you do that in a media landscape. I do know that Jake was working on the show right up to that evening and the pairing of the two most renowned showrunners in television must have worked. So, despite your differences, if you can put personal issues aside, I know you will find a way to continue Madeline's achievements.

'If you do not, and the show begins to lose its syndication or its moral compass, then the Kane Foundation's financial board will make the decision of whether to sell the network to a new owner. The Kane Foundation is funded by my father and is strong in family values and deeply religious. I doubt anyone will want to keep the show alive as much as Madeline did, so if you want *Falcon Bay* to continue, then I suggest you do your best to get along.' His handsome face showed a smile that didn't quite reach his sad eyes and then with a brief farewell he was gone.

Helen switched the conference line off and picked up her bag, then turned to Amanda.

'See, how could we have prepared for that?' she said in despair, then buried her head in her hands.

Chapter 9

Hours later, in the beach house she'd rented since the separation, Amanda finally gave up on the idea of sleeping. Not even Dan's solid arms, which she usually snuggled into and drifted off in, offered her any comfort from the nightmare she now found herself in.

Around five in the morning, she slipped out of the sheets, quietly went down to the kitchen, opened the fridge, and poured herself a glass of wine. She took it out onto the deck and watched the sun rising over the tranquil waters of St Augustine's. After the hell of last week had subsided, this very same space and view had once again seemed so peaceful. She and Dan had taken Olivia for a picnic on the beach, where she'd watched as he'd made a sandcastle for her chubby little hands to pat. She'd finally thought she had it all: a man who loved and respected her, as well as the child she'd always believed she'd never be able to have. Finally, after years of putting up with Jake's tyrannical behaviour at home and at work, she'd been totally free, and she'd never been happier.

Under her control, *Falcon Bay* had become a place where

everyone had a smile on their faces. Even actors, who were never happy, seemed at peace. The whole atmosphere was one of hope, especially after their award wins.

Ross Owen was missed by no one, and had provided only a day's office gossip about how badly he'd behaved at the party. Like Helen, she wasn't happy to have been involved in yet another cover-up for Catherine, who seemed to be St Augustine's walking albatross these days. But having come so close to losing the show they loved and their homes on the beautiful island they inhabited at Christmas, and after the combined exit of Jake and Aiden – toxic alpha male presences – she'd somehow turned this already perfect location back into a true paradise. And now it was all about to be destroyed again.

Even if Chad had gone for Helen's suggestion of them sharing the showrunner's job, like they had years before, during the happier years of their marriage, when it came to Jake, teamwork was only ever spelt with a capital I. She sipped the cold Sauvignon Blanc and pulled the cashmere blanket that was on the porch swing around her as she contemplated what to do. Upstairs, sleeping soundly in their beds, were the two things she cared the most about in the world – but in the distance, over the vast beaches, like a mirage in the desert, was the third. Only her beloved *Falcon Bay* TV studios were real. She'd lost them once, when she'd quit under the strain of Jake and Madeline's tyrannical plot to oust Catherine from the show. If she'd survived that, she told herself, somehow, she wasn't sure how yet, she must be able to survive this.

The next day, Catherine entered her dressing room and flicked the switch on the wall, which lit up the lights on the elaborate make-up table. Taking her red Valentino coat off, she placed it down along with her matching bag, then took a seat in the pink oyster-shaped chair that she'd been studying her reflection in for forty years.

Staring back at her was the face of a woman who knew what was coming. Sheena had rung her mobile after Helen had called her late last night with the news. She'd been fast asleep, thanks to her Xanax, the same pills she'd thrown into the ocean, determined to take back control of her life, just moments before Ross had attacked her. In the seven days and nights since that awful moment, she was now taking more and more of them.

She hadn't listened to the voice message until she was making the short walk from her condo to the set. As soon as she'd deleted the voicemail, she'd searched in her bag for the strip of pills she had ready. She'd restricted them to just when she was going to bed, for fear she should wake from a nightmare, and after taking two, she'd settle back down. Well, she accepted, this was a nightmare of sorts, and if she wasn't going to be able to wake up from it, the least she could do was take its edge off.

That was the wonder of Xanax, she mused, as she began to prime her skin, ready to apply her foundation. The pills had some sort of magical ingredient that could make you feel calm even when you were under attack. Which is why Sheena's voice message, which had a hint of panic in it, saying Jake was coming back, wasn't the worst message that she could have heard. She'd been expecting *the call* she'd been dreading since Christmas Day and had doubly panicked about it when Ross's body had been washed up, so all other bad news seemed tolerable.

Although she wasn't close to Jake – after he was promoted to sole showrunner, his usually manageable ego had become unhinged – they'd worked relatively well with each other over the decades. It was Madeline's twisted revenge plot he'd been dragged into, she reasoned, as she rubbed cream into her neck, not his, that had seen the two of them go head to head last year. Surely his return should be no different than the way he was before Madeline's arrival. He was dismissive of her age, unsupportive of her role as the show's leading lady and generally irritating to be around, but *not* a specific threat. Sure, he was a sexist, ageist pig, she thought, as she imagined him striding smugly around the set, fanning out like a preening peacock showing off his feathers to the ordinary chickens in the hen enclosure. But she'd rarely met a man in power in television who wasn't the same.

Well, apart from Harry Pearson, who had set up CITV and *Falcon Bay* four decades ago when she'd first been hired to play Lucy Dean. But people like him didn't exist any more, she thought sadly, as she expertly filled in her eyebrows using her favourite dark-blonde Lancôme pencil.

No, she decided, Jake would know better than to single her out on the show for trouble. It was poor Amanda who would be the one in the firing line. Just the thought of them having to work together made her stomach flip for Amanda. She glanced down at the shooting schedule for today. She had three wordy scenes, all inside the bar, thankfully.

As it was early March, she dreaded seeing the word EXTERIOR marked on her script. As the show was shot out of sync, she'd often find herself outside in freezing weather wearing clothes for episodes for summer, or vice versa. But that was the world of soaps – nothing was ever as it seemed, on camera or off.

After she'd finished blending her base, she reached for her Dior Sugar and Spice blush and gently swept the brush against her high cheekbones, then started on her eyes, applying two coats of jet-black mascara, before adding the winged lashes that created the infamous Lucy Dean feline look. She'd stopped going into the make-up department years ago. No one knew her face better than she did, and it always took them forever to make her look even half as good as she could do herself in fifteen minutes. Plus, she couldn't stand listening to all the gossip and speculation on recent events. Especially when she knew the truth.

She patted some pore minimizer on either side of her nose. HD television picked up the most minute flaws, which the best fillers, facelifts or soft lighting in the world sadly couldn't hide. She used a tiny brush to blend it in.

She was scanning the script again to check the scene order whilst she selected the lip gloss that would complete her routine. A quick slather of YSL's Rouge Pur and a brush of her long golden hair and she was ready to go.

Chapter 10

Meeting Room 6 wrapped around the highest level of the main tower of the CITV building, with floor-to-ceiling panoramic views of the glorious Jersey coast and the exterior bayside sets. It was packed to the rafters. Its long white table with twenty seats was full, bar one seat, with several people, including junior members of the team, standing at the back by the cast board. The board had photos of all the actors currently in the show – pinned onto a large-scale map of *Falcon Bay*'s layout, with their characters' family trees connected to the internal studio set. A table underneath the board was laid out with an assortment of waters, teas, coffees, and a huge plate of mixed pastries that still had the cellophane wrapping over them, showing they'd gone untouched.

No one in Meeting Room 6 was in the mood for nibbling. When Amanda had written the email marked *urgent – full heads and assistants of all departments meeting* while sitting on her porch, the 5.30 a.m. sent time hadn't gone unnoticed by its recipients, hence the lack of appetite in a room full of people who would usually strip a snack table dry in under five minutes.

Helen sat at the far end of the table, resplendent in a red Hermès fitted suit, the same shade as the glasses she was wearing. She had arrived early and had already been the subject of a barrage of questions from the team wanting to know exactly what was going on. She'd denied any knowledge, keeping one eye on the door and one on the clock.

Amanda was always punctual, and the email had said 10 a.m., meaning there was just a minute to go. Any moment now the heat would be off her and she could feign surprise at Amanda's revelation along with the rest of the team's genuine shock. Helen knew it was never good to show your hand on the set of a long-running show. If everyone knew how close you were and to whom, they never spoke freely around you, so Helen, Amanda, Catherine, and Farrah all made sure to keep their closeness as discreet as possible.

She was surprised Farrah wasn't here. As head director and writer of the show, she'd usually be in every meeting, and Helen was certain after everything that had gone on between Farrah and Jake that Amanda must have pre-warned her, just as Sheena had done with Catherine. But as Farrah was technically still off sick, maybe she'd used this news to further delay her return. It was strange, Helen thought, that Farrah hadn't been in touch, and very unlike her. She decided to keep her in the loop by taking a quick video of the room and sneakily panning her phone gently in her hands, pretending she was checking its signal.

The transmission tower that had been installed to beam the show live to destinations all over the world for the Christmas special had still not been dismantled. Bizarrely, even though they were high up, it was playing havoc with mobile reception, so luckily no one noticed what she was doing. She sent the video via WhatsApp to Farrah's mobile. *Look what you're missing . . .* she said – but before Helen could see if the two blue ticks appeared, meaning Farrah had read it, Amanda appeared at the door.

'Good morning, all,' she said, as she smiled around the room, making sure to acknowledge those at the back.

She was wearing a cream cashmere polo-neck dress, which discreetly made the most of her curves. Helen recognised it because she'd had a similar one in black years ago from United Colors of Benetton, when they were the height of fashion. She'd bought it two sizes too small though, so it had been much less discreet in showing off her own assets. Seeing the way Amanda's dress showed off her body, she wondered if hers was somewhere in the back of her wardrobe, and she made a mental note to have a look for it when she got home.

Helen looked up at the chorus of greetings that met Amanda's arrival. As Amanda approached, she grabbed a bottle of water from the catering stand, then made her way to the one empty seat clearly reserved for her. After sitting down, she took a sip, then placed her laptop in front of her and readied herself to speak.

'Sorry about the short notice, but I need to give you some interesting updates from the Kane family and what they mean for the future of *Falcon Bay*. As you all know, they now own CITV.' Amanda spoke in the most upbeat tone she could muster on two hours' sleep. She was still processing the news Chad had delivered, which was about to turn her world upside down once more.

A room full of curious faces looked at her with expectation. Her choice of words was interesting, Helen thought, as she aimed her gaze just above Amanda so as not to throw her off her stride, knowing that whatever she was going to say was clearly going to have more than hint of a spin on it.

'Late last night, I was informed of the good news, and I

think we can all agree that this is good news. The family are not intending to sell the network.'

Candy and Dustin, the assistant producers, watched intently. Dustin's expression showed he was clearly thrilled. Candy, who had long perfected the art of the poker face, looked beautifully icy. The rest of the team let out a series of relaxed sighs. The assumption after receiving the email was that the network was going to be sold again. That very same topic had been the subject of the production WhatsApp group from the moment Madeline Kane had died on Christmas Day, so the mood in the room at the news this was not going to be the case visibly lifted as soon as the words left Amanda's mouth.

Pausing to let them enjoy the good news before she delivered the bad, Amanda gave her best smile and prepared herself to deliver the kicker.

Once Jake had been sacked last year, team members who'd been too frightened to ever voice their opinion of him whilst he was in power had enjoyed letting loose their delight at his exit. Amanda knew that the announcement of his return was going to lead to an immediate shift from elation to paranoia should some 'suck-up' on the team be more than happy to point out exactly who had been rejoicing at his departure. It would most likely be Candy, who had always been close to Jake and, Amanda suspected by her lack of reaction, probably already knew he was being reinstated.

There was no way round it; this had to be said. So, she took a sip from her bottled water and fixed an even wider smile on her lips, ready to say the words that already felt like they were going to choke her.

'So now we officially know the Kane family are keeping us running, it's only to be expected that they'll be making some changes.'

She was just about to start off a speech with the lies she'd rehearsed, about how they wanted to bring back Jake and Aiden to the network because there were rumours they were about to start working on *Falcon Bay*'s TV rival *Heartlands*. *Heartlands* was the show Amanda herself had been poached by briefly before Sheena had blackmailed Madeline into sacking Jake and giving her full control on Christmas Eve. It was currently doing really well in the ratings after *Falcon Bay* had been off-air for six weeks following the Christmas Day fiasco. She'd reasoned the story she was about to weave had an air of authenticity to it, and was just about to give it her all, when the double doors of Meeting Room 6 swung open with such force that papers on the desks flew up in the air. Her hair, which had been softly resting on her shoulders, blew across her face. As she straightened it, she saw all eyes move to the entrance. She didn't need to look to know who it was; the expressions in the room said it all.

Helen, still wanting it to look like she was part of the group, followed the team's gaze to take in the sight of Jake Monroe, staring them down in his usual skin-tight black jeans, cowboy boots, white T-shirt and leather jacket. *Here we go*, she managed to think to herself before his familiar voice rang out.

'It's good to be back, guys,' he boomed. He stepped inside, but left the doors wide open behind him, no doubt wanting anyone who wasn't in the room – or hadn't spotted his arrival via the corridor that led to Meeting Room 6 – to witness his return.

Amanda slowly turned to face him, ready to switch to the Stepford wife tone she'd been practising on her walk over to the studios across the beach. She was beaten to a greeting by Candy, who predictably was in immediate suck-up mode. Amanda watched Candy, in a skin-tight lemon jumpsuit and matching heels, and with her annoying blonde curls that bounced when she spoke, spring from her chair.

'Mr Monroe!' she exclaimed, in her broad Australian twang, as if Jesus himself had risen from the cross and entered the CITV building. 'On behalf of all of us at CITV, we're thrilled you've returned to join us.'

She started a round of awkward applause that neither Helen nor Amanda joined in with. Helen was watching her little act too. Candy reminded her of the doll Rainbow Brite, which was popular in the seventies and eighties: all garish and in your face. Helen was fantasising about pulling her head off to see if it was as hollow as a doll's would be when Jake's laugh cut into her brain.

'Oh Candy, still as sweet as your name.' He winked, which made her blush, then began a slow saunter towards Amanda's side of the table whilst addressing her.

'Hello, Amanda, it looks like I've been missed,' he said with a wink, getting closer.

Oh my god, Helen thought. Was he actually going to try to embrace her? What on earth was he up to? Desperate to save her friend from having to scrabble for a reply, she decided to play Jake at his own game. Before he could reach Amanda, Helen was out of her seat and striding towards him.

As she weaved through the crowded room, flashes of her red outfit caught his attention in the same way a matador's muleta would draw the bull towards him in the ring. But Helen didn't need a sword; her words would be weapon enough. Unlike Amanda, who had planned to pretend to be on board with Jake's sudden return, Helen had decided to go full nuclear. Everyone knew they'd been sworn enemies for decades. They'd always let rip at each other in public meetings in the past, so today was as good as any to be upfront about her opinion on his return. The two met in the middle of the room, which fell silent once again as Helen reared up on her six-inch stilettos to nearly match Jake's height.

'Unlike some in here,' she said, giving Candy a withering look, 'I'm not going to pretend I'm glad to see you back.'

'I'm not pretending,' Candy stated with a smile as the room looked on.

'Well, Helen,' Jake said with a smile of his own. 'I'm glad you feel able to be open about your feelings. There was too much repression going on before I took my break, so I'd like to take this opportunity to thank you for being so upfront. I hope it will help us get along better this time around,' he finished, then smiled again.

Amanda watched the exchange in fascinated horror. What the hell was he up to? The same man who'd blackmailed his way back onto the set of the show was now playing Mr Charming, actively welcoming being insulted to his face and in front of most of the team. This didn't make sense. Before she could further question his demeanour, Jake continued.

'Helen,' he said calmly. 'I want you to know that whilst I do intend to make major changes to *our show* with immediate effect' – as he said the words 'our show', he looked around the room as if to include everyone in the sentence – 'I want you to know, all of you, that I have returned to help keep this show in its number-one slot.' Again, he looked around, this time allowing his gaze to fall on Amanda for a moment longer than the others. 'And for that reason alone.'

Helen knew that whatever game Jake was playing, he already had the upper hand in the room, so if she had continued with her planned outburst, his calm tone and friendly demeanour would instantly make her appear to be an overemotional shrew. As head of casting, she could spot an actor from a mile off, and whilst he might have the rest of them fooled, she wasn't going to fall into the trap of showing herself up by calling this charade out. As angry as she was to see him, she was clever enough not to take the bait.

'Glad to hear it,' was about as much as she could manage to deliver, as he leaned in to kiss her on both cheeks as if he were some long-lost French lover.

She stiffened at his touch, and as soon as he released his grip on her, walked away and returned to her seat.

Amanda knew if she didn't speak soon, she'd lose the respect of the team she'd been in control of up until just a few hours ago. She decided to match Helen's direct approach and got out of her seat and headed towards Jake. Every step she took felt like she was walking towards the edge of a cliff, but she was determined to stop the sinking feeling that had filled her soul and style this awkward exchange out as best she could.

'Jake,' she said, extending her hand for him to shake, intending to stop him getting anywhere near as close as he had got to Helen. 'We appreciate your candour and commitment to continuing our show's success, and with that as our common goal, I know we will all aim to work as one committed team.'

As the skin on their palms met, the familiarity of the fingers that once roamed her body, and the hand that once held hers at the altar when they'd said 'I do', made her feel physically sick.

'That's a great attitude, Amanda, considering my return means you are no longer in charge. I appreciate the way you are handling this,' he said, with another smile and the faintest hint of sarcasm.

God, she wanted to kill him, Helen thought, as she squeezed her mobile phone between her hands under the desk, imagining it was Jake's neck. Demoting and belittling

130

Amanda in one go was one speciality Jake had certainly not lost, but hiding it under a faux friendly demeanour was definitely a newly acquired skill. If this was Jake mark two, then they were all in for a new adventure, she mused, trying to make subtle eye contact with her friend to send some sort of telepathic support.

'Right, team,' Jake continued, still stood in the middle of the room, addressing them. 'Let's hit the ground running, shall we? I know the show has only been back on air two weeks since the hiatus, and the live episode threw all our story arcs out of whack. Of course, the tragedy of what happened meant certain characters were not able to tie up storylines that I remember from the grid before I took my break. So, who wants to give me a quick recap on what's happening with our surviving members of *Falcon Bay*?'

As he finished, he walked over to the snack table and perched on the end. Candy, realizing there were no empty seats, took the opportunity to show her delight at his return once more.

'Well, Mr Monroe,' she said, standing up and carrying her chair over to him whilst she carried on talking, 'due to the *situation* we found ourselves in following Honey Hunter not joining the show . . .'

She placed the chair down and Jake sat in it. As she continued talking, the mention of Honey's name took him back to the night he'd returned to the villa they'd been sharing nearby, in preparation of her joining the cast, and brought back the passionate memories of their time together. Candy's squeaky voice bringing him up to speed pulled him from his memory.

'So that's where we are now,' she finished with a smile. Having not heard most of what she said, Jake had no choice but to nod in appreciation.

'Thank you, Candy,' he said, then walked over to the storyline board next to the cast photos and set layout.

A quick scan brought him up to date enough to cover what he hadn't heard when his mind had wandered. With his back briefly to the room, and all eyes on him, Helen and Amanda took the opportunity to exchange glances that made it clear they couldn't wait to get the hell out of there.

After he'd scanned the board once more, he ripped off the covering from the pastries and went straight for a Danish. Jake always ate in times of stress. The mention of Honey had thrown him and in almost one go he devoured the delicate treat like a hungry wolf, wiped his mouth with a napkin, then picked up the tray and walked over to the desk, placing it in the middle.

'Dig in, people,' he said. 'We'll need our appetites if we're to rescue *Falcon Bay* once more.'

'Considering we're still in the number-one slot Jake, I don't think *rescue* is exactly the right word,' Amanda said, unable to help herself. She'd done an excellent job at hiding her feelings so far but couldn't help but react to the wording Jake had chosen.

'Exactly,' added Helen, backing her up. 'I hardly think we are need of rescuing.' If she was going to have to watch her friend be demoted publicly, she wasn't going to let it go without some sort of defence. 'On Christmas Day, we reached a global audience of a billion people and you were not even here,' she began, but Jake cut her off and turned his back to Helen and focused on his soon to be ex-wife.

'Amanda, with all due respect, I do not think company members should be referring to that episode as a success. The wife of the man who owns our company lost her life live on screen in a horrific stunt gone wrong,' he said, then turned his attention back to Helen with a withering look.

Suddenly enraged, Amanda's Stepford wife act went out of the window.

'Jake, everyone in the room knows that the only reason we had a bloody real-life shark on this set was because you suggested it in the conference and Madeline herself turned down all the brilliant CGI effects. It was quite frankly a ridiculous idea, but she was the one who sanctioned the marine to bring that thing onto the set. It was to fulfil your idea. So whilst I might no longer be in charge, I will not stand here and have you accuse any of us of being the reason for that tragedy—'

'Do calm down, Amanda,' Jake cut her off, back to his calm over-friendly demeanour. She knew it to be as fake as the height the four-inch Cuban heels on the back of his boots gave him. 'I wasn't attacking *anyone*; I was simply saying that the audience figures for the tragedy of that episode are not a real-life bar we can set ourselves.'

Helen noted he didn't deny Amanda's correct accusation of exactly how events had led up to the mess of Christmas Day.

Jake took a step back from Amanda and sat himself back down in the chair Candy had brought him. This action made Amanda look very awkward, stood alone in the middle of the room, but she had no choice but to stay where she was and wait for him to continue. Dan had been right, she thought to herself.

Last night, when she'd told him Jake was coming back, he'd pleaded with her for them to pack their things and leave the island. As much as she knew Dan had her best interests at heart, and she loved him for it, the career woman in her just couldn't let Jake win so easily. As she refocused on Jake's smug face, she steeled herself to not react to whatever subtle gaslighting comment was due out of his mouth next.

Jake knew his wife's face well. He was enjoying the mental

torture she was clearly going through, but he had a longer game in mind to play out. He wanted revenge on her and the other bitches that had seen him dethroned from his kingdom, and he wasn't going to go about it publicly. Chad Kane was too much of an ethical goody-goody for his liking, and although that had worked a treat at getting him reinstated, he'd much preferred the steeliness of his wife Madeline before she'd strangely turned on him on Christmas Eve. Now she was dead, he figured he could allow himself to admire her once more, for she had been one ruthless woman. In fact, the most ruthless he'd ever met. Before his mind could wander further to how attractive Madeline had been, and how he wished he'd had the chance to bang her, Helen Gold's irritating voice cut into his thoughts.

'Well, I have to get back to auditioning,' she said, as breezily as she could manage, leaving her seat and heading towards the doors.

'Wait one moment, Helen,' Jake replied, with a hand gesture that suggested she sit back down. 'What I'm about to say very much includes you.'

Helen sat down and once again exchanged looks with Amanda.

'What fresh hell will this be?' she muttered under her breath. Candy looked on excitedly like a woman in the know.

'The last time we were all in this room, we brainstormed that *Falcon Bay* needed a new bitch. Whilst things didn't go quite according to plan, I think we can all agree that it was in principle a very good idea.'

Helen was fuming. Everyone in that room knew the 'new bitch' idea had been hers and not a collective one, but there was little point in chipping in with a reality check as Jake clearly felt he was on a roll.

'So, despite what happened, we all agree that in theory the

idea of a new character coming into *Falcon Bay* to shake things up is what the audience wanted, right?'

A room full of enthusiastic nods and agreements met his question; only Helen and Amanda stayed silent.

'During my time out, I've been working out what we need now to keep our ratings up and satisfy the audience. They were disappointed in the lack of consistency we had due to that storyline not running its course. We also need to grab headlines that actually come from the show, not the death toll around it.' Jake raised an eyebrow, which suggested he was talking about Ross Owen as well as Madeline.

Helen looked at her phone – no reply from Farrah. It was actually perfect that she wasn't here to witness this because there was no way that, as head writer, she'd have managed to keep her cool at what Jake was saying. Showrunners asked the writers for storylines, not the other way round; it was industry protocol. Not that Jake gave a shit about anyone's opinions other than his own.

'And I think after all the darkness of late, and the bad headlines, we need something sexy to spice life up on the Bay.' He smiled.

Amanda knew what was coming. No doubt some twenty-year-old, big-busted bimbo whom Jake would install behind the beer pumps in Lucy Dean's world-famous seaside pub. She'd be designed to make Catherine feel and look every year of her age. God, he was so predictable, she thought, as she readied herself to hear exactly what she'd envisioned.

Jake went over to the archive stand, which had the *Falcon Bay* characters' family relationship history marked out in five-year blocks. He pulled out the file marked 1990, then began to flip through it.

'Lucy Dean has been through so much; I think the audience

would love to see her find some happiness for a change,' he said, still flicking through the pages.

Helen was glad he wasn't looking at her because she hadn't been able to stop her eyes widening in disbelief at the words coming out of his mouth. Jake had spent all of the previous year slagging off Catherine Belle's portrayal of Lucy Dean, the matriarch of *Falcon Bay*. He'd been practically full of glee at Madeline's storyline, which was supposed to see Lucy leave the show and have her role taken over by her lost daughter, to be played by Honey Hunter. So 'Lucy needed a bit of happiness' were words she truly never thought she'd hear come from his lips. Amanda, as shocked as Helen, also looked on in grotesque fascination of what appeared to be the biggest U-turn in history.

Jake looked up from the file but kept his finger between two pages.

'I mean, she's been through hell, as an actress and as the character, right?'

The room nodded.

'And when the audience vote came in on whether to save or kill her character, it was such a close margin. It was probably screwed up by those wacky online fanatics who just wanted to see a bit of gore without thinking about the consequences of losing the *biggest star* on our show. I think it's only fair to say that after keeping her *alive* we need to ensure she now has a storyline befitting an actress who has, after all, given forty years of her life to our fans.' He smiled again as Helen and Amanda continued to look at each other in disbelief.

What the hell is he up to? Amanda texted to Helen on her phone. Both women had them under the table and on silent.

No fucking idea, came Helen's reply.

Candy, who had spotted what they were doing, gave them

dirty looks, thinking it totally disrespectful that they were on their phones during what was clearly an impassioned speech from their returned leader. She then turned her gaze back to Jake.

God, he was handsome, she thought, as her eyes wandered down his toned body and she imagined kissing his lips and running her fingers through his slicked-back blonde hair once more. He'd always reminded her a bit of Sting, and she loved Sting. The lyrics of *The Police*'s 'Don't Stand So Close to Me' were just starting to go off in her head as her mind wondered if next time they did it she could persuade Jake to try tantric sex. She wasn't even really sure she knew what tantric sex was, but if it was good enough for Sting, she wanted to try it. She could feel the faintest flutter of excitement building between her legs at the very thought of them both naked. Jake's voice suddenly changed tone, refocusing her on what he was actually saying rather than what she'd like to be doing with him.

'So, we'll keep our newcomer idea from last year – to introduce someone with a strong past connection to the show, someone long-time viewers will be happy to see again, but equally that our new viewers will be fascinated to watch walking across our infamous sandy shores. I've decided that Lucy will find her happy-ever-after with none other than her true love and father of her dead daughter, a daughter who was once excellently played by our Farrah. Where is Farrah, by the way?' he questioned the room, as he scanned the background to see if she'd placed herself out of vision.

'She's off sick,' Candy answered.

The penny of Jake's plan dropped in Amanda and Helen's heads as they locked eyes, realising the implications of what Jake was saying. Without missing a beat, Jake clocked their reaction and continued his impassioned, clearly well-rehearsed monologue.

'Yes.' He smiled triumphantly, like an athlete about to bring home a medal for his country in the Olympics. 'It's time for the return of Lee Landers.' As he said his name, he turned the file he'd been holding round to show the room a photo taken of young Catherine Belle in the arms of a stunningly handsome black man, who was holding her tightly whilst giving a perfect smile to the camera. The backdrop was the exterior harbour set, and the year was marked 1992. Lucy Dean and Marcus Lane's engagement party.

Helen's mouth went dry. It was well known to everyone that Lee and Catherine's character romance had spilled off the set and into real life, even mirrored in the fact that they too were engaged. In the late eighties and early nineties, they'd become the tabloid darlings of the show. In an era when a mixed-race couple was still considered taboo, it had helped break down prejudice when *TIME* Magazine in America, where they shared a joint cover, hailed them as TV's golden couple. None of the women had ever seen Catherine so happy – that was, until Lee had suddenly broken off their real-life engagement with seemingly no warning.

He'd declared their off-screen life to have become a circus in an explosive interview with a major Korean tabloid that had been profiling them. Saying that showbiz was no longer for him, he'd abruptly handed in his notice to leave the show, refusing to give Catherine, whom he never spoke to again outside of his final scenes, any further explanation.

The heartbreak and devastation had caused her to take six months off after having a breakdown. Lee's character was written out in an off-screen boating accident that allowed Lucy's character to leave the Bay long enough for Catherine to recover. Everyone on the set, especially Amanda, Farrah, and Helen, knew never to mention his name again for fear of bringing all the heartache back to her. Not once in thirty years had anyone mentioned his name, not even Sheena, who'd done an excellent job handling the horrendous media mauling of her 'dumping' at the time. They'd all behaved like he'd never existed, on or off camera. His character was never referred to on screen.

All the women had gone along with Catherine's description of French Claude, the stud who owned Claude's restaurant, which they often used to visit, as being the one who got away. In reality they all knew it was Lee who was the man that had broken her heart so badly she'd never really allowed herself to love again. Instead Catherine had given her all to the very show Lee had abandoned, and Jake was now proposing he not only returned but came straight back into scenes directly opposite the woman he'd jilted.

Fuck, Helen texted. Amanda read it under the table and replied with a head-exploding emoji – both of them knowing that this was designed to cause maximum damage to Catherine, who was still fragile from the Christmas fiasco. It was absolutely clear, if only to them, that this new Jake performing his act in front of the packed meeting room was nothing but a façade. This was a man with a serious vendetta, and they knew Jake well enough to know that today's goal was obviously the further undoing of fragile Catherine. There was little doubt that it wouldn't be long before they were next on his list, along with Farrah and Sheena too.

Jake sensed he'd been read by Helen and Amanda. Whilst the rest of the room were genuinely salivating at what they saw as a no-brainer of a winning storyline, he was enjoying seeing their awareness of just how subtly clever his plan was. He couldn't help but break into a broad grin at the absolute wickedness of it. As the team congratulated him on his brilliant idea, he couldn't resist a little goading to see if he could get the women to bite back in the midst of his adoring audience, showing themselves up as the bitter bitches he knew them to be.

'And in this era of inclusivity, I think it's good to remind the viewers that *Falcon Bay* was leading the way with diversity decades ago. Ladies, don't you think so?' he said, looking left and right to meet their gaze with just the hint of a smirk.

With his use of the diversity card, both of them knew he'd handed them a trapdoor to hover over with any objections. Choosing her words carefully, Amanda was first to reply.

'There's no doubt this is a sensational idea, Jake,' she said as earnestly as she could muster, determined not to give him the reaction he wanted or reference the issues he knew it would cause Catherine personally. 'But,' she continued cautiously, 'didn't Lee famously swear off ever returning to commercial television? Stating the very reason he left was to be a *serious actor*? His words, I seem to recall, at the Emmy Awards, when he won Best Actor for us. He went into the foreign press tent announcing he'd never do a soap again and actually called *Falcon Bay* a factory that churned out shit.'

Helen smiled. Pow. Good on Amanda for remembering that. She spotted a distinct drop in Jake's smile at that blow. Now it was her turn to attack.

'Yes, it was quite the scandal. I think the speech is still on YouTube under "Ultimate Cringe TV Moments" or something similar.' She picked up her phone and searched for it as she was talking, and without stopping found the clip, connected her Bluetooth to the room's internal speakers, and let his words boom out for all to hear. A few audible gasps rang out as 1992 Lee Landers let rip at the very show everyone in the room was still working on.

Jake, momentarily thrown, didn't get the chance to interrupt, so Helen barrelled on. 'I remember that night so vividly. I don't think you'd have been at the awards, do you, Jake? You were only a researcher at the time, weren't you?' She allowed the dig to fester in the air to make anyone in the room who'd only known Jake as the boss become aware that, although in a less powerful role than he, she knew way more about *Falcon Bay* than him. 'God,' she continued, 'we were absolutely ripped to shreds worldwide over it. Definitely one of our lowest moments before, well, this Christmas,' she said, pulling a grimace at the memory of both, designed for the whole room to realise just exactly how bad what Jake was suggesting would be. 'Perhaps a re-cast of the role would be better?' she said with a straight face.

Continuing the double-edged attack, Amanda picked up the verbal baton.

'I agree. There's so much new talent out there – we could even find the next Idris Elba. Come to think of Lee, I seem to remember he was absolutely emphatic he'd never return to our show anyway?'

Helen nodded as Amanda continued.

'I lost track of his career years ago. Is he even still working? That independent art film he did straight after leaving pretty much ruined his credibility. Wasn't he playing all twelve of the characters himself, and the critics savaged him for the ego of it all?' She threw the bait back to Helen, who immediately ran with it.

'Oh god, yes,' she said, shaking her head with embarrassment on his behalf.

Jake was trying to control his anger now, which was rising at their clever undermining of his plan. He could even feel the vein in his neck starting to bulge, the one that was known by everyone on the lot as the precursor to the moment he

141

would usually lose it, throw a chair or sack someone in the peak of his rage. But he would not rise to it. Taking deep breaths out of the side of his mouth like a ventriloquist gearing up to speak, he was determined to keep his composure under bitch-fire.

Amanda was watching the vein in his neck pump. She knew he was close to rage and wondered if whatever Helen said next would be enough to tip him over the edge. That would expose that the Jake Monroe that had been thrown off this show for being an egomaniac nut case, and had led to them nearly being cancelled in the first place with his and Madeline's ridiculous ideas – which they'd all been forced to go along with – was in fact the very same man now masquerading as a reborn, caring leader interested in the show's ratings rather than his own personal glory. *Come on, Helen*, she thought. One more poke and the beast would bite.

Helen eyed her, then went in for the kill.

'According to the internet,' she said, brandishing her mobile up high for all to see, as if it was the suddenly discovered missing murder weapon in an episode of Poirot, 'if he is still alive, he hasn't worked since 1995. So, whilst I *totally* agree with you that the audience would love to see Lucy get her happy-ever-after, especially after what happened, do we even know what Lee Landers looks like any more?' She smiled, knowing at the very least that between them they'd created some serious doubt in the room over Jake's messianic proposal.

Jake had been listening silently to Amanda and Helen's passive-aggressive, ping-pong-ball style of attack across the table. As it came to an end, he geared up to speak. But Amanda couldn't resist one last dig.

'We've seen recently that there's huge media coverage to be garnered by casting high-profile names. That's probably the way I'd go *if* I were going to pursue the idea of giving

Lucy a new love interest,' she said, as emotionlessly as she could manage. She would deliver the final kicker that they'd quickly texted about under the table after she'd done a quick check on *Falcon Bay*'s Wikipedia page for one vital fact – so far not addressed.

'But if you are *really* set on having the character of Marcus Lane back, there is one more vital problem we'll need to consider,' Amanda said, in a sing-song voice that could have rivalled any Disney movie, clearly enjoying the battering she and Helen were giving Jake's bullshit idea. 'How are we going to deal with the fact that the character is not only dead, but that he was decapitated in the boat crash? It was how we got away with not filming his face, as he refused to honour his exit contract. The on-screen funeral we filmed for him was watched by eighty million people around the globe. We all know how loyal our audiences are, and they have long memories, especially when it comes to who is meant to be alive or dead. And our writers, who of course are absolutely brilliant, do too,' she said, gesturing around the room with a flourish, which brought on several smiles, especially from newer members of the team. 'But I'm not sure even with their creative talents we can ask them to write for a character that has no head?' She let out a little laugh, then, sure she had at the very least thrown one giant spanner into Jake's obviously devious plot, leaned back in her chair and let her previously tense shoulders relax into its padded comfort.

Candy watched intently as Jake appeared to be processing Helen's take on what she thought sounded like a great idea. Helen was snide; in her opinion anyway. She smiled at Jake to let him know that he certainly had her support. Catching her eye, Jake smiled back.

'Helen, I've got to hand it to you, if we had a scoring system in here, that would definitely be worth at least ten merit points just for memory.' He turned to the younger members of the team. 'See, you should never ignore how valuable the older members of our CITV team are. They're a source of almost biblical information that you younger people can always learn from.'

What an absolute twat, Helen typed into her phone, furious Jake had pulled his usual ageist card when there were only two years between them.

Pig, Amanda replied as he continued on. He was aware he'd applied the perfect dig, one designed to needle Helen, who was well known for being sensitive about her age and was always first in the queue to try any procedure or plastic surgery designed to turn back the clock.

'On those *very valid* points, I have three answers that I believe will allay any fears. One, I have before me the best imagination of any continuing drama department in the world, and we all know that bringing characters back from the dead is a well-trodden and popular part of the soap cannon, when it's done correctly of course. Our viewers will expect to suspend their disbelief in order to see a fan favourite back on their screens – after all, we are a fictional drama, not a documentary series, right?'

Candy smiled, and Dustin nodded.

'Two, as was quite correctly mentioned, as eighty-five million avid viewers watched his character "die", we know for sure we are in for humungous viewing figures. They'll want to see him rise from the dead – that alone will also generate global media buzz, because to have the original actors back always generates more publicity than a recast.' He threw that line towards Helen and then kept his gaze on her side of the table.

'Three, and you can thank me for this one later, Helen, as technically this should be your job – you've admitted you're off the boil when it comes to Lee Landers' career or

144

whereabouts. I've saved you the bother. I spoke to his former agent myself this morning and he is, I'm delighted to say, able to confirm that Lee Landers is not only alive and well, but he's up for coming back to finish what he started. I also FaceTimed him myself, and it's fair to say he's lost none of his charm or looks, unlike some of our long-term cast. Our audience will still see him as a catch, so I'd say Lucy is one lucky lady.'

He laughed as Candy started another round of applause, which Jake did not discourage. Yes, he thought, the mood in the room amongst the team was now firmly back in his corner. Only Helen and Amanda sat stony-faced amongst a room buzzing with excitement.

'So, now we have a plan, I'm going to leave you *creatives* to work on his return. Helen, I'll let you deliver the good news to Catherine that not only will she be front and centre of our wonderful show once again, but she's also getting her most successful on-screen partner back. I guess we could call this a late Christmas present, as I wasn't around on that fateful day where it all went so horribly wrong. Perhaps this can be our way of making it up to her?' He smiled again as he let his gaze land on Amanda to emphasise where the blame for Madeline's death should lie.

'Right, I'm off to get back to *my* office,' he said, giving Amanda a wink that resembled the way a crocodile's eyes flickered in the dark just as it was about to attack its prey. 'I want you to know that my door, just like these,' he gestured to the still wide-open entrance, 'will always be open. This is a new era of *Falcon Bay*, where I want us all to be united. I'll be taking two weeks off at the end of the day, as I've obviously been working very hard to bring you this new plan ready to be worked worth with. When I return, I look forward to seeing the full storyline and schedule to see our new vision

145

come to life. I know you won't let me down.' And with that he strutted off down the corridor, looking like Mick Jagger at the end of a Rolling Stones concert. Candy immediately followed him.

After about fifteen minutes, everyone had left Meeting Room 6 apart from Helen and Amanda, who were looking at the picture of Lucy and Marcus Jake had left on the table.

'Well, this is going to tip her over the edge,' Helen said grimly. 'And she's only just about getting level again after Christmas. Sheena said she was on the verge of a full-on confessional breakdown at the funeral in Louisiana. God knows how she'll handle this news. Lee fucking Landers of all people. I'll give that ex-husband of yours one thing, and it's not a compliment,' she said placing her hand on Amanda's and giving it a squeeze of reassurance. 'He's a clever bastard. He knows what effect this is going to have on her.'

Amanda squeezed her hand back. She knew only too well just how devious and clever Jake's twisted mind was.

In the old days, when she'd loved him, it had just been the clever side that ruled him. She wasn't quite sure at which point he'd gone over to the 'dark side' – a bit like Darth Vader in the *Star Wars* movies he'd made her watch over and over again when they were first dating. Today was a sure sign that there was definitely no turning back.

'And us,' she said flatly, knowing they were once again in a battle to save the Bay they loved so much, and its leading lady, from yet another attack designed to take them down. 'You call Sheena and deal with Catherine and I'll head over to Farrah's to break the news.'

'Deal,' Helen said. The women hugged then went their separate ways, both sad in the knowledge they were about to ruin two of their best friends' days.

Part 2

Chapter 11

At the Durand Pledge Hospital, 5,000 miles away from St Augustine's Cove, where the world-famous rehab centre sat high on Mulholland Drive, Los Angeles, drugs were running through the veins of another woman. Despite her location, she could not see any of the outstanding views of San Fernando or the Hollywood sign in the distance. She was deep in the windowless basement, which sat at the far end of the lowest corridor and housed the facility's most disturbed patients. Strapped to a bed by her arms, her legs were being held apart by two men wearing nurse's uniforms, whilst a third one lay on top of her. As her body rocked against the only piece of furniture in the otherwise empty room – the white leather bed – the men cheered each other on as they abused her, whilst a fourth man stood watch at the door.

'Hurry up, man,' the one to her left shouted as he reached up her body and roughly squeezed her breast. 'It's my turn next.'

The men laughed as the one on top howled as he climaxed, then stepped back breathlessly. 'I never thought I'd get to bang a Disney princess,' he said, as he pulled the used condom off himself, wrapped it in some tissue and put it in his pocket. As the man who'd been urging him to hurry up dropped his trousers and moved towards her shaking body, he put a hand on his shoulder. 'Wear a rubber, man, or they can get your DNA,' he said, handing him one.

He took it, then heaved himself onto her half-naked body. 'I bet you love this,' he whispered menacingly as he pounded her flesh hard, reaching up to pull down her nightdress so her breasts were now fully exposed. The third man cheered him on as a single tear ran down one of her cheeks. 'Give it to her, man,' he laughed, as all three of them jeered. After the third man took his turn, they turned to the nurse standing guard.

'It's your turn now, buddy,' one of them called out whilst pulling his trousers back up. 'We've warmed her up nice for you.'

The man at door looked at his watch and shook his head. 'We need to get back to the wards. We've been down here too long,' he said solemnly.

The nurse pulled up his fly and looked surprised.

'Your loss, man, she's got the sweetest pussy you'll ever bang.'

'You can go first next time,' one of the others added. 'And I'll keep guard. You can't miss out on banging her, man. We're in this together, right?'

The man at the door nodded.

Happy they were all in agreement, the others, now fully dressed, began to wipe her body down, spraying her skin with disinfectant before retying her hospital gown back up, putting her legs back together, and refastening the ankle restraints that matched the ones that were intact around her delicate wrists.

One of them noticed her hair had bunched up from where

her head had rubbed against the gurney. 'You better brush her hair, man.' He gestured to the man who'd been the first to re-dress. 'If Durand ever finds out what we've been doing to his princess here, we'll all be in for it. That dude is crazy.'

The first man combed Honey's hair and used his thumb to wipe away the tear on her face. 'Hey, she's been crying,' he said, looking to the others in panic. 'Shit, do you think she's awake?'

Man Number Two approached her and looked deep into her eyes; her pupils were still dilated and they didn't flicker as he studied them. 'Nah, she's well out of it.' He smirked, then pulled a small bottle from his pocket and a needle from the other, injecting it into the bottle and filling the syringe. He tapped the air bubbles out and leaned towards the drip that was strapped to her left arm. 'Just to make sure, I'll dose her up.'

He inserted the needle into the bag that carried the fluids directly to her veins, then, laughing once more, they tidied the room and themselves and headed towards the door.

'Thanks for a great time, your highness,' the one who'd been last to take advantage of her body said as they began to exit into the white corridor. 'I might watch one of your old movies with the missus tonight.'

'Sleep well, sugar tits,' said another as they left, locking the door behind them.

In her drugged state, just above the fog in her brain, the throbbing pain in her body made Honey Hunter want to scream. But just as her eyes began to focus on the ceiling above her, the injection in the drip hit her bloodstream and she was gone again.

Chapter 12

When Lee Landers's former agent had called saying *Falcon Bay* wanted him back, if he hadn't been determined to play it cool, he'd definitely have dropped the phone in shock. It felt like another lifetime since he'd left the show, and considering his character Marcus Lane was supposed to be dead, this was a call that no actor would ever expect to get. Especially nearly three decades to the day when he'd told the world's press at the Golden Globes that not only would he be leaving the show, but he'd never go back, proudly declaring his time in the 'soap world' was over for good.

It hadn't taken long, however, for him to realise that like so many before him, he'd misjudged his popularity and the power of the show. Within a year, not only had the phone stopped ringing with offers, but due to the sheer embarrassment of being unemployed yet constantly recognised, he'd decided to flee to the one country in the world that had never broadcast *Falcon Bay*: the Netherlands.

With the money he'd made from his five years on the show, he'd bought himself a large barge, which was moored in the Oud-Zuid on one of the quieter sides of Amsterdam.

It wasn't long before months stretched into years and then into decades. He'd grown to enjoy his relative obscurity, and he ran barge boats for tourists along the gorgeous canals of Amsterdam. In the early days, occasionally drunk tourists, mainly Americans, would tell him how much he looked like that '*Falcon Bay* actor', but with his skill in the Dutch language he'd always managed to throw them off. Having been used to learning six scripts a week, he'd picked it up fast. Eventually, though, even that stopped, and he believed that 'Marcus' was well and truly in his past – that was, until the call that had woken him early in the morning two weeks ago.

His former agent Swifty Bagshaw had called, telling him that the boss of CITV, Jake Monroe, personally wanted him back. As off-the-grid as he was on the riverboats, not having a TV himself, he saw the newspapers passengers left on board, and overheard the chatter, especially last December when the show's disastrous Christmas episode had even been an item on the only radio station he still listened to: BBC Radio 4. It had been a double shock, as they wouldn't normally reference anything so lowbrow, but it made him well aware that *Falcon Bay* was once again the most watched show in the world, albeit not for all the right reasons. Catherine Belle, who played Lucy Dean, his former partner off-screen and on, was still very much at the heart of it.

He paused for a moment whilst studying his handsome face in the boat's bathroom mirror, checking out his profile from side to side, imagining what the cameras would see. Thanks to his family's mixed Jamaican and Moroccan heritage, his skin was still as firm as it had been all those years ago when he and Catherine had been smiling together on the covers of magazines, on the racks of newspaper stands all over the world. He'd seen pictures of her being taken away in an ambulance after the shark attack, and although she was soaking wet, crying with a blanket wrapped around her, she still looked just as easy on the eye as she had done all those years ago.

His mind wandered back to the days their bodies were entwined as one, making passionate love in the hidden coves of the *Falcon Bay* set between takes. Back then, they'd barely been able to keep their hands off each other. Well, during the good times anyway. The memory of Catherine's exquisite body and perfect breasts on top of him as he thrust himself into her against the rockface instantly made his cock harden.

He took another look in the mirror and pretended it was a camera on set, practising the stare that used to make millions of viewers go weak at the knees.

Chapter 13

One of the best protocols Amanda had introduced as soon as she had taken control of *Falcon Bay* on Christmas Day was on-site drug tests. In the live call with Chad, he'd given them the devastating news that not only was Jake returning, but he wanted to bring back his drug-addled sidekick, the Bay's former lead director, Aiden Anderson.

He'd been ejected from the show once before, after being arrested in a tabloid drug scandal that could have given Pablo Escobar a run for his money. Jake had used his power as showrunner to allow his best mate to return after a faux public apology during their live 'Bitch Party' episode. The press had lapped it up, but Amanda knew it was more contrived than any prime minister's speech and there was no way he'd change. The new rules at CITV applied to everyone, even her. So if Jake tried to bring him back on board, her one solace was that there was a chance that one of them would fail. Deep down she prayed they both would. But cocaine had never been Jake's drug of choice; power and the degradation of others were what gave him his high.

Whilst it were beyond frustrating that neither she nor Helen had been able to reveal the real reason behind how they'd got Jake off the show last time in order to stop his return this time, in a follow-up email she'd flagged the show's new drug-testing rules. She knew that Chad's values were beyond reproach, but he'd agree the last thing the show needed right now was another scandal. Amanda had had no doubt that Aiden would use a friend as a stand-in and do the pee test for him – to give him no chance to do so, they'd had the CITV medical team arrive at his hotel without telling Jake, meaning he'd had no time to warn his buddy.

The result was exactly as they'd both expected. Sadly Jake was clean; it was a shame you couldn't test for toxicity in blood, Amanda had thought when she saw the results. But she smiled at the email she'd been able to send on to the Kane Foundation, cc'ing Jake, confirming Aiden had, as expected, failed with flying colours. There had been enough drugs in his test to guarantee that no third chances were coming his way, giving her the first sense of relief she'd had since this new nightmare began.

That was one down, with the added bonus that Jake wouldn't have his toxic wingman with him. Although judging by the way Candy had chased after him when he strutted out of Meeting Room 6 like a demented peacock, she felt sure he had already found an equally dubious sidekick.

Each morning now, Amanda woke with a migraine. Just trying to work out how the hell she was going to get through being on set with her estranged husband had also caused her to start grinding her teeth when she did sleep. It was the not knowing when that day would actually come that was making the build-up worse.

Despite Jake saying he'd be back in a fortnight, it had been a month now since they'd last set eyes on each other, and he still hadn't showed up – just sent a barrage of emails adding pressure to the ridiculous storyline he'd landed them in. As she removed the mouth guard the dentist had recommended, she reasoned that without his physical presence around the Bay, it had at least given her more time to enjoy feeling like she was still in charge of her precious show before having to hand the reins back to her maniacal estranged husband.

Even though she'd enjoyed the day-to-day satisfaction of the responsibility of running the team she saw as her extended family, the last month had been far from peaceful. Despite it being gone midnight after she and Helen had finished the live call with Chad, she'd gone straight over to Farrah's condo, determined to deliver the bad news herself. Even though Farrah was officially off sick, Helen knew that she would still be monitoring the crew's WhatsApp group chat. There were only hours to go until the team meeting where she'd be sharing the bad news. She knew if she didn't get to Farrah, who hated Jake almost as much as Amanda did, her finding out about it via the group chat would only make things even worse.

Despite it being 1 a.m. when Amanda pressed the buzzer at Farrah's condo, she'd answered immediately, and within minutes she was facing Farrah, whom she hadn't seen in weeks. As she went to hug her friend, she noticed she was uncharacteristically wrapped in a large, oversized dressing gown. That was odd as Farrah was much more the Agent Provocateur silk robe and cami type. Even for a girls' night in for cocktails and movies, Farrah rarely looked anything but Victoria's Secret-runway perfect. Amanda took particular notice because as much as she loved her friend, she'd always suffered body envy of her model-like figure. It wasn't even unusual for Farrah to open the door fully naked if Amanda arrived early and they were due to head out somewhere for the evening.

155

Amanda, however, wouldn't be caught dead stood up in the buff with the lights on. Not even her gorgeous boyfriend Dan, who made it clear that he adored every curve of her figure, had seen her without at least some sort of negligee on. Even as she followed Farrah up the stairs of her condo, the Spanx she had on under her shift dress chafed on her thighs.

Amanda entered the main living room, which was on the upper level where her vast balcony with gorgeous views of the ocean was. Amanda was shocked to see that Farrah's usually pristine showroom-style home was untidy, with food delivery boxes cast aside on the sofa and clothes strewn across chairs. Amanda wondered if Farrah, who'd gone into the bathroom, had a sixth sense about what she was thinking, because as Amanda moved a pizza box to sit down, Farrah called out from behind the door.

'Sorry about the mess. I've been too ill to let the cleaner in. I'll be through in a moment. Help yourself to anything you want, there's loads of ice-cream in the fridge.'

Farrah was usually offering to crack open a bottle, day or night, good news or bad, so the offer of ice-cream had Amanda tossing the words around in her head. What on earth was going on? Moments later, a downcast Farrah appeared and took a seat next to her friend on the now cleared sofa.

'You look terrible,' Amanda said, reaching her arm out to touch her friend's hand.

Farrah took her hand and squeezed it. 'I am,' she replied, but before Amanda could ask her why, she continued. 'But so do you, and if you're coming round here at this time without any warning then something bad must have happened. What is it? Please tell me it's not what I think it is. I saw they'd announced Ross Owen's death as misadventure. I knew it wasn't safe to call or text about it, and as I haven't been out of here, I couldn't see what you thought – but that's got to be good news, right?' Farrah fixed her with a slightly manic, hopeful stare that was like an interrogation lamp. Amanda squirmed in her seat.

'Yes, that's good news,' Amanda started.

'Oh, thank god.' Farrah smiled, grabbing a piece of cold pizza off the table and taking a bite.

'But . . .' Amanda said.

'But what?' Farrah said, with a full mouth. 'Oh, please don't tell me it's about Christmas—'

'No,' Amanda cut in.

Farrah let out another sigh of relief then took another bite.

'But it is bad news.'

'Oh god, what now?' Farrah said, getting off the couch. She walked to the fridge, where Amanda assumed she was about to open a bottle of chilled wine. It would be helpful to share one whilst they commiserated about a return to a time on the show they believed had died along with Madeline. But instead, she retrieved a tub of Häagen-Dazs from the freezer, grabbed a couple of spoons and flopped back down in her seat.

Farrah, aware Amanda was eyeing her, took a mouthful and turned to face her friend.

'Before I hear your bad news, I've got some that's so bad, I've stayed off sick trying to find the words to tell you.'

'So you've not been sick then?' Amanda said, leaning towards her.

'Oh, I'm sick all right, and I doubt that what you're about to tell me is going to make me even sicker than I've already been. Now it's not just the mornings I've been being sick, it's all day and all bloody night.'

Amanda leaned back in confusion; she couldn't mean . . .

'Yep,' she said, looking Amanda in the eyes as she pulled open her robe to expose her rounded belly. 'And that was pretty much the first face I pulled when I realised too.' Farrah dug into the ice-cream pot with her spoon and took another mouthful. 'This is the only thing that it seems to want – clearly got a sweet tooth like its bastard dad.'

Amanda reeled back in horror at Farrah's words as well as the vision of what was clearly the beginnings of a baby bump forming on her friend's perfect body. 'But you had an abortion,' she managed; her throat tightened as the words left her mouth.

'Yep, but it turns out, just like one of our twisted storylines, it didn't work. I stupidly didn't take the second set of pills in time, plus I mixed them with booze. I just assumed they were guidelines, and I'm such a fucking idiot that not only am I still pregnant, but I didn't even realise until I was six months gone. When my periods stopped I thought it was the menopause, which I didn't really want to talk about, and it's too late to do anything about it.'

Farrah ate another mouthful and continued. 'It didn't even show any signs it was in there until two weeks ago, when my jeans wouldn't fasten and suddenly I was craving this shit – and now I've ballooned.' Farrah gestured to the tub. 'You know me, I don't even fucking like ice-cream,' she said, suddenly letting her anger at the situation rise in her voice. 'I didn't want to tell you until I'd had the scan, which was yesterday. The hospital take no responsibility because I didn't follow the instructions, so there I was thinking I'd got rid of his evil seed, and all the time, like *The Omen*, it's been in there growing.'

Amanda was speechless. Farrah had slept with Jake just one time. Tensions had been high between everyone, but the women had overcome it; their friendship was much stronger for it. The news that Farrah had become pregnant as a result, then taken the medical abortion pills immediately after, had closed that one break in their twenty-year friendship. The irony, if she could find any at the time, was that it had taken ten years of IVF when she was with Jake for her to conceive Olivia, and she'd had several miscarriages along the way. Each one was still marked in her diary with a date and the name she'd have chosen, each still a baby she loved. She imagined that one day, when her time on earth was up, she'd be reunited with all her lost children. She believed in every woman's right to terminate a pregnancy, so even though her road to mother-hood had been horrendous, she'd supported Farrah.

And now, sat right opposite her, inside one of her best friends, was a baby that not only had her ex-husband created but was so strong it had survived medical intervention. Her head felt woozy. She wanted to run from the condo, out onto the beach, and let out a scream, one so loud and full of pain it would echo across the ocean. But right now she needed to hold her emotions together. She'd already forgiven Farrah and they'd repaired their relationship; she was feeling she had to be there for her friend who was clearly on edge.

'I can't get rid of it now, it's illegal at this stage,' Farrah said, looking down at nature's time bomb, which was ticking inside her. 'You know I'm not the maternal type anyway. I wouldn't have wanted it, no matter whose it was, but to know that there's a part of him inside me makes me want to be sick. If I wasn't already being sick night and day, that is. No offence to Olivia, obviously,' she added, registering Amanda was reeling in the same way she had been when she'd first got the news herself a few weeks earlier.

Amanda was still too shocked to speak, so Farrah pulled her dressing gown closed, placed the ice-cream down and continued. 'I don't want anyone to know. I've no idea how I'm going to cover this up as it gets bigger.' She gestured to her stomach once more. 'But it's all arranged. I'm having a caesarean at thirty-eight weeks if the baby hasn't been affected by the drugs and booze, which I've stopped,' she said, waving the ice-cream in the air. 'Hence why I'm on this crap instead. They say looking at the scans and blood tests it seems fine, so I'll have him removed from me and then he'll be adopted. No one must ever know.'

'It's a boy?' Amanda said quietly, the realization of Farrah's plans sinking in. The shock of it all, whilst not subsiding, adjusted enough to allow her to take in her words and plans fully.

'Well, it would be, wouldn't it? It's so annoying they told me the sex. I said in advance I didn't want to know, and some stupid young trainee was in the room watching the scan and let it slip,' she said, with more than a hint of anger. 'Anyway, it's not "a boy" in my mind, it's not even a baby, which of course sounds stupid and I know it is, but for the sake of my sanity until they can take this out of me – it's an it.'

Amanda found relief washing over her that however unwanted this baby was, it would get a chance to be born, but the brutality of Farrah's description made her stomach turn. Farrah, too wrapped up in finally being able to get this secret burden out into the open, carried on unaware.

Farrah continued as if she were talking about moving house. 'I've got twelve weeks to go until I can get my life back. I'll come back to work next week and I'll work as long as I can manage to cover this up for. Then I'll book some "creative time off", and we can say I'm working on future storylines or something. By the time I get back, it will all be forgotten about. I won't ever want to talk about it again. I need you to promise me that you won't tell anyone about this, not even Catherine, Sheena or Helen – and it goes without saying Jake must never find out.'

Amanda looked at her, trying to work out how best to

160

deliver what she'd originally come to say before she'd been floored by these revelations.

'So that's mine.' Farrah gestured with her delicate hands for Amanda to continue. 'What's yours?'

'Jake's coming back.'

'What?' Farrah screeched in a pitch so high Amanda was sure it would wake the neighbours. Farrah jumped up and headed towards the balcony, pulled the door open, and took a deep breath of the sea air as the sound of waves against the rocks filled the room. 'How is that even possible?'

She was clutching the door handle with a grip that could strangle a python. She spun round back towards her friend as the wind coming through the now open balcony door blew her dressing gown open.

'When will that bastard get out of our lives?' she raged.

Amanda recounted the live call with Chad that she and Helen had had earlier as Farrah stood in the breeze, listening. When Amanda had finished, there was a pause. It seemed like Farrah was processing the information.

'Well, just when I thought things couldn't get any worse,' she finally said, her face more deflated than Amanda had ever seen it. Farrah closed the balcony doors and returned to the sofa to sit next to her friend.

'Fucking hell,' she said.

'Yep, that about sums it up,' Amanda replied, before promising to keep Farrah's secret, however much it would eat her up.

And eat her up it did, over the next two months whenever she saw Farrah on set, wearing long flowing robes, which Helen remarked made her look like she was some sort of seventies tribute act.

Amanda hadn't breathed a word. Not even to Dan, which killed her. The idea that she was keeping something so important from him made her feel bad each night when she went to bed, looking at his sweet face. She'd been in a relationship of lies for years and she didn't want to recreate that ever again. She'd reasoned this was not her truth to share every night when she tucked Olivia into bed – who'd been the last of her viable eggs during the IVF process. Just a few hundred yards away, in the womb of one of her best friends, Olivia had a brother, destined to be given away to strangers that she'd never know about.

The knowledge that her miracle baby was destined to grow up as an only child meant over the course of the last few months, she'd barely slept.

Chapter 14

Catherine Belle's last few months on the set of St Augustine's had been far from peaceful. Every time she went to bed, the nightmares would return. Each night they'd be the same: either fighting Ross off as he tried to rape her, or staring into the shark's jaws, with Madeline's mouth full of blood as she screamed Catherine's name. Sometimes, worse than the dreams she was having based on reality, other dark areas of her mind let Ross have his way with her, or she'd find herself in the shark's mouth with Madeline pulling the hand that could have saved her away – just like Catherine had.

She was emotionally exhausted every moment she awoke, feeling like she'd run a marathon of horror.

She was adding extra concealer under her tired eyes when there was a double knock at her door. Before she could answer, it opened to reveal Helen and Sheena. She barely looked up from what she was doing to her eyes, as she knew whenever two of their close circle of friends showed up at her dressing room together, and unannounced, it was never a good sign

Once she heard the reason they were here, to say she

completely lost the plot at the news of Lee Landers's return to the show wouldn't have been an understatement.

'Why would he do this to me?' she shrieked, smashing all of her make-up off the counter with the swipe of a perfectly toned arm, causing one of the illuminated mirrors to smash.

Helen did her best not to react, but genuinely felt shocked at the damage Catherine had caused. Helen knew how much she loved her workspace, and that the illuminated glass she'd smashed had been here as long as she had. She approached her gently and tried to assure her that she and Amanda had fought against it with Jake, but ultimately, he was once again in control. They hadn't been able to stop him. Sheena tag-teamed her with the fact that despite the personal issues and their past, which were obviously going to affect her, the team had ultimately come up with a good storyline. It would work for the show and see her front and centre.

As Helen cleaned up the mess, there followed several rounds of tears, despite Sheena's best efforts reiterating that Amanda had done everything possible to create an upside to the storyline. Amanda played her the recordings Helen had made for Farrah from Meeting Room 6. They captured the moments after Jake had left: Dustin and the team working out an authentically feasible way to return Lee to the show in the most convincing storyline possible.

Inevitable drama was guaranteed to go on off-camera the moment the two former lovers came face to face. Amanda's measured voice, captured on the tape, reassured Helen and the team that after the brainstorming, she was now confident they'd found a way to realistically reunite them, on screen at least. After several duff storyline suggestions, including two quite frankly deranged ones from Candy, who'd returned from whatever she'd been doing with Jake towards the end of the conference and was suddenly way too opinionated for Amanda's liking, they'd finally agreed on what the new back-story would be.

Catherine repaired her make-up from the tears. Her reflection in the shattered glass now reflected the way her brain felt at the latest absurdity being thrown at her character and ultimately her.

It was going to be revealed that Marcus's character had been leading a double life when he was last on the show: despite being engaged to Catherine's character, Lucy Dean, and being the father of their daughter, Tiffany Dean, once played by Farrah – it would turn out that he was already married. New scenes would now be filmed and presented as flashbacks to Marcus's double life, and due to the wonder of anti-ageing editing technology, which Hollywood studios had invented to allow their most bankable stars to keep playing roles way younger than their years, they'd look authentic, as if they'd been filmed years ago. That would give the audience a credible belief that *Falcon Bay* had planned this as a long story arc.

They'd written it so that Lee's character, Marcus, believed the only way to avoid telling his first wife that he was already married was to give up the love of his life, Lucy, jilting her at the altar, by faking his own death in the motorboat explosion, ensuring both women thought he was dead. This was why the viewers had never seen his face, because it hadn't been *his* body that was retrieved, but that of a bit part player, a surfer called Todd. He'd taken Todd in the boat with him. Between that and some other links between the men – which had seen them fighting over Lucy's attentions in the earlier days in old story arcs that would be edited in from the archives – Amanda felt they had just about enough to keep the show's audience convinced of its feasibility.

Since that day, Amanda had spent weeks going through old episodes, finding as many threads to weave together as she could. Social media had such a powerful effect on TV programmes these days. Fans could be so aggressive and, unlike the old days of weekly reviews, feedback was instant. If the public didn't like something you did with one of their favourite characters, you could find yourself in the middle of 'cancel culture', and Amanda didn't want the Kane Foundation on her back as well as everything else. So she'd left it to Helen and Sheena to convince Catherine that despite her own personal misgivings, she should trust that with her showrunner hat of experience on, she genuinely felt storyline wise this would work.

Catherine wasn't interested in the upside spin Helen and Sheena were using to try to convince her that this appalling plan would see her leading the show once more.

After she got them out of the room under the guise that she needed time to reflect on what they'd said, she went over to her filing cabinet, which sat in the far end of her dressing room, and pulled out some old cast annuals.

She hadn't kept a single photo of herself with Lee from the relationship they'd had when they were working together. But she knew there would be some inside the faded pages of the special hardback books that people used to buy as presents, when life was simpler, and her heart was less scarred. She remembered the long queues there would be when the cast would be sent to some huge department stores to do signings for the fans, and for a moment, she reminisced on how much kinder the world seemed back then. These days, fans wanted to know all the dirt on your personal life, specu- late about what surgery you might have had, and would even graft your head onto fake pornographic images on the internet to no doubt use for the same disgusting reasons they would create fantasy X-rated blogs, where they'd write filthy sex scenes between the characters and share them online.

The press office had warned her not to look, that the internet was a Wild West that no one could control. But curiosity had got the better of her after hearing some of the younger cast revelling in being fantasised about. One day, she'd made the mistake of googling herself. After what she saw, she wouldn't be doing that again, that was for sure.

When she found the 1992 *Falcon Bay* annual, she pulled it out of the file and sure enough, there he was. Well, there they both were, embracing, with full smiles and young faces, looking happy, like they had the show and the world at their feet. She'd believed they had.

Just like Lucy had loved Marcus, she herself had loved Lee. When the tabloids had exposed that he had been caught cheating on her with an actress from rival soap *Heartlands*, it had been yet another blow to her self-esteem and encouraged her belief that perhaps true love would always evade her, on screen and off.

As she looked at his handsome face on the pages of the book, she wondered how she would feel seeing him in the flesh. If it hadn't been for what had happened on Christmas Day, and at the awards ceremony where she'd seen Ross Owen's skull smashed into several pieces, she'd have handled this news much differently. She'd have marched up to the head office and threatened to quit the show if they re-hired an actor who had not only broken her heart in real life but also shown no loyalty to *Falcon Bay*. After all, he'd abandoned his role on the network in the same cavalier manner that he'd abandoned their relationship in real life. But, still numb from what she'd been through and almost on autopilot, she didn't have the fight in her. Besides, times had changed. No one upstairs, not even Amanda – now once again below Jake in the power chain – would be able to help her.

With a sigh, she put the book back into the filing cabinet and pushed the drawer closed, then went over to her smashed dressing table and picked up the earrings that had been left out for her by Brad from wardrobe, for continuity filming. She placed them on and then looked at her reflection, seeing several of herself reflected back in the shards of what remained of the mirror.

'I will not show him that he has any power over me,' she said to herself in her soft and mellow voice.

She repeated the sentence three times whilst she stared into her own eyes. She'd read about *The Secret* recently and had been using this technique since they'd got back from Louisiana. The affirmations she'd been using on the platform when Ross had attacked her hadn't worked, but she was grasping at anything she could find now to help keep her sane. She hadn't bought into everything in the book, but this one element seemed to help calm her. It reminded her of the rhymes they used to warm up years ago before a scene, in the days when dramas were filmed with proper rehearsals and in several takes, rather than crammed into what felt like a never-ending factory production line.

A few moments later, after doing her eyebrows and giving her hair a brush, she was finally feeling calmer. She picked up her scripts and headed for the door.

The call sheet had shown that Jake was on set today. It would be the first time they'd crossed paths since last year and she was determined not to let it show that his presence or his plans to return Lee Landers to the set had rattled her. With one hand on the door, she slipped the other into her coat pocket, pulled out a strip of Xanax, raised it up, and expertly popped four pills out of the silver foil into her perfectly lip-glossed mouth.

That was four times the dose she was supposed to take, but god, how she needed them. Affirmations were very good for the average hellish days, but it would take a decent amount of her trusty class-C drug to keep her composure around that piece of shit.

Chapter 15

The dockyard set of *Falcon Bay* had never looked more beautiful. Spring always seemed to create the perfect atmosphere. Spring days on the Jersey coastline were usually sunny enough to make it look like early summer, which was when the current batch of episodes being filmed would air, but the temperature was much more comfortable to film in.

Catherine walked towards the platform above the decking that led up to her character Lucy Dean's famous beach bar, The Cove. The exterior camera crew were set up there today. She noticed that they'd also brought in the crane, which they used to capture sweeping shots of the island that gave their viewers all over the world a full-on look at the paradise they were lucky enough to not only work on but live in too. In the distance, she could see Farrah, who was directing this episode in a flowing black jumpsuit with her braided hair in a high ponytail. She was briefing the cameramen on positioning as one laid a board across the sand to stop them sinking into the beach.

Catherine thought Farrah's outfit a strange choice for such a bright day, but she and Farrah, who'd been incredibly close for nearly three decades, had barely spent any time together since that night up on the cliff edge. She'd got the distinct impression Farrah was avoiding even coming close to her. Usually she'd have been with Helen and Sheena when they'd come to deliver good or bad news, but as they'd barely crossed paths, she didn't think making a joke about what she was wearing, like she might have in the past, would be a good idea. So, instead of what would usually be a hug, she waved. Watching Farrah wave back then look away made Catherine's heart ache with what felt like loss. To anyone watching it looked like they barely knew each other. Maybe after everything that had happened, that was now true, she thought sadly.

Today's scenes were all set on the veranda of The Cove and were part of the backstory of bringing Lee Landers back in. The scripts were good, so even though she still hated the idea she was, as ever, determined to give the scenes her all and not show him an ounce of anything she was feeling personally about seeing him again. She'd managed to pull off two police interviews about two suspicious deaths without cracking, so his return, as much as she wished it wasn't happening, couldn't possibly be on their level, she reasoned, as she looked for her mark on the floor to stand on for the first shot.

The script called for Lucy to open a letter that had been left for her at the bar, which said that 'Marcus' was alive and wanted to see her but didn't have the courage to turn up in person, for fear she would reject him. The irony of the wording wasn't lost on her; the second part could definitely have come from real life. If by any chance, in any small way, he so much as tried to rekindle their off-screen romance, she was ready and very much looking forward to telling him exactly where to go. But on screen, Lucy Dean sadly didn't have the same resolve Catherine did.

171

In order to get Lee back on screen asap they had, in her opinion, rushed Lucy into being too forgiving too early. In the old days when they only filmed two episodes a week, a storyline like this would take months to mature, allowing for a believable turnaround in her feelings. After all, Marcus was a character who, for over twenty years, she had believed to be dead. In 1993, on screen, to an audience of 100 million, she'd been given the news of his fatal boating accident whilst stood at the altar. She'd run towards the ocean in tears in her wedding dress, then collapsed at the sight of his lifeless body being carried out of the sea.

As her mind ran over the scene, a shudder ran down her back at the similarities between Madeline's real-life death in the same exact spot of their famous ocean. Unlike that day, where Lee Landers was concerned, Catherine Belle was definitely the innocent party. Now the whole backstory would be played out over just one week and, looking at her schedule, she could see her first scenes with Lee in person would be on Friday, meaning she had just two more days to prepare herself for their on- and off-screen reunion.

Farrah's voice rang out, breaking into her thoughts.

'Make-up checks, please.'

Brad appeared next to Catherine and began adjusting her hair. Since Christmas, he'd been alternating between hair and make-up and the wardrobe department, which again was a new sign of the modern age, doubling up people's jobs to save money. In the old days there would have been a strike if either department stepped on each other's toes. She remembered one incident where a props man had called in the union as she'd moved her own bar stool inside The Cove, and the union had actually sent her a warning telling her not to do it again. At the time she thought it ridiculous and bizarre that something so minor could be treated so preciously but now, with all the unions dissolved and a multi-tasking attitude being taken by nearly everyone in production, she looked back on it fondly and wished she could rewind time. For once she wasn't thinking about how she looked.

Brad finished combing her hair and gave her a smile.

'You OK, Catherine?' he said, in his friendly voice, which matched his sparkly eyes.

'Yes, my darling,' she replied, patting him on the arm. She turned to Farrah to show she was ready. Farrah noticed and called action.

Falcon Bay Episode 3004 Scene 12, the Cove exterior

Lucy Dean has read the letter from Marcus which explains his regret and cowardliness at abandoning her by faking his own death. A shocked Lucy reads the end part of the letter out loud then clutches it to her chest and gazes out across the ocean.

LUCY

'. . . I want to explain everything to you. Please allow me to visit and tell you in person why I had to do what I did. I still love you, Lucy. I hope you can find it in your heart to forgive me. Yours forever, Marcus.'

Farrah signalled for camera two to zoom in on Catherine as she turned towards them and, as scripted, dropped the letter as she finished reading from it.

LUCY

'Dear God, can it be true? Is he really alive?'

As Catherine delivered the last line, a tear fell from her eye. An impressed Farrah was just about to shout cut when a solo round of applause broke out. She was desperate to go over and tell Catherine how amazing she was, but was terrified she might spot the bump under her clothing. As she was about to send a message to her earpiece, she noticed everyone on the studio floor turn. She followed their eyes to see Jake Monroe, with Candy by his side, striding towards Catherine on the set. *Fucking Jake*, Farrah fumed.

'Cut,' she yelled, then turned towards him.

'Jake, you bloody well know that is unprofessional when we're in the middle of a scene,' she said, barely able to contain her anger, but trying desperately to stand still on the gantry so the fabric of her jumpsuit stayed loose. Jake, still clapping as he neared Catherine, shot a few words in her direction.

'Sorry, Farrah, just a bit excited to be back on set as you can imagine. I wasn't sure if that round of applause was for me or Ms Belle.' He laughed as Farrah stared him down. 'Besides, our star here had already finished her dialogue, word perfect and still a one-take wonder, I see,' he said, finally reaching Catherine, who was now facing him, having turned back from the sea on hearing the commotion.

'Hello, Jake,' she said as cordially as she could.

'You look wonderful,' he continued, insincerity dripping from his mouth. Catherine had been acting all her life; she knew a performance when she saw one. When he reached her, he kissed her on both cheeks. As his lips met her skin, she wanted to retch. God, he made her skin crawl, but, determined to be professional, she pulled on her own skills to go with his fake flow.

'Thank you, it's always easy to do your job when the quality is as good as these current storylines,' she said, smiling and at the same time manoeuvring herself so she was out of the sun's glare and into the shade. She figured if she was going to have to play silly games with Jake she might as well protect her well-preserved skin as well, if not her dignity.

Clever cow, not biting, Jake thought as he stepped back to survey the *Falcon Bay* lot. But he had another piece of bait up his sleeve that was sure to rattle her.

'Oh, I am so pleased you're happy with the new direction we have for Lucy,' he said, beaming. 'Amanda and Helen felt you might find it a *bit* too emotional having to work with Lee Landers again.' He registered that for a nanosecond the smile she'd plastered on her face to match his slipped down briefly before returning to a full upswing. 'But I said they were being disrespectful to your professional capabilities – I mean, you've been doing this job since God was a boy, haven't you? And after the way you survived Christmas Day, in more ways than one, well, the return of an old flame who dumped you is hardly likely to ruffle your feathers, is it?' He laughed as the crew and Farrah looked on awkwardly.

Catherine kept her smile up and casually reached for her script and phone, which she'd placed just out of shot.

'Exactly. If anyone understands what it's like to work with someone who dumped you, it's you, Jake. So when they said exactly the same about you coming back after being fired I said, no, not Jake, he can handle it,' she said with a smile, and patted his face gently. She used the stage voice she'd once projected whilst performing plays above the grotty little pub where she was discovered by *Falcon Bay*'s original casting executive, the late Caroline St James. Caroline had rescued her from obscurity and brought her to St Augustine's forty years ago.

Jake's face stiffened as she continued.

'It must be difficult seeing Amanda so happy with her lovely man, Dan. They seem so well matched,' she added, loud enough for everyone to hear.

The awkwardness of the crew intensified, but Farrah was grinning from ear to ear as she watched Catherine's masterclass in rebutting a put-down. Jake was struggling to think of a witty reply when Catherine decided to leave it on a high.

'Anyway, keep doing what you're doing, stiff upper lip and all that. Thanks for checking on me though. Oh, and if you ever need to speak about how *you* feel, my dressing room door is always open.' She gave him another smile, then began to walk across the sand as Brad, who had been watching in awe, followed behind her.

As she passed Farrah, the women's eyes locked and Catherine decided to throw in a parting shot.

'And Jake, make sure someone from make-up gives you some factor fifty. Don't forget how terribly ageing the UV rays are around here,' she said, then disappeared into the shadows of the studio set, leaving Jake awkwardly alone in the full glare of Farrah and the crew.

'I'm not sure about the sun, Ms Belle, but you certainly gave him a proper burn,' Brad whispered in an excited voice as they both entered the internal lot. 'You are a true sass queen, gurl,' he said, pulling the door open for her to enter, and bowing as if she were regal.

She didn't know exactly what he meant, but this caused Catherine to laugh. She loved 'the gays' as she called them – you could always rely on them to have your back.

As she made her way to studio B for the next scene, she smiled in the knowledge that whatever happened next, at least round one had gone to her.

Chapter 16

For someone who'd spent her career successfully digging up dirt on celebrities on both sides of the Atlantic, Tabitha Tate was finding her lack of progress at discovering the whereabouts of the missing actress Honey Hunter beyond frustrating. Every contact she had worldwide, and she knew everyone, had come up with nothing.

When Mickey had made finding Honey a condition of her tell-all scandal book on *Falcon Bay*, she'd accepted it because actresses with booze and men addictions like she had were pretty easy to find, in her experience. They were usually under the spell of some no-good toyboy who'd whisked them away, at the star's own expense, keeping them out of the public eye long enough to snaffle away at whatever money they had left, or tricking them out of it with a scam that anyone with half a brain would cotton on to before it was too late.

The case of Chrissie Martin, the lead singer of the legendary eighties girl group The Thunder Girls, sprang to mind. Tabitha had read an exposé where Ross Owen had taken great pleasure in splattering pictures all over the front cover of

The Herald of her crying, recalling her disastrous wedding day. Chrissie had tried to keep it quiet, but Ross had managed to get all the dirt he needed.

She'd never been a fan of his when they'd had to share office space. She found his way of doing things so slimy, not to mention sweaty. But she had to hand it to him, when it came to digging the dirt on a distressed diva, Ross had had a particularly good shovel.

She was flicking through his old notebooks to see if Mickey had made the same request about Honey to him for the book deal that she'd now taken over. But there was nothing, not in his scribbled notes, or on his office computer. She would have loved to have access to his cell phone, but it was presumed to have been washed out at sea when his body was floating for days, and had never been recovered. Being well known for his paranoia of anyone hacking into his iCloud to steal his exclusives, he hadn't backed anything up in years. She knew this because she'd already hacked into it, and all that was there was his list of contacts, which might turn out to be useful at some point but wasn't helping her right this minute.

Googling images of Honey at the book signing last year with Mickey, she'd have put her in the same category as Chrissie, assuming she'd fallen for a similar love interest scam, but all her money was still in place, and if anything, she was still earning plenty. Getting access to her bank accounts was technically illegal but that didn't bother Tabitha. She knew every way there was to get in and out of someone's private life to steal their privacy, without leaving so much as a digital red-painted, pointy fingerprint.

Not only did Honey have several million in the bank, but it was being topped up by hefty royalties still coming in from Fonda Books from the continued sale of her autobiography.

Nothing had been spent since she'd paid for that one-way First Class ticket to Los Angeles on Christmas Eve. Not a single transaction had gone through any of her accounts since that, apart from old direct debits, certainly nothing of interest.

Has-been stars, even ones with Oscars, didn't usually agree to join a soap opera after years out of the spotlight if they had access to those sorts of funds, so that in itself was a bit mysterious. After she'd got over exactly how much money Honey had, which itself would have made a great feature if she was around to talk about it, Tabitha began to concentrate on her LA contacts.

Being American, she had a vast contact list of people who tracked down others for a living, and not just paparazzi. She'd used bounty hunters in the past, the really low-down, ask-no-questions, do-whatever-it-takes-to-get-paid types. One in particular came to mind: Vlado Slavica, an ex-military Serbian guy she'd used when she was tracking down a missing politician's daughter in New York, who'd disappeared with a circus worker and a crack pipe. It had been a few years since she'd spoken to Big Vlad, as she had him in her iPhone, but she was pretty certain he'd still be working. He loved the thrill of the chase as much as the cash. However, his services came at a big price, at least $100,000 which, with exchange rates being so shit, would be half her advance. But he always got the job done and there would be royalties to make up for it.

As she looked at his number in her phone and started a text, she decided to have another look through some of her cheaper contacts, just in case there was a more cost-effective way. Ross had barely had the chance to start his search before his death, so perhaps Honey could be found with a dig of her own shovel.

'Think, think, think,' she said out loud, as she twisted

her long hair around her finger and closed her eyes to concentrate.

Usually, the best places to track celebs down in the States – if Honey had stayed in LA where her plane landed – was the party planners. Everyone in the industry was on the make over there. Check in to anything – from a five-star hotel to a motel dive bar on a highway, or even a hospital – when you were a star, and you could guarantee a bell boy, concierge, cocktail waitress or nurse would either tweet you'd been there or tip off a pap for a backhander. Fallen stars sold just as well as current ones, and with Honey being the rare combination of the two – a fallen star who was back in the A-list – it just made no sense that not a single person in the showbiz know had tried to sell the information to any of her sources. It was known that before she'd disappeared, Honey had fallen off the wagon and had been drinking again, but not one of the extensive list of rehab facilities she'd attended over the decades had her registered either.

Annoyed that the search for her was taking up too much of her time, she decided if she had any chance of getting this book published whilst the misery of Falcon Bay was still a hot topic, she had to bite the bullet.

Job for you . . . she typed, then pressed send to Vlad's WhatsApp. She preferred that to texting as she could always tell when a message had been read. His profile picture on the app was a close-up of one of his giant biceps, which had a tattoo of a gun on it. Tabitha found that so tacky, yet somehow on someone so brutish as Vlad, it was kind of horny, in a hate-yourself-for-even-thinking-it way. Although in the past she'd done more than just think about it.

Her memory floated back to the time they'd got it on during a late-night stake out. She hadn't planned it, as he wasn't her type at all. She liked tall, long-haired, surfer or digital tech geek dudes, whereas Vlad was short, his hair shaved to a zero buzz cut, and solidly built like a tank. His accent was so thick she could barely understand him. But that one cold night in Manhattan, they'd spent six hours in close proximity, just the two of them. The sheer brutishness of him, combined with the strange aftershave he wore that mingled with his sweat and sent out an oddly intoxicating scent, had sent her clit pulsing with desire as their bodies lay close together in the back of a blacked-out SUV. Before she knew it, they were kissing and her clothes were off. After working his way down her body, he'd held her legs apart and went down on her in a way she'd never ever experienced.

Vlad's tongue was as strong as his tattooed muscles, even stronger than the most powerful vibrator in her collection, and she had quite a few. A girl in her line of work had little time for relationships, and having switched the US for the UK, she hadn't quite compiled her 'little black book' of booty calls yet. Even remembering Vlad's zig-zag oral sex technique, where he alternated the rhythm with a combination of sucking her clit and swirling his tongue around it, had her getting hot at the recollection.

On the night it happened, by the time his rough hands had travelled back up her body, squeezing her nipples whilst he ate her out like a man who hadn't had a meal in months, she could hold back no more, and she came all over his face as her body shook so strongly she felt like the car must have rocked. If he hadn't placed a hand over her mouth, the moans of ecstasy she'd let out would definitely have blown their cover. As the waves continued to flow down her body, she went to pull him close, so he could enter her, but she was surprised when she looked down to see he had already returned to his post and was looking though his night-vision goggles to spy on their target.

181

When he'd noticed her expression, he'd raised an eyebrow and said something she'd never forgotten.

'Pussy was snack, now back to job.'

At that very moment her phone pinged. It was him.

Send details was all it said. She smiled. It would cost her, but it was a weight off her mind to know that she could now put some of her concentration back into other areas of the book she knew was going to be the making of her. It was, after all, called *The Curse of Falcon Bay*, not *Finding Honey Hunter*, so she needed to get on with the wider arc of her soon-to-be bestseller.

Logging back in to The Vault, she scrolled back to the photos and footage of Madeline Kane's death. As she studied the footage from all the cameras that were filming the exact moment she'd fallen into the water and into the jaws of the shark, there was still something bothering Tabitha about the angles in the files. She'd seen it all at the time – a screaming Madeline Kane being bitten in half, whilst Catherine Belle fainted. It had been on every front page across the world and trended as the number-one social media topic for weeks. When she'd glanced at it over her coffee in Madison Square Gardens in New York, two weeks before she'd arrived in London for her placement at *The Herald*, she, like the rest of the world, had looked at it in shock.

Now, however, she was studying the images with a different eye. The Vault contained copies of everything the police had on the case, which had been officially closed months ago with the verdict being recorded as accidental death. The coroner must have felt that there was nothing suspicious in the evidence. She watched the full ninety-second clip of the moment the two women fought just before Madeline fell into the water, over and over again. She clicked the sound onto mute; there were only so many times she could bear to listen to the bloodcurdling scream as Madeline was dragged underwater by the giant beast. She was just about to switch the laptop off and go for walk around the office to get her steps in for the day and clear her mind of the bloody images when it suddenly came to her what it was about the footage and photos that was odd. The shots from the cameras from above didn't match the footage from the underwater ones with the same time codes. There were several frames missing and each one of them was exactly around the moment the nation's heroine, Catherine, was leaning on the boatside decking, extending her hand towards a flailing Madeline just before the shark teeth's bit her gorgeous body in two.

As she paused on two frames in particular and studied the differences between them, a big smile spread across her Dior-glossed lips.

Chapter 17

The main tower of the CITV building sat right in the middle of St Augustine's coast, its panoramic windows showcasing the best views the island had to offer. Farrah was on her way to the script department when she spotted Jake coming out of the large office he'd taken back from Amanda when he returned.

Farrah was rounding the last corridor, which would lead her into the huge open-plan suite of the production office. It would be crammed with desks, filled with teamsters chattering away on phones, tapping away on laptops, or brainstorming in the 'think-tank' – which was actually just the corner of the office opposite the terrace, leading to the fire escape, and had been repurposed with several bean bags and a coffee machine to create a less formal environment. Well, that's what it had been described as in the annoyingly worded email Candy had sent on Jake's behalf about a week earlier.

Desperate to avoid running into Jake, Farrah instead stepped into the first office door she could find, which happened to be the office of the head of accounts and Amanda's boyfriend, Dan.

Before he could call out to greet her, Farrah put her hands to her lips to quieten him, then closed the door behind her. Dan looked handsome in a fitted grey suit that showed off his muscular frame, and the silver highlighted tones of his salt-and-pepper hair glinted in the light as he looked up at her in surprise.

'Are you OK, Farrah?' he whispered, unsure as to why he was whispering at all.

Farrah smiled and made her way gently over to one of the chairs opposite his desk. Ever since her bump had started really showing, she'd developed a sort of gliding motion to the way she walked, designed to give whatever she was wearing the chance to float and not lie flat against her stomach. Considering she'd spent her entire career at CITV strutting around in six-inch heels and killer suits, it had caused quite a few eyebrows to be raised. But with her new hair extensions in, rather than the famous severe crop, at worst it looked like she was trying a new look, one she was quickly marking off on her calendar and would be happy to burn in a beach bonfire the moment the spawn of Satan was out of her and she was back to her old self.

'Didn't want to speak to *you know who*,' she said carefully. She leaned to one side and crossed her legs in a way she'd once taught one of the actresses who was pregnant in real life when the show didn't want the audience to spot it.

'Ahh,' Dan said, his blue eyes sparkling with understanding of exactly *who* she meant. God, he *was* handsome, Farrah thought, as she took in his chiselled but kind face. Amanda had certainly upgraded with him, compared to Jake's sharp face and annoying blonde hair that was well due a cut, but he kept long because Candy actually told him in one of the production meetings that he looked like a young Sting.

'How have things been for you?' Farrah said, knowing it

185

couldn't have been easy dealing with Amanda's emotions. They were never very stable whenever Jake was anywhere near, let alone with all the secrets she was now forced into keeping.

'Oh, you know,' he said. 'Ups and downs.'

Farrah nodded. She was impressed that Dan was so discreet. Another mental tick in the winner box for him. 'Yes, I can imagine,' she replied. Leaning her chair back, she craned her neck to look out of the side window of Dan's office, which had a clear view of the corridor. Seeing Jake was now nowhere to be seen, she stood back up and headed towards the exit.

'All clear,' she said with a smile.

Dan stood, came towards her and opened the door. Blimey – good looking, charming, discreet and he had manners, Farrah thought. Amanda really had hit the jackpot with this one. She wasn't jealous though. If anyone deserved a decent man it was her. She smiled, happy in the knowledge that although they might be back in a war zone at work, at least Amanda had someone at home who was looking after her.

After waving goodbye, she headed into the corridor and took the long way round via the photocopying area where the scripts were compiled and stapled for the cast each day, so as to avoid even passing Jake's office window. She was just one row away from Dustin's desk when the distinct Australian twang of Candy's voice rang out.

'Farrah,' she said, dragging each letter out in an authoritarian tone. It made Farrah want to stick a ball gag into her mouth – she had one in her wardrobe somewhere from one of her more adventurous previous lovers. 'Jake would like to see you in his office.'

Shit, she thought. Then, practising her gliding move again, gently turned to face Candy.

'I'm about to have a meeting with Dustin,' she said. She

knew Dustin was also not a fan of Candy, especially since she'd become Jake's girl Friday. She eyed him, signalling him to back her up, but before he could chip in, Jake appeared.

'I'm sure Dustin can wait for you, can't you, Dustin,' he said in a tone that made it clear it was not a question.

With a forced smile, Farrah glided as slowly as she could towards Jake, hoping he'd turn round and head into his office so she could follow. Annoyingly, he just stood waiting for her to reach him, then walked alongside her as they headed into the gorgeous office Amanda had lovingly decorated.

Farrah's eyes were drawn to the terrace, the biggest of the whole building with a direct view overlooking the whole of the exterior sets. God, how she wished she had a parachute so she could just jump out of the window now to avoid whatever *this* was going to be about. Her eyes focused on the very sofa where she'd made the one decision she was going to regret for the rest of her life – the very place she'd stupidly had sex with Jake the day he'd told her she was going to be directing the now infamous Christmas Day live episode.

On hearing the news, she had for some unknown reason, which to this very day she still couldn't understand, become so overjoyed at landing the gig, she'd let a man that she not only loathed but was also married to one of her best friends inside her body. She shuddered at the memory of Jake slobbering over her breasts and the grunting sound he'd made. Unbeknownst to her, the sperm he'd shot inside her had had the precision of a loaded gun, with the bullet heading straight for – miraculously, as she was forty-eight – one of her last fertile eggs, creating the unwelcome visitor now invading her body.

'Candy, you can leave us to it.'

Jake's words broke into her memory, which actually did her a favour. She was beginning to wonder if she might recreate the time Amanda, hungover during the days when they used to spend their evenings partying, had projectile-vomited not only all over the office but also over one of the show's actors, Adam Roscoe. He'd been due to be fired, but thanks to the threat of a lawsuit of actual bodily harm by being covered in her fluid, was still woodenly acting his way through scenes on *Falcon Bay*. That was apt considering the role he played was that of the local handyman.

Candy's face showed that she was far from happy to be asked to leave, but she did her best to cover it with a forced smile. When she closed the door behind her, there were just the two of them in the room.

Jake, now seated behind his desk, leaned forward and handed Farrah the shooting schedule for the next two weeks' episodes.

'I don't need this,' she said, bemused. 'I know what's on it. They're my blocks, so I just did the grid.'

'There have been some changes,' Jake said with a smile.

'Since when?' Farrah replied, as she flicked though the pages, looking for whatever bomb Jake had clearly hidden within them.

'I've been speaking with Chad. He's a very moralistic man – of course you know that, as he was behind my return to the show after you and the other witches somehow convinced his wife to oust me on Christmas Eve.'

And so, the act was dropped.

The *true* smirking Jake was finally baring his teeth. Farrah smiled. She preferred this version of him, as she knew how to deal with the real him much better than the faux one. As all niceties and pretences were clearly now out of the balcony windows showing the beautiful view, she was ready to bat back.

'If he had any idea of just how lacking in morals you are,

he'd have made sure you never set foot on this island ever again,' she said with another smile.

Jake eyed her – there was something different about her. It wasn't just the change in her appearance, which in his opinion was doing her no favours. She'd always been a bitch, but at least she used to be hot. Now she wasn't even that. But no, it wasn't just her new look. It was something in her eyes that showed she looked like she wanted a fight with him, and the one thing Jake hated was giving any woman what she wanted – so he immediately changed tack.

'There's something else that's been bothering him.'

'Oh yes?' Farrah said, joining Jake and switching back to the professional tone. 'Please do tell.'

'It's the result of the public vote. It's come to his attention that it was actually Lydia Chambers who the audience voted to join *Falcon Bay* as our latest leading lady.'

Farrah took a tiny breath at Lydia's name. She knew exactly what was coming next and exactly what it was designed to do.

'He's decided – well, with consultation with myself of course – that we will now be honouring what should have been an offer to Lydia to join our family here. I notice she's no longer represented by your vile old cauldron stirrer Sheena McQueen, so at least that's one less reason for her to come flouncing down here for constant set visits the way she did last year.'

Sheena storming the set to intervene in Jake and Madeline's plans to kill Catherine's character off unchallenged clearly still rankled with him. Farrah didn't bite. If he wasn't going to go directly for her jugular, she'd join him in this game of cat and mouse.

'Who is she going to play?' she said as impassionedly as she could manage. 'I'm assuming that whoever it is, you've shoehorned some references to her into these shooting scripts and that's what we're here to discuss?'

Damn her. Always beating him to the punchline. Jake took the cat role again and went after her tail.

'I would have consulted you earlier,' he said in an exaggerated half whisper, as if the people on the other side of the glass, including Candy, who were watching them, could hear, 'but it's been a bit of a nightmare trying to undo all of Amanda's fuck-ups. I know she's your friend and technically my wife, but she's really dropped the ball in the story arcs. *Falcon Bay* must continue to break new ground and stay fresh if we're to keep our lead in the ratings post the Christmas high.'

'Will she be arriving on the back of a shark then?' Farrah added dryly. 'Or have you decided to introduce a crocodile to our shores instead this time?'

Jake smirked.

'We won't be going *there* again.' His words hung in the air and they both looked at each other; beyond the banter, the subject was still sensitive for everyone.

'She'll be playing Marcus's first wife, the one he couldn't admit existed to Lucy Dean all those years ago, causing him to flee. She'll arrive two weeks into his first on-screen reunion with Lucy and really put the cat amongst the pigeons.' He smiled smugly.

Farrah could see right through Jake's plans. They were once again designed to unsettle Catherine's position as *Falcon Bay*'s leading lady, so there was no point in giving him the further satisfaction of letting him deliver more news to her. She very gently rose from the chair, clutching her scripts, and wafted towards the exit.

'Right, just so I'm clear, we've now got to redo all the new scenes to incorporate . . .' She flicked through the schedule to find the character's name that Lydia would be playing. 'Claudia Raymond? I know you've been away for a while, Jake, but I'm sure you remember that Helen Gold is our head of casting. Since she hasn't sent me a brief, nor have Catherine or Amanda mentioned they know about this, I'm guessing you're giving me the pleasure of delivering the news to everyone?'

As his grin broadened and each one of his bright white veneers poked out from his thin villainous lips, Farrah imagined knocking each one out with a hammer like a game of head croquet.

'Correct,' he said.

After exiting the office in angry silence, she walked down the corridor, trying to decide who to visit first. Helen to have a bloody good moan about the sheer unprofessionalism of Jake taking over casting, or Catherine, telling her that another queen bee was about to be let loose to swarm over her manor. From her quick scan through the proposed storylines, it appeared Lydia's character Claudia's main aim on the show was to upstage Catherine's Lucy Dean.

With Claudia being nearly two decades younger, Helen could just imagine the digs Jake would be authorising her to dispense at her on-screen rival's expense. As she reached the lift, she decided to go to Helen as at least they'd be able to work out how best to sell this latest time bomb to Catherine. Farrah and Catherine had barely spent a moment alone together since the night they'd fled from Ross's dead body splattered on the rockside, as it had coincided with her discovering her pregnancy and wanting to keep her distance.

She was sad that their friendship had thinned out to the point it had. But it had started even before Ross's death and her mission to hide her ever-burgeoning bump had pushed them even further apart. The Christmas Day pact they'd made

191

to protect her had backfired when Catherine had started threatening to confess all and drop them all in it. All Farrah had done was try to help keep her friend out of prison, so that had been the deepest crack in the chasm that was now between them. She still couldn't shake off the anger at how selfish she felt that sort of attitude from Catherine was to those who'd tried to help her. As she hit the button that would take her to the floor Helen's office was on, she was suddenly aware of a weird stabbing pain in her side.

As the doors closed and the lift descended, she felt it again. With one hand, she gingerly ran her fingers over the protruding flesh of her tummy, hidden under her layered top, and placed them on her skin. Moments later she felt what was definitely the baby that was growing inside her – its first kick.

'Oh god,' she said out loud as Jake's DNA made its presence clear. 'Give me the strength to get through this and not lose my mind.'

She wasn't usually religious, but then she wasn't usually pregnant. As the doors pinged open, she looked around to make sure no one was looking, then, abandoning her gliding tactics, rushed to the first loo she could find. She locked the door, then pulled off her clothes to look at her naked body in the mirror. She could actually see movement happening under her skin as the baby shifted position. With a horrified fascination, she studied it and found herself placing her hands gently on the area the activity seemed to be coming from and pressing gently down.

Her heartbeat began to race at the realisation that whatever she'd been telling herself, right there, in that very moment, there was no denying the baby she could feel moving inside her body was part of her too. She hadn't bargained on feeling this. Right up to that kick, she'd been able to categorise this as exactly what it was: a problem she had a plan to deal with.

In true Farrah style, she had organised its exit from her life with unemotional military precision.

But as it kicked again, emotions were unlocked in her that there seemed no way to keep back. Feelings were flooding her, like a dam that was about to break. They flooded out of the place at the back of her mind where she'd kept the wood firmly in place to stop even a trickle of them from seeping through. Now the flood barriers had failed and she was suddenly swept overboard as a tidal wave of what she assumed was maternal love rose from her tummy into her heart.

As she cradled her bump again, she looked down as words tumbled out of her mouth that she'd never planned to say. 'My baby,' she said softly as she felt it kick again. She raised her head back up to look herself directly in the eyes in the mirror.

'Fuck,' she said.

Farrah was fully away that her crafty use of wafty clothing and her ice-skater's gliding motions to hide the fact she was pregnant from everyone at *Falcon Bay* had just drifted off into St Augustine's deep blue sea.

Chapter 18

It was a few weeks earlier. Whilst lying on her chaise longue and having a tropical-inspired pedicure done by Lina, her favourite beautician, in her central London mews house, Lydia Chambers got the call from Jake Monroe that every actress over fifty dreamed of. She knew it was going to change her life.

She already believed she'd used up what she thought was the last of her nine lives when she'd pulled out every trick she had in the bag during the live Bitch Party episode last year. She'd won the quite frankly borderline humiliating public audition to join *Falcon Bay* last year. But despite her agent at the time, Sheena McQueen, assuring her that the role was as good as hers, it was announced that it would go to Honey Hunter, whom she hadn't ever seen as real competition. Devastated, humiliated and angry at the deceit of it all, in a fit of rage she'd not only sacked Sheena but had lashed out publicly at the corruptness of CITV's casting decision, appearing on several TV shows saying exactly how she felt. After all, as far as she was aware, there were no more bridges to be burnt. She was toast.

She knew roles like Claudia Raymond were as rare as the fabled pot of gold at the end of the rainbow. At her age, in TV terms, she was considered by male executives – who still seemed to hold all the power – as deader than the hound that once played Toto in *The Wizard of Oz*.

But now, six months, one missing actress and one dead network controller later, it seemed the showbiz deck of cards had suddenly been dealt in her favour. She was going to have her second chance after all, and she absolutely couldn't wait.

Chapter 19

Ever since Catherine had been told about Lee and Lydia's imminent arrivals, she'd found it hard to conjure up the same love for *Falcon Bay* that had coursed through her veins last year, when she'd battled to the death to stay on-air and on the island that had been her only true home.

Now Jake was in charge again and her friendship with the other women, even her agent Sheena, was forever changed, she felt alone and out of place. She walked barefoot through her open-plan kitchen and onto her balcony, sitting in one of the bamboo chairs under the canopy and looking down on the place she'd called home for nearly forty-one years. She kept her eyes away from the rocks where she'd fought with Ross, and away from the spot on the boatside where she'd battled with Madeline, and focused on the beach set and her beloved bar, The Cove.

Crew members were setting up tables for the party scene she was due to film later that night. It would be the first time she or indeed her fictional character, Lucy Dean, would set eyes on Lee Landers's Marcus since 1993. Her heart seemed to beat loudly in her chest as she remembered the day she'd woken up in this very apartment, the one that they'd once shared, to find his note saying he'd left her. She'd sat in the same place as she was now, night after night, re-reading the note and trying to understand how he could have been so callous. In many ways he'd mirrored what his character had done on the show. Only neither of them were dead, fictionally or otherwise, and both were about to come waltzing back into her life and onto the show, bold as brass, as if they'd never done anything wrong.

'Men,' she said, crying as she took a sip of her wine. 'Real or fictional, they're all bastards. We'd be better off with you all gone.' As she looked down on the crew again and remembered how sweet some of the long-term workers were, who'd looked out for her over the years, she mentally told herself not to be so bitter. 'Apart from you – the good ones,' she said, raising her glass to toast them in the distance, which mentally she figured undid the voodoo-like curse she'd just laid upon the male species.

She had still been reeling at the news she'd be coming face to face with her ex-lover on screen when Amanda and Helen had come to her repaired dressing room. She hated the new mirror they'd given it; it had no charm like the one she'd sadly shattered. They'd come to deliver the news about Lydia joining the show.

She was in no doubt this was the cherry on top of the revenge cake Jake had been baking for her since his return to power. It wasn't that she had a problem with Lydia. During the search for *Falcon Bay*'s new bitch last year, before she realised whoever landed the role was due to take over from her as the show's leading lady, she'd already considered she might be working with Lydia. In truth, she'd have preferred Sheena's other client, Stacey Stonebrook, who was also up for the show. Catherine felt the wine she was sipping mixing with the Xanax she'd popped earlier to keep her mood level. In a twist of irony that wasn't lost on her, it was the very same mix of pills and booze that had knocked Stacey out of the competition, leaving just Honey Hunter and Lydia Chambers in the running.

She took another sip and quickly glanced at her phone's clock to check she still had enough time to get down to set, which she did. It was odd, in a way, she thought, that out of the three women who were most likely to land the role that Madeline eventually took herself, two of them were now nowhere to be seen. Stacey, humiliated from falling off the boardwalk during the live episode, had totally left the business. Catherine seemed to remember seeing something about her going into property management or something, obviously wanting to step away from the humiliation altogether, which was understandable but sad as she was a talented actress.

But the mystery of Honey Hunter's disappearance was still big news. Photos of her had been in *The Herald* again earlier that week, in a strange article by Tabitha Tate, stating she was now officially listed as missing with a tipline tagged onto the online feature. She'd read it on her laptop; they were offering money for information that might lead to her whereabouts. Such a strange thing for a national newspaper to do, Catherine had thought. Much more the sort of thing one's family did for a missing teen, rarely for a woman in her fifties that everyone knew had enough money to stay on a private island and wait for everyone to forget she'd run away from *Falcon Bay*, no doubt filled with nerves, before she'd even filmed her first scene. It was sure to be embarrassment that had caused Honey to go into hiding.

That was the thing about a soap opera. You might have an Oscar but filming one movie every few years was very different to six episodes of a soap a week – for that you had to have stamina and commitment. Catherine was certain that Honey had bolted at the last moment knowing she'd never handle the pressure. She'd seen it so many times before, so she didn't judge.

Stacey was a different kettle of fish. Given the choice, Catherine would have picked her to play opposite her every time, and she had even given Stacey her backing to Helen, who at the time they wrongly believed had the power to choose. Such a gentle soul. It was no surprise that she too was trying to keep her life private. She hoped *The Herald* wasn't going to try to spin Stacey's absence from the media into her being missing as well and create some sort of whodunnit, which would bring attention back towards the Christmas live. They'd milked Ross's death almost as much as Madeline's. She thought back to the coverage Ross had run on her after Christmas. Day after day, she was on the front covers, and the way he'd reported on her life, you'd have thought she was Princess Diana. Unlike Madeline – she genu- inely wished she'd been able to change the outcome of their battle – she was glad Ross Owen was dead. He was a piece of shit, and she didn't feel at all guilty about her part in it.

Despite the Xanax and wine, just running over the blood trail she'd unwittingly left on the island over the last year had caused what she knew was a tension headache coming on. Damn, this was the last thing she needed. Not with the scenes she had to film tonight.

Placing her glass down, she went back inside, found some paracetamol and popped two along with another Xanax just for good measure. She let her silk robe fall to the floor, then slipped on her costume, which she'd brought home with her, not quite in the mood to get into Brad's excitement zone in the wardrobe department. No, tonight she would get herself fully ready. She'd already done her make-up and spent an hour alone adding as many lashes as she could fit on her eyes to really make them pop. Some hot rollers had given her hair just the right amount of bounce so it gently bobbed around her perfect shoulders.

The dress she was wearing was a canary-yellow, gypsy-style one with a split up one side and a cinched-in waist that really showed off her figure. Happy with her appearance in the full-length mirror in her walk-in wardrobe, she went over to the dressing table and reapplied her lipstick, placed some large gold hoop earrings on and took a deep breath. There was no getting away from it now, she thought, as she texted Brad telling him to send the buggy to pick her up from her condo's walkway and ferry her to The Cove's outdoor set.

Minutes later, as the buggy hurtled across the sand, the breeze in the air made Catherine's hair blow like she was in an eighties rock music video. As the crew watched her approaching, she could tell by the appreciation in their eyes that she looked good. Brad was on the walkway waiting for her.

'How are you feeling?' he said, as he reached out his hand for her to hold as she navigated the few small steps in Lucy Dean's infamous six-inch heels.

Fans all over the world were captivated by how she managed to stay upright in them on the show's sandy beach. Even Cher had once tweeted *How the hell does she do it?* Brad had thought that was amazing and had it as his screensaver on his mobile. The secret was sand-coloured wooden boards a few inches into the beach. It had been her idea in the eighties. Being only five foot four, she'd got sick of always having a crick in her neck after hours of filming with her head tilted up to taller male co-stars because they had her barefoot on the beach. Once the boards were installed, she'd been able to get her stance back; she hadn't realised that one small idea would fascinate people for generations. But that was the power of a soap opera. Everyone all over the world watched them, even if they didn't admit it. She'd recently noticed that that bitch reporter Tabitha Tate was now using the technique every time she hosted a sneaky blog about *Falcon Bay* from outside the studio.

'Is *he* here?' she said to Brad, ignoring his question.

Brad nodded.

'How does he look?'

'Honestly?' Brad asked.

Catherine gestured for him to continue.

'Hot!' he exclaimed. Then, realising that Catherine wasn't impressed with his choice of words, started to backtrack. 'Obviously he doesn't look as good as you—'

She cut him off. 'You mean for my age.'

'No, well, yes, but you know what I mean,' Brad said awkwardly.

He hated it when Catherine disapproved of anything he did; he idolised her. But hot was definitely the right word to describe Lee Landers. A few hours earlier, Brad had been on his hands and knees in the wardrobe department altering the hem of the linen trousers Lee's character Marcus was to arrive in in tonight's episode. He'd been fantasising about what it must be like to pull them down and enjoy what was clearly a very full package. He was desperate to ask Catherine how hung Lee was, but knew that was absolutely out of the question. Besides, the way the linen had clung to his shape and the fact that Lee was clearly going commando in the trousers had pretty much already given him the answer. From what he could tell, the man was packing an anaconda.

As he walked a silent but composed Catherine over to The Cove's terrace set and towards her mark, he tried to get his mind off Lee's length and back into support mode for his favourite actress . . . 'That dress looks amazing on you,' he said as he fixed Catherine's hair, which had lifted from the buggy ride.

Catherine smiled. She knew he was trying to be sweet but she didn't have the tolerance for chit-chat tonight; she needed to save all her energy for the scene.

'I'll be fine now,' she said, gesturing for him to leave. She waved at Amanda, who was talking to Farrah up on the director's platform. 'You go and enjoy looking at him,' she said, then, as he was walking away, added, 'Oh and Brad, I think you meant, *I* look amazing in *this* dress,' she said with a wink.

'My bad, Queen,' Brad said with a laugh and walked away, planning on doing exactly as Catherine had said and getting another good look at Lee Landers.

Amanda, in flip flops, smiled at him as they crossed paths in the sand and she headed up into The Cove. Catherine looked sensational as the combination of the dusky night sky and the studio lights made her exposed skin glow like the surface of a pearl.

'How are you feeling?' she started.

'How the fuck do you think I'm feeling?' Catherine hissed, causing Amanda to almost stumble on the final step that would bring them face to face. 'I would have at least thought *you* might have asked *him* to come and see me away from the cameras before we filmed tonight's scene,' she said quietly, but curtly enough for Amanda to know she meant every word.

'Jake's been with him all day,' she replied.

'So your marital awkwardness has stopped you doing your job, has it?' Catherine snapped, her tone a level higher so that those in the surrounding areas picked up on the exchange. Farrah also looked up from her monitors, craftily swung an overhead mic towards them and slipped in an earpiece so she could hear what looked like an intense conversation.

'No, but—' Amanda tried, but once again Catherine cut in.

'But nothing. Let's be clear, no one in power on this show has done any professional behind-the-scenes etiquette of re-introducing two actors who have a difficult working history, let alone a personal one. Those actors are now about to come face to face onscreen in front of the whole crew, half of which have worked on the show long enough to remember what he did to me in real life.' Amanda was silent as Catherine's perfectly made-up eyes stared harshly at her. 'Does that answer your question on how I'm doing?'

Amanda decided to stay silent; she could tell it was a rhetorical question and that Catherine's lambasting of her was far from done.

'You could have at least had the decency to try and arrange that,' Catherine spat out of the side of her perfectly made-up mouth. 'Any producer worth her salt would have *made* him come to a read-through with me at the very least, or a meeting with all of the cast, to apologise for his unprofessional behaviour of refusing to even film his exit scenes. He left before your time here, so you probably don't even know that I had to film all my last lines to his character with an extra standing in as his bloody body double. Putting his and my personal life aside, if you can call it that, he's an actor who has returned to a show he slagged off all over the world. That requires some modicum of apology – even if he doesn't mean it. This showiness, fakeness I can do, Amanda. I would have gone along with it and played the game, to at least get that first moment out of the way, but the very first words we will exchange will be this shitty dialogue in front of dozens of people. Do you think that's right?'

Amanda once again stayed silent, knowing Catherine wasn't waiting for an answer.

'I'm a bloody good actress, Amanda, but even I'm going to

struggle with this,' she sniped, now aware she was being watched, the last half of the sentence delivered in a much lower tone. 'Well?' Catherine asked, signalling that she was indeed now done and was expecting Amanda to provide her with a defence.

Fully aware they were in the full glare of *Falcon Bay*'s night crew, Amanda didn't really have one. She knew everything Catherine was saying was true. What Catherine didn't know was that she had tried to get Jake, admittedly via Helen, to do all the things Catherine had listed, but Jake had said there was no way he was going to 'make Lee think he was unwelcome' and dismissed it. In a phone call with Sheena, they'd also discussed how else to find a way to make the situation better but neither could bring themselves to admit that, for the moment at least, the men had the better of them. And unlike them, but very like their co-workers, they'd taken the coward's way out of letting the reunion happen on set tonight. Sheena herself had not even turned up, so the brunt of it was left at Amanda's door and she knew there was nothing she could say to make herself look any better to Catherine for her part in this, as there was no excuse.

Seeing as how she'd let her friend down and, humiliated by the public assignation, a part of her just wanted to run down the steps, across the beach and all the way to her house, grab Olivia and jump with Dan in the car and get them all the hell away from this island. But another part of her was determined to at least brave this public confrontation. She was steeling herself up to reply when a shadow broke into the light where they were standing.

Catherine didn't need to look to know it was him. She could feel his presence and, all these years later, if she was not mistaken, she could smell the same cologne he'd worn back in the day. It had a blend of aromas that she'd smelt on others, but it only truly seemed to come alive on him. When coupled with the sweat on his skin an unmistakeable musk would radiate from the mixture. And whilst it might have been decades since she'd last seen him, she knew one thing: if he was sweating, he was nervous.

Suddenly her anger at Amanda was forgotten. As his shadow grew closer to them, she raised her body up and puffed out her shoulders, slipping one leg out of the side split in her dress and very gently moving herself into the stronger lighting a few inches away from where she had been stood. After forty years on this set, she knew exactly how to find 'the light' and she quickly gazed up at Jimmy in the overhead rig, who was aiming her favourite set of bulbs, the amber ray, directly over her. *Bless him*, she thought, then readied herself for action – and she didn't mean the scenes in the script.

Farrah reached for a Danish pastry she'd been snacking on and took another bite as she watched Catherine posturing. She suddenly pretended to look down at her script as Amanda looked over to her as Lee Landers approached.

Damn, he was fine looking, she thought, as she took another bite and looked down on the monitor showing him in close-up. She'd never have dreamed of snacking on the podium before – it looked so unprofessional – but this baby inside her had a sweet tooth and when it wanted sugar it let her know. Ever since that day in the bathroom after her confrontation with Jake, where it had kicked its way into her heart as well as her waistband, she'd been gearing herself up to reveal she was pregnant to the rest of the crew.

Amanda had agreed she'd be there with her when she did it. First, they were going to get Helen, Sheena and Catherine together so she could tell them, but messages in their joint WhatsApp group about meeting up had been lacklustre to say the least. She'd toyed with the idea of just dropping it

205

into a text and having done with it, but seeing the words *turns out I'm still pregnant with Jake's baby and I'm keeping it* looked even more preposterous than tonight's script, where Lucy would forgive a man who dumped her and who she also believed was dead, all in the space of one episode.

Farrah had decided her news could wait. She didn't want to hang on much longer though, she was sick of all this layered clothing and bag carrying she'd been doing to hide her bump. With May's weather hotting up, ready for what looked like a super hot early June, she knew she'd be boiling if she didn't ditch the swamp gear for her old look and get the news out. She'd actually tried on some fitted jumpsuits and luckily all the cravings she'd had seemed to go only to the baby bump, so the rest of her body was still as toned and fine as it always had been. Dare she even think it, she looked kind of hot pregnant. Her boobs, which had never been that big, but were very pert, had grown at least two cup sizes, so she looked truly Amazonian with her curves encased in fitted silk. She could even still manage her heels. As the last bite of the pastry went down her throat, she came out of her mind's haze and back to the moment. This was it. Lee and Catherine were now face to face. She put the headphones on both ears and listened in.

'Hello, Catherine,' Lee Landers said, in deeply rich velvety tones that matched his glowing ebony skin.

He looked around the very set he'd last stood on nearly thirty years ago and then back to face the woman he'd once loved but ultimately left. His eyes couldn't help but cast down her body and back up to her beautiful face. She looked sensational, as if the clock the last time he'd been this close to her had stopped and she'd stayed exactly the same. As her eyes lifted from her script to meet his, he found himself under that famous gaze, the one that millions of viewers tuned in for all

Guilty Women

over the world. They were the same eyes he used to stare into as they lay in bed, exhausted after hours of love-making. How could she look exactly the same? he wondered. She was still breathtaking.

The whole set watched in fascination, waiting for Catherine to speak. Amanda had rejoined Farrah in the safety of the director's box.

'Here we go,' Farrah said, as the two held hands, hoping for the best and expecting the worst.

Then, after what felt like a whole advert break, Catherine finally spoke.

'Welcome back,' she said, leaning forward to place a kiss on his cheek.

As she got closer the scent of his cologne took her back to those long evenings where he'd hold her on the balcony of her condo and they'd watch the sun go down. She could feel that the physical chemistry that had always crackled between them, even when they'd argued – actually especially when they'd argued – was still there. Suddenly, inside her the rage she'd been feeling about the sheer nerve of his audacity in returning began to mingle with lust at memories of the times they'd been entwined together. He'd been an excellent lover, one of her best. She couldn't believe that that was what was on her mind. She'd planned a full-on snide speech about how his career had flopped and how embarrassing it must have been to come crawling back to the very place he'd once sworn never to return to, but all that had dissipated from her mind.

It wasn't just her senses that were tingling. She could feel that familiar gentle buzz between her legs activating. Her vagina remembered him too and was making it clear to her that despite *her* rage, *it* was pleased to see him back. Lee looked as taken aback by Catherine's friendliness as Farrah and Amanda, who were both watching in confusion from afar.

207

Lee's shoulders dropped into an easier position; they'd felt so tight as he'd prepared himself for a big confrontation, but it seemed that wasn't going to be the case. As she'd clearly created a welcome space for him to speak, he decided to use it to make his mark.

'Firstly, I need to apologise to you, Catherine,' he said, looking deep into her eyes, and she stayed absolutely still. 'I wanted to come and see you privately, but Jake said you didn't want me to, which of course I fully understood.'

Amanda leaned into Farrah in the director's box 'The wanker. God I hate him.'

Farrah's face showed she agreed as she added an 'Amen' and they went back to watching Lee and Catherine on the soundstage.

'I'm humbled that you have allowed me to return and have the honour of working with you again,' he continued.

Catherine watched him, trying to work out if this was a performance or the real deal. Then, she remembered that whilst he'd been a world-class lover, he had only ever been a so-so actor, albeit one the cameras loved. He'd never acted this well, so no, she realised, as she listened in fascination, this apology was the real deal. A gentle tilt of her head gave him the courage to continue.

'I know it will take time to explain why I was the way I was back then, but if you'll let me, I'd like to share that with you, when we're away from the cameras. I just wanted you to know that I am a changed man, personally and profession-ally. I know we have a lot of scenes together, so if you'll let me, I will do my best for you on the show, and if you can find it in your heart to forgive me for the way I treated you *off* the show, then I hope this can be a new start for us.' As he finished his last word, he leaned forward and returned the kiss on the cheek that Catherine had greeted him with.

The crew stared in fascination. Brad was doing everything he could not to burst into tears with the sheer emotion of it and lamented it was a shame the real scripts of the show were nowhere near in this league. His thought train was derailed by crackling on the monitors.

Ever the professional, Farrah decided it was best to start filming, before this amazing chemistry she was witnessing dissipated. With a nod from Amanda, she decided to go for it before anything could go wrong. In the scene, which was shot out of sequence, Lucy had left the party, which they would film in a couple of hours when all the extras they'd hired for the night shift had arrived. Lucy would meet Marcus on The Cove's rooftop balcony alone, to hear him out after the letter she'd read in the previous episode. Amanda, hoping that what appeared to be a positive reunion might have dissipated Catherine's anger with her, spoke down the mic into Catherine's earpiece.

'Catherine, are you happy for us to begin?' Amanda said. Catherine, who still hadn't replied to Lee's statement, turned towards Amanda and nodded, then as Farrah directed cameras two and three to change position she spoke quickly to Lee.

'They're about to start,' she said softly, still taking in his words, his smell and his deep chocolate eyes.

'But are you ready to start? Are you really OK with me being here, because if you are not, I'll leave. I do not want you to feel forced into this,' he said solemnly, again with what seemed like genuine intent.

Farrah's voice rang out, cutting in. 'People, places please.'

Suddenly a haze of activity went on around them as scripts were moved off set and Brad reappeared to powder Catherine's brow, which, with the sheer physical energy of their reconnection, had given her the finest hint of sweat.

'Catherine?' Lee said again, gently pushing for an answer.

She found herself nodding, then felt emotionally taken aback that, as she watched him walk out of shot to find his mark, she realised she actually meant it.

'Action,' Farrah called as the crane camera panned over the pink night sky.

Falcon Bay **episode 3005,** exterior Cove, night-time

Lucy Dean is gazing over the bay of St Augustine's Cove, watching for the figure of the man she hasn't seen in decades to reappear. Visibly on edge, she is taken aback when she hears footsteps on the terrace and turns round to see Marcus is now facing her. Close-up on Marcus's face shows he's nervous too. Neither speak for a moment as Lucy takes in the sight of a man she believed to be dead. She takes four steps towards him and stares again.

LUCY DEAN
It can't be you.

MARCUS
It is.

LUCY
But I—

MARCUS
Thought I was dead, yes, I know. But I'm not, I'm right here in front of you.

LUCY
This must be a dream; I saw your body.

MARCUS

You saw a body. It wasn't mine.

Lucy takes two more steps towards him and now they are within touching distance.

LUCY

How is this possible?

MARCUS

I can explain, and I will. What I've done is unforgivable, but I beg of you to hear me out.

Lucy reaches her hand out, still in disbelief; as her fingers touch his face she realises this is no vision.

LUCY

It really is you.

MARCUS

Yes.

They look at each other as Lucy continues to stare in disbelief. The camera cuts away from them ready for the ad break.

Farrah was just about to shout 'cut' when Catherine raised up her hand and slapped Lee hard across the face. Amanda took a sharp intake of breath.

'Oh my god, this isn't in the script,' she said frantically, looking at the order, which showed the scene definitely should have ended on Lee's stunned expression.

'Roll with it,' Farrah whispered. 'Remember I played their

daughter. They used to go rogue all the time back in the day. She doesn't do it now but he's a method actor, it's one of the reasons he left. He'll follow her lead, just watch.'

Lee stood back as Catherine stared him down as Lucy Dean. The energy he felt in his veins was like a volcano. Not only was he back on the set of the show that had once made him a global star, but he was opposite the woman he felt sure there was still a connection with, one he'd never felt with anyone but her. Now, just to take it to the next level, she'd abandoned the script and set their characters free whilst the cameras were still rolling. Fuck, he felt so alive. He took Catherine's bait and stayed in character. Brad, who was watching from the side with Candy, looked like he was going to faint at the sheer drama of it all.

MARCUS
Do it again, I deserve it.

Catherine struck him again, even harder this time. As she did so, her eyes flashed with passion and her cleavage heaved as she threw her full power towards his body.

MARCUS
Again.

Once more she slapped him; the sound echoed around the studio with the sheer force she inflicted on his handsome face. Her eyes widened and her glossy lips trembled as his muscular hand went up to touch his reddening cheek, all the time not taking his eyes off her.

Amanda and Farrah continued to let the cameras roll. The whole set was transfixed by the monitors, which showed that these were no stage slaps. Catherine's handprint was marked on his face. Candy looked on disapprovingly; she couldn't wait to report to Jake that Catherine had broken health and safety protocols. Farrah switched cameras so they were now on a two-shot, with the water of the ocean swirling up and crashing against the rocks, seeming to match the passion that was spilling over onto the set.

With his other hand, Lee reached out for Catherine Belle's quivering Lucy Dean and grabbed her by her tiny waist.

LUCY

No!

She struggled, beating her hands on his chest as he pulled her into him.

MARCUS

Yes!

The camera focused as they got ever closer. Marcus's lips were suddenly full on Catherine's and the two began to passionately kiss.

Candy's face was incandescent but Amanda was transfixed, lost in the moment as these two actors and characters burnt up the monitors with the heat of their clearly passionate embrace. When they finally stopped kissing, Catherine burst into tears as Lee held her tightly.

LEE

Let it out, my darling, let it out, you'll never cry again. I'm here for you again now. And I'll never leave you again.

As Farrah signalled the crane camera to pan out to the silhouette, she yelled 'Cut!'

A rapturous round of applause, started by Brad, rang out across the set. Lee and Catherine separated, almost reinhabiting themselves and stepping out of the characters to turn to see everyone in the vicinity, including Amanda and Farrah, on the podium clapping.

Catherine looked at him and he returned her gaze – neither spoke a word but both knew the magic that had made them one of the world's favourite couples on screen and off was still there. Lee gestured for Catherine to take a bow, which she did, then she returned the gesture and he did the same.

Brad let off a wolf whistle in appreciation of the sheer drama he'd just witnessed, sure that when this aired the whole world would be just as in awe as he was when they saw just how dynamite this reunion was. Candy stomped off, dialling Jake's number on her mobile.

As the applause died down, Catherine looked at Lee's face, which was still marked from her slaps.

'Did I hurt you?' she said coyly.

'No more than I deserved,' he replied, his eyes glinting with a passion that made her knees weaken.

If it hadn't been for the fact they were under a dozen sets of eyes, she'd have ripped his clothes off right there and then and fucked him with every ounce of anger in her body. Anger that he'd left her with in the first place. She was angry that he'd had the nerve to come back and that there was absolute clarity in her mind – that kiss had given her no doubt that she wanted him back in her life, in every way possible.

She turned away and walked off towards Brad, who was practically jumping up and down. She passed him and jumped in the empty buggy that had brought her to the set and got in the driver's seat herself. Lee watched from the set. She turned to him and gestured for him to join her. Within moments he'd bolted down the steps and into the cart. Seconds later, with the push of her high-heeled foot onto the accelerator, the buggy sped towards her condo, and they disappeared from view. The moment the door was closed behind them they both knew they'd be making love.

As Amanda and Farrah watched them disappear, they looked at each other with raised eyebrows.

'Well, that's the rest of tonight's shooting schedule well and truly fucked.' Farrah laughed.

A smile ran across Amanda's face. 'It won't be the only thing that is, either,' she replied, and they both burst into laughter.

'Sod it,' Amanda said. 'Jake will go mad but screw him. He clearly thought Lee would be an unwelcome presence for Catherine and it looks like it's going to be the complete opposite.'

Farrah laughed. 'Yes, he'll hate that!' She picked up the mic that connected her voice to the main speakers that echoed around the set. 'That's it for tonight, people, early wrap.'

With that they headed out of the director's box and Farrah pulled off her multi-layered top that had been disguising her bump. She made her way over to the craft table, gently pushing the extras, who were always nibbling at the on-site catering, aside with a loud cry of 'Let me through, baby on board,' before picking up a Danish pastry.

Her words, alongside the clearly visible bump, led to audible gasps around the set, and one from Brad. His was less about the fact she was obviously pregnant but more that she was no longer in the hideous smock-like top that he – as head of wardrobe – would rather burn than see on a clothes rack, let alone a gorgeous woman like Farrah.

Amanda looked at Farrah. They'd been friends so long they

had an unspoken bond; each knew what the other was thinking without having to ask. Farrah nodded.

'You're *keeping* it!' Amanda said.

Farrah nodded, then took another bite of the cinnamon Danish.

Amanda pulled her into a hug whilst the crew, who were still gawping, began to gossip.

'And Jake?' Amanda ventured, whilst Farrah seemed in a good place to broach the unspeakable connection to her beautiful baby bump.

'You can tell him that he'll be having absolutely nothing to do with it. You'll enjoy that,' she said, with a glint in her eye. She reached out and picked up a cherry muffin from the back of the table.

Amanda smiled. She certainly would.

Part 3

Chapter 20

In the month since Lee Landers's return to set, the show had rarely been out of the headlines, fuelled by shots of Catherine and Lee practically eating each other's faces off during their reunion.

Tabitha Tate made sure she'd got the most exclusives. Aware of the book deal she had, Jake had made the decision that they were to allow her not only to wander alone all over the island but also to interview its stars. Considering the number of vitriolic stories she'd written, this was totally unheard of and had caused several internal bust-ups with the ones who'd refused, two of whom had been sacked by Jake in a full-on villainous rage.

Before the latest shit hit the showbiz fan, in yet another Meeting Room 6 bust-up, Amanda had argued this was madness, considering the PR pre-order blurb on Tabitha's book on all the sites described it as 'a shocking exposé of the curse of *Falcon Bay*'. Jake, with Candy by his side, had over-ridden her. So, day after day, bombshell after bombshell came from 'within the set', smugly reported by Tabitha, who was now even filming her blog on Lucy Dean's Cove set. This had sent Catherine, understandably, into a total rage, but with the public still fascinated after last year's Christmas Day live episode, and Ross Owen's body being washed up on their shoreline, the cast's lives were now more in the public consciousness than their characters. In fact, it was now easier to get a headline out of someone who worked on the show rather than about anything that happened in it. And no longer was it just the actors that were of interest; the execs' and even some of the crew's real lives, thanks to Tabitha's digging, had set social media ablaze.

The whole world's press was now reporting on what had essentially become a soap within a soap. There had never been a situation like it before coming from a mainstream drama. Even *Variety* in LA had called it 'a modern media phenomenon'. The situation was making all the women feel sick, especially when director Farrah's pregnancy had been reported under the headline 'show exec who slept with colleague and best friend's husband is keeping the baby but denying him access'. Clearly that was why Jake had wanted to stay on Tabitha's good side. Farrah had been ripped apart by all the militant #FathersForAccess groups and the mummy blogs were up in arms too over the broken girl code revelations, meaning she was getting it from both sides. #SackFarrahAdams had trended for three solid days. The women had tried to assure Farrah the headlines would die down, whilst a smug-looking Jake lapped it all up.

Tabitha Tate was, it was fair to say, truly having the time of her life. Thanks to her tipline, Vlad had made huge progress on Honey's whereabouts, which was keeping Mickey, her publisher, off her back. It was also thanks to a new union she'd formed with Candy. She'd initially underestimated her because of her bombshell looks, but once they'd spent some time together it became clear she was as savvy as she was sexy. With Candy onside, she was getting even more out of being in the *Falcon Bay* bubble than she could ever have dreamed of.

The more time she spent with her, the more she really liked Candy. Maybe it was because they were both from other sides of the world, and were so passionate about their careers that they'd left loved ones behind to climb the career ladder. Or maybe it was that they recognised that in a media world still dominated by men, women sticking together was powerful. In order to pull off the scoop, they had to be the enemy.

Candy had acquired a leaked set of photos for Tabitha, of Catherine Belle and Lee Landers having sex down by the waterside late one night, captured by security cameras. Tabitha had landed a global syndication rights bidding war. Once Tabitha had done a hefty deal with the Hollywood foreign press association, she'd split the windfall with Candy. They'd both loved seeing the zeros on the money transferred into their accounts more than the naked pair splattered all over American magazine covers, although both agreed Catherine's body was impressive for her age. Equally easy on the eye was the naked Lee Landers thrusting behind her.

The smouldering images were the first set since the shots of Madeline Kane's body in the shark's mouth at Christmas to finally knock the British royal family off the front pages, which these days was a nigh on impossible task. Candy joked that they might get damehoods for giving Prince Harry and William's wife wars a break in coverage. Media frenzy aside, Tabitha was secretly floored that the drama behind the making of this once nearly insignificant coastal-set soap had become *the* topic everyone around the globe wanted to know about. When a picture of herself appeared alongside one of her exclusives from the show on the front cover of the *National Enquirer* as well as *The New York Times* on the same day, she knew her tell-all book was a dead set international bestseller. She just needed to find the missing pieces of the puzzle to get it finished.

Back in the beachside apartment that Jake had given her free rein to use whilst she was working, Tabitha lay in the hammock on her terrace and looked out at the ocean. It was the calmest she'd ever seen it. With a perfect blue sky and birds soaring overhead, she could understand why the 'old hags' as Jake called them had loved living here for so long. She didn't think of them that way herself. She wasn't ageist or naive enough to think that one day she too wouldn't also be an older woman, despite their attitude towards her, which was understandable. She pulled their lives apart for her own gains. She had a respect for their resilience, but she couldn't let them know that or it would get in the way of a good story. And instinct told her they were definitely hiding something; she just wasn't sure what.

When she saw the way Jake spoke to them it went against her grain not to reprimand him but she wanted to keep in his good books after he'd given her such amazing access, so she simply wasn't able to show them any support. As a huge gull cawed above her, she looked around at the paradise of St Augustine's, then lowered her eyes to scan a much darker place as she flicked open her MacBook and opened her book files.

She'd written most of the puff pieces that would fill out the story arc and spine of her tome, once again mainly thanks to Candy, whom Jake had been fucking like a rag doll whenever it suited him but giving her no commitment. Candy told Tabitha she'd gone along with his selfishness, hopeful that he'd realise what he had with her. That was until one day she overheard him describing her on the phone to his old pal and ex *Falcon Bay* director Aiden Anderson as 'an easy piece of Aussie pussy' that Aiden should try. She'd arrived at Tabitha's apartment in tears. They'd made a pact that, in return for Tabitha taking Candy to the States with her, if Candy continued to help her with her book, she'd play Jake like a fiddle, leaking more secrets than a spy being interrogated. It all made great fodder and Tabitha relished the idea of Jake, who thought he was going to be portrayed well in her book, seeing his true persona revealed for all to see and hate.

She was still missing the MacGuffin – a phrase Americans used to describe the heart or the most sensational part of the story, the middle of the cake, or the icing on top. The big scoop. From the coded info Vlad had shared on Honey Hunter's situation, she could possibly be it, but there was a worry that Mickey being overprotective could stop the best, or actually the worst, of what she may or may not have been through from going in. Plus, Vlad hadn't actually located her in person yet, so she couldn't bank on that.

Conspiracy theories sold well but hard facts were where the real money was at, so she knew she still needed to find out why that camera footage of the last moments of Madeline Kane's life had not been handed over in full. What was on the cameras from angles inside the tank, which were missing? There was some sort of foul play at hand, but try as hard as she could, no matter which database in the CITV system she searched, she could not access the hard drives that housed them.

Thanks to Jake, she'd interviewed all the women involved that night, several times; all told the exact same story word for word, which was no use to her. As good a source as Candy was, the access she needed now was way beyond her level. For this, Tabitha had done the unthinkable in the tabloid world she inhabited – she'd made contact with Chad Kane in Louisiana.

Widowers were usually off limits, even when she'd actually been honest about what she was looking for. There was the chance that perhaps he, wanting to protect his wife, had had certain frames deleted before they were all locked down in the vault forever. It was a long shot as she couldn't imagine there was anything more gruesome he could have edited out than what was left in, but it was a question she had to ask, and explain why she needed the answer. As she'd prepared to make the call, she'd braced herself for a massive lawsuit and lockdown on her book that could end her dreams of the Pulitzer Prize and stop a single page ever going to print. After all, the Kane Foundation were the ones who'd paid *The Herald* to vault the images of Madeline, which now lay next to the Red Room files. Knowing what that had cost to do, it was clear that their pockets were deep, so she wouldn't be able to fight them. But the only way to shine a light on what really went on that Christmas Day was to access the CCTV footage archives, deep within the building and not on the main system. According to Candy, they could only be accessed digitally, and she'd have to reinvestigate the set and everyone who'd been present on Christmas Day step by step, which even Jake couldn't enforce. No, it would have to be Chad.

Chad had insisted on a recorded Zoom call and made Tabitha sign an NDA before he'd speak to her. When she finally got through, after an initially wary start she was able to be open about her suspicions over the missing frames. She underlined that, with the police case closed, probably his only real way of truly knowing if any foul play was related to his wife's death was if he agreed to grant Tabitha the access she needed. Shortly after, she received a written letter between their lawyers and Fonda Books, which was watertight and guaranteed that Chad had overriding approval of any information discovered on Madeline. Tabitha found this intriguing and had yet another sense that something else had gone on, which Chad himself wasn't even sure of, so with Mickey's approval the new deal was done.

It was a risk to allow Chad that level of approval, but Tabitha reasoned if her hunch was right and something underhand had happened on that day, she'd at least get an interview for the book on Madeline out of him. Then she could spin that into something that would make people still want to buy into a conspiracy theory about her death, even if it turned out there was nothing relating to it in those missing frames and it was just a tragedy after all.

Yes, it had been a very good month indeed, she thought, as she gently swung in the hammock. The online #FindHoneyHunter tipline campaign she'd run had been a risk in case it had sent anyone else on the chase, but the results it had brought in had given her some bargaining power with Vlad's fee. It had taken some time to follow up on all of the tips, as things at *Falcon Bay* had been kicking off so fast that she'd had to juggle that with trying to keep to the book deadline. Of course, over 90 per cent of the tips were cranks, nutters looking for attention, or people genuinely mistaken, but it only took one or two calls to make all the difference and the useful ones had come.

The first was from a male nurse who worked at one of the rehab facilities Honey had last stayed at in the nineties, which was actually one of the first she'd enquired with. She'd asked who she'd checked in for treatment with, only to be told she hadn't. It turned out, according to him, she had been logged in the system but wasn't a patient in the main building. She was still there.

The second had been from a cab driver who had dropped her off at the same facility exactly around the same time she'd gone missing. It was amazing what a bigger than usual payoff could do. The cab driver had been happy with a couple of hundred dollars for his tip but the nurse was much more nervous. He wouldn't give his details, saying that they'd have to meet in person and negotiate the deal. This guy was a totally different kettle of fish to the cabbie. He knew exactly what he was doing. Considering the rehab facility was in LA, she could have cut Vlad out altogether and investigated it herself, but a trip right now to the States was hardly ideal.

Once Tabitha had laid eyes on the photo he'd sent from an untraceable email address, of an out-of-it Honey in a hospital room, she'd authorised Vlad's expenses to get the next flight over. She hadn't told Mickey; even with the pictures she wanted to be sure first. After all, photo editing could do wonders these days. But once Vlad had confirmed it was her, she'd give Mickey the news he'd been praying for, that she'd found his missing icon and that she'd tap him up for the extra advance money he'd promised. If it didn't turn out to be her, she'd be pretty pissed off at the nearly ten grand Vlad had already quoted her to get access to the building. Her gut told her it was, and with Honey finally located she could relax and enjoy putting the rest of her book together, maybe even start thinking about her author photo that would go on the back.

When she was a little girl, she used to look at her mum's collection of Jackie Collins novels and, although they were not exactly to her taste – she liked things a bit grittier – she always thought Jackie's author photos were on-point. She drew the line at leopard print but she definitely wanted to recreate that Lady Boss Bitch vibe her mum and so many other women had loved in her. Even a quarter of her mammoth sales numbers wouldn't be bad either, Tabitha thought.

With a big smile on her face, she got off the hammock, pulled her silk kimono around her and padded barefoot into the kitchen. She took a bottle of Cristal from the fridge, popped the cork, and stuck a straw into the bottle, not even bothering with a glass. With access to CITV's deepest level of security granted and Vlad on his way to prove Honey Hunter was alive and provide her whereabouts, she was tantalisingly close to having it all. She'd already drafted the 'found her' email to Mickey, which was sitting in her Drafts box, along with the invoice for the extra advance agreed on locating the missing golden goose. She was very much looking forward to pressing send on that.

'Oh yes,' she said out loud. She ditched the straw, then took a full-on swig from the bottle, before placing it to the side and heading back out to the hammock to watch the sun begin to set. Everything was going her way indeed.

Chapter 21

Jasmine candles lit Catherine's bedroom, casting soft shadows around the queen-size four-poster bed on which two naked bodies writhed and clawed at each other's skin. Lee Landers and Catherine Belle were naked and moaning in ecstasy. Catherine was on her back, her head thrashing around her white silk pillows, the ones designed to stop your face wrinkling when you slept on them. Sleeping was the last thing on Catherine's mind as Lee buried his face deeper between her legs. His tongue expertly flicked at her clitoris in a motion that had her whole body trembling. She let out a moan as Lee's tongue went faster and faster.

Apart from her French lover Claude, no man had ever made her body feel more alive than Lee, and as he switched his lapping motion to sucking on her, she knew at any moment the fireworks she felt all over her body were about to ignite. Even after decades apart, Lee knew Catherine's body well enough to feel the tension in her thighs as they clamped around his face. He instantly ran his hands up her slim waist and placed both hands on her round breasts, gently pinching her erect nipples between his thumb and forefinger, then darted his tongue faster and faster until Catherine could hold back no longer.

'Ohhhhhhhh,' she screamed as her body released a flood of wetness, which seemed only to excite Lee even more as he drank her in. He wasn't finished with her yet though.

'One more,' he breathed, then squeezed her breasts again whilst sliding his tongue around her labia, which felt more alive than Catherine could remember. His mouth darted down towards her bottom, gently biting her buttocks, then suddenly he pushed the tip of his tongue deep inside it.

'Oh my god,' Catherine squealed.

Lee proceeded to tongue her lower hole at the same time as flicking his finger rhythmically at her clit, and he didn't stop until she'd climaxed again. As her body arched after reaching its second climax of the evening, she felt unable to speak. She tried to catch her breath. She felt Lee's lips working their way up her body, inch by inch.

'Now you are ready for me,' he whispered.

His mouth reached her neck and she felt the engorged head of his perfect cock push against her soaking wetness, then as his lips brushed hers, he was inside her. She gasped as she felt the full length of him opening her up, and she slid her hands over his pert buttocks, clawing her French-tipped nails into them, urging him to let himself go. She wanted every part of his DNA inside her, mingling with hers, turning what was once a barren desert back into a lush rainforest. As they kissed passionately, tongues roaming each other's mouths, she dug her nails in deeper and felt him tense as his motions sped up. She felt the bed moving from the sheer force of his body grinding her down into the soft sheets.

'I'm close,' he whispered, then licked her neck.

'Give it to me,' she breathed.

Three deep thrusts later he let out a roar that would rival

a lion that had just conquered a pride of lionesses in the wilds of the jungle. His seed flooded inside her and she held his now quaking body as every drop left his body and entered hers.

For a moment they lay still; he was still inside her. Gently he slid out and spooned his body around hers, and they lay in silence, their skin glistening from their spent energy. Catherine couldn't believe that from the moment they'd raced back to her condo after that first scene together on set four weeks ago, they'd not only been inseparable, but it had truly been like all the decades they'd been apart and the resentment she'd held against him for the way he'd humiliated her had never happened.

After that first time they'd had sex, Lee had shocked Catherine by bursting into tears, as he told her of his regret at his behaviour and how lucky he felt now fate had brought them together again. He'd promised that if she could bring herself to trust him, he swore he'd prove to her that not only had he changed, but if she'd allow him to, he'd never leave her side again. Catherine could count the times she'd seen a man brave enough to cry in front of her, for real, on one finger, and it was once, on that day. So, despite Helen, Sheena and Amanda's advice to be wary, she'd reasoned that with only months to go to her seventy-first birthday, just to feel this alive was worth the risk of having him shatter her heart all over again. Once a heart had truly broken, she'd told Sheena, no matter how badly you hurt it, you could never damage it the same way twice.

Emotional scar tissue had formed around every molecule of hers back then, when he'd abandoned her. Even though a new layer of scarring had formed over her part in Madeline and Ross's deaths, her heart felt like its blood flow was restricted to beating just enough to allow her to work each day since those dreadful nights. Every moment she spent with Lee, she felt the scars loosening, allowing it to beat stronger, blood surging through its arteries in a way that it hadn't since the nineties. For that alone, it was worth every moment of the risk. But so far there was no sign of a risk.

Lee had told her night and day that he loved her, stood up for her on set and never left her side. Not once since his return had he done a single thing to cause her any unrest. After everything that had happened over this last year, she of all people now knew that life really was too short. She was *in* this hook, line and sinker. And the way she felt right now, as his warm hands held her close, to feel this alive again was worth the chance of drowning if it went wrong.

Chapter 22

The calm sea and clear blue-sky view from Meeting Room 6 at St Augustine's definitely did not match Jake Monroe's mood. He was pretending to study the new exterior island set designs that were pinned on the storyline boards.

In recent weeks, he'd authorised a hefty spend to incorporate the new rival beach where Lydia's character Claudia Raymond was due to do battle with Lucy Dean in a catfight across the sandy dunes. Although not exactly ground-breaking territory, a war of glamorous rival female business owners was always a ratings winner. For some bizarre reason lost on Jake, their audiences seemed to love seeing older women going head-to-head, especially if it involved a slap or two. But not even the thought of seeing Catherine acted off the screen, let alone whacked in the face by sexy Lydia, was enough to lift his spirits today.

Once Tabitha Tate had told him that Chad had now given her triple-A access to all areas of CITV, he felt wrong-footed. By going over his head to Chad, he now felt that Tabitha clearly couldn't be trusted, not that any tabloid journalist ever truly could be. The clever ones rarely bit the hand that fed them, but now it was clear that, like a smiling python, Tabitha had decided to slither towards the main man for her meals. And he didn't like that one little bit, especially right after he'd been the victim of a recent media mauling due to Farrah fighting back against Tabitha's pregnancy reveal.

At an open press conference as big as any cast announcement, and organised without his knowledge, Helen and Amanda had flanked a tearful Farrah. Farrah, holding hands with her supposed foe Amanda, told and showed how united they were in their friendship and hatred for Jake. They'd both taken great glee in slating his parenting skills to the world's press. If that wasn't bad enough, Tabitha, who'd been sat front and centre, had done a piece where she publicly apologised for a previous article saying she now understood that Jake was a classic gaslighter. Farrah had used her old acting skills to burst into tears at being cleared of being a heartless bitch, Tabitha's previous description in her first pro-Jake piece, which was in his opinion absolutely correct.

He'd raged and thrown two Emmy awards out of his balcony as the mainly female press pit lapped up their statements about how their friendship was strong enough to help them co-parent the latest child of an 'unfit father'. Since 'Woman Power' was the main headline spun out of his apparent uselessness as a parent or partner, he'd been the subject of attack after attack by the radical feminists. He'd been *cancelled* – that was the word Candy, who'd recently stopped giving him daily blowjobs, saying she now wanted to keep things professional, had used. If he wasn't mistaken, she'd looked rather pleased when she'd said it. He'd have had Tabitha frogmarched off the island in a heartbeat, but now she was reporting to Chad he was powerless on that front, and being powerless was not something that suited Jake at all.

Trying to take his mind off the fact that he'd made a real

fuck-up with Tabitha, he studied the luxurious terrace that had been drawn up for Claudia's bar. Even after the rebuild following the Bitch Party fire last year, it was clearly far superior to Lucy Dean's bar, which looked rather shabby, in a sea-shanty style way. That gave his thin lips the faintest of upturns, but as his eyes cast over the photo of Lee Landers on the cast board, it turned into a snarl.

Before returning Lee's character to the show, he'd searched through all the archives, determined to find a guaranteed Achilles heel that was sure to wrong-foot smug Catherine Belle. With her and Lee's toxic history, the stuff of showbiz folklore, it had been a no-brainer that he would be the perfect grenade to throw in her direction. Jake had taken great pleasure in his rehiring, feeling that by doing so he'd theoretically pulled the pin. So how on earth she'd welcomed him with not just open arms but open legs absolutely infuriated him.

Why were things just not going to plan? he wondered.

Lee's arrival should have caused her to storm up to his office and demand her usual 'it's them or me' policy, one he'd been gleefully ready to reply to by saying that this time, it was definitely toodle pip to her. It would have appeared to be her own decision, meaning his hands would look clean to the Kane Foundation. Everything might not have been going his way but he'd find a way to get his plans back on track. He always did. As he looked at the new press shots of Catherine and Lee's characters Lucy and Marcus holding hands on set, he felt the anger rise again. She was positively glowing in the photos and wherever you went on the island you'd spot the two of them holding hands, walking around like they were at a couples' resort, totally inseparable. The pictures of them having sex in the American tabloids had made her a heroine, with Jane Fonda, Oprah Winfrey and Sharon Stone declaring her an icon for putting older female sexuality back on the map.

That had sent him straight to Lee's agent Swifty, an old friend from decades ago who loved a bit of a revenge as much as Jake and had been well and truly on board with the plan. When it became clear that, far from Lee unsettling the actress he desperately wanted toppled from her crown, somehow they'd created a geriatric version of love's young dream, Swifty was as blind-sided as Jake. Neither of them had seen this coming and if *that* kissing scene that had already aired and the sex hadn't been enough to turn his stomach, considering they had a combined age of nearly 150, then the 'at home' feature in *People* magazine was. It showcased the two of them now living together in Catherine's condo, and had finally been enough to put him off his beloved Danish pastries for days.

Reading between the lines of the article, he could see that while she thanked Mr Monroe for bringing them together again, it was a clearly a dig designed to flaunt the fact that his plan had backfired. He'd hurled the magazine towards the bin in a rage and begun to wonder if that hack Tabitha Tate's book blurb about 'an alleged curse hovering over *Falcon Bay*' was right. But if it was a curse then it seemed to only wrong-foot the men and somehow always gave the witches of the island the power to keep coming back stronger and stronger.

What the hell Lee saw in old Catherine was a mystery to him, especially as he'd had a reputation as quite the ladies' man back in the day. Although he was no longer in the first flush of youth, Jake felt sure that if he wafted a bit of fresher meat right underneath the old leopard's nose, eventually nature would take its course and he'd bite and abandon the old mutton he was currently nibbling on. After all, old leopards never changed their spots. Jake should know, he was one himself.

He couldn't believe that one fuck with bloody Farrah had knocked her up, when he'd had to put up with ten years of

Amanda's constant whinging and moaning through IVF. On his way down to Meeting Room 6, he mused it was no wonder that by the time Olivia finally arrived in their arms, he was too exhausted to emotionally invest in her. It wasn't that he didn't love her. He felt something that he assumed was love. But babies were pretty boring if you were being brutally honest. Until she could talk and make up her own mind as to which of her parents she actually preferred, which of course he was sure was bound to be him, he didn't mind missing out on first teeth, the first walk, first word and all that rubbish that sap Amanda had shacked up with seemed to live for.

'Bloody accountants,' he said as he ruffled his blonde hair back. He ignored everyone on his way to the snack table and wolfed down an apple Danish pasty in one go. He'd finally got his appetite back when planning for the *emergency* conference he'd called just hours earlier.

He might have misfired with Lee Landers, but from the late-night dinners he'd had earlier this week with his other signing, Lydia Chambers, he was sure he'd scored a bitch bullseye. She'd made it very clear she was a woman with no intention of befriending Catherine Belle and every intention of getting very friendly with Lee Landers, who was currently the show's most highly published actor. And Lydia loved publicity. She'd surprised him with just how hot she'd looked when she'd rocked up for dinner with her breasts barely contained in a corseted nude dress. She'd been wearing the same gold six-inch sandals she'd worn on the night of the *Falcon Bay* live episode last year, which had given him a stiffy at the time. They had exactly the same effect when they made a reappearance at the meet-up.

At fifty-five, Lydia on paper was a bit old for his usual taste but the excellent work she'd had made her look at least ten years younger. Compare that to Catherine being twenty years older and he felt certain – it might not have been the way he'd planned it, but old Catherine's heart and spirit would be breaking again very soon one way or another.

Finally ready for them, he brushed off the pastry crumbs and turned to face them. 'Right, people,' he said, staring the packed table out. 'I'm going to cut straight to the chase. If headlines made audience figures we'd still be number one, but sadly they don't, and as we are now languishing at number three, we clearly need to make some drastic changes and fast.'

Helen Gold was in her usual seat at the furthest edge of the table. It meant she had the most distance between herself and the place where Jake liked to stand to take centre stage. She was looking down at her phone in the middle of a sexy text exchange with Matt. Jake eyed her and the room, which was minus Amanda and Farrah, who, thanks to a complaint to HR, now refused to attend meetings with him citing emotional pressure.

'Ms Gold, when you are ready,' he said loudly, with more than a hint of sarcasm.

Amy, who was taking meeting notes, which were now sent to the Kane family once a week, began her shorthand. Helen tapped a few more times on her iPhone, placed it down and then finally looked up.

'Oh, I'm ready,' said Helen, who was dressed in one of her famous power suits. This one was bright green with the hint of a white cami peeking out under the tailored jacket. 'But I'm surprised I'm even invited to these meetings any more, Jake. Over the last few months, we've had two new signings to the show, and despite the sign above my office door and the title that states that I'm *Falcon Bay*'s casting director, I have not been involved nor consulted on either of them. By the way, that actually breaches my CITV contract terms.'

She threw a look in Amy's direction, making sure she was

taking down every word as Jake stared at her in barely concealed fury.

'So, since you seem to want to do my job for me these days, I'm wondering if I'm actually even needed here? Or whether you'd like Candy and me to return to the press office and continue to try to handle the circus show Tabitha Tate living on the island has caused? Which was your decision,' she finished with a smile.

She knew he was still raging about the press conference she'd organised for Farrah and Amanda. She sat back in her seat, as if offering him the floor back for his answer. Candy, who was sat opposite, looked a bit flustered for the first time ever. She and Helen had never been close but working together recently she'd come to see her in a new light, not that she wanted Helen to know it.

Jake's eyes flicked over to Amy's note-taking, which had suddenly become much more rapid. *Fucking clever bitch*, Jake raged internally, knowing Helen had chosen her words for the ultimate written effect. Determined not to lose his composure, he took a discreet breath and the room watched him take a step back before answering.

'Ah, well, you see, Helen, Amanda appointed you as acting press officer last year, which by the way was actually against your CITV contract,' he said, echoing her tone and exact choice of words from earlier, then casting his eyes over to Amy to make sure she was noting his response down. 'I felt it was only right to ease the burden on you whilst I did some internal reshuffling. You've been so busy handling the press lives of our behind-the-scenes staff rather than the cast on our world-famous show, which I doubt is in your CITV contract either. I can safely save your time as doubling up on roles is now over.' He gave a smile that was in fact real, imagining the fictional baseball bat he'd just used to whack an imaginary ball thrown hard right into Helen's plastic face.

'Very kind, I'm sure,' Helen continued, unrisen. 'Well, if we are—'

Determined to stop Helen in her tracks, and before any more notes could be taken, he cut her off mid-sentence.

'You'll be pleased to know that as of today, Candy's sole role on *Falcon Bay* is that of chief press officer,' Jake said.

All eyes around the table including his and Helen's swung to Candy, who, judging by look on her face, was also hearing this news for the first time. Before she could contradict him, and before Amy from HR could say it hadn't gone through the correct channels, he walked over to her side of the table and continued.

'Candy has proven she knows what's best for our show, on and off screen.' He smiled and rested a hand on her shoulder as he reached her chair. 'Let's have a round of applause for her promotion.'

Slowly the table, including Helen, half-heartedly clapped as Candy, due to the eyes on her, felt obliged to stand up. She didn't know what was going on. For a second, she wondered if Jake was playing some sort of game with her and was perhaps aware that it was her who'd been leaking so many stories to Tabitha Tate, but if he did, he'd clearly decided on the old adage of 'keep your enemies close'. Not that she'd considered Jake an enemy until she'd overheard him calling her his 'easy piece of Aussie pussy' on the phone to his creepy mate and practically offering to pimp her out. She might not have been able to work out exactly what Jake's motives were for this sudden 'official' promotion but as ambitious as she was, she wasn't going to look a career gift horse in the mouth and picked up Jake's lead.

'I'm thrilled the news is out,' Candy said, pretending she

knew what was going on, as she addressed the team with a big smile.

Helen eyed her suspiciously. In her skin-tight jeans, knee-high boots and off-the-shoulder top she was tall, thin and perfectly proportioned for shit-stirring.

'I think in the ever-changing media landscape we find our show in, it's time someone took a firm grip of the reins and stemmed this negativity. It seems to have been seeping out of late, overshadowing the wonderful work our show is actually doing,' she said. She tried hard to keep a smirk from appearing on her face at the deliciousness of the knowledge that she herself had been a key player in most of the damaging head-lines. Tabitha had already told her she would soon be ready to leave as she had nearly everything she needed. Candy decided to spin it. 'I'll be making a lot of changes to the way we do things round here, starting with ending Tabitha Tate's constant access to the building, so you can all stop looking over your shoulder and start to look forward to a new public profile that suits our glorious show.' As she finished, a wide, perfectly white-toothed grin spread across her apricot lip-glossed mouth.

Jake, quite frankly taken aback by her statement, stepped away from his seat and back towards the middle of the table so he could move things on before she managed to keep the floor. He'd only said it as he really fancied her again now she wasn't interested and he'd hoped the promotion might have had his balls back in her mouth by the time they were back in his office. If she thought she'd be able to get Chad to do as she wished, she really was more stupid than he'd described her to be to Aiden.

Helen never took her eyes off Candy. With her wealth of acting experience she was well aware an improvised performance had just been given. But with her casting hat on, as much as she found Candy irritating, she felt had she been

238

an actress trying out for a guest role on the show, and after seeing that Helen may well have actually hired her.

'So, as you can see, we are moving forward positively,' said Jake, forcing a smile for Amy from HR, who was still typing the minutes. He pulled out one of the empty chairs that Amanda or Farrah would usually be seated in and appeared to relax. This meeting hadn't gone the way he'd planned, so he decided to do some improvising of his own.

'Now the restructuring is out of the way, let's talk about our new star, Lydia Chambers, and her entrance to the show,' he said prompting Dustin, chief storyliner and assistant producer, to lean forward and read out the story arc.

It was based around the unveiling of her new hotel, which would eventually be revealed to be more a bar than a guest house, designed to see her do battle against Lucy Dean to reign supreme as the most powerful businesswoman on the island. Lydia's character Claudia would fall in love with the show's handyman Adam Roscoe, who'd not had a major storyline in a while but with his ripped physique was a firm favourite with their audience, which was mainly made up of housewives and gay people. A couple of the women writers chipped in, explaining the strain Lucy would find herself under, giving great scope to develop her reunion with Marcus and make it even stronger. Jake listened as Dustin rounded up by divulging that the first reveal of Lydia's character on the show would see the two women initially agree to work together, before their friendship took a darker turn when it became clear Lydia's character wanted to take over all the businesses on the island and didn't want to work together at all. And it would end up being couple against couple to reign supreme as King and Queen of the Bay.

As Dustin finished off with a couple of minor strands surrounding supporting characters, the room had a low hum of chatter, generally sounding happy about the way the summer had been planned.

Even Helen, whose nose was most definitely out of joint, was excited about seeing Lydia on the main *Falcon Bay* set. From the rushed backstory filming, Helen could see she still had the magic that had once made her one of the soap genre's most famous actresses of her time. Her starting role as a soap bitch on a long axed but fondly remembered show had seen her as one of the only threats to Catherine as Best Actress at awards shows over the decades, and she'd even managed to pip her to the post once or twice. Her acting ability was never in doubt, and anyone who could act was always welcome on the show as far as Helen was concerned, even though Lydia had a reputation for being a bit difficult. But then which actress worth watching wasn't? Yes, this could work well and it was great to have two mature actresses in leading roles on the show together.

Helen still loved *Falcon Bay* so Tabitha going was also going to be a huge relief. Helen genuinely cared about their audience and was sure they'd love the Lydia vs Catherine pairing. They'd reacted positively to Lydia in the public vote in the last season and by rights the role of Honey Hunter had been corruptly cast and should have been hers. Whilst it might have been an unconventional way for her to arrive, she'd finally made her way onto the show. She was no longer a client of Helen's close friend Sheena McQueen, which could have made things awkward if she had in fact cast her herself. The upside to Jake's sneakiness was that because he'd hired her himself, it meant she'd be out of Sheena's firing line, which was always a good thing. No, she reasoned, it was always good to see an older actress have another bite of the showbiz cherry, especially when she was as talented as Lydia. She just hoped after years out of the spotlight she'd have lost some of the diva traits she'd been known for at the height of her fame. Her imaginings were broken into by Jake's annoying voice, which rang across the table once more.

'Right, well, thank you, team,' Jake said as he got out of his chair. There was an almost audible sigh of relief that the meeting seemed to be over and had gone relatively well. But instead of Jake walking towards the exit, he made his way back over to the cast wall and set layout.

Immediately Helen's stomach flipped. After a moment's silence where he ran his fingers across the large-scale map, tracing the characters and the storyline arcs connecting them to each other, he made a loud 'hmm' sound, then turned back. Every writer and production team member at the table visibly stiffened apart from Candy who, still buzzing from her promotion, was looking forward to whatever Jake was about to reveal. Knowing him as she did – and even though she no longer saw him through rose-tinted glasses – she knew he would most likely be about to cause waves on the show bigger than the ones crashing on the shore outside the widows. Even Helen, who was used to Jake's dirty bombs, held her breath.

'I'm thinking that putting Adam with Lydia is a waste of her talent,' he said, casting a side eye at Candy, who he already knew by default was back in his corner. He was really hoping a post-meeting blowjob would be on the cards.

Dustin was startled by a statement that could see them having to alter at least six weeks of filming schedules, which were already planned, if Jake suddenly threw the whole pairing out. But, being used to Jake's whims by now, he leaned back in his chair, ready to hear whatever nightmare changes he'd be charged with having to fix. As much as he despised Farrah for abandoning the writer's team to join the directors, especially now it was clear she'd got there by shagging and getting pregnant by the very boss about to cause him a massive

241

headache, the one thing he'd always admired her for was her ability to call Jake out on his storyline changes in conference. Mind you, it helped when your best friend was the second-in-command, Amanda, and you were also pally with Helen. He never thought he'd miss the presence of those three united in this room, but as he prepared to hear Jake's new proposals, he suddenly found that he did.

'I've been looking at the backstory,' Jake continued, his voice as even and businesslike as he could manage. He wouldn't put it past Amy to note down tone as well as what he said in those bloody meeting notes for the Kane Foundation. 'And I think I've found a much better backstory and eventual reveal for Lydia. It will not only make the most of Catherine's ability as our long-standing leading lady but will also bring out the best in our latest acquisitions, Lee and Lydia.'

Helen kept her eyes firmly on him as she gently flicked her phone onto mute under the desk and hit the audio record button. Whatever was coming next, Amanda, Farrah, Catherine and possibly Sheena would need to know, so she wanted to make sure she captured every word of whatever twisted new plan Jake had been cooking up. Candy was taking notes but in a much more obvious way, already making her new role clear to the room and that she was ready to action whatever revelations were about to be revealed.

'Interesting,' Dustin managed, again determined to stay calm.

After a pause in which Jake felt he had the whole room's attention, he went on to describe a new storyline that would see Lydia's character revealed to the audience as the very wife that Lee's character Marcus had left Lucy for all those years ago. After extensive plastic surgery to alter her appearance (and discovering that Lee had gone back to the woman he'd originally abandoned for her), she was now back on the island, determined to seduce him as her new alter ego. After failing to win him back, even with her stunning new appearance, in a fit of rage she would set fire to Lucy Dean's Cove bar, leaving Lucy and Marcus trapped inside.

Marcus would save Lucy but perish in the fire by doing so. Lucy Dean's newfound happiness would be over; her heart would be broken. Lee's contract would be paid off early, meaning that the audience would be losing the very man they'd already fallen back in love with on-screen in a plot that also involved an insurance scam accusation. Claudia would sleep with the investigator to make sure Lucy Dean's finances were left in ruins and that she was unable to rebuild The Cove, forcing her to clean for Lydia. Claudia would then be the queen bee and star of the show, with her new bar its focal point, where Catherine would be scrubbing the floors.

When he'd finished the room sat in silence. Even Candy, who'd been ready to cheerlead what she was sure was going to be something fabulous, wasn't sure what to say. Helen knew exactly what to say, as did Dustin and everyone else on the team, but no one chose to say it.

Jake, blindly unaware of just how badly that had landed, stood up and announced his exit.

'Right, so that's our new plan. I know it will involve some juggling, but I know you're all up to the job. Let's get this show back to the number-one slot, people.'

Then, after doing a strange almost military salute as if he were a sergeant major addressing the troops, he left the room. He was followed by Candy, who gestured for Amy and her assistant to follow with her, aware that what was going to be said the moment Jake had exited the meeting room shouldn't make it onto the minutes list.

When they were gone, it was Dustin, totally out of character for someone known as a serious fence sitter, who broke the silence.

'Well, this show is fucked,' he said, meaning every word.

Helen wearily put her head in her hands.

'We've only just got the storyline on an even keel after what happened at Christmas,' he said, taking a pause. The whole room knew exactly what he meant. 'Lucy Dean and Marcus are our most popular characters. Lydia's Claudia hasn't even been tested with the audience yet, but now she's going to become the star of the show. The Cove Bar, something our show is known around the world for, is going to be destroyed? All these stories of hatred just as we're finally getting back to some feel-good drama that people are enjoying. Number three in the ratings is bloody good when it's based on the feel-good factor and not the circus show that saw us reach the top slot.'

A chorus of muttered agreement went around the table as Dustin's face looked more exasperated than anyone had seen him in a meeting before.

'And now he wants us to put Lucy Dean's life in peril *again*, just six months after the last time. Whilst Lydia plays a dual character, we never met her in the first place, so the audience won't care about her. And if this is all a revenge plot aimed at having Lucy on her knees when she's only just got back up – if we have the women at each other's throats – then it's basically exactly the same storyline Madeline introduced minus the fucking shark.'

'Oh, we still have a shark,' Helen said flatly, clearly refer-encing Jake. 'It's just not in the script – well, not yet anyway,' she finished with a roll of her eyes.

'*Seriously* though,' he continued, running his hands through his coarse red hair and adjusting his glasses. 'Without Amanda in charge, how is anyone going to be able to stop him from driving this show off-air? If these storylines go out, we won't hold onto number three. We'll be out of the top slot a week after they're aired, then we'll drop right off the charts. We all know soap audiences expect us to be "out there and over the top" but this stuff just isn't even in the realms of believability – not for this day and age. In the eighties maybe it would work, but now, competing with series on Netflix and Amazon? No chance. We'll be laughed at and cancelled and if that's the case I'd rather go now. I suggest everyone in the room have a serious think about your own future job prospects before we play a hand in this, because if we do as Jake says, just having this show on your CV will mean none of us will ever get decent work on television again.'

He took his glasses off as he finished and rubbed the bridge of his nose, clearly stressed out. The rest of the team's silence echoed Dustin's raw honesty. Helen watched him with sadness. Even though technically as casting director she had no responsibility to try to help the producers, as the only one of the old guard in the room she took it on herself to try to offer some words of comfort to the team. Standing up from her chair, she brushed her pink suit down and picked up her phone – she'd stopped the recording.

'Look, if we can survive Christmas, we can survive this,' she said as reassuringly as she could manage.

Dustin pulled his head back up and looked at her intently. 'Helen, I respect you, I really do. I'm going to say this the best way I can without being insensitive to the deceased, but I'd rather be eaten by the same fucking shark that bit Madeline Kane in half than have my name on this.'

Helen looked at him, then around the room. The whole team looked as broken as Dustin; this was serious. God, how she wished Amanda was here. She placed a hand on his, which was in front of her on the desk.

'Just try and keep calm heads and let Jake think things are running their course.' She looked up and addressed the room.

'And remember, we have the Kane Foundation overseeing the direction of the show now. If they mean what they say in the latest memo that I've seen, they are not happy about all the bad press. In order to counteract it, we need to keep a high moral value to the show's content. Jake must have seen it so I'm not sure what he's playing at, but as soon as they get wind of this change of direction, well, things may not play out exactly as Jake might like them to.'

She knew it was a risk mentioning private memos or talking about Jake. Revealing her true thoughts or sharing things that even she shouldn't know about was effectively showing her hand in a room full of the whole team who all reported to Jake, not her. She intended to make the Kane Foundation fully aware of Jake's directly opposing plans. But without Candy the snake or the minutes and HR girls in the room, she felt pretty confident, as she looked at their dejected faces, that after today's meeting the very least she could leave them with was a shard of hope.

'So do your best to look like you're patching Jake's "new vision" together but slowly stall the storyline out as far as you can. Use excuses for re-coordinating the cast's shooting roster and schedule – even Jake knows that's a nightmare for last-minute changes. That will buy us a bit of time whilst I get this new plan under the noses of the true powers that be.'

She headed into the corridor and towards the lift that would take her down to the floor her office was on. She knew what she had to do. But it certainly wasn't without its risks or repercussions. With Tabitha having got her claws into Chad, and Melissa now blocking the gateway, she could think of only one other woman who might be able to interact with him.

Chapter 23

Later that night, Helen sent the audio she'd recorded of Jake's plans to a new WhatsApp group chat she'd set up with just her, Sheena McQueen, Farrah and Amanda. Afterwards, the four women were seated in a private area of the dockside restaurant the cast and crew often frequented half a mile away from the *Falcon Bay* set on St Augustine's. They had a separate WhatsApp group that included Catherine, but Helen felt it best to keep her out of the loop until they had had a chance to come up with yet another plan to save her carefully maintained skin.

The sun was setting and in the distance. Dolphins passed by in the deep blue ocean. Farrah had already polished off two portions of the famous freshly caught whitebait whilst they'd replayed the whole of Jake's speech on Helen's iPhone speaker. She was now tucking into some walnut bread smothered in thick butter and talking with her mouth full.

'God, I hate him,' she said as she swallowed another bite.

Amanda took a piece of the bread herself. 'Join the club,' she said in a weary tone.

'She's already in it!' Sheena said, pointing at Farrah's bulging stomach.

For a moment the women giggled at the absurdity of Farrah's situation. To any of the staff who were stood at the far end of the bar out of earshot – but in view, ready to be called over if needed – they must have just looked like four old friends enjoying a catch-up dinner on a warm summer's night. But Sheena's joke was to be the last laugh of the night. Casting her eyes around the restaurant to check no one they knew was within earshot, Helen dismissed the waitress who'd started to approach, thinking her look had been a call for attention. After she'd topped up their glasses with wine, Helen started to speak.

'So, what do we do?' she said, addressing the group but keeping her eyes on Amanda for longer.

In her role as second-in-command to Jake, Amanda should not only have been at the meeting she'd had to record and share, but should now be the one leading this very dinner to try to work out how the hell they could thwart him again. Considering how publicly supportive of Farrah's pregnancy she was, and her now having to work alongside the estranged husband she despised more than any of them, which was saying a lot, Helen was trying to give her a pass.

Always astute at reading body language, Sheena, who'd travelled by helicopter down from her London office the moment the dinner had been suggested, could sense some tension between Helen and Amanda. Knowing they needed each other to overcome this, she was aware this was not a good place to start, so she decided to chip in.

'Well, let's get the elephant in the room out of the way first. I'm guessing you all think that because I went to Louisiana and spent time with Chad, the only way to stop all this madness is me contacting him, suggesting he comes down here to show him that Madeline's vision for the show is about to be destroyed. We know that's his Achilles heel. That's what this dinner is really about. You want me to be the one to prepare Catherine for his arrival, right?'

The women nodded.

'Then you couldn't be more wrong. In fact you sound crazier than Jake.'

The women looked surprised at her reaction.

'Look, I was the only one of you that was with Catherine at Madeline's funeral in Louisiana. It took all I had to keep her from confessing to him. She was a wreck when she was anywhere near him. If she gets within ten feet of him, this show won't just be over. Our freedom will too. I'm telling you – around him, she's a ticking truth bomb. If she goes off and confesses to what happened with Madeline then I have no doubt she'll confess to what happened with Ross, so we'd be doubly fucked.'

'But she's so much calmer now with Lee around—' Amanda began. Sheena held up her sharply manicured finger, with a huge set-in emerald diamond on it, to silence her.

'Trust me,' Sheena said in a tone that made absolutely clear that she meant every word that came out of her mouth, 'when I say the one thing we can't do is bring Chad Kane down here. I mean, we cannot bring Chad Kane down here at any point. Not if we value our freedom. Lee or not, she'll lose it and take us all down with her – and how much would Jake love that?' She widened her eyes as she said his name.

The women looked on as Sheena, resplendent in a zebra-print jumpsuit with her jet-black hair poker straight, continued, echoing the seriousness of her previous words. 'When I say she was on edge, I am not being dramatic. I didn't tell you all just how bad it was, because as soon as I got back, we were all caught up in the bloody Ross Owen fiasco. At one point on the bloody funeral boat she was just about to tell him *everything* and I only just caught her in time. If I had got back from the loo even a minute later, it would have been too late. I'm telling you she's a liability around that man and I'm a loyal agent and friend, as you all know.'

Sheena scanned all their faces, knowing they all knew that she knew things about each of them she'd never shared with the others. 'I draw the line at *doing time*, especially because we've all inadvertently got involved in accidentally covering up the truth about the deaths of not one, but two of the most hideous people we've ever known.' Helen went to speak but Sheena carried on, just to make sure her point was well made. 'So I am not exaggerating. She can't be trusted around him at all.'

When she finished, she picked up her wine glass and took a big slug of the chilled rosé, then grabbed the bottle from the ice bucket by the table again and filled up her glass, which emptied the bottle. She tapped it with her red nail, making a pinging sound, which caught the attention of the waitress, and she signalled for her to bring another one.

'So bringing Chad is not an option,' she said flatly.

'I've been talking to Dan—' Amanda began, before Sheena cut in.

'Not about . . .?'

'No! Not about *that*,' she said, as all their eyes darted at each other in panic, fearing the secrets that they'd sworn never to reveal outside of their circle had been passed on to an *outsider*. 'I'd never tell him those things. He's the sweetest, kindest man I've ever known. I don't know if he could forgive me,' she said sadly.

The waitress arrived and Sheena took the bottle from her, dismissing her quickly so they could carry on their conversation.

250

Farrah eyed it widely. 'God, what I would give for a glass of that,' she said, then frowned as Amanda pushed the water bottle towards her and picked up where she left off.

'I've been talking to Dan about leaving,' she said.

Helen looked at her in shock. To hear that she'd confided such a huge decision in her boyfriend before sharing it with the group felt like a betrayal of their sisterhood, and with the irony of the man she was dating being a serving police officer. Of all the men to fall in love with, and at any stage of her life, it had to be a policeman at the one time she was technic-ally involved in the cover-up of two suspicious deaths. One could possibly be considered understandable, as she'd only kept her silence on Amanda's edit of the camera shots, but she'd actually watched Ross Owen's dead body be pushed into the sea and waited for it to be discovered. There was no way out of that one if Catherine confessed to the lot. Amanda saw the look in her eyes and headed it off.

'He's been suggesting I leave since it was announced Jake was returning. I swear I have not said a word.'

The women all looked at her, and then each other; once it was clear they believed her she felt able to carry on.

'Look, you all know how much I love this place and all of you, and what I've done rightly or wrongly for us to stay here.'

There was another pause as Amanda's sentence – packed with the guilt she felt – fell on the table. If she hadn't have told Helen or Farrah about the underwater footage she'd hidden from the police – which showed Catherine pulling her hand away from Madeline as she reached out for help in the water – then they wouldn't even be involved in her crime of perverting the course of justice. If they hadn't done that, maybe they wouldn't have feared revealing the truth about Ross's death in case it made the police reinvestigate

Madeline. It was all such a mess. The women looked at her, aware of what her words meant versus what she was saying.

'And if I could turn back the clock, I'm not sure I would do the same again – it's this island. I used to think it was worth risking everything for.' Amanda's voice quivered with emotion.

'We all did,' Farrah chipped in, placing her hand on Amanda's.

'But it's become a living nightmare and I've got Olivia to think about. It's not healthy for her. She can sense the vibes in me. I'm just not happy here anymore. You can't make a move without Tabitha Tate popping up at every turn, and God knows what's in that book of hers.'

They all looked at each other with joint concern at the mention of it.

Amanda let out a deep sigh before saying something she'd never imagined she would say. 'The truth of it is, I don't think I've got it in me to fight Jake or whoever our latest enemy will be when that book's released, all over again.' She gestured for Sheena to pass over the fresh bottle of rosé that was positioned next to her and filled up her glass.

Helen was taking in Amanda's words when Farrah, after eating the last two bites on her plate, decided to say her piece.

'If there was ever a time that I didn't need more stress it's now,' she said, placing her hands on her belly. 'It wasn't what I planned and lord knows, certainly not *who* I'd have planned it with, but it has happened, and I think the only way I'll ever truly be able to love this baby *unconditionally* is by getting away from its father.'

She reached out to Amanda and squeezed her hand again, both in the understanding they now shared a bond that the others would never be able to fully comprehend. Helen stayed quiet, again surprised that Farrah seemed to be on the same page as Amanda and yet hadn't discussed her feelings with her. She'd known they'd been spending a lot of time together due to the pregnancy but it still hurt to feel excluded from a friendship that she'd always thought was equal up until now, especially as she'd known Farrah longer. She was just about to speak when Sheena started.

'The thing is, if your heart isn't in it any more, then what's the point? We've had a good run. If Jake wants to run this ship into the ground, we *don't* have to be on it, do we? And if there's no show, the interest in whatever that shitty little witch Tabitha has got in that book will already wane by the time she gets it out.'

Amanda and Farrah's faces showed they liked Sheena's train of thinking, but the casualness of her tone visibly irritated Helen.

'So let me get this straight. You've dragged me into not one, but two cover-ups that could land me in jail because you all wanted to be here so much and keep the show going,' she said, in a voice that made it clear she was most definitely not happy. 'But now you've all already mentally checked out of this place, you want to head off with your new man, you with your new baby, and you no doubt to cash pay cheques on other soap operas, and nobody cares about being here any more?'

'It's not that we don't care,' Amanda tried to explain, but Helen was not to be stopped.

'Might it not have been nice of you to bother to tell me rather than letting me attend these bloody meetings and support the team and deal with Jake whilst you've both avoided him?' she said, staring at Amanda and Farrah, who both looked sheepish. Her gaze turned back towards Sheena. 'And why you even let me bother calling this meeting, thinking I was trying to help come up with a way to stop that maniacal bastard's latest plans to sabotage your client, is a mystery. You don't seem that interested either.'

Sheena looked at her face. Helen rarely snapped but was definitely on the verge of losing her rag.

'I came down here the moment you called, so it's not that I or we don't care,' Sheena said firmly, 'and I'm sorry if all three of us have surprised you with the same sentiment tonight. To be honest, it's a surprise to me to hear that I'm not alone in just not feeling as passionate about risking everything all over again. I guess what's happened has changed us; I don't know what else to say,' Sheena finished with a shrug of her shoulders.

Helen looked at her and then at the others. She could tell by their faces they'd taken no enjoyment in sharing the fact they felt ready to throw in the towel. Perhaps it was the stubbornness in her, which had always been on her school reports, that stopped her from doing the same. After all, she could have just walked out of that ridiculous meeting earlier that day rather than rallying the troops, thinking they'd want to do the same as her and defeat their common enemy. The table fell silent as they all looked at each other, aware they were no longer united in the battle to control *Falcon Bay*.

Eventually Sheena spoke.

'Catherine really is happy with Lee. They seem in a really good place. If we tell her Jake's plans to attack her role on the show again, I feel sure she'll want to go rather than fight it. Maybe this is just the right time for us to get off the ride. I mean, come on, Helen, be honest with yourself. You don't want to lose face, none of us do, by letting that bastard think he's driven us away. But do you really want to stay on this island with him running the show into the ground with those crazy storylines you played us on that message, plus the stress of Tabitha constantly trying to catch us all out?'

Helen shook her head. She hated admitting defeat, but as strong as she was, she couldn't mount a fight against Jake alone and nor did she want to. Perhaps the others were right and it was time to go, but the pride in her couldn't agree to go quietly.

'Well,' she said firmly. She gestured for Sheena to top up her glass and pushed her dessert, which she now had no appetite for, towards Farrah, who'd wolfed hers down ages ago. 'It looks like the decision had been made then.'

Amanda looked at her with worry. 'Are you mad at us?'

'No,' Helen said, and meant it. 'Look, I'm not so desperate to stay here that I'll put up with his shit. I just didn't know that we were no longer battling to stay together.' She gestured to Amanda and Farrah. 'But maybe our time as one here has come to an end, and I'm sad about that, as you know how much I love you all.'

The women all held hands as emotions ran high at the table.

Helen, determined not to cry, took a deep breath and continued, 'At least once I go, I will never have to deal with him again, unlike you two, who are stuck with him forever. Imagine how much worse he'll be if he has the fact that he's driven you off the show to throw at you from now until the kid's graduation days.'

Farrah and Amanda looked each other, then back to Helen, with an exhausted understanding of what she meant. Then Helen turned to Sheena.

'And I'm guessing that even though you think Catherine would rather leave here, there's also that small fact that you don't want to be involved with a show whose new leading lady just so happens to be the ex-client who sacked you,' she said flatly, with no edge of malice, but clearly enough for Sheena to understand she was being called out.

'True. I wouldn't enjoy being here whilst Lydia Chambers turned Catherine's character into her dogsbody and enjoyed me being powerless over it, no. I'm not ashamed to admit it,' Sheena said, with an open expression.

'So, between you, one way or another, you all want out, but if we are going, we need to go out on a high, not a low, right?'

The women nodded.

'Then we need to come up with a plan that works for all of us,' Helen continued. 'I don't mind leaving *Falcon Bay*. I never thought I'd say this, but I've actually got real feelings for Matt and to be honest, with him in London and me here, we don't get enough time together. If your hearts are no longer in this, then we're not in it together any more, so I'd rather be with him and see if I can turn what we have into something serious, rather than spend my days solo trying to prop this chaotic mess up.' She looked at Farrah and Amanda reassuringly. 'And that is not a dig.'

Amanda smiled. 'I can't believe you're saying you want to settle down.'

'Neither can I.' Farrah laughed.

'The cougar has finally been tamed,' Sheena threw in with a giggle as Helen felt a slight blush come to her cheeks.

'Let's not go that far,' she said with a smile. 'But yes, I do like the idea of seeing where it's going to go and I can always work freelance. I don't need to give my life to a show any more. The business has changed. We can work remotely. I'll learn to change with it,' she said, raising her glass and gesturing for the others to join her in a toast. 'But Dustin was right in that meeting that you all heard. If Jake gets to wreck the show, even if we've left it, our legacy will be tarnished and that's hardly going to make any of us hot properties, is it?'

The women looked at each other as she continued. 'And as much as we're all saying we're ready to do new things, let's be real here, all of us are career women. Maybe it won't be here any more, or in the same way, but we all know we'll be working in this business till the day we die and loving it – because showbiz is in our DNA, or we wouldn't have done what we've done to last this long in it.'

The women nodded.

'So, we won't be leaving this show in Jake's filthy hands,' she said with a glint in her eye.

'What do you mean?' Amanda said, genuinely clueless as to whatever Helen had in mind.

Farrah also eyed her with interest. Anything that was going to fuck up Jake's plans was going to be worth involving herself with, even if it was for the last time. 'What have you got in mind?' she said, digging her spoon into the crème brûlée Helen had passed her down the table earlier.

The answer she gave caused Farrah to drop the spoon.

Chapter 24

When Sheena had pressed Catherine's buzzer at 11.30 p.m. later that night, she knew that, as she hadn't even told her she was on the island, whatever she'd come to say would be serious. And it was. Catherine had been lying in Lee's arms on the sofa in post-coital bliss and her phone was switched off, so she hadn't seen the dozen or so missed calls that had come before Sheena had made her way over to the side of island where Catherine lived in one of the luxurious condos.

'Come up,' Catherine had said into the intercom, instantly alarmed.

Knowing Catherine wasn't alone, Sheena had used the excuse that she was smoking, which Catherine abhorred even on her balcony, to get her to come down. Lee had practically ripped off Catherine's white maxi dress earlier and thrown it to the floor in a moment of passion, so it was crumpled when she'd thrown it back on. She pulled on a large silk wrap. A few minutes later, Catherine was standing next to Sheena on the water's edge.

One of the things Catherine had always loved about the positioning of her home on the island was that practically as soon as you exited the building, you were on the glorious seafront, and even in the dark of night, the moon highlighted the gentle waves that lapped the ocean. It was a tranquil setting, but something in Sheena's expression made her anxious that a new storm was brewing. She eyed Sheena's outfit, which was far too glamorous to have travelled down in just for an impromptu meeting with her.

'Where have you been?' she said suspiciously as Sheena, true to her word on the intercom, lit another cigarette, took a long drag, then leaned back and faced her.

'Dinner with Farrah, Helen and Amanda,' she said, and took another drag.

'Without me?' she said, looking hurt. Sure, they hadn't been as close as before Christmas and she'd been spending all her spare time with Lee, but a girls' dinner without even inviting her was a painful thing to be told about. Sheena, having known Catherine thirty years, could see the spiral of rejection most actresses could fall into at just the merest thought that . anyone might not want their presence at an event, and decided to save her from herself.

'You weren't invited because we wanted to work out what to do before coming to you, which I've done, as your agent and friend, immediately. We left the restaurant and I came straight here.'

Catherine looked at her intently. Whatever Sheena was about to say next was definitely not going to be good and it made her wish she had a Xanax in her kimono pocket. Before Lee had re-entered her life, she could have reached into any of her clothes and found an emergency tablet, designed to take the edge off whatever attack was heading her way next. But after telling him she had a prescription drug problem, he'd helped her go cold turkey, and she truly was amazed at just how easily she'd come off them. She'd been taking them daily since the doctors had given them to her at the hospital she'd been admitted to for recovery, after her altercation with Madeline Kane on Christmas Day. But from that first night she and Lee had spent together, all her anxiety and fear had subsided and with his help, she hadn't needed a single one. She still felt as calm as she had been when she was on them.

'Right,' Catherine said quietly. 'So what is it this time?'

Sheena took a final drag on the cigarette, then flicked it into the sea and faced her.

'Jake's on another one-man mission again to bring you down,' she began.

Catherine studied her face as she spoke. In the moonlight, Sheena looked almost as young as she had done when she herself had been an actress years before making the move to representing the talent rather than being it. Catherine couldn't help but think that if she wanted to, Sheena could still cut a striking figure on screen. Sheena, noticing Catherine didn't seem that interested in what she'd said, decided to reinforce her statement.

'Do you understand what I'm saying?' she said slowly, assuming Catherine was probably numb with her usual mix of prescription drugs and wine. The way Sheena spoke caused Catherine to laugh as the air coming off the sea made her clutch her wrap tight for fear of it blowing open.

She smiled at Sheena. 'Up there,' she pointed to her condo's balcony, 'is the love of my life. I didn't know it,' she said, looking wistfully in the direction she knew Lee's perfect and warm body was. She already couldn't wait to get back to him. 'And I certainly wasn't expecting it, but I've never been happier, Sheena. Whatever Jake has got planned for me this time, on screen or off, with Lee by my side, I know I can handle it.' She reached out and patted Sheena's high shoulder pad reassuringly, then added, 'And no, it's not the Xanax talking. I don't take anything like that any more,' she said with a smile.

'Well, you might want one in a minute when I tell you that Jake is planning to axe Lee, burn down The Cove and turn your character into some sort of beggar woman, beholden to Lydia Chambers's Claudia for work. From what Helen said, mainly cleaning toilets,' Sheena said, watching Catherine's smiling face turn to horror.

'What? Lucy, a cleaner? And Lee dead? Surely he can't. Lee's so popular,' she began, her voice now definitely not calm.

'Listen, you and I know better than anyone else, he can, and he will.'

Catherine was agitated. She looked up once more towards where she knew Lee was, a sense of dread filling her at the very idea of Jake's plans being actioned. Her being the show's skivvy was one thing but she knew how much Lee loved his work on *Falcon Bay*. He had mellowed and he wanted to stay on the show this time around. This would devastate him. He couldn't handle being axed after such a triumphant return, and Catherine knew that no matter how in love they were, his male pride would mean he would leave the island if he was booted off the show. He was not a man who could live in a woman's shadow, even if, by the sounds of what Sheena was saying, that woman would no longer be the queen of *Falcon Bay*.

She turned away and looked towards the sea and out along St Augustine's coastline. It glittered like stardust had been sprinkled all over it. She took in the lighthouse at the far end and watched its amber glow reflecting in the waters, then cast her eyes over towards the Lucy Dean Cove Bar set, which she could just about make out in the distance. Eventually, she turned back to Sheena.

'I don't want to put you in an awkward position, Sheena,' Catherine said, speaking slowly in a tone Sheena didn't quite recognise. 'But if you've spent the evening planning an elaborate plot for us to fight back, just so I can stay on the show, then you've wasted your evening and come all this way for nothing.' She touched Sheena's shoulder again, with apologetic affection.

Sheena looked at her in surprise. Just six months earlier these very same two women had fought for their professional lives like tigresses against Jake and Madeline Kane's constant attacks to end Lucy Dean's reign as *Falcon Bay*'s leading lady. The mere suggestion that Jake had her in his revenge sights again would usually have brought the Sunset Boulevard out in her, causing her to fizz with rage and extol her hatred for the man who seemed to make it his life's work to fuck up her life on the show she'd been so loyal to. But right now, Catherine's facial expression showed a very different woman to the one who'd fought to the death and won on Christmas Day. Sheena went to speak but Catherine wasn't done.

'I know it's un-PC, certainly not feminist and probably unthinkable for you to hear,' she continued, again her tone even, her manner calm, 'but feeling these feelings that I thought I'd never feel again has made me realise there really is more to life than work and war. If they don't want us here any more, then I'd rather be touring in a play with Lee, like Elizabeth Taylor and Richard Burton used to do. Or even just be on his barge in the Netherlands, rather than staying here on this island under attack. I certainly do not want to be here at all without him.'

Sheena looked at Catherine, once her most ambitious of clients. The very thought of her ever declaring her love for a man could be stronger than her desire to retain her showbiz crown was once unthinkable, but she could tell she meant every word.

Catherine could see Sheena was taken aback by her state-ment. In truth, she hadn't really realised it herself until she'd said it but she knew she meant it. Being with Lee had changed her perspective and helped her find herself again. If it was weak to admit that she felt stronger in a couple and that love was now finally, after forty years of being married to her career, more important to her than work or maintaining her success, then she was proud to show her weakness, because being with Lee made her feel the strongest she'd felt in years.

'We both know *life* here has never truly been the same after what we've been through,' she said solemnly. 'I'm still living with the guilt of what I've done, but it's gradually getting better, and I'll always be grateful for what you all did for me, twice, which I know has changed us all forever. I can only imagine it will be much easier to try and forget it al-together if we don't have to see the very place it happened or be in the place it happened over and again. This time, I don't want to fight whatever Jake has in store.' Catherine had a smile on her face that seemed genuine. 'So it's time to go.'

Sheena looked at Catherine, who, either by chance or sheer instinct, had somehow managed to end her speech in the perfect light. It was hitting her high cheekbones and luminous skin. She certainly looked like a woman in love and for a second Sheena felt jealous.

Amanda had Dan and Olivia, Farrah seemed to be focused on being a mother, even if it was the spawn of Satan, Catherine was clearly so content with Lee that she wasn't even interested in her career any longer and Helen, the only one of them that she'd have put money on joining her in the 'single girls till they die' club, seemed like she too had fallen hook, line and sinker for Matt. She wasn't jealous in a bad way. She loved the women and wanted them to be happy, and Catherine's admission tonight would certainly mean that she didn't even have to persuade her to join in with their plans. But seeing how happy she was to go off with Lee, she couldn't help feeling alone in the fact that it was only her now in the group that seemed to be truly on her own.

She'd spent the last six months having random sex with nameless women she met on the internet, mainly married women who were known for their love of experimentation. Sheena had always been happy to oblige, knowing that once they'd ticked their lesbian experience off their mid-life bucket lists they'd always go back to their husbands. But with Amanda and Catherine seemingly deeply in love with their partners, Helen not far behind, and Farrah opting to make motherhood her focus, suddenly she felt the urge to find something real for herself. Sheena reminded herself that it wasn't the time to think about that, for right now, she must do her job and deliver Helen's idea so Catherine knew exactly what they were doing, as she'd need Lee onboard too.

'Well,' Sheena finally said, sensing Catherine had finished her statement and was ready to listen rather than talk. 'That's actually going to work out perfectly with our plans.'

Catherine, knowing Sheena was never one to give in to Jake's whims, had been expecting a battle, so stepped back and eyed Sheena curiously.

'How so?'

Sheena pulled another cigarette out of the Vogue Super Slims packet, lit it with a flick of her crystal-covered lighter, then began to explain.

Chapter 25

On the balcony of Catherine's condo, a naked Lee Landers was looking down at Catherine and Sheena, who were talking intently by the waterside. Looking at his watch, he saw it was gone 1.30 a.m., meaning Catherine had been down there for hours. What on earth could they be talking about?

Feeling a chill on his skin, he walked back into the apartment and retook his place on the large L-shaped sofa he and Catherine had been making love on earlier. He turned on his phone and was about to text Catherine when he spotted she'd left hers on the side. *Damn*, he thought. They had to be on set at 6 a.m. for their first scene with Lydia Chambers in the morning and he didn't want to rock up looking like he'd barely slept. Especially when Lydia was such a hot piece of ass.

He'd remembered her from the awards ceremonies they'd both frequented back in the day when he was on the show the first time around, and he'd always thought she was a stunner. When he'd seen the recent pictures of her in the papers CITV had released, in her new role as Claudia Raymond, he'd felt the blood in his impressive penis flow until it was at its full height of ten inches. He'd had to whack off in the dressing room right there and then at the thought that if he played his cards right, he might finally be able to have a crack at slipping her his length.

The condo monitor, which was linked to the CCTV outside the building, showed Sheena and Catherine were still deep in conversation. He decided to have a quick google of Lydia, and typed *Lydia Chambers porn* into the search box. It was amazing what came up. Suddenly images of Lydia on all fours being spit-roasted by various men alongside solo shots of her using a vibrator on herself filled the screen. They were fake, of course – all celebs were the victims of computer trickery these days – but the imagery was so good that it was easy to let himself believe he was looking at the real deal. As his cock sprang to life again, he picked his favourite one, one where her face had been grafted onto a porn star's body, with her legs wide open, her fingers inside herself. He reached for his hard cock and began to wank, imagining that soon, in one of the trailers, he might get to see that image for real.

Brad, the queen from wardrobe, had told Lee a story that Lydia had been late to the *Falcon Bay* Bitch Party episode the previous year because rumour had it that she'd let the driver assigned to bring her to the show fuck her in the back of his limo. Lee was sure Brad had told him the story to see if he got a boner or not. He knew when someone wanted him, male or female; the desire was always obvious. The story had worked, as he'd seen Brad's eyes widen as his cock snaked itself down the side of the trousers Brad was on his knees adjusting for him. He saw the desire in his eyes and that turned him on almost as much as the thought of Lydia being shafted by the driver. If it hadn't have been for the CCTV in wardrobe, he'd have unzipped it right there and then and fucked Brad's mouth, imagining it was Lydia. Brad would have loved that, no doubt. Lots of gay men, in his experience, loved a straight man more than any other. Forbidden fruit, after all, always tasted the best – he'd learnt that in Amsterdam.

But no, he wouldn't be feeding Brad's desires. A quick blowjob from a random mouth wasn't worth losing the set-up he had with Catherine for. But being paired up with Lydia, well, that was an altogether different situation. If he'd let Brad suck his impressive cock, he wouldn't have considered it to be a bisexual act.

Over the years on his boat, especially on a cold winter's evening when there were not many women out travelling, and with the area being so well known for its gay scene, eventually he accepted one of the many offers he had. He'd decided a mouth was a mouth, despite who it belonged to, and as long as all he did was let them do the work, well then, his sexuality was never in doubt. If anything it just proved what a stud he was. If someone wanted to go down on him until he shot his load from his equally impressive and ever-full balls, well, he wasn't going to say no – it was better than a wank. In fact, if Brad had been here now, Lee decided he'd have let him service his throbbing hardness as he took a closer look at pictures of Lydia and imagined it was her. He wouldn't even have looked down; well, maybe just a quick glance.

The thought of that alongside the quickening of his rhythm as he tugged at himself brought him to a climax. He carefully lifted his body backwards so that his cum splattered his body, and not on the precious sofa Catherine was always so careful to cover with sheets before she'd let him fuck her on it. She was so annoying and unspontaneous, which was one of the reasons he'd had no qualms about leaving her the first time all those years ago. When he came back, he knew the only way to get the most out of this second ride on the showbiz merry-go-round was to put in the performance of his life off-screen as well as on. He'd calculated his approach to their first scene, but even he'd been surprised at just how quickly Catherine had fallen for it. She must have been desperate to feel loved to have accepted him back into her life so easily. He wasn't complaining; it had made his return to the big time all the sweeter and easier for the last few months, but boredom was starting to set in, so the timing of Lydia's arrival was right on schedule.

He grabbed some tissues from the side and wiped his stomach clean, then padded to the bathroom and flushed them down the loo. He wouldn't put it past Catherine to pull them out of the bin if he'd discarded them there. She was so needy, even worse after she'd proudly announced that thanks to him, she'd been able to come off the prescription drugs she'd tearfully confessed she'd become addicted to. She'd told him that one night after a late dinner on the terrace, in an emotional display that if he didn't know better, he'd have thought was one of their scenes from the show. After telling her how proud he was of her, he asked her to give him her stash so he could dispose of them, to avoid temptation ever getting the better of her. She'd thanked him when he took them. Little did she know that from that day on, he'd been grinding them up and putting double the amount she'd said she'd been taking into the freshly squeezed orange juice he brought her in bed every morning, meaning Catherine was constantly in an unbeknownst Xanax haze.

He smiled at that. 'Stupid bitch,' he said out loud, then washed his hands before heading into the bedroom, where he popped a couple of sleeping pills and slipped under the covers.

He'd set the alarm on his phone and placed it right next

to his side of the bed, so he knew that despite how strong the pills were and that he'd be asleep in minutes, the sound of the phone would wake him up in time to make sure he was looking sparkling fresh for Lydia. With a final grin at the idea of the two of them being together, he drifted off to sleep.

He didn't hear the sound of the front door go when Catherine re-entered the condo after finally saying goodbye to Sheena an hour later. Sensing he was asleep, Catherine crept to the bathroom, where she took off her make-up and applied a thick layer of VI Derm Intense Hydration, her favourite moisturizing serum, then tiptoed into the bedroom and slipped under the covers and next to Lee's warm, naked body. As she looked at his angelic face as he slept, she whispered some words.

'I love you, my darling, and whatever becomes of us outside of this bubble, I'll always be happy just to be by your side.' And with that she gently kissed him on the cheek, excited that when they woke up, even though she'd sworn to Sheena that she wouldn't share Helen's plan with Lee just yet, they'd be one day closer to being free from the terrible pressures of showbusiness and could venture into the real world hand in hand.

As she drifted off to sleep, a smile crossed Catherine's lips, knowing she'd truly found her happy-ever-after and that she couldn't wait to start their new lives away from *Falcon Bay*.

Chapter 26

In upscale Brentwood, on Cherry Tree Lane amongst the houses of celebrities, was the home of Dr Durand. His family had lived there long before the area became a hot spot for the fame whores, as he called them in the handwritten diaries he'd been keeping since the day he first saw Honey Hunter on a movie screen in the 1970s. He knew she was a real star, not like the ones of today, with their huge tacky cars and reality shows. Brentwood was once home to true Hollywood legends, like Joan Crawford and Marilyn Monroe, so it was only fitting that Honey should be in the small part of Santa Monica that for years he'd built into a shrine for her.

Behind the white shutters of the three-storey wooden house, each wall was covered in pictures of Honey throughout her younger years, when she'd first made her name as a teen star in Hollywood. On the top floor, in the master suite, a naked Dr Durand lay gently caressing a sedated, sleeping Honey Hunter, who was covered in white bandages. 'Vide Cor Meum' played out from the surround-sound speakers. As he looked down at her angelic face, he took in every detail of it, trying to savour every second they would have together.

For the last seven days, he'd been enjoying every moment he had left with Honey. He hadn't reported to the rehab faculty; he knew that time was running out. Despite his behaviour, he was no fool. The media speculation – in the same filthy tabloid rags that had led to her downfall in the first place – had been going on for the last few weeks and they were offering money for her whereabouts. He was fully aware that this would, eventually, result in someone at the rehab facility tipping them off. And he'd lose her forever.

He ran his hands down her body, then touched the Glock 19 handgun that was on the dresser next to the lacy, embroidered bed they were lying on. He hoped that there truly was a heaven because that's where his angel deserved to be, not in this rotten world obsessed with fame, fortune and looks. On the black market in America, if you had the money, there was nothing you couldn't get, so he knew that now there was a bounty on finding her, time truly was of the essence.

He'd taken her out of the back exit of the facility, the one they used for private ambulances for suicidal patients who, after achieving their goals, often with his help, left the facility in body bags.

'I'm going to get you away from those male nurses,' he'd whispered soothingly to her as he put her into the car. 'Touching you with their impure hands.'

He'd taken her to a once very well-known plastic surgeon he'd been friends with for years. Dr Zimmerman was no longer practicing thanks to an indiscretion he'd had with a minor, but Durand didn't judge – everyone had their sins and vices, or in his case, obsessions.

Zimmerman was still practicing, but illegally, and most importantly discreetly, in his home in the Hollywood Hills, behind several gates. It resembled an impenetrable compound. It was there that, at Durand's request, Zimmerman had

271

removed Honey's breast implants and restored the bump to her original nose, which once graced screens all over the world when she'd first found fame as one of Disney's young stars. He'd removed the fillers she'd had put into her lips, and had taken out the extensions in her hair, cutting it back to the way it had been when Durand had first fallen in love with her as a teenager.

Zimmerman hadn't questioned him. If anything, his expression when Durand explained what he wanted to do showed he was excited at the project, and for 100,000 dollars in cash he'd restored her.

And now, with the bruising gone, and her soft shape back, she looked like his Honey once more, back to her true original condition, the way she should have been all along before she was damaged by the world of beauty obsessions. He was so sad that it was already nearly time to say goodbye. The moment he'd broken his Hippocratic oath, this was only ever going to end one way. Maybe he should have reached out to her the first time she'd checked into the rehab facility in Mulholland Drive in Los Angeles, connected with her, not watched her spend years ruining her life before fate finally drew them back together when she stepped back through those doors a decade later. He knew the moment she reappeared that this time he wasn't going to miss his chance. He'd loved every single second of caring for her.

Alerts on his security system went off one by one, signalling that someone was in the grounds, then inside the lower level of his house. Then the final alarm went off, which signalled that they were on the staircase that led up to the master suite, where he was holding his baby. He knew it was over, but he had no regrets, other than that he wished they'd had longer. With one hand, he held her body close to him and with the other he picked up the gun. As the bedroom door – which had several deadbolts across it – started to shake from the sheer pressure applied to it, and the noise of it breaking began to fill the room, he turned the music up to the highest level. This had always been his favourite aria.

He gently sang along to the words, with his mouth against Honey's ear . . .

> Lo sono in pace
> Cor meum
> Io sono in pace
> Vide cor meum

Then he translated the words, knowing Honey didn't know Latin. 'This is our song, my darling,' he said gently, as the door's hinges began to break.

> I am in peace
> My heart
> I am in peace
> See my heart

He sang whilst cradling her, with his finger gently resting on the trigger.

As Vlad and his team of heavies finally broke the door down, Honey's eyes suddenly opened just as Durand's gun went off.

Chapter 27

The helicopter carrying Sheena McQueen took off from St Augustine's helipad and flew over the island, starting the journey that would take her home to central London. She looked down at the place that housed the fictional world that had dominated her professional life for so many years.

It was hard to believe, she thought, as the pilot increased the speed and the world-famous location disappeared into the background, that only last year, keeping Catherine in this exotic location had felt like the most important moment in their professional lives. That was saying a lot when you'd represented someone as long as Sheena had represented Catherine, over three decades, and seen all the drama on-screen and off that came with life on a serial drama and its globally famous leading lady.

She thought back to the day when she'd watched Madeline Kane step onto the dockyard set in Lucy Dean's high heels, under the world's gaze. None of them were aware she was just moments from a death that would change the women's destinies forever. She wondered what she'd think of them all abandoning the ship that she was so desperate to control, that the desire that burned inside her to be the star of it had actually killed her – well, sort of.

Sheena looked out of the window and at the sea below, the same waters she'd pushed Ross Owen's dead and broken body into on the night of the awards ceremony. She wasn't particularly religious but if there was a heaven and a hell, she was pretty sure both their vindictive souls had headed down, not up. As she weighed up Helen's plan, she was at least certain that this was one counter-attack Jake Monroe wouldn't see coming. Had she been alive, even Madeline Kane herself would have marvelled at the sheer Machiavellian genius of it. If they pulled it off, that was. Helen had a huge task ahead of her. Around the dinner table when she'd explained her plot it had sounded extreme, but when she'd found herself recounting it to Catherine outside her apartment later, and with a couple of hours to digest it, she really believed it would work.

Helen was a lot smarter than anyone who didn't know her gave her credit for. You didn't work your way up from being a casual assistant to being the sole casting director on a globally syndicated show and stay in your job for over thirty years if you didn't have a certain amount of creativity. And whilst her job wasn't related to the storyline department, it had been her idea to cast the bitch role last year, which had kept the show afloat amidst its first sign of sinking in the ratings. None of them could have imagined when Jake stole it and claimed it as his own that CITV's new owner Madeline Kane would turn the fiction in the plot into fact. And what a bitch she'd been. Venomous, vindictive and vengeful. All great traits in an onscreen character, not so much in a real-life one.

Even so, Sheena hadn't wished her dead. In fact right now if she had the power to bring her back to life, even her villainous presence would be better than the idea of the four women who'd covered up Catherine's part in her and Ross's demises potentially paying the ultimate price for it and losing their freedom. A cold chill ran though Sheena's body at the very thought of their cover-up ever being exposed. She wasn't built for prison life. Sitting in a helicopter that had cost five grand for the evening and wearing fifty grand's worth of diamonds whilst it took her back to her penthouse flat certainly compounded that.

No, Helen's plan had to work. They were better off away from St Augustine's. They'd all vowed that once it was over, they'd never return to the island again, closing the door on the past once and for all and securing a worry-free future, especially if they could do it in time to derail interest in Tabitha Tate's shitty book. Financially, she wasn't worried about losing *Falcon Bay* as a home for any of her talent from the McQueen Agency. She had clients in every major soap and drama in the world. No, *Falcon Bay* had always been Catherine's domain, and if she was also happy to finally flee the toxic nest then the end of this era had truly come. Sheena thought back to how calm she was when she'd explained Jake's sabotage plans and Helen's exit strategy; if she hadn't known better, she'd have sworn she was still self-medicating. She'd had that calmness that downers and alcohol always gave stars, and being a former addict herself, she knew it when she saw it. But if Catherine wanted her to believe she was clean, Sheena wasn't going to contradict her. After all, who wouldn't need a tranquilizer or two to cope with the stress of living and working on that trapdoor set? No, Sheena reasoned, Catherine would free herself of them when she was ready, or admit she needed help at some point, and when she did Sheena would be there for her, just like she'd always been.

As the chopper dipped, causing Sheena to clutch her snake-skin Fendi, a little treat she'd picked up for herself earlier that day in Bond Street, she wondered how long it would last with Lee. Although they'd only crossed paths once since his re-arrival, when Sheena had popped down with some fashion endorsement contracts for Catherine to sign, he'd seemed to have mellowed from the egomaniac who'd once thought he was king of the universe. It was amazing what life outside the soap bubble could do to someone, Sheena mused, as she thought about his changed temperament.

Soap operas were a bit like greenhouses. Each actor was like a seed germinating in the climate. Some would bloom big and wither quickly, a bit like herself when she'd been a child actor on the now defunct *Second Chances*. She'd been Britain's version of Lindsay Lohan during her worst times, but once outside of the system and post recovery, she'd reflowered back into a much better version of herself. Others were like evergreens, sturdy and solid, never running into trouble, always guaranteed to be relied on. And then there were the orchids, which needed to be treated with kid gloves. They wouldn't always be the star of the show, but once or twice a year, they'd be given storylines that would see them bloom as brightly as the rarest types, and just like the Phalaenopsis orchid, could last for months and provide pleasure for millions.

Catherine was the most unusual flower of all, a hybrid of all the best of every type of seed. Sturdy and constant but capable of bursting into colours that would mesmerise you. Sheena was sure that once the idea of bumming around in a canal barge in the Netherlands had worn off – which, knowing Catherine's taste for the pampered life, wouldn't be long – she'd soon be asking Sheena to find her a new creative home where she could be re-rooted, ready to flourish again. And if Helen's plan went as everyone hoped, Sheena would have absolutely no problem achieving that for her.

Chapter 28

The Zoom call with Melissa Kane was organised for midnight, St Augustine's local time. Amanda had suggested they do it in Meeting Room 6, even though it was dark, as it would give them the backdrop of the island and the *Falcon Bay* set that she, Farrah and Helen deeply loved.

Amanda was the first to arrive and took a seat at the long white table that had been their power hub for decades. In this very room, characters and the actors' fates had been decided on-screen and off. She thought back to fifteen years earlier, fresh into her marriage, when she and Jake would sneakily hold hands under its shiny white surface. It was hard to believe that a man she'd once loved so much that she'd put herself though twelve rounds of IVF to give him a child – which it quickly turned out he really wasn't interested in – could turn into a monster. He now lurked with vicious intent around the corridors of this CITV building. He did it in the same way the shark he and Madeline had installed, in what was supposed to be the protective tank by the dockside near Lucy Dean's bar, had stalked its prey, but unexpectedly got fed a different dinner. She was imagining being in Dan's arms the moment this meeting concluded, and telling him the news she hoped he'd be happy to hear, when Helen and Farrah walked through the door. Amanda looked at her Swatch watch, a cute retro gift from Dan. She smiled at the thought of him at home with Olivia.

'You can't say I'm late tonight.' Helen smiled.

'And I should be given extra credit for being here at all.' Farrah puffed. 'Bloody maintenance have got the lifts being serviced overnight – we had to take the stairs!' she said, taking a deep breath. She checked out the leftovers from one of the storyline conferences that must have happened in the room earlier in the day, before deciding nothing took her fancy. She slumped her ever-burgeoning bump into a chair and placed her coat behind her to make herself comfortable.

Helen rolled her eyes. 'Erm, not only are you in flats, but I am in six-inch heels, Farrah. And, not that I look it, but I'm a *bit* older than you and you don't hear me complaining,' she said, also taking a seat. Amanda smiled again, watching her dear friends one-up themselves on who had it the hardest. It was a welcome distraction from the grim task they had coming at midnight, that was for sure.

'Yes, but you're not pregnant, are you? Unless you've got something to tell us,' Farrah cracked, determined to win the banter.

Helen slipped off her bright red jacket and took a seat between the two of them.

'Still trying but no sign as yet!' she said with a wink.

This caused both Amanda and Farrah to laugh.

'Seriously, I never thought I'd say this but if I were five years younger . . .'

Farrah laughed out loud. 'Fifteen years, you mean.'

Helen rolled her eyes.

'Whatever, my point is, I don't know what it is about being

with Matt, but it's different. I feel different,' she said, looking longingly into the night sky as the stars above the Bay twinkled.

'It's called love, Helen,' Amanda said with a wry smile.

Helen pulled her vision back into the room and tried to regain her usual carefree, where it came to discussing men, expression.

'I never said that,' she said quickly, as she poured herself a glass of water then filled the other glasses up.

'You didn't need to,' Farrah added. She'd reached back over to the muffin basket that had been left on the table and, after prodding several, found one at the bottom that seemed to be edible. She picked it out then took a bite. 'It's written all over your face,' she said, with her mouth full.

Amanda looked at what she was sure was a blush sweeping across her friend's face and for a moment almost forgot what they were here for. It was just like old times, when they were happy, when it looked like they'd be together forever, doing a job they loved in a place they'd all called home. But events beyond their control had meant that that's all these moments would ever be now, relegated to memories, for the future would never be the same again. Feeling a catch in her throat and a tear in her eye, she cast one last look out of Meeting Rooms 6's windows and gazed at the moon, which seemed more beautiful and brighter than she'd ever seen it. *Right*, she said to herself, *let's get this done.*

As she turned back to Helen and Farrah, who were looking at photos of Matt on Helen's iPhone, she tapped her watch. It now said they had just five minutes before the large screen Helen had had temporarily put up for the evening over by the cast board would beam live to Louisiana and bring them face to face with Melissa Kane.

Helen nodded as Farrah finished her muffin and wiped the

crumbs off the table, readying herself for the international meeting they all hoped would protect their legacy, even if it was in the most unconventional way.

'Considering she's Chad's sister, they look nothing alike,' Helen said, as Amanda fiddled with the laptop, which had Melissa's Zoom picture on the screen, ready to go live. She logged into the system and did a test to make sure the camera angle featured all three of them, jostling her seat a bit closer to Farrah's so they all filled the screen evenly.

'Let's hope the crazy father's not in this meeting. Some of the things Sheena said he said about her being gay were disgusting. He clearly knew about and had an issue with Madeline's past as well, so no doubt he'll be a true bigot and probably racist too. Those religious types are always the worst, preaching love and compassion when behind closed doors they're usually the vilest.'

Helen nodded.

Amanda, aware they only had minutes left before the meeting began, was keen to check Helen was still happy for her to take the lead.

'Are you sure it should be me?' she said.

'Absolutely. It doesn't matter which of us came up with the plan, you are the most senior here, apart from Jake, so she's hardly going to listen to me *from casting*,' Helen said, mocking the way Jake always described which department she was supposed to be representing, when nine times out of ten the best ideas in the conference room always came from her. 'And listen, I'm not exactly after credit for the plot I've come up with for tonight, but we all agree it's the only way, so you'll stick to it exactly as we planned, right?'

Amanda nodded and looked down at her extensive notepad full of points in the order Helen had designed the discussion to go. Helen then looked at Farrah.

'And no sly digs about Jake, no matter what she says.' Helen eyed her seriously. 'If she thinks this is not legit and there's any personal motivation rather than professional, she won't buy it – and I'm not being funny, but you two have a lot of work to do in this chat to show that it isn't personal from your sides. I'm sure you know what I mean.'

Farrah looked down at her bump then back to Amanda. 'No problem,' she said dryly.

Helen eyeballed her. 'No, I'm deadly serious – this *has* to work.'

Farrah reached her hand out and squeezed Helen's and Amanda's hands with affection.

'One for all,' she began, before the others joined in: 'And all for one.' They squeezed hands one more time and exchanged emotional smiles. Amanda looked over to Catherine's headshot which was staring at them from the cast board wall.

'I still can't believe Sheena said she took it so well,' she said wistfully. 'What a difference a year makes.'

Farrah was just about to make a quip that Catherine was probably up to something way more exciting with Lee Landers right now than anything they'd ever given her in any of her scripts here when the Zoom call began to ring and *Melissa Kane group meeting* flashed up on the screen.

'Well, that's love.' Helen managed to slip in a comment. The others wondered how much of it related more to herself than Catherine, but Amanda, aware they were now on the fifth ring of the Zoom call, hovered over the join button.

'Ready?' she said, and, holding a glass in her other hand, took a sip of water.

Farrah and Helen nodded in unison as Amanda clicked accept and Melissa Kane filled the screen.

The Zoom link had the very slightest of delays. Melissa

was wearing a grey jumper dress, which Amanda thought an odd choice for what was certain to be sweltering heat in America at this time of year. After a polite but brief introduction from Melissa to them all, and vice versa, Amanda was just about to begin their well-rehearsed speech when Melissa beat her to it.

'Ladies,' she said in a soft Louisiana drawl that more than matched Chad's, but with none of his charm. With her brown hair in a high ponytail, no make-up on and glasses, she bore absolutely no resemblance to her brother, who was without doubt one of the best-looking men any of the women had ever set eyes on. 'Whilst it's pleasant to put faces to the names I've been seeing on our production wage sheets, may I ask why Jake Monroe is not at this meeting when it appears to be only senior staff in attendance?'

Her directness threw Amanda, so Helen, unplanned, stepped in to buy her some time.

'Well, Melissa, we didn't feel we could be so open with Jake being here because the truth is—' she began, before Melissa cut her off again.

'Ms Gold, I just need to make you aware that I have a software system running that takes down all the minutes of our meeting as we are speaking. It sends them directly to the board of investors of the Kane Foundation, including my father, who as you know have the power to grant or decline any CITV requests that are filtered via me. The full Kane Foundation investment board are all also online via our software system. Chad will be sent the transcript when we conclude. But before we proceed, I would like to ask you: are you happy to continue with whatever your sentence was going to be now I have made you aware that everything we say here will be recorded?'

Her tone was businesslike and unemotional.

Amanda was aware that it was now Helen who was stuck for words and Farrah was staying silent for fear she might say something personal she'd been warned repeatedly not to. Amanda straightened in her chair and faced Melissa.

'I can confirm that all three of us are happy for this conversation to be recorded and documented word for word,' she said confidently.

Melissa looked at her after the time delay and appeared to type a few words into the keyboard in front of her at the other end of the Zoom. The room Melissa was broadcasting from was very different to Chad's ornate office with pictures of Madeline on every wall. It had clean white walls and filing cabinets behind her. It was almost as plain as she was, Farrah noted.

'Now that's clear,' Melissa continued, 'please begin.'

'How is Chad, by the way?' Amanda asked, with genuine concern, as they all liked Chad.

'He is as expected,' Melissa replied, then gestured for her to continue.

'Good. I don't mean good, I mean – oh, I'm sure you know what I mean,' Amanda said, in a fluster as Helen nudged her under the table in a way that suggested she needed to get a grip. 'Well, I am glad it's you we are able to speak to tonight as what we have to say wouldn't have pleased him. I can speak for all of us in this room and at CITV when I say, none of us want to displease your brother.'

Helen and Farrah nodded.

Melissa seemed to appreciate the clear affection they had for her beloved sibling and took off her glasses as Amanda continued.

'A few months ago, before he began dealing directly with Jake – which was also before he handed control over to you – he was very clear with us that he did not want

Madeline's vision of *Falcon Bay* to be destroyed.' Amanda emphasised the word *destroyed* strongly. Helen was impressed with her tone.

Melissa tilted her head gently to one side with what appeared to be the first sign of genuine interest.

'He told us that if *Falcon Bay* could no longer maintain the high standards that Madeline's restructuring had bestowed on us, and keep its success in the ratings, that she alone was responsible for . . .' As the words came out of her mouth, she felt like she could choke on them. In reality it was Madeline's very 'revenge-filled reboot' of their beloved show that had sent it into a spiral of decay in the first place, but truth had no place in tonight's meeting, so she pushed through. 'I know there have been several internal memos reinforcing that statement recently, especially since Tabitha Tate was installed on the island, so it is with sad regret that we have called this meeting tonight with the aim of being true to our promise to your brother's wishes. I am sure you will be aware that not only have we slipped another ten places in the ratings, meaning we are now outside the top ten, but we've also lost ten of the countries Madeline's power had regained us.'

'I am aware of these facts,' Melissa said, emotionless, 'and we were due to discuss them at our scheduled conference call next week.'

Amanda sensed a snip of irritation that Melissa's planned meeting had been brought forward but was also pleased she was talking to an open door, in that the failings of the show had already been noted.

'Jake assured us that this was normal coming off what happened at Christmas,' Melissa said, again emotionless about how the Christmas episodes had achieved their historically high ratings.

Amanda decided to continue before Melissa could repeat

any more of whatever lies Jake had obviously already started to spin.

'That is true about Christmas,' she continued, 'and please understand that the next statement I make, the one Helen was going to begin, is in no way related to my personal connection to Jake . . .'

'Or mine,' Farrah threw in, painfully aware she hadn't spoken at all and felt that if anything was a safe line to say, it was that. She could have sworn she saw Melissa's eyes cast down towards her bulging baby bump briefly as she lowered her head to tap something into her keyboard, perhaps responding to a message that had popped up on her computer.

Helen threw up her hand as if they were in school. 'Or mine, by the way,' she said quickly, then leaned back into her seat, making it clear Amanda had the floor.

'Noted, please continue,' Melissa said, scanning all three women's faces as she spoke.

'But that is not the reason our show is floundering. Nor is it because of all the terrible press, which hasn't helped. The real truth is *Falcon Bay* is from a different era. The world's viewing habits have changed. Madeline knew that, which was why she was she was so ambitious in shaking up our format to make us relevant, and her plans worked whilst she was here. But without her, we are sinking faster than the *Titanic*, Melissa. As much as it pains us, all of us,' she gestured around the room, then over to the cast photos where Catherine's face still appeared to be watching over them, 'we believe that the time has come to end *Falcon Bay*'s reign whilst it is still as close to Madeline's vision as she wanted. Let's preserve its legacy for future generations and honour her memory of the show she was so passionate about.'

Her words reverberated around the room, which with only Helen, herself and Farrah in it seemed vast and empty, and there was a slight echo as her words hung in the air. Melissa, who showed what Amanda assumed was the first sign of surprise they'd seen in the whole meeting, took in what she'd said. Then once again she appeared to be typing into her keyboard, responding to questions Amanda assumed were coming in from the board.

'How does Catherine Belle feel about this decision?' Melissa said when she raised her head. 'From what I've been told, she is as passionate about *Falcon Bay* as my brother's wife was.'

As head of casting, Helen decided to field this one. 'It is her true love of the show, like your late sister-in-law's, that sees her in agreement. She is by far our most highly paid star and is still under a two-year deal, yet she has confirmed she'd rather sever her contract with no penalties or payouts from us early in order for us to send the show off on the high it deserves. We have no doubt that the rest of the cast will follow her. They all have the same desire for *Falcon Bay*'s legacy to be kept intact so future generations can look back on its forty years on-air and see it as the legendary show it was, rather than the one it's about to become.'

'And this is where you want to reference Jake, I assume?' Melissa said, not looking at them, but typing into her keyboard as she spoke.

'Yes, Jake wants to keep working on this show at whatever cost to the quality of output,' Farrah said, keeping her tone even and as emotionless as possible. 'I am happy to send you his latest plans for our future storylines. All, if you will allow me to be to be crude, are moral cesspits. Not only will what's left of our audience switch off in droves, but our syndication will desert us, and as the others have highlighted, do unfixable damage to our legacy and brand.'

'And you all feel this is the only way forward?' Melissa asked once again, without looking up.

'Yes,' the women said in unison.

'Ladies, please excuse me whilst I consult with the board,' Melissa said, then flicked the meeting into pause and muted her microphone.

Sensing they had a few minutes to discuss, Amanda clicked mute on their end of the call too for fear of being overheard.

'What do you think?' she asked anxiously.

Farrah shrugged, but Helen looked more positive. 'If she's consulting with the board, it means they must have been watching our decline. When she comes back on let me lead. I've got an idea I think might just seal the deal.'

Amanda nodded, then they all watched the screen as Melissa unmuted and un-paused the meeting and her face returned to the monitor.

'Thank you, ladies,' she said. 'Whilst it is our true desire to honour my brother's wishes, we do have to consider the shareholders in CITV. *Falcon Bay*, although clearly not what it was under Madeline's reign, is still the network's only syndicated show. If we were to cease production, we would effectively be ending CITV's revenue stream, which would be a bad business decision, and the Kanes do not make bad business decisions . . . The board believe if you truly feel our show has peaked and that no new blood can restore it, it would be a better financial decision to sell the network immediately – with *Falcon Bay* still running as an ongoing concern – perhaps into new hands that could keep the show going.'

Amanda's heart plummeted at the thought of yet another set of owners coming in, probably falling for Jake's usual lies, and them all being in an even worse situation then they had found themselves in. But Helen was ready to pick up the baton.

'Forgive me for interrupting here, Melissa,' Helen said

straightforwardly. 'I mean this with all respect. The Kane Foundation, including Chad, have been open with us from day one that apart from Madeline none of you have either the interest or experience in television drama content.'

Melissa, slightly taken aback by Helen's directness, nodded, wondering where she was going next.

'So, what you won't know is that when a huge show goes off-air, on a high, not a low, if it's still in syndication – which we currently are – then those international sales go through the roof. Nostalgia sells way more than anyone's current output. You only have to look at *Friends*, which has made 100 times more in repeats than it ever did during its original run, because there are no production costs. Everything is pure profit.'

Melissa seemed interested and typed a few more words into her laptop, which Helen took as a sign for her to carry on.

'It is my suggestion that you cease production on *Falcon Bay* whilst it's on a high, then sell the repeat syndication globally before you sell the network. That way, your shareholders will retain all of the indefinite profits, with none of the costs, and then St Augustine's and the CITV buildings can be sold separately. For decades fans from all over the world have been wanting to visit our private island and the sets they've known and loved from our glory days. The profit alone in a company that will want to initially run the island as a tourist destination will see the Kane Foundation make back ten times what Madeline invested in its purchase. Trust me when I say this is the way to go. As much as it hurts us to admit it, we've reached the end of our course on an ongoing production, but it would hurt us more to denigrate *Falcon Bay*'s brand until it was worthless, and then none of these profitable options would be available to you.'

Melissa watched Helen, who was in full flow, and as good as any of the show's leading ladies in what would definitely have been a season finale episode.

Before she could comment, Helen went in with her killer line.

'I feel sure it's what your brother would want for Madeline's memory and that's why we are here sacrificing our own lives in a place we love to be honest enough to say that we want to preserve what he cared about most, his wife's wishes. This is all of our opinions, including the whole of the production team, except Jake. We want to be honest and reveal we have not consulted him because, as we said earlier, with no personal malice, his vision of what is considered a successful show is one he can cash a paycheck from for as long as possible, at whatever the damage. That's very different to what Madeline would have wanted. So, we hope you will take our honesty and integrity seriously. As you can imagine, we have not presented this option lightly. It will be life-changing to all the cast and crew here on the island that we like to think of as family.'

If Jake could see us now, he'd explode, Farrah thought, stifling the desire to laugh out loud. Even Farrah herself couldn't have written a better speech than Helen had just delivered, nor could Catherine have acted it half as well, and that was saying something.

'Please hold for a moment, ladies, whilst I consult with the board,' Melissa said, then paused and muted her end of the call. Amanda turned their camera off and turned to Helen and hugged her.

'That was amazing,' she said, smiling.

'It really was,' Farrah added, and patted her on the back.

Helen was about to speak when she noticed the mute button on their side was not activated. She gave the women a smile and whispered quietly, 'Stay quiet, we're about to find out if it's worked or not.'

Amanda turned their camera back on. The three women held hands under the table and, after what was at least ten minutes, Melissa finally reappeared on the screen and her mute button was unsilenced.

'Ladies, firstly I want to thank you for the selfless way you have presented this option to myself and the board.'

As her words rang out, Helen worried they sounded like the beginning of a well-rehearsed speech she would use at open casting calls for talent when they were casting new roles. She always said thank you before delivering the harsh blow that none of them had impressed her enough to make them stars. She steeled herself for the brush-off and her mind began to whirl as to what they would do next now this had failed.

Amanda and Farrah looked on in silence at Melissa. They couldn't tell if she was enjoying the pause before the next part of what she was about to say, or if it was still the slight time delay in the connection. They readied themselves for the worst.

'I have consulted with the board and my father. We will of course have to get consent from my brother, from a legal point of view – as you know, he is still the actual owner of CITV – but we at the Kane Foundation agree this sounds like the right decision at the right time.'

Had they heard right? The women all looked at each other, then back to Melissa for reassurance.

'Which part?' Amanda said gingerly, hardly daring to tempt fate in asking for specifics.

'All of it,' Melissa replied, emotionless. 'We will cease production, bring in the finest syndication experts to sell the show into the nostalgia market and then put the island and the buildings up for sale.'

291

None of the women could speak. So Melissa carried on.

'All that is left now is for you to decide how *Falcon Bay* goes out on a high deserving of my brother's wife's wishes. Ms King, we grant you the power to deliver the news to Mr Monroe. After your display of openness at your own cost this evening, we trust you to decide the way our loyal audience will wave goodbye to a cast Madeline liked to think of as an extended family. We will send him an official letter, confirming that you are once again the official show-runner. But for the sake of lawsuits, he will stay on, if he so wishes, up to the last episode, as your second in command – is this understood and accepted, before I start the ball rolling?'

Amanda, in shock that she'd now got one over on Jake again, albeit just for the last few months of production, nodded.

Melissa then turned to Farrah and Helen. 'Ms Gold, we've seen Mr Monroe's promotion of Candy Cooper into *Falcon Bay*'s press officer. But you know the show the best. With no casting left to be done, and now the decision to cease production has been made, are you happy to finish your role at CITV by resuming the press officer role and making sure the world sees us go out with the attention you all deserve?'

Like Amanda, Helen was also speechless and nodded; that would really piss Candy off, she thought, trying not to grin.

Finally, Melissa's eyes turned straight to Farrah. 'Farrah, I am aware that you are our finest director, and I know you are due to give birth late in the summer. But it only feels right that, after being such a driving force in this decision – and also suffering the way you must have with the things you saw directing the Christmas episode – we feel that you should direct our cast's goodbye. The board would like it to be a live episode.'

'Live?' the three women said in unison.

Melissa smiled. 'Yes, ladies. Let us go out in the most spectacular way you can think of. I will leave you to come back to me with details, but,' she looked down at some notes, 'with Farrah's due date being in eight weeks' time, I suggest you get cracking on the finale of all finales.'

Farrah smiled and rubbed her bump. 'You have my word. I will work to the very last moment possible,' she said, feeling excitement that she'd been given the honour of directing what was going to be a show that would go down in history. She just prayed this baby wasn't planning on arriving early.

Melissa smiled again. 'I believe that concludes tonight's business. Emails will be sent confirming plans tomorrow, so that gives you twenty-four hours to deal with it on your end before this becomes knowledge within the building.'

Again, the women nodded, still not quite believing they'd pulled their plan off.

'I'll bid you goodnight,' Melissa said, and with that she was gone and the live feed cut.

Amanda was the first to speak. 'Well, that's it then.'

Helen, sensing she was already regretting what they'd done, leaned towards her.

'Remember we talked about this. It was the only way we could leave here on a high. Don't start fantasising about what we've lost. That had already gone. Start thinking about what we are now going to achieve and what that will do for us in the future – we've managed to dock a sinking ship and save its brand. You know it will only be a matter of time before someone decides to bring the show back, and when they do, they'll come for us, the women who saw it go out on a high.'

Amanda nodded tearfully. She knew Helen was right but it still stung to think the show she'd risked her freedom for twice was about to be cancelled, and at their own hands. Farrah, sensing her spiralling thoughts, attempted to lift her spirits.

'Stop that, and keep remembering, all shows like ours get rebooted,' Farrah said confidently. 'I give it two years before Apple, Netflix or Amazon are wanting *Falcon Bay – The New Generation*. It's happened with all the big shows a few years after they come off-air. It *will* happen to us, and when it does, with new bosses and no toxic past, we'll get a fresh *Jake-free* start.'

Helen nodded. 'She's right, the *Dynasty* reboot is already in its fifth season and it's global. We'll be back, this isn't the end. It's just a break before our new beginning. And remember,' she added with a grin, 'you get to tell Jake that not only is he working for you again, but in about eight weeks, he won't be working here at all.' She smiled and gave her a wink, which Amanda returned as she nodded, hoping her friends were right.

The three women rose from the table together and walked over to the window of Meeting Room 6 to look out onto the beautiful night sky. It was lit by the hugest moon they'd ever seen. After a moment of taking in the view, they scooped themselves into a group hug, then, hand in hand, made their way out of the room. They were ready to set the wheels in motion that would begin the end of their lives on the island and the show they loved with all their hearts.

Part 4 – The End?

Chapter 29

Amanda had been amazed at just how free she'd felt in the eight weeks since the decision had been made for *Falcon Bay* to come off-air. After their midnight meeting with Melissa and the Kane Foundation, she'd spent the night crying in Dan's muscular arms, mourning the other baby she'd fought so hard for. That's what the end of *Falcon Bay* felt like to her, like the loss of one of the many babies she'd tried desperately to keep alive, before she was eventually blessed with her gift from God, Olivia.

It didn't mean that all the others before her were not still on her mind though. Sometimes late at night she'd log in to the chat forums for women who'd suffered miscarriages or, even worse, stillbirths, and take solace in knowing she wasn't alone in her grieving or the guilt she felt that she'd eventually got her little cherub. Olivia was getting bigger and more adventurous by the day, whilst the others had not.

One morning, when Dan was feeding Olivia, she'd called him Dada. It was one of her first proper words, and although technically she'd been wrong, in Amanda's heart she knew Olivia was right. Jake might have provided the DNA but in the nearly a year she'd been with Dan the three of them were more of a family than she'd ever been with Jake. As she snuggled deeper into Dan's arms as he slept, she looked up at his handsome face and wondered if the price for Olivia and now having found the true love of her life was the loss of *Falcon Bay*. As her eyes studied his rugged profile and thick eyelashes, which moved ever so slightly as he slept, she decided if that was the deal then she was happy with the trade-off.

That midnight Zoom conference had sealed *Falcon Bay*'s fate, and since then everything seemed to have gone in a blur. She'd been expecting resistance at the secret team meeting with every exec apart from Jake, where they'd delivered the news that, forty years and seven months after the first episode, July 4th was going to be the last day they would be on-air. Helen, with the help of Dustin, had done a sterling job of getting everyone on side, including the crew, who were notoriously difficult, especially if they'd decided to bring in their unions. But somehow, they'd done it. The crew had even made the whole process easy, suggesting that going out on a high rather than a low, and with the team's reputation intact, would make it all the more easy to find work in television again, rather than lumber to a halt in an embarrassment of Jake's design. They had almost cheered when the news was announced that they would cease production. There had been tears too, but they were happy ones, ones that came when people realised they were making the right decision, albeit for the wrong reasons.

In Amanda's opinion, if Chad hadn't reinstated Jake, she felt sure she could have kept the ship afloat. But she was wise enough to know that the world had changed. Even in the eighteen months since Madeline had acquired the network with the goal of taking them back to number one, they'd been in trouble, and as much as she hated Jake she couldn't even lay it all at his door, just a lot of it.

Falcon Bay cost millions per episode to make and with reality TV being the most popular, and cheapest, programming around these days, eventually their number was always going to be up. Even in America there were only two long-running soap operas of *Falcon Bay*'s magnitude that were still in production. It was as if overnight they'd been relegated into dinosaur territory, but without the *Jurassic Park* ratings.

She breathed in Dan's gorgeous scent, and she smiled as she thought about how sure Helen was that they'd be back. After a few off-the-record chats with some of the biggest on-demand producers, she now believed it too. It would be on a much smaller scale, and probably in a shorter run, and definitely away from the gorgeous private island of St Augustine's, which she could see through her beach bungalow's windows, looking more beautiful than ever. But as her mum had once said, all good things came to an end, and as much as she hated to accept that, sometimes that was true.

There was still the positive that thanks to Jake's absolute fury at being ousted from the top power position *again*, he'd hardly been seen in the production office from the moment she arrived in their former shared office. She was barely able to conceal her excitement at having the power over him once more to deliver the news, even though it was essentially bad news for all of them.

She'd dashed up the stairs to Jake's office after hosting the meeting. Everyone but Jake, Candy and Helen were present as she'd officially announced she had pulled the plug on production. With Amy from HR noting down the minutes, she knew she only had moments to get to Jake before those minutes got uploaded and shared in the central notes system

– then reached Candy's iPhone. She'd no doubt be scanning it constantly while they were in the meeting.

Helen had craftily arranged not only to stall Candy from sharing the news with Jake, but to steal Amanda's thunder. Helen also planned to explain the gravity and global interest that the demise of one of TV's most famous shows was going to be met with from the press. It was going to be way above her experience, so despite the recent promotion Jake had given her, which would have seen her in charge of the stampede of requests from around the world about to head their way, Helen herself would now continue on in her acting role as official press officer. She would allow Candy to assist her, essentially giving her another skill on her CV to help her find work after the whole of CITV found themselves unemployed after the last episode wrapped.

Amanda hadn't even had time to find out how Candy had reacted by the time she'd appeared at Jake's door. Her peach jumpsuit was feeling tight as her skin glowed with the effort it had taken to ascend the five floors in her six-inch Stella McCartney heels.

'Menopause?' Jake said dryly from behind his desk, noticing her flushed face, as she entered without knocking. 'It's not a surprise really, is it? Without all those IVF drugs, which cost me a fortune, you'd have probably been through it years ago,' he said with a smile.

Fuck, how she hated him. There had been a moment, just a brief moment around the third floor, when she'd wondered if despite everything that had gone on, that maybe, just maybe, when he heard it was over, that they'd somehow connect over their love of the show. Like Darth Vader in a *Star Wars* movie, she knew that despite his power-mad, alpha-male mode – which he'd been in ever since he was promoted – somewhere there must have been a shred of the man she'd once said 'I do' to, and that had once held her hand in the IVF clinics in the early days.

She'd given up trying to reach him long ago, and with Dan by her side, certainly had no desire to ever try to reconnect to what they'd once had when he was a decent human being. But for the sake of Olivia, and the baby he'd fathered by Farrah, which was just weeks from being born, she'd prayed that for their sake something good was still left in him. Even though Farrah and Helen had goaded her into rubbing his nose in the news when she reached him in his office, she really wasn't planning on doing that. He might have sunk below a surface that she recognised, but the night she'd covered up what had happened on Christmas Day and jeopardised her freedom, all for her obsession of keeping *Falcon Bay* alive, had shown her that that level of obsession with being in power was dangerous. It wasn't somewhere she ever wanted to find herself again.

'I think you'll be the one who is sweating in a minute, Jake,' she said with a smile, as she flopped into one of the armchairs by the terrace. She made a mental note to check if she could take them when they cleared the offices. After all, she had found them in a local reclaim store and had them re-covered in a gorgeous blue leather that mirrored the dazzling ocean they faced.

Jake raised an eyebrow as Amanda grabbed the aircon control and flicked it onto max.

'And I ran up the stairs, actually,' she said.

'Ah yes, still fighting the baby weight,' he snipped. 'That's one thing I'll say for your friend Farrah, she's still kept her figure around *my* baby's bump. It hasn't spread out everywhere like it did on you.'

His words stung her and took her right back to how vulnerable she used to feel, being naked with him after Olivia's pregnancy had changed her shape. It hadn't been until Dan had made love to her on the private beach that belonged to her house that she'd truly been able to understand just how damaging Jake's criticisms of her body had been. For months, she wouldn't even let Dan see her naked, made sure every light was dimmed, or candles were on, and only with the strategic use of lingerie had she felt able to share her body with him. She hadn't felt confident enough to expose it. But one early evening, with Olivia asleep and after several cocktails inside her, she'd found her clothes had fallen away as they rolled around the sand. She'd reached for her discarded sarong. Dan had gently held her hand back, worked his lips along her body and kissed each of her stretch marks. He hadn't said a word. He didn't need to. She knew what he was saying by his actions and they made her feel loved and worthy of love, the opposite of how Jake had made her feel. Remembering how much Dan loved her meant Jake's arrows missed their intended target of feelings, but she was about to score a bullseye.

'I can't stay long, but if you check your email, you will see the minutes from the meeting downstairs,' she started.

'What meeting?' Jake asked, clearly thrown.

'It's all in the email,' Amanda said with a smile as Jake looked down at his computer screen and started scanning his inbox.

'Well, it better not be anything major, because nothing on this show happens without me greenlighting it,' he began in his pompous manner. Amanda continued to smile, knowing that any moment now the email with the minutes would tell him that there wasn't going to be a show any longer.

'What the fuck?' he exclaimed as he looked up from clearly having discovered the news.

Amanda got out of her chair and walked over to his desk,

which was still covered with some of the nicest-looking trophies *Falcon Bay* had won over the years. They were supposed to go in the display cabinet but of course Jake wanted them to look like they were won by his hands alone, so he always kept the Emmys and BAFTAs around his computer.

'Yep, we're coming off the air, and I'm in charge again until we do. It's all there in black and white and there's no point in going whinging to HR or the legal department because you're still getting the showrunner's wages and your contract paid out. You just won't be running the show because I will – well, until there isn't one to run any more,' Amanda said, enjoying knowing not only that Jake was reeling from the bombshell news, but also that clearly he was the last to know. She reached across the desk and for a moment their eyes locked.

'And you know what, I'm glad it's over,' she said. She grabbed the biggest Emmy on his desk, which said *Best Serial Drama 1999*. She'd always been proud of that one because it had been her storyline that had won it for them.

Jake was, for once, speechless, so she took the opportunity to step back with the award and begin her exit.

'I'm taking this, as well as taking control of our entire exit storyline,' she said, as she made her way towards the door. Jake watched her, open-mouthed. 'Our final filming date is July the fourth – it's a fitting date, isn't it?'

She reached the door and gave Jake a smile. 'Although I'm obviously sad we've come to the end of our journey as a show, I am thrilled to know that professionally at least, I'll never have to see you again. Obviously, if you ever want to see Olivia then I won't stop you. I can't say the same for Farrah. That's down to her to decide, although with your track record I doubt either of us will have to be dealing with you for access visits.'

She let that land; Jake remained silent. In all the years she'd known him, this was a first.

She gestured out towards the view from the balcony, with the Emmy in her hand. 'I won't lie,' she said with genuine affection. 'I will miss St Augustine's Cove forever and it will always be in my heart, just like *Falcon Bay* will be, but unlike you, I'll be leaving here with a partner who loves me and friends who will always be in my life. I know for a fact you won't be doing the same, so as much as it pained me to be the one who brought our once glorious show to an end—'

Jake suddenly rose from his chair and cut in.

'You?' he said, his tone incredulous.

Amanda stepped back into the room so they were a little closer; she was ready for the kicker now.

'Yes, *me*. When it was clear that once again your reckless disregard for not only our show but its audience was going to ruin a legacy for those of us with respect for our craft, I simply could not allow it. So I was the one who persuaded the Kane family that it was time for *Falcon Bay* to flee its nest and soar into the sky with the best of TV's golden memories. Rather than be dragged down to the depths of the ocean, lower than that heinous shark you brought here last year when the true rot of your poisonous ways made it clear the only way for us to protect what we all love so much was to take it away from you for good.'

Jake just stared at her. It was all too much to take in. For once, he couldn't think of a single thing to say.

'So, for absolute clarity, as I already said, even though you'll continue to be paid the showrunner rate, you'll have no say in the way *Falcon Bay* is ending. Attend the production meetings if you want, or go home, cash your cheques and work out what you are going to do with the rest of your sad little life. Either way, I'm not bothered.'

She smiled again, enjoying what she was sure was a slight slump in Jake's ever-high shoulders.

'Oh, and I know how you hate to be left in the dark, so, just in case you can't face Meeting Room 6, the entire production team was behind me on this and everyone made sure you were excluded. I'm guessing you might feel a bit uncomfortable going in to look at the storylines for our exit. I can assure you now that we'll be going out on a high. Our grand finale will be an uplifting, gloriously positive happy ending. For the world's favourite leading lady. And one that our cast, crew and most importantly our audience deserve after all these years they've stayed loyal. They'll be no monster lurking on the day we go *live*,' she finished, with a smirk.

'*Live?*' Jake spoke, as if finally registering what she was saying.

Amanda's face finally broke into the huge grin she'd been holding back since witnessing the shockwaves that were battering him – just like the waves on their glorious beach did against the rocks below the very office they were stood in.

'Yes. I may not have agreed with your storylines last Christmas, Jake, but I'm professional enough to recognise a ratings winner when I see one, albeit not with the tragic ending yours had.' She wasn't going to tell him the live idea had come from Melissa, deciding Jake wasn't the only one who could steal a great suggestion.

Jake eyed her. 'So what is our final storyline then?' he said, almost sounding defeated.

'Lucy Dean will marry Marcus Lane, meaning she'll get the happy-ever-after the whole world, apart from you and Madeline Kane, have always wanted for her. And in a lovely twist of fate, which I am happy to be the first to reveal, as

303

it's another piece of top-secret information you were not aware of, Lee has proposed to her in real life, so we'll actually be witnessing true life unfolding, as life imitates art. Because when Catherine and Lee say 'I do' as their characters do, it will also be for real and forever, making television history as well as capturing a wonderful moment of love on screen and off. There won't be a dry eye on the sound stage, let alone around the world, and the press will go mad for it. It's a perfect ending,' she said. Then she added an extra kicker: 'And to think, had you not brought him back, this might never have happened, so I guess there's one thing to thank you for. Making Catherine Belle happier than ever.'

Beyond the shock, anger and betrayal Jake felt at the Kanes allowing this to happen behind his back, and seeing Amanda gloat at regaining the power he loved so much, deep inside, even with his hatred for all of them, the TV man in him knew this was a juggernaut ending that not even the best of his put-downs could pull apart. In fact, it was genius, and if he didn't despise Catherine Belle so much he'd have loved to take credit for it himself.

He thought for moment as to whether to comment on it or not. He wasn't used to Amanda having the upper hand. It reminded him of that dreadful Christmas evening when Madeline had called him into this very office and dismissed him with no explanation as to why. All he'd known was that Amanda and the other bitches of *Falcon Bay*, Helen, Farrah, Catherine and her bitch agent Sheena, had found some way of getting control over her, and somehow they'd done it again with the Kanes. As he watched Amanda waiting for his reaction, he considered if it was worth showing that he wasn't ready to just take this lying down. He decided there was more power in working out what, if anything, he could do in the few weeks they had left before *Falcon Bay* joined the rest of the world's once mega soaps in the annals of history and went into syndication.

'So now you know I'll be off.' Amanda's words cut into his thoughts. Jake nodded as once again she began to leave. 'Oh, and one last thing, I've signed the divorce papers. My solicitor says you still haven't. Could you get on with it, as I'd like to leave St Augustine's with only good memories with me, not the bad?'

'What's the rush?' he replied, surprising himself at his honest question. There had been flashes of the strong defiant Amanda that he'd fallen in love with all those years ago during the showdown in his office. Why was he only seeing it now? he wondered, as she hovered in the doorway.

'Oh Jake,' Amanda said, almost with sympathy. 'Didn't you notice this?' She held up the Emmy award again and angled it so her engagement ring was flashing in his face. His eyes took in a single, solitaire diamond set in platinum.

'I thought not.' She laughed. 'Dan asked me to marry him. There must be something in the air! Obviously, I've said yes, so the sooner we can get everything tied up the better.'

She took one last look around the office, which had been witness to the best and worst times that any marriage or work environment could ever imagine and certainly way more dramatic than most of the scripts that had played out on their famous sets. She looked him straight in the eyes.

'I don't hate you, Jake,' she said softly, and for a minute he wondered if she was suddenly feeling that same strange stirring feeling he'd had for her just a moment ago.

'I *pity* you,' she continued from the doorway, as she looked down on him in his chair behind his desk. 'You threw away everything we had and could have had in the future and sent this show on course for disaster with your obsession of being in control, whatever the cost. You've ruined everything that

305

was good in your life and all so you could be the king of this castle. Now, just like the water lapping at the shore outside, it's all being washed away from you – so roll on July fourth. I don't think Independence Day has ever been more appropriate,' she said with a wide grin.

And then she was gone.

Chapter 30

In her dressing room, Catherine Belle was re-reading the scripts Farrah had written for *Falcon Bay*'s final episode ever. She'd already learnt them, but knowing the episode was going to be live somehow made every letter of every word mean even more than they usually did.

Catherine always gave every script that featured Lucy Dean her all, but seeing the words *Falcon Bay Episode 3025 – The End* really made it hit home. Despite the excitement and confidence of the others that the show would be brought back by a new production company in a few years, she knew that whether it did or it didn't, this truly was the final episode of the show that was once so important she'd killed for it. Yet it no longer filled the void in her heart anywhere near as well as being united with Lee.

She realised now that as much as she loved acting, it had been one long escape from her past or broken relationships. Even all those years ago, when *Falcon Bay*'s original casting director Caroline St James had discovered her acting above a pub in Dublin in a cheap production of *The Importance of Being Earnest*, she'd only been in it by accident. She'd never even dreamt of being an actress, let alone a star. She had fled to Ireland to escape a violent gaslighting ex who'd battered her heart and self-confidence, and was only on the dirty pub floor stage playing the part of Gwendolen as a favour because one of the usual am-dram players was ill. It had been fate that Caroline's nephew had been in the production and the only role on the soon-to-air *Falcon Bay* they hadn't cast was that of Lucy Dean.

Looking back, when they'd offered her a new stage name, a trip to London's Harley Street for a tweak to her nose and breasts, and a new home on the stunning private island of St Augustine's, it had all seemed like a dream. And it had been, for decades, before Madeline Kane had turned up and revealed herself to be the blast from Catherine's past she had never been expecting. By the time she'd been on *Falcon Bay* thirty-nine years her broken romance with Lee had been replaced by a dedication that she was married to the show. At least it couldn't hurt her, abandon her, or betray her. Well, that again had been the case until Madeline had turned up and things had never been the same again.

When you'd looked into the eyes of a woman as she died you were never quite the same – or seen the brains spill out of a man's head, crushed by the battering it had taken on the rocks. Less than a year after she'd fought to the death to stay here, Catherine was surprised at how relieved she felt to be leaving. *Bizarre*, she concluded. Then she smiled as she looked down at her gorgeous ornate, twenty-four carat emerald engagement ring. It sat raised in a little cage above a diamond-covered rose-gold band. She lifted it to her face and kissed the stone. She'd always believed gemstones had special powers, so when Lee had popped the question when they'd been told the news that their final show would be their characters' wedding, it seemed fitting that the real ring he'd given her (but that she'd paid for) would be the one that would be seen onscreen by millions. Two happy-ever-afters combined in one. Her heart had nearly burst when he'd asked her. The knowledge that this live episode would go down in history for all of the right reasons helped Catherine push memories of that dreadful Christmas Day with Madeline, and her fight on the platform with Ross, from her mind, but still every now and then they crept back in.

'Happy thoughts,' she said out loud three times.

She tapped her chest in the way her therapist had taught her to deal with the anxiousness she'd suffered since giving up the Xanax. Although, despite her doctor's warnings that she'd suffer panic attacks and withdrawal effects for months, she'd barely felt any different. Again, she put that down to Lee; he had a calming effect on her that was better than any drug.

'Yes,' she said out loud, turning to admire her reflection in the mirror. 'Everything will be behind me when I'm off this island. I'm ready to start again.'

She smiled and began practising the delivery of her lines. Her final scenes would be a TV first. Her wedding to Lee's character Marcus on the beach would be done without them using their character names. Instead of an actor playing the role of a marriage officiate, they would have a real one, meaning the ceremony that millions would watch was a dual one. As Lucy and Marcus said 'I do', so too would Catherine and Lee. It was not only a truly romantic gesture of Lee's, but it was a genius idea, so much so that Lee suggested they present it to Amanda and the team. They too thought it was a fantastic way for the show to go out with a heart-filled bang; it just all felt so right.

Lucy Dean, the character she'd played for over half her life, deserved a happy ending. Thanks to Lee's love showing

Catherine that there was more to life than pretending to be someone else, she finally allowed herself to believe that she deserved this too. After the scripted on-screen celebrations, Lucy had one final speech, which was part delivered to the cast of characters who lived and worked in the fictional cove of St Augustine's. They would gather around to wave Lucy and Marcus off, ready for their new life away from the Bay, thus bringing a close to one of TV's longest-running shows. It was a magnificent speech, the kind an actress could wait a lifetime for and never get, and it was partly delivered to the audience at home, too.

'I may be leaving the Bay,' Catherine practised, looking in the mirror and using the soft accent she used for Lucy Dean, 'but you'll always be in my heart. Wherever I go, wherever I am, you will always be in my heart and thoughts. You've always been there for me, for the good times and the bad, and I hope I've been there for you too. You'll always be my family. You only have to think of me and I'll feel it. Our bond is unbreakable and I'll always love you.'

In the script, this line was directed as down the barrel. It was so rare in drama to break the fourth wall and appear to speak to the audience at home, but again, Farrah had pitched this just right. Every word in the speech was true for Lucy *and* Catherine. As the final directions had her waving goodbye, Lee would pick her up and carry her off down the boardwalk as the credits rolled. She knew that even she'd struggle not to cry.

She placed the script down, then turned her attention to the elaborate Vera Wang wedding dress that was sparkling under the reflection of her make-up mirror's light at the far end of the room. Again, she'd been willing to pay for the dress. As much as she adored Brad, she didn't want the moment that was also going to be *her* moment too to have been anything less than perfect.

Brad had surprised her – he'd contacted Vera's press office only to find she'd been a fan of *Falcon Bay* all her life and had gifted Catherine the most stunning dress she'd ever seen. She'd cried when he'd told her. All these years hadn't been for nothing. She'd brought pleasure to people all over the world as she'd played out Lucy's tragic but heroic life in the show's arc, from the poorest viewers in shanty towns – where the show was dubbed on cable – to what she imaged was probably the most beautiful New York townhouse where Vera Wang had watched. They'd all rooted for Lucy. She was so pleased that, unlike Madeline and Jake's horrendous plans to have her character killed off in the most humiliating way last year, fate, as twisted and as guilty as she still felt, had intervened and given Lucy the farewell she deserved.

She walked over to the dress and ran her fingers over the soft lace of the neckline. She imagined Lee kissing her exposed flesh and felt a tingle between her legs at the sheer thought, then let out a little sigh of excitement at the image of them being alone again tonight after filming.

After placing Lucy's famous charm bracelet on her arm, and picking up her red crocodile-skin Hermès and her script, she headed out of the dressing room and down the corridor to the large doors. When she pressed the giant red button to the side of them, they opened to reveal the exterior beach and boatyard Cove set, which was covered in sunshine.

Her toes hit the sand as she walked towards the crew. A huge smile spread across her face as she took in the sign above *Falcon Bay*'s world-famous beach bar, The Cove. Yes, she thought to herself, as some of the crew waved and she waved back, she really was finally ready to close its doors forever. And finally, in her new life with Lee, far, far away from the place she'd done something she'd never believed she was capable of, she hoped that her future would help her finally forget her past. She wanted to be the good woman she knew she was, not the woman Madeline Kane had forced her to become, or the one Ross Owen, or that vile Tabitha Tate, had tried to portray her to be. She knew now that only a fresh start could set her free and she was literally counting the hours until she could finally close those terrible chapters and the guilt that still plagued her night and day, forever.

*

A mile away from where Catherine was about to start filming, in the Blue Lagoon hotel on the outskirts of St Augustine's, Sheena felt a shadow cast over her on their gorgeous terraced bar. She'd been seated there to enjoy her mimosa and scan the menu. She'd usually have stayed with Catherine when she was on the island but didn't want to disturb her and Lee's love nest. They'd barely spent any time together since Catherine had rekindled her romance. With the way things had been back at Madeline's funeral in Louisiana, and then with the tension of the aftermath of Ross's death pushing them even further apart, it was sad but probably a good thing that their relationship had reverted back to more agent-and-client than best friends.

She'd booked to stay at the Blue Lagoon for the last week of *Falcon Bay*'s production and luckily she knew Serge, the owner. He'd given her the biggest suite they had, which over-looked the whole of the glorious bay, with the exterior set of Lucy Dean's Cove bar just about visible in the distance. Once she'd settled in, she'd turned the aircon on to full whack; the weather was unbearably hot this summer. After unpacking, she'd arranged via text to meet Catherine for dinner later that night after she'd wrapped. Serge agreed to lay out a table in a private corner further away from prying eyes or ears. And, Sheena was desperately hoping, away from Lee and the hustle and bustle of the bar downstairs.

Once alone, they could reconnect, and maybe she'd be able to change Catherine's mind about the bombshell she'd dropped when Sheena had said she was coming down to discuss the future. Even Catherine uttering the words 'retiring from the spotlight' seemed unthinkable, but for the reason to be so she could go travelling around the world with Lee at the exact time when she was at her hottest and most marketable was utter madness. Even though she was secretly dead set against the marriage, she'd done her job and the honeymoon deal with *People* magazine Sheena had negotiated was worth a million alone. It proved that when you were fresh out of one of the biggest episodes of any TV show ever aired, in love or not, this was no time to be doing a Greta Garbo.

From the moment Amanda had confirmed the show's end date, she'd been sourcing a whole host of juicy contracts for Catherine to cash in on now she'd be free of the network's code of conduct for advertising. It meant she'd finally be able to make millions from endorsements from everything she wanted. And everyone wanted a piece of her. Sheena was sure that later that night, when she showed Catherine all the offers on the table, she'd be able to change her mind. She'd gently remind her that the moment you were off TV, the cash clock was ticking on how long the good offers would roll in. She'd insist that Catherine needed to strike whilst the iron was hot. The 20 per cent she'd make if she agreed to all the deals she'd brought contracts for to the hotel alone would buy her a gorgeous little villa in St Tropez, which she'd had her eye on. She'd decided they would dine alone, rather than inviting Amanda, Helen or Farrah to catch up as she usually would, so she could really concentrate on her pitch when she had Catherine alone.

Aware she was still being hovered over, she finally looked up, expecting it to be an overzealous waiting staff member wanting to take her order so they could free the table up for the hordes of journalists, press and fans that had booked pretty much every single hotel upon or anywhere near the island. They were all desperate to make sure they didn't miss any exclusives on TV's biggest show's farewell. She hadn't seen St Augustine's this packed since Christmas Day, and at least there was no chance of a repeat of what happened that day. The memory of the shark clamping its jaws on Madeline Kane's body as she screamed sent a shiver down her spine. She was about to politely but firmly say she hadn't decided what she wanted yet when she realised the face staring down at her when she finally raised her violet eyes – framed by her famously applied catlike winged liner – was not that of a waitress. It was Lydia Chambers, her ex-client and *Falcon Bay*'s final hiring.

In her entire career as an agent, she'd only been fired once. Well, technically it was twice, but it was Lydia Chambers and another ex-client Stacey Stonebrook, and they'd teamed up to do it together, so she only counted it as once. And Stacey had never worked a single day since she'd allowed herself to discount her entirely. Lydia, however, had rarely left the head-lines. She'd milked the demise of her losing the role on the now infamous Christmas Day episode – it went to the then missing Honey Hunter, who Lydia had even done a bizarre on-air appeal for on one of the morning TV shows. She'd stated how worried she was for her and, explaining that fear of failure and mental health amongst actors must be more respected, urged Honey to make contact with the fans around the world who loved her. She'd carefully cried just as the presenter wrapped up the feature.

It was one of many unsubstantiated rumours said to be the reason that Honey had fled the set hours before she was due to film her comeback role as Tania Dean, the part that ultimately Madeline Kane had taken for herself. Nothing had been confirmed, so Sheena had thought it was pretty distasteful to jump on the bandwagon of a woman she knew Lydia hated anyway. But when she saw her milking the tragedy of Madeline's death for all it was worth too, using the line that she had been due to step in for Honey, which was untrue, she'd begrudgingly had to tip her hat to her.

Now the truth of what had happened to Honey had been revealed via that scurrilous little shitbag Tabitha Tate, she wondered if Lydia felt guilty about using her for publicity, when it turned out she was the one living in a true nightmare. The thought of what she'd read in Tabitha's reveal still sent shivers down her spine. But being a queen of spin herself, Sheena had to admit that at the time – and being unaware of the horrendous truth, which was spinnable matter – it was quite a clever move on Lydia's part. Even when it was announced that Jake Monroe had hired Lydia to play Catherine's latest enemy in the show, Sheena hadn't held it against her.

Lydia of course crowed about 'her big return' and repeatedly mentioned doing the deal herself on her Twitter page, taking several public digs at Sheena online. Tweeting 'why have an agent when you can do it all yourself?' and using the crown emoji. Considering Sheena knew Lydia was a blind-as-a-bat technophobe who could barely work an emoji or write a text, let alone run her own social media, she knew it would be one of the fans who ran her websites who'd posted it. But Lydia would have sanctioned it. As annoyed as she was that she'd let that one slide too and not tweeted back, she'd had bigger problems to deal with. And with her mind firmly on trying to persuade Catherine against her plans to disappear,

Lydia taking a seat at her table for the first time they'd set eyes on each other since that day in the Langham in central London where she'd humiliated Sheena was not going to be on today's menu.

Before Lydia could speak, Sheena coolly said, 'Can you move, please, you are blocking my light?'

Lydia was wearing huge sunglasses, her perfect figure clad in a red maxi dress with exposed décolletage, and had her hair in soft curls bouncing on her shoulders. Sheena thought she looked a bit like Farrah Fawcett in the seventies. She moved out of Sheena's light but straight into the seat opposite her at her table.

'If I was unclear, let me explain what I meant – fuck off,' Sheena said curtly but quietly.

With so many industry bods on the island, the last thing she wanted was a rehash of the headlines surrounding the departure of two of the McQueen Agency's biggest names. Several so-called social media influencers had gone to town saying 'the queen of soaps' was losing her touch. The media had nicknamed her that for years, for having represented more actresses on long-running soap operas than any other woman in the business.

'Please hear me out,' Lydia said quietly. Always one to read a room's temperature, she'd followed Sheena's lead in aiming to keep the conversation they were having in public as private as possible. She didn't take her sunglasses off, hoping that if they were papped, perhaps no one would spot it was her.

Sheena picked up her mimosa and took a sip. She'd looked after Lydia for twenty-five years. She knew her body language inside out and the presence opposite her wasn't that of the gloating diva she'd been watching on TV before it was announced *Falcon Bay* was to be axed. Suddenly a lunch guest didn't seem such a bad idea, especially if humble pie was what she'd be eating.

'You've got fifteen minutes then I have a meeting.'

Lydia looked around over the rims of her vintage black Prada sunglasses, then, catching a waitress's eye, gestured she'd have the same drink as Sheena. It would save them being interrupted before she hit her full flow.

'Look, I know what I did was wrong but I am truly sorry,' Lydia began.

Sheena, unable to see her eyes, studied her, trying to work out if it was a performance or the truth. After all, Lydia had been a nightmare client to deal with, one of her most demanding in fact, but as an actress she'd been one of her best, so it would take a while for Sheena to work out which one she was seated with.

'Take off those glasses,' Sheena said firmly.

Lydia hesitated, then removed them to reveal the blue eyes that had graced a thousand magazine covers in the nineties and early two-thousands. Under Sheena's guidance, she'd become one of the highest-paid soap actresses on television. Her ego had seen her written out and turned into a laughing stock thanks to a writer's revenge of seeing her once glorious character die under a stampede of cows.

Eye to eye, the women both paused. Sheena was first to break the stand-off.

'Twelve minutes,' she said, tapping her Cartier watch. It sparkled on her slim wrist, a few inches up from the morganite cocktail ring Christie, her former married lover, had bought her during happier times.

'Don't be so ridiculous,' Lydia snapped.

'Well, that apology didn't last long.' Sheena laughed. 'You might as well go now.'

Lydia leaned closer and kept her voice low. 'Listen, Sheena,

I've said sorry and I mean it. I've come to talk to you about business and whether you're ready to accept it's genuine or not, I know you well enough to know that money certainly helps speed up the forgiveness process with you.'

The waitress arrived with Lydia's drink and Sheena signalled that she was ready for a top-up too.

'Go on then,' Sheena said with a smirk.

It was true, there wasn't much a few zeros couldn't do to change her mind about how she felt about working with someone, even someone who'd publicly betrayed her. One of the pieces of artwork in Sheena's office was a Banksy that had the words 'Everyone has a price' sprayed on it. She'd paid 100K for that in his early days and it must now be worth millions, but she wouldn't part with it, because in her case it was certainly true.

'I have it on good authority that Catherine is retiring,' Lydia started.

'That's not true,' Sheena said, in the same tone she used to use when Ross Owen used to call her office with a story on a client that *was* true but knew he didn't have the proof to print it – she would call his bluff.

'It is true. *Lee* told me, and if anyone would know, it's him.'

The way Lydia said Lee's name made Sheena's ears prick up. Sharing Catherine's private affairs was not a good sign, especially at such a vital time.

'Anyway, *how* I know is not important.' She looked down at her own watch, which was built into a gorgeous emerald-encrusted Cartier bangle. 'If I've really only got ten minutes to talk to you, I better cut straight to the chase,' she said, then took a sip of her drink and tossed her famous golden curls.

Sheena nodded for her to continue.

'Talk is that *Falcon Bay* will be coming back as a reboot.

I'm assuming you've seen the new story arc they've given my character for our official exit?'

Sheena nodded. She studied all the scripts that her talent did; it was the former actress in her. She still found them fascinating. Plus the fact that she represented Farrah too, who wrote most of them, meant she had a doubly vested interest in knowing what was going on.

'When Jake hired me, they promised me a two-year contract and the usual showbiz blah blah, but we both know that they know when a production ceases, there's no way to make them honour that.'

Sheena raised an eyebrow, as high as it would go with the amount of Botox she'd recently had pumped into her perfect forehead, to show that she did indeed understand what Lydia was saying. She was surprised she was talking about money. She knew Lydia wasn't short of cash, thanks to some very clever investing in prime real estate during bumper payday contracts that Sheena used to negotiate for her when she was one of the most famous faces on TV.

Sensing Sheena's train of thought, Lydia continued, 'But there's one thing they are honouring, even if it's just for the exit, and it's exactly why I've come to see you.'

'Go on,' Sheena said, genuinely interested.

'In the final episodes, my character still takes over The Cove Bar as well as most of the businesses and men of St Augustine's. Even though the old show is going off-air, I'm the one character left in prime position to open the new one when it comes back. With Lucy Dean gone it leaves Claudia as *Falcon Bay*'s leading lady, and you know the fans love me in this role. I've still got it, I still want it, and I'm prepared to wait for it to come back. When it does, I want you to handle the deal.'

'Don't you mean *if*?' Sheena countered, even though she

knew that Amanda had had some very positive meetings about bringing the show back as a limited series for the binge-watch generation in about eighteen months' time.

'We both know it will. And you know these reboots always feature new leading characters. Although I was furious at the idea of coming off-air so soon after I've just got back on it, you know how much I've wanted to work.'

Sheena dropped her shoulders a little, remembering how hard it had been for Lydia during the years no one wanted to see her, and felt a chink of the connection she'd once felt for her during their glory days.

'I do,' she said more softly, 'but just because Catherine is saying she wants a break, doesn't mean that when the call comes for the reboot, if they want her, she won't do a U-turn and want to come back.'

'I understand that, as an actress of course I do. But as an agent you must be able to see the fact that I'm twenty years younger than her and the show is going out with my character in control of it. That must leave me in a prime position to be the lead, and we've made a lot of money in the past together, Sheena. You know when it was good it was great.'

Sheena nodded.

'So I've come today to say if you will take me back, I'd like you to represent me from right now. I don't want to miss a moment of anything from the second that live episode comes off-air. I want you to be using the heat it's given me to keep the flames alive. I couldn't bear to lose it all again, I really couldn't,' she said with genuine emotion. Tears welled up in her perfectly made-up eyes, and Sheena knew them to be real. She reached across the table and squeezed her hand.

'*If* we do this and things get rocky again, or we hit a dry patch, or *Falcon Bay doesn't* come back, do you swear that

you'll never do what you did to me in the Langham again?'
Sheena couldn't bring herself to even use the words of that
dreadful day.

Lydia reached out both hands to hold Sheena's and looked
her dead in the eyes.

'I promise, as long as you'll have me, I will never leave the
McQueen Agency again.'

Sheena's heart felt a little flutter. She'd never had children
and even though she and Lydia were very similar in age, there
was something very parental about the responsibility of being
someone's agent. That's why it had hurt so much when Lydia
and Stacey had left the way they did. Whilst they held hands,
she reasoned that if Catherine really was intent on a hiatus
from the spotlight, she might very well be able to shift a fair
amount of these contracts she'd sourced for her over to Lydia.
Maybe that South of France villa would still be coming her
way after all. She pulled her hand back from Lydia's and
picked up her glass.

'OK, you're on.' She smiled and raised it to gesture a toast.
'Let's forget what happened. It's been less than a year anyway,
let's just move forward and get you some juicy deals going.'

Lydia let out a girly squeal that sounded decades younger
than it should have coming from a woman in her fifties. She
knew with Sheena back on her side and the power of the live
episode round the corner, those horrible dark worries that
had kept her awake at night with the idea that no one wanted
her again when production wrapped would be well and truly
banished from her mind.

'Thank you, I won't let you down. I'm really ready to go
for this. I want it more than ever and this time round I'll
appreciate it more than ever,' she said, raising her glass.

Sheena met it with hers with a loud clink. That alerted a
table of press and paparazzi, who'd been eating the hotel's

famous locally caught swordfish, and they suddenly realised they were just feet away from two of the tabloid's favourite women.

'Whoops,' Lydia said coyly, seeing the pap grab his camera and point it in their direction.

Sheena laughed. 'You never change.'

Lydia winked at her. 'Well, it's good news, isn't it? Let's let the world know who to call when they want Lydia Chambers.'

With that she stepped up from the table and addressed the packed room.

'Ladies and gentlemen of the press and real people, if there are any of you in here . . .' She laughed.

Row after row of chairs turned to face her and Sheena, who had now also stood up and was alongside Lydia. Her zebra-print jumpsuit and long dark hair complemented Lydia's look and together they were quite the picture.

'I know you are all looking forward to *Falcon Bay*'s live episode. I'm honoured to be leading the way as we guide this wonderful ship into the waters of TV history for one last voyage. But I want you to know that you haven't seen the last of me. My wonderful agent, who I know you all know, Sheena McQueen, already has some fabulous projects lined up for me that sadly we can't tell you about yet. But let's just say the end of *Falcon Bay* is just a new beginning for me. Watch this space, I'm back to stay!' As Lydia finished her speech, she pulled Sheena in for a hug.

The paparazzi flash bulbs went off all around them and Serge the hotel owner smiled from the far corner. The Blue Lagoon was the furthest hotel from the *Falcon Bay* set and usually the last to get booked up. As he gestured for the paps to change their angle to capture the hotel's sign – which was on the ceiling just above the two women – he felt sure the tourists who'd be visiting the soon-to-be abandoned CITV set buildings for the next few years would be making it the first on their to-stay list.

As Sheena smiled for the press, she wondered how Catherine would feel about the news she'd taken Lydia back on. There was a buzz about Lydia's enthusiasm that excited her though. If Catherine really was determined to set off into the sunset with Lee, maybe she shouldn't try to dissuade her. She was due a happy ending after everything that had happened and maybe with her gone it would finally sever the terrible memory of guilt that fell on herself and the others who had covered up for her. But she was going to make damn sure she made the commission off those honeymoon pics as a parting shot.

As more flash bulbs went off, Sheena smiled, deciding that Lydia's return to the McQueen Agency must have been fate. Her true calling had always been to fight like a tigress for her talent but it only worked if they wanted it, and Lydia did. Soon, away from the blood-stained memories of this beautiful but toxic island, and back in the safety of her beloved Langham Hotel the moment the live episode concluded, that's just what she intended to do.

Chapter 31

Tabitha and Fonda Book's MD Mickey Dean were already five hours into the eight-hour flight to Los Angeles. Thanks to the onboard Wi-Fi in First Class, she received the exact address of the secret location Vlad had moved Honey Hunter to. Even though the seats reclined into fully luxurious beds, Tabitha was sat bolt upright in hers and had refused the complimentary snacks and finest wines on offer. After what she'd seen, she couldn't face a thing. Turning to her side, she watched Mickey stuffing his face, and then when he'd finished, lying back, pulling up the blankets and quickly drifting off to sleep. She stared at him in disbelief that he could keep anything down, let alone now be snoring, after she'd shown him the recording of the video call Vlad had made to her from inside Durand's blood-splattered bedroom just before the police arrived and cordoned it off as the crime scene it was.

The moment Mickey knew he had Honey back, he'd told Tabitha to drop any further digging on Madeline Kane's death (which had been useful as even in the deepest of the CITV archive logging system there was no sign of those missing underwater footage frames). He said with Honey's story they now had more than enough to make tens of millions in sales. Tabitha, who had never ever been speechless in her life, and was certainly no saint, did not know what to say about his commercialisation of his supposed lost lamb's ordeal, before he'd even seen or spoken to her. She did however know evil when she saw it. There was evil on what she'd seen on that video call, and she recognised a flash of a similar evil in Mickey's eyes when, rather than focus on the horror of what Tabitha was explaining to him, all he'd been interested in was making Honey's kidnapping and torture the main story in the book.

He wasn't interested in keeping the horror of what had happened to her private, giving her time to recover; that's if she could ever recover from this. No, he was rubbing his hands with glee at sharing her ordeal blow by blow in the pages of the book Tabitha's name would be on. He wasn't interested in *Falcon Bay* at all, not now he had Honey's story in his fat greasy clutches. When they'd arrived at the private hospital Vlad had taken Honey to, she desperately wanted to run into her room and warn her that she might have just escaped the clutches of her predator within seconds of losing her life, but she was already under the surveillance of another.

Sweet Mickey Dean, the man who'd tempted Honey back into the limelight with his promises of love and care for the star, had finally been revealed to her for what he was, a heartless user. She'd scanned through all the archives to spot it was Mickey that had handed her the glass of champagne, caught on camera in behind-the-scenes footage of Honey's book signing. She'd watched the scenes over and over and saw Honey, who'd been sober for more than a decade, refuse twice before Mickey persuaded her 'one little one wouldn't hurt' – well, it certainly did.

Following the timeline, that's when she'd fallen off the wagon and began her descent into losing control of her sobriety so badly that, in desperation, she'd fled her starring role on *Falcon Bay*, just hours before she was due to film her grand entrance. She'd caught a similar flight to the one they'd taken, to LA, where, determined to get herself back on track, she'd arrived at the Durand Pledge Hospital to dry out, having no clue that the doctor who'd treated her more than a decade before had been waiting, hoping and praying that one day she'd return so he could enact his sick fantasies on her.

The crime scene of his house was covered in her photos, which she'd already, under Mickey's insistence, done a buy-up of via her police insiders. The pictures of Durand, who had shot himself in the face when Vlad had kicked the door in, were gruesome, as were the testimonies to the police of the so-called nurses who had been entrusted with looking after her. But nothing could have prepared Tabitha for the sight of Honey, who'd been botched by plastic surgery in an attempt to turn her back into the teen star the deranged Dr Durand had been fantasising about. As they entered the room where she lay, sedated but aware, she started crying when she saw Mickey, who in turn did the same, but Tabitha, who had taken a sharp intake of breath just at the sight of her, knew his tears were fake.

'My angel,' he said over the sobs. 'I never thought I'd find you.'

He cradled her as she wailed, telling her she was safe now. As Honey sobbed and held onto his wobbly body, Tabitha desperately wanted to run over and drag her away from him, but she couldn't because of the deal she had with Mickey. The book that was with zero doubt going to get her all the things she'd ever dreamed of – the money, the awards, the plaudits, the fame and glory – was going to come with a very heavy unexpected cost.

The sickening realisation hit her that she'd signed a deal with the devil, and if she wanted all those things, which she did, there was no way out. She turned her back as a tear dropped down her cheek, and she left the room desperate to get some air, for fear she was going to be physically sick.

Chapter 32

Helen's office had once been covered wall to wall with stars of the show past and present, casting awards, and all her mirrors, which had now been taken down and boxed up ready for leaving the room that had been her second home for thirty-eight years. The bare walls made the already impressive-sized room look even bigger. All that was left were the sturdy metal-and-leather desk, laptop, chair and phone, where she'd made calls that changed people's lives for the better and the worse. All that remained on the desk was a photo of her with her best friends Catherine, Farrah, Amanda and Sheena, taken for the show's twenty-fifth anniversary.

Helen picked it up and looked at their young faces; in truth, thanks to the wonders of plastic surgery, Helen, who was due to turn 63 soon, didn't actually look much different than she did in the photo. But the energy that they all radiated in the snap had definitely changed compared to the way they were around each other now. Still close, but that hope that had been caught in the moment had been knocked out of them.

She looked out of the windows of her balcony, which over-looked the candy-coloured cottages that were built into the cliffside running along the famous waters of St Augustine's. Helen forced herself to think back to all the good times she'd had on the island. She didn't want her exit to be defined by the present, and reminded herself that this was not goodbye, simply au revoir, as she truly believed they had a strong chance of getting the show back on air later via a streaming service down the line. Candy had broken down in tears when Helen had told her of her demotion but rather than enjoy her downfall, she'd embraced her, and Candy had told her all about how Jake had used her, to which Helen had told her she wasn't the first, and she wouldn't be the last, and that she mustn't blame herself. Candy had looked so shocked that Helen was being kind to her that she delivered a bombshell that in different hands could have meant that Helen had never got the chance to stand here and say goodbye to the pod of dolphins that swam past her office every day.

As her eyes followed them, knowing it was for the last time, she noticed one break away and seem to do a little dance in the ocean, as if it knew she was watching. A simple act of nature was all it took to bring a smile to her glossy lips, just like a simple act of kindness with Candy had made a lifechanging difference. She was just about to get her phone out of her bag and take a video of the dolphins as a memory when the door to her private shower, which was off the main office, opened and Matt, still naked from their love-making session, re-entered the room.

'Stay back over there.' Helen laughed, gesturing to him not to come near the windows.

She wouldn't normally have been concerned. She'd lost count of all the lovers she'd had in this office in front of that window, safe in the knowledge that no one could see them as the cottages were fake fronts for filming purposes – no one was ever able to overlook her. But to mark the end of production they'd positioned some cameras inside them to capture shots of the set and the bay that had never been seen before so that Lucy and Marcus's exit shot would truly look unique as they headed off in the distance. She was aware that today she could easily be seen.

'You come over here then.' He beckoned and held out his hand, which she took, and he pulled her into an embrace.

His hands roamed her body and he kissed her passionately. The silk dress she'd only just put back on after they'd made love on her desk was once again on the floor. With the strength of his powerful arms, he lifted Helen onto the edge of the desk and within seconds had entered her body, which was still wet. She let out a moan as he inched his way into her and ran his lips down her neck. Of all the lovers she'd had in this room, none had been in Matt's league, and that was saying a lot. Helen had had at least a dozen of the men who'd featured in *Vanity Fair*'s sexiest-man-alive polls in here, as well as a variety of hungry ambitious young studs who loved a cougar always on the prowl the way Helen had been.

But that was before she'd met Detective Sergeant Matt Rutland. Since they'd started seeing each other she only had eyes for him. Gently, he lay down on top of her, then rolled them over together until she was on top of him. As she felt him throb inside her he squeezed her breasts before pulling her down into another kiss as his rhythm intensified. He whispered something in her ear that she was sure she must have misheard. She pulled herself back up as she rode him, feeling she was getting close to climax. Her eyes met his and she pulled the face he knew meant she was nearly there.

'Say it,' he said, as he bucked his body underneath her.

He rubbed her clitoris expertly with his thumb in the circular motion that he knew drove her crazy. Every fibre of her being was trembling, not just at his expert handling of her, but at the words she knew he'd said and now he was urging her to say back. She hadn't heard or said that sentence in decades, allowing herself to believe that sex with younger men was all she needed. That and her career had kept her more than satisfied before Matt had arrived. His thumb movement intensified and with his other hand he pulled her bum hard down onto his thick thighs, meaning every inch of him was now pulsating inside her.

'Say it,' he said again, breathless. She could tell he was as close to coming as she was.

'I love you too,' she said.

The words seemed to float above her, as if they'd left her lips but someone else had said them. His eyes flashed with excitement as he let out an almighty moan as he flooded her with his seed. Helen came at the same time and allowed her body to collapse onto his, and they both lay naked, sweating, writhing as they kissed again, tongues roaming each other's mouths. As she lay in his arms, he held her tight. She was still breathless and could feel him still inside her as he whispered again.

'I really do, Helen; I want this to be forever.'

She was almost too scared to turn her face to look at his. Feeling such raw emotion was alien to Helen so she kept her lips buried in his gorgeous neck, the veins of which she could see pulsing hard.

'It will be,' she replied softly, deciding that it really was time to let a man nearly her own age love her in a way she'd always resisted. As they kissed again, in their frenzy she didn't notice the picture of her and the girls fall to the floor and the glass shatter around their faces.

Chapter 33

Farrah was gingerly making her way up The Cove set stairs when Amanda appeared from one of the stage doors and rushed over.

'You know you're supposed to use the ramp the insurers put in?' she said firmly but with affection.

'It's embarrassing!' a now-huge Farrah exclaimed, whilst continuing to struggle up the last two steps leading to Lucy Dean's terrace in four-inch stilettos. Amanda stayed close behind her as she alighted, then took a seat at one of the bar's chairs.

'Farrah, you are due to give birth in seven days, you shouldn't even be here.'

'There was no way I was going to miss this,' Farrah said, reaching the top then discreetly slipping into one of the Cove's bar seats. Amanda eyed her shoes and raised an eyebrow.

'Don't even say it,' Farrah started. 'If I am going to look like a python who swallowed a goat the very least I can do is keep my fashion dignity with my Stellas. Besides, these are actually very comfy,' she lied.

They'd been killing her all day but she felt they sent out

the exact message she wanted them to say: that she was strong, she was stylish and she was still sassy. In reality she was absolutely exhausted and the extra pressure of the shoes tilting her back with her massive baby bump was pushing her pain levels to new territories she'd certainly never visited. But with just twenty-four hours to go till they went live, she was determined to sashay away in the killer heels, fresh from her success of directing the last ever episode of *Falcon Bay*, rather than waddle. She had, however, started fantasising about the Terry towelling slipper boots she'd been given at last week's surprise baby shower in Catherine's dressing room.

She'd been adamant she didn't want a fuss and it had taken the trick of suggesting a rewrite to one of her scripts, something that always raised Farrah's hackles, to get her to be in the right place at the right time. Exhausted or not, she cared about every minute detail of her work, so she'd headed straight over to find Helen, Amanda, Catherine and Sheena, who'd travelled all the way from London to be in on the surprise for her. She'd cried at how much trouble they'd gone to and it reinforced just how much she'd missed seeing them daily.

It had cost a fortune to let the insurers continue to allow her to work on the show at thirty-nine weeks pregnant. It was thanks to a historic case of a former major cast member, the late actress Silvia Smith, who'd had such a leading role as barmaid Stella in The Cove Bar in the show in the seventies – and was needed in so many scenes – that they'd let her work right up to the day before she'd given birth. It was a good job they'd been able to shoot her from above the bar tops because if she was anything like the size Farrah was now (she'd googled the episodes to have a look at how well they'd hidden her bump), then it must have taken at least three barrels and four beer pumps to disguise her imminent arrival.

As she cast her eyes around the set, she could see there were now at least three extra health and safety team members, as well as CITV's resident doctor and nurse, dotted around in booths at the edges of the sound stage. All no doubt were ready to pounce if she should suddenly go into labour before they'd wrapped. But despite the constant twinges she felt, which did seem to be getting stronger, Farrah was determined that this baby was not coming out of her until those credits had rolled and she'd given her best to the show she loved as much as she'd come to adore the baby growing inside her. Despite never being able to forget its origin, after that very first kick, she was smitten with it, and truly knew she'd always be able to love it.

Since the show's cancellation she'd agreed she'd stay with Amanda and Dan for the first six months after the baby's birth, which Amanda said were the best and the worst all rolled into one. It had been Dan's idea. What a lovely man he was, Farrah had thought, when he and Amanda came to see her with pictures of the cottage they'd rented on an island about fifty miles from St Augustine's. It had an annex where she'd have her privacy, but they'd be on hand to help her through the sleepless nights, which Amanda had described as more brutal than the worst of any hangovers – and Farrah had had a lot of hangovers.

'I'm fine, honestly,' she said, hoping to allay the worried look on Amanda's face. 'And remember I'll be seated in the directing box all day tomorrow. I only wanted to climb up here one last time to take in the view.' She looked out to sea and the panoramic view of St Augustine's in all its glory. 'After all, we don't know who is going to buy the island, do we?' she said in a tone that caused alarm to rise in Amanda. 'This view could be blocked by high-rise hotels in a couple of years.'

'But Helen thinks it's bound to be turned into a set location destination. She thinks Disney might be interested and I've had at least three positive chats with on-demand production companies who definitely think we've got new life in us after a rest,' she countered.

'*Think* isn't actually fact, is it?' Farrah continued. 'Let's be realistic, the Kane family will take the highest offer for this place and an island like this is ripe for a developer to knock this all down and turn it into real estate.'

Amanda's face paled at the thought of all the history they'd created on St Augustine's being bulldozed to make way for the mega rich who wanted its views of their glorious ocean, which on a clear day you could see all the way over to France.

Farrah was aware her words had settled in Amanda's brain.

'I don't want to be pessimistic,' she said, seeing her friend's face flatten with the reminder that in showbiz, talk really could be just that, talk. 'I'm just saying, drink it all in like I'm doing.' She gestured out at the dockside bay set and along the boardwalk, which had been decorated with a wedding chapel, covered in bows and fairy lights, ready for the scene where Lucy and Marcus – as well as the actors playing them – would say 'I do' in front of an audience of millions. 'Because this may very well be the last time we get to see it like this. *If* we do somehow get Falcon Bay back on air it will never be on this scale, that's for certain. The backdrops will most likely be CGI.' Farrah rolled her eyes at how their industry had changed, then put her hand on Amanda's and gave it a squeeze as Amanda followed Farrah's gaze and looked around at the studio set they loved so much.

They both sat in silence, allowing the hubbub of the crew members moving around behind them to fade into the background as they listened to the water lapping by the dock below. As much as she hated to admit it, Amanda knew Farrah had a point. A permanently purpose-built set on a private island in one of the most expensive areas of the world would never happen in this day and age. If the show was rebooted, most of it would be green screen. There were hardly ever any real extras these days; computer trickery created the people needed to stand behind any show or movie's stars. Amanda felt it was sad that this was the future of TV, but the businesswoman in her understood that it certainly cut down on the production costs. After all, 'ghosts' as she called them didn't stuff themselves silly at the catering vans or have to be dressed by wardrobe. Yes, Farrah was probably right, they'd had the very last of the golden era of television and for that she wanted to be grateful. For a few moments she just drank in the scenery then eventually turned away from the sea and back to her friend's tired, beautiful face.

'Are you 100 per cent sure you're up to this tomorrow?' she said softly.

'I wouldn't miss it for the world, Amanda. I am absolutely certain.' Farrah smiled then patted her bump gently. 'And I've told this one that if he wants to come early, he's welcome any time, but only from the moment those credits have rolled and we've left this building. Not a moment before, or he's grounded till he's eighteen,' she said with a laugh.

'Well, let's hope he takes direction better than his father,' Amanda said dryly.

'*Sperm donor*, you mean; we don't use that word around here,' Farrah corrected her.

Amanda nodded. Though they both wished it wasn't true, Jake Monroe was both their children's father, whether he deserved to be or not. The one upside to this awful twist of fate was that Olivia would now have a blood sibling, something she'd thought would never be the case, as Jake had caused her remaining embryos to be destroyed by not paying the storage costs, without even telling her. Pushing the pain from her mind, Amanda decided she just had to focus on the upside; there was no other way round it.

Farrah sensed Amanda's mood had been jarred by the talk of Jake, which was understandably still a raw topic for both of them, so she decided to bring up the other elephant in the room that all the women had been worrying about. They'd already discussed the horrendous headlines that Tabitha Tate had leaked about what had really happened to Honey Hunter. Their understandable horror at finding out about her ordeal had sidetracked them from discussing Catherine's announcement that she wanted to wed Lee for real in the live episode.

Due to the chaos of organising the show's grand farewell and their desperate desires to go out with their heads held proud on an enormous high, and with so little time or budget allowed to make it the spectacular ending they wanted to give the show's fans, it had seemed like a PR gift. So they'd professionally rushed it through with little chance to discuss what they really thought of it, away from its obvious benefit to their careers and *Falcon Bay*'s fans.

As she went to speak, Helen, looking flushed in her pink silk dress, which was very creased, descended the upper staircase. It led down from the press gallery built for tomorrow's farewell episode. She entered The Cove Bar through the side set doors and joined them at their table.

'Ahh, here you are,' she said with a smile, taking a seat close to the huddle. 'Nice shoes,' she said, taking in Farrah's gold heels, which made Farrah pull a smug face at Amanda, who looked at Helen disapprovingly.

'Just cos she's up the duff doesn't mean she can't keep her edge! Sheena's waiting for us,' Helen said with a smile. 'She's just finished dinner with Catherine *early* and said we should meet her at the Blue Lagoon bar. Shall I call a buggy? I have massive news to share too, but I want it to be all of us together.' She was well aware that her heels were even higher than Farrah's, and didn't fancy navigating the beachfront walkway to where the boat was moored, in which they could sail up to the Blue Lagoon's waterfront entrance.

Farrah smiled, then thought about it again. She so didn't want to show any sign of weakness, but she'd had a late tech run tonight with Lee and Catherine, who'd insisted on running their vows over a dozen times, essentially using the rehearsal for their own benefit, and there were the ever-growing pulsations she could feel deep in her baby bump. She knew that if she was going to be on top form for tomorrow's big day this was one invitation she was going to have to pass on.

'Not for me,' she said, which made Amanda smile at her being sensible for once.

'OK, understandable,' Helen said, with a wink towards her bump. 'Then I shall deliver the good news now.' She looked around the set for floating mics and signalled for the women to turn off their headsets, so they could not be overheard.

'You will not believe what happened in the meeting I had with Candy during the coup,' she began, in hushed tones.

'It was weeks ago,' Amanda said. 'Why are you only just mentioning whatever it is now?'

Farrah pulled an expression that suggested she didn't understand either.

'Because it's taken this long to get something off her that she said she would give me. I didn't want to mention it until I was sure she was going to, and now she has. We all know she isn't in our trusted circle. Well, she wasn't, but thanks to this she is now.'

Amanda pulled another face, which Farrah copied.

'What are you talking about?' they both said in unison.

338

Helen smiled, then reached into her Fendi handbag and produced a battered and cracked, water-damaged phone.

'This, exhibit A – or it would have been had Tabitha not broken her promise to Candy to take her with her, and had Jake not treated her even worse than he did you two, if that's possible. She's sided with us, which is why we've now got this. She's promised never to tell anyone about it. Don't you understand? This is great news. We're in the clear, girls. We can leave the island with no worries that anyone is ever going to link us to Ross's death. All the footage from that night, including all of us with his body in the water, was captured on this and it still works,' she said, smiling.

'I wasn't actually there, remember? But I do understand your point, this is bloody great news,' said Amanda.

The colour returned to the women's faces, and Farrah loosened her protective grip on her bump as Helen got closer.

'So there's now nothing to worry about. I know we never liked her but she's actually done a good thing. I'll tell you the full story when we've got the live episode out of the way, but in short, the man you married and the one you let knock you up,' she said, eyeing them both, 'has been using her for sex, and treating her like shit. It turned out she'd been working for Tabitha Tate on that book from the inside.'

Helen carried on. 'But now, with poor Honey Hunter's ordeal being the main focus of Tabitha's filthy tell-all, she's no longer interested in us. Candy came across Ross's phone, the one Sheena was looking for that night, which would have given Tabitha what she was after the whole time she was here: something to link us to one of the mysterious deaths on this island. If Tabitha had honoured her promise to take Candy to the States with her and not just left her behind, Candy would have given it to her and we'd all have been fucked.'

Amanda gasped again at the realisation they had,

unbeknownst to them, been within a sharper-nailed handover of evidence that could have blown their lives apart. Helen was quick to try to finish her story and to get to the point she was trying to make.

'So, given what Tabitha and Jake had done to her and the news the show was coming to an end, when I gave her the demotion in the meeting she had a full-on breakdown. I genuinely felt sorry for her, and we connected, and I said I'd help her get work. She was so grateful and surprised because I could have kicked her when she was down, and then that's when all this came out.'

Farrah rolled her eyes. 'And we're trusting Candy Dace now, are we?'

'In this instance, yes,' Helen said firmly. 'I'm going to keep her under my wing workwise. And I was there, she's been damaged by broken promises and she finally understood, having been on the receiving end of the worst of Jake herself, what we've been going through. So she's on our team now, and most importantly, it's over. There's nothing that can go wrong now, or come back to bite us. Sorry, wrong phrase, as I'm just about to go into the Madeline Kane section,' Helen said, trying to rush her words out, aware there was a lot to say and not a lot of time to say it. 'So, to wrap up, she told me Tabitha could find nothing suspicious on Madeline. We're clear on that. And now I have the only copy of Ross's recordings, which link us to him, and I'll be destroying that later tonight. We're free, we can leave with no worries. It's over, in every single way,' she finished with a huge smile, and pulled the women into a hug.

Amanda and Farrah looked shell-shocked as the realisation of what Helen had recounted sank in. Eventually Farrah let out a huge breath that she hadn't realised she was holding in.

'Are you OK?' Amanda said, looking worried.

'I am now,' Farrah replied. 'God, I didn't realise how stressed I was about that until Helen just told me it's over. I'd been pushing it to the back of my head, but it was always there, you know, the worry.'

Amanda nodded, as did Helen.

'And you are sure we can trust Candy?' Farrah said.

'Yes, I am. You had to be there to see it. She was broken and I was in the right place at the right time to connect with her. It must have been fate because now we're leaving this island free women, with nothing hanging over us,' Helen said, beaming again. 'I can't wait to tell Sheena and Catherine! Speaking of which,' she said, changing her tone, as if what she had to say next was even more important than the bombshell news she'd just dropped. She pulled her phone out and showed the girls a text from Sheena. 'Look at this Sheena sent me earlier about the dinner she had with Catherine.'

She's brought bloody Lee with her to our meeting and he's chipping in on every suggestion or job I have for her, acting like her agent. I could scream. See you later, I need to get drunk.

She'd signed off with an angry-face emoji.

Helen grimaced. 'Not a good sign, him getting involved with her deals, is it? And I know you're not coming now, Farrah, which is understandable, but apparently Catherine has just texted her saying she's missing our farewell dinner too.'

Amanda and Farrah looked at each other in agreement.

'I can't ever get her alone these days, can you?' Helen asked – both of them shook their heads. 'He's with her 24/7. Even when you ask to meet her for a coffee he turns up. The only time he's not there is when he's in scenes without her – and even then, he has her watching him act from the sidelines,' she said, raising an eyebrow.

'Maybe it's just the way they are together,' Amanda said with hope in her tone. 'I mean, they have so much history and they've waited all these years to start again. I guess it's understandable they'd be inseparable.'

'*Inseparable* is one thing,' Farrah added, fishing in her handbag, looking for a snack she'd taken from the catering table earlier. 'I know it's a brilliant coup for the show, so I am absolutely *not* criticising you for jumping at their offer of it for our final twist. We've all more than gone along with it and I was thrilled to write it.' She paused and took a bite of the frosted cherry muffin as she looked in Amanda's direction. 'Let's be honest, if we didn't want to leave the show on a global high, which we know *that* stunt will achieve, and if we weren't all *so* desperate to get off this island and put what happened here behind us, we'd never have supported the idea, let alone agreed to air it. We'd have staged an intervention and told her it was way too soon and way too public.'

Helen and Amanda watched Farrah in full flow, talking with her mouth full, both aware that everything she was saying was true.

'If it goes wrong and he leaves her as soon as she's not the hot telly star any more, she'll be humiliated globally. They'll never take that clip off YouTube, like they did with the other one,' she said darkly, referring to the infamous footage of when Catherine and Madeline Kane had gone to battle by the very waterside the women were seated just twenty feet from. 'And if she chooses not to work, that's her choice, but he's really just a middle-aged man, who thanks to a good set of genes and plenty of workouts still has a pretty face, isn't he? His acting's only so-so – no one's going to be knocking down his agent's door trying to sign him up for another gig like this. Jake only brought him back to cause trouble, which certainly backfired, but now he's had a taste of the A-list life again, who knows what he'll be like with her in a few years, or even months down the road when his profile drops? She's actually turning down jobs, or worse, for him. Still, if she does change her mind and work again but no one wants him, we all know how bitter they get when they feel unwanted.'

Helen raised her eyes. She knew only too well how needy and nasty a male actor could be to his more in-demand actress partner if his career had turned cold yet she was still desired. She'd seen it a million times.

'OK, so we've taken our eye off the ball,' Amanda said, holding her hands up in a way she'd always done when she knew she was in the wrong. 'But in our defence, I think we've all done above and beyond for Catherine by covering up for her. We put our freedom on the line *twice*; if that's not a show of friendship then nothing is. I think we can be forgiven for not looking this real wedding gift horse in the mouth even if it does go wrong. You know I wouldn't normally say something like that, and I love her, like we all do. So much so, we all risked going to jail for her, so on balance I think it's a fair swap.'

Helen looked around, making sure no one was within earshot, and Farrah gestured for Amanda to be quiet, raising her eyes to the overhead mics above The Cove Bar. They should be turned off, but one could never be too careful on set.

Amanda took the hint and dropped her voice. 'So let's be hopeful, give him *and* them the benefit of the doubt and get behind *her* choice. Tomorrow when she says 'I do', in character and as herself – let's make a pact to wish for the best. Remember, we're used to seeing the worst in men; maybe he'll prove us wrong. Like Dan did for me.' She smiled.

'And Matt has done for me,' Helen added, her cheeks flushing.

Farrah laughed. 'Well, I knew it was serious when you didn't send us a pic of his cock in the WhatsApp group – you've never not done that before!'

Amanda let out a giggle. She'd never share a picture of Dan's gorgeous manhood but she had used to enjoy looking at the slew of Helen's conquests, who were only too happy to pose for the camera, fully aware she'd be showing their prize assets off to her friends.

'*No one* but me is seeing Matt's monster, not now, not ever,' Helen said with a smile.

'Blimey, it must be good,' Farrah said. 'Cos I never thought I'd see the day the cougar of St Augustine's Cove would be tamed.'

'And I never thought I'd see the day *Falcon Bay*'s most unmaternal woman would not only be happily up the duff – *but* by the man she hated most on this earth,' Helen replied in a tone that was clear she was having fun with her and not in any way making a dig.

'Touché,' Farrah said, pulling a grimace at the reference to Jake. 'But can we stop this talk of sex, please, as this has been an understandably dry spell and I don't want any excitement down there right now. If my la la wakes up she might pop him out early!' she said, and moved in her seat, which showed the others how much her back was hurting.

Amanda stood up and tapped her watch. 'Right, you get to bed, Farrah. We'll go and meet Sheena at the Blue Lagoon and tell her the good news! God bless Candy eh? Who knew she'd be the one to ease our minds in the eleventh hour?' She kissed Farrah on the cheek and Helen did the same.

'Do not use the stairs to get down. Promise me you will use the ramp,' Amanda said sternly.

'Yes, Mum,' Farrah replied, and let out a sigh. Helen helped her out of her chair and she tottered in her stilettos towards the ramp under the watchful eyes of the set medics, who were following her every move and would escort her back to her condo.

'And don't start till midday, we'll handle the tech,' Amanda called after her. 'You can log in to the gallery from home and give your directions to the crew. We'll use the remote system we installed during the Covid pandemic. We've still got it, it will save your energy for our big night.'

Farrah actually thought this was a brilliant idea, giving Amanda the thumbs-up as she went down the ramp. She smiled at the thought of wearing her slippers all day before having to squeeze her swollen feet into the crocodile-skin Gucci high-heeled mules she'd promised herself she was going to wear as she took the helm for the most important day of their professional lives so far. She wished Amanda had said it all a bit more quietly, though; she hated anyone thinking she was taking it easy.

Twenty minutes later, Helen and Amanda had filled Sheena in on the news. She was looking stunning in an emerald-green linen suit with just a hint of a black lace bralette underneath. She too was relieved that another link in their freedom chain was now secured, and took the phone off Helen, saying that thanks to dozens of client misdemeanours being caught on camera over the years, she had more experience of making sure every part of its memory was destroyed, so she'd do it herself.

The three women sitting at The Blue Lagoon's best table on the dockside looked and felt happier than they had in longer than they could remember. After all the online coverage Sheena and Lydia's impromptu photo call had brought to the hotel, Serge the owner had insisted on taking their table closer to the water than any of the others. So they not only had privacy but were all wonderfully lit by the gorgeous pink and gold lanterns that lined the jetty that led any dinner guests arriving by boat up to the entrance. The waterside was vast and as the women celebrated the turn of events whilst eating dinner, several boats came and went in the background. It certainly made for a perfect final evening setting.

'It's absolutely rammed in here,' Amanda had said in surprise at the queues of people trying to get in.

With it being the furthest hotel from the set on the island, it was one she rarely went to. Helen pulled her phone out and flashed her Twitter page at Amanda, showing Sheena and Lydia posing up a storm here just hours earlier. Amanda had rarely looked at social media since last year's embarrassment. Footage of her accidentally being sick – due to the worst hangover she'd ever had – on one of the show's actors, whom she was sacking, had been leaked from CITV's security cameras. She'd trended as a GIF. Now, she looked confused.

'But you hate Lydia Chamb—' Amanda began.

'Before you say another word, it's just a good business decision. She's apologised and we're giving it another go,' Sheena said, pouring everyone a drink.

Farrah surprised them by arriving at the last minute, back pain and bump spasms aside, wearing Gucci flip flops she'd disguised under the longest maxi dress she owned. She'd decided she couldn't miss the farewell dinner, even if Catherine did, and had turned up just in time to hear about Sheena's U-turn on Lydia Chambers. A glass of Cristal, which was chilling next to their beautifully decorated table, looked so tempting, but sadly she couldn't partake, opting for water with lime.

'You're here, Farrah!' Amanda exclaimed. 'We were just talking about Lydia Chambers.'

'To be fair, she's not been any problem on the show,' Helen said. 'She's a very good actress.'

Farrah and Amanda nodded. Both things were true, but it had been a very public humiliation when Lydia had sacked Sheena, and knowing Sheena held a grudge, there was still genuine surprise around the table about her U-turn.

Sensing they wanted more reasons, Sheena decided to give them.

'Catherine is adamant that she's quitting showbiz, so it was an obvious swap.'

'She's leaving you?' Helen asked, ripping off a piece of walnut bread, which she'd smothered in butter. She hadn't eaten a thing since she'd shagged Matt in her office and suddenly realised she was really hungry.

Sheena bristled at the choice of words. 'Not leaving the McQueen Agency, leaving the business,' she said with clarity.

Amanda, who was also tucking into the bread, having watched Helen go back for a second piece, chipped in. 'She won't mean it. Give her a year off and she'll soon miss the buzz. It's all she knows. She's been famous too long to give it up. She's just in love; after the honeymoon phase she'll want it all again.'

'Exactly, and when she does, she'll call me and I'll get the fires going for her again. But in the meantime, Lydia is going to clean up because she definitely wants it. It means at least all the effort I put into finding brilliant gigs for Catherine to keep her busy after we wrap tomorrow can now go to her. So my time has not been wasted,' she said, grabbing her glass and gesturing for the others to join her in a toast. Before she could do one Farrah butted in.

'How will Catherine feel about that? You know how territorial they get.'

'She actually said she was pleased for Lydia to get another

bite at the cherry. I guess it's easier to pass on a meal you don't want to eat.' Sheena shrugged. 'At the end of the day, it's her decision. I mean, look at the fact she's missing tonight and even you've made the effort to come,' Sheena said, touching Farrah's arm affectionately. 'But she said she wanted to spend the night with Lee.' Her words dripped with sarcasm. 'As if she's not going to be spending enough time with him from the moment we leave St Augustine's for the last time tomorrow,' she added dryly.

There was a pause between the women which acknowledged the sisterhood the five of them once shared was sadly missing one of its founder members.

'But anyway,' Sheena continued, trying to sound positive, 'I was about to propose a toast, wasn't I?'

The others nodded.

Sheena raised her glass once more. 'So this one's for Catherine, long may it all work out for her and Lee,' she said, with what the girls could tell was genuine affection. They all raised their glasses and chinked them together.

'To Catherine's new life,' they said in unison.

'And now we know the nightmare of the last year's events are behind us, to ours,' Sheena added. 'Particularly in your case,' she said, pointing in Farrah's direction. 'And to your romance,' she said, winking at Helen, who for once looked coy. 'And finally, to a proper fresh start for you,' she finished, looking towards Amanda, whose cheeks gave a rosy glow. She was thinking of Dan and Olivia waiting for her at home and how much time they'd all get to be together when the next twenty-four hours were over.

Helen picked up her glass again and tipped it towards Sheena. 'And what are we toasting for you?'

Sheena laughed. 'Oh, you know me, I never change. Work, fuck, work, fuck, work – and in that order. So basically, let's toast me being me – but without the worry of an unflattering mugshot looming now.' They all laughed too.

'Well, that deserves another cheers,' Farrah said, raising her sparkling water.

The others downed their glasses with a smile. At exactly the same moment the last of the champagne tricked down her throat, Sheena's eyes were drawn to three figures alighting from a boat that had just moored by the restaurant jetty. As her focus became clearer, she began to cough in shock, causing the last few drops of her drink to go down the wrong way.

Amanda leaned over and patted her back as the others looked on.

'Are you all right?' she said.

Sheena tried to gently cough and clear her throat without bringing too much attention to herself from other guests. She knew they included many members of the press who'd be reporting to news channels all over the world from the press balcony of *Falcon Bay*'s last ever show tomorrow.

'You've gone very pale, Sheena, what's the matter?' Farrah added. Now all three of the women were studying their friend's face, which had lost the cheerful glow she'd had just moments earlier.

As Sheena continued to quietly clear her throat, she used her violet eyes to gesture for the women to follow her gaze down the boardwalk to see what had made her choke.

Helen, Amanda and Farrah turned in unison to see Melissa and Chad Kane standing on the far end of the restaurant's jetty.

'Oh shit,' Helen whispered out of the side of her mouth. Farrah put down the piece of bread she'd been nibbling on and Amanda grabbed the Cristal, topped just her own glass up and took a huge sip.

'Exactly,' Sheena managed to say, finally having got her voice back.

The four women plastered smiles on their faces for the Kanes, who were heading their way.

'If Catherine loses it like Sheena said she did when she was near Chad in Louisiana, we're all fucked, and she doesn't even know we have Ross's phone yet either,' Helen hissed out of the corner of her mouth, as expertly as a top ventriloquist who'd worked the variety scene back in the day when that sort of entertainment was popular.

Sheena, despite noticing them first, was actually seated the furthest away from the Kanes, who were now just moments away from reaching them, and whispered back. 'I'll have to warn her he's here and fill her in on the Ross situation. Even with that sorted we can't leave her alone with Chad for even a moment. I'll go over to hers now. We've got to get her through tomorrow without confessing anything to him that could fuck us all up.'

The shift from calm into full-on panic mode had spread through all the women's bodies in seconds. They followed Sheena as she got out of her seat, grabbed her purse and headed towards the Kanes. Helen's heart did a triple beat at the obvious consequences of Catherine blowing the secret they'd managed to keep so well locked down in the eleventh hour. The thought of Matt even knowing she'd been involved in covering up the truth behind Madeline's death, and the inevitability of what that would mean for their relationship considering his job, was unbearable.

'I can't believe this,' Amanda said under her breath. 'I spoke to Melissa last night and she never said a word about them coming over.'

Farrah was the next to speak. 'Well, they're here, so everyone be on your guard. Just stay calm. As long as Sheena can get Catherine to keep her mouth shut, in twenty-four hours we'll be out of here, and home and dry forever.'

She watched Sheena have the briefest of interactions with Chad and Melissa as she made her apologies for leaving, jumped into one of the restaurant's speedboats and moved out of sight.

They all waved and did their best to look happy at the surprise heading their way. As Farrah turned to gesture a greeting, a pain ran through her bump, which was so intense it made her want to let out an actual scream. But she swallowed it down as the Kanes were now standing right in front of them and there was nowhere to hide.

Chapter 34

The next day, during final rehearsals for *Falcon Bay*'s last ever episode, which would air in just a few short hours' time, Candy paced the press area like a pop star enjoying the power she had over an arena of people who had come to see her perform. Scenes were being blocked out on the stage below the viewing platform the press were seated on, and several reporters were already doing live links with actors in view of the show's famous backdrop. She'd felt really bruised when that bitch Tabitha Tate had flown off to LA, breaking her deal to take her with her, without so much as a text message. If it hadn't been for Tabitha's exclusive on finding Honey Hunter that she'd seen on CNN, she wouldn't even have known she'd gone.

'Bloody Yanks,' she'd said under her breath.

But then, though Tabitha didn't know it, she'd actually fucked herself over too, because if she'd kept to their bargain, when Candy had discovered Ross Owen's phone in the lost and found archives deep in the basement, she'd have given it to her. And as horrific as the Honey Hunter headlines were, and they truly were, what Candy had seen on Ross's mobile footage would have given Tabitha even more to gloat about. It would also have been exactly what Jake had been dreaming of: a way to finally take down every woman on *Falcon Bay* that he hated.

So again, it was a bizarre twist of irony that the way they'd both treated her made her determined to make sure he didn't get his final wish before the curtain fell. When she first realised what she had, she was amazed it had survived weeks in the sea, and that no one, not even Tabitha, or the police when they'd first investigated his death, had bothered to check the lost and found area. Next, she started imagining all sorts of book deals of her own, showing Tabitha that two could play at that game, but the kindness of Helen Gold, who had not needed to be nice to her at all, when she'd lost it, caught her off guard.

She'd decided that karma, something her mum back in Australia was a big believer in, would eventually pay off if she did the reverse of what Tabitha or Jake would do. Knowing she'd helped the women escape being fucked over by the two people she now hated the most was worth missing out on any power she could have held over them with the evidence. Blackmail wasn't really Candy's thing. She'd always hated Ross and from what she could tell from the footage, he wasn't just a sleazy pest, he was a potential rapist, so it looked like karma had stepped in high on that platform too. It looked like an accident, the way he fell off the balcony when Catherine had fought back against his vile advances, so on balance, she decided that having Helen's guiding help with her new career, now that Tabitha had dropped her, was a better trade-off.

And Helen was already coming through for her, having given her the leading role in tonight's live episode press conference, which she was determined to take advantage of, deciding which members of the press got the best ringside seats. Usually it was strictly forbidden for them to be this close to the action, and they would all remember it was her, Candy Dace, who'd given them preferential treatment, leaving the door open for some useful networking ahead. She'd been scanning social media and had seen she'd featured in many of the reports and shots being filmed behind the scenes, so as promised by Helen, her profile was already on the rise. Yes, she decided to herself, she had done the right thing. As she flicked her eyes over digital media, she saw that on every headline news outlet around the world, #FalconBayTheFarewell was the hottest topic. The show was trending globally on Twitter. Even TikTok, which was usually a bit young for their demographic, had gone into a frenzy of parodies with people acting out their favourite scenes from episodes over the decades – it really was quite intense.

Light entertainment TV show news hosts had been ruminating all day about the risk of the show daring to broadcast fully live, and if this was wise after what happened last Christmas. They questioned whether the show should be running a two-minute delay, should some other tragedy befall the allegedly 'cursed cast', as *Falcon Bay*'s main players had now been dubbed by the media. Candy actually thought that if something unexpected did happen as they played out their final storylines, a delay on the feed was a good idea. She'd been here that day and still remembered the horror of what the world witnessed, but she'd read a memo from 'upstairs' advising it was indeed to be fully live with no delay. That instruction had come direct from the Kane Foundation, so, wanting to impress them, even though she knew the network was about to be sold, Candy emphasised this point with a new press release. It had caused even more publicity and interest from viewers everywhere.

Maybe Chad or Melissa might invite her to go and work

for the Kane Foundation in Louisiana. She'd always felt she'd
go down well in the States, which was why she'd teamed up
with Tabitha Tate in the first place. Even her name, thanks
to her mother's love of sweets, sounded perfect to fit in in LA.
A small frown crossed her frosted peach lips as she thought
about Tabitha's betrayal, but then she remembered she still
had the money from the pictures they'd sold into syndication.
That was enough to get over there and set her up for six
months if she did dare take the leap alone, so she decided to
stay in the present, determined to enjoy her big moment.

She scanned her phone again to see if there were any more
shots of her, hoping if there were, two-faced Tabitha would
see them and realise she hadn't seen the last of Candy Dace.
It might take her a bit longer and she'd have to take a different
route, but she was still determined to make it in the States
and when she did that duplicitous bitch would certainly know
about it.

The press screens were on the wall next to all the world
clocks, which showed the time they were going out in all their
syndication zones, so she could see reports of the live show
being aired all over the globe regardless of what hour of the
day or night it was in the territory. Global networks were
going absolutely crazy for it. In Australia, her friends had said
the gay bars were running 'Falcon Bay' theme nights and she'd
seen at least a hundred Catherine Belle drag queen lookalikes,
all dressed in wedding dresses, tweeting drunken pics as they
geared up to send their idol off. It seemed like at least half
the world was either talking about it or getting ready to
watch them go out with a bang. From A-list stars like Beyoncé
through to the royals. William and Kate had even tweeted it
would be a sorely missed feature from their schedules.

Not everyone was so kind though; some of the trolls had
been posting bets on which actors might fluff a line or stumble

on set. Candy knew that even the slightest mistake would cause extra Twitter trends, so was secretly hoping that there would be several. With her being based in the press pen all evening, it would be her they'd be coming to for quotes, so every fuck-up would boost her new profile as a leading drama show publicist, which in this digital age could only be a good thing.

She'd never planned on being a publicist but she was loving it, and mused about what would have happened if she hadn't spent the last few years sucking off Jake or putting up with moody Dustin and his lame ideas as a lowly assistant producer. When Helen had given her the third set of bad news in a row, of her demotion, following her betrayal by Tabitha and Jake, she'd hated herself for crying in front of Helen, whom she had never liked. If the high-heeled shoe had been on the other foot she'd have taken the opportunity to gloat at Helen, but instead she saw a side to her that she'd never seen before.

After the way Helen had comforted her, she was mad with herself that she'd seen the older women as the enemy before, and looking back could see that that was Jake's brainwashing, which was all behind her now. Tonight was the start of her new life, and what better launch pad than to be at the forefront of what was going to go down in history as one of television's biggest moments? The buzz she felt knowing she had some of the world's most esteemed reporters and online influencers hanging off her every word made her certain that with the esteem and credit of tonight on her CV, this was the very step-up she'd be going after the moment *Falcon Bay* was off-air.

'If you look over the balcony,' she gestured, 'you'll see our star couple have just arrived.' The reporters all swung round together to look and Candy felt the weight of their collective movement sway the platform ever so slightly, which made her

356

feet wobble. 'Please don't lean over the edge,' she said, and they began to sit back as she continued. 'Catherine Belle and Lee Landers will make history tonight for the first time ever for a serial drama, when their characters Lucy Dean and Marcus Lane say 'I do' as part of our plot, and they will actually be legally married at the very same time – isn't that wonderful!'

A round of applause rang out through the press pack, which sent another ripple of powerful excitement up Candy's spine and another wobble through the press galley. She'd borrowed the pink Chanel suit she was wearing from the wardrobe department. Brad, the bitchy stylist, said, when she'd put it on, it made her look like she was in the Reese Witherspoon movie *Legally Blonde*. She knew he meant it as an insult, but the admiring reaction from the faces in front of her made her certain she'd made the right decision, and she felt powerful in it, and power was what she'd learnt television was about. She adjusted the buttons on her jacket to show a bit more cleavage, then smiled as she turned towards the reporters, who had live feeds on their cameras. She knew that people were watching her right now online and on TV station feeds around the world.

'In order for this to happen, the casting team had to seek out an actor who was also legally able to perform ceremonial duties during Catherine and Lee's characters' vows scene, which as you can imagine is a rare combination. But Helen Gold, our head of casting, did a wonderful job in finding David Kartner, a fine actor who also, away from his acting work, loves to help couples legally seal their moments of true love. If you look towards the wedding area stage, you'll see him in character as Lucy Dean and Marcus Lane's registrar on the set. The book on the register beside him is a legally binding ledger and not a prop. Thanks to the clever script

357

and some humanist wedding language options, our director and head screenwriter Farrah Adams have crafted dialogue that allows the characters and the actors to be sealed in matrimony on screen and off – seamlessly.'

She'd decided to throw some namechecks in as, after all, it was the last time she'd be working with these women, and despite being at war for years, they were now on the same side, as part of a secret sisterhood. She also thought it looked good to show she knew exactly what she was talking about as she explained how the legal aspect of tonight's show would work, rather than have to do a barrage of Q&As about it when she already knew time was running short to wrap up before silence would be called for.

'As you all know, in our forty-one years on screen, *Falcon Bay* has consistently provided our loyal viewers with drama unrivalled by any other long-running serial. So as if going fully live with no safety delay wasn't enough excitement, thanks to the love of our leading stars echoing that of our lead characters, we're able to witness the true waving off of the world's favourite couple into the sunset for real. Which those of you who know CITV's history will understand has major resonance with our programme's origin.

'The island of St Augustine's was first bought and chosen as a destination to make quality programming by the husband and wife team Tina and Harry Pearson in the 1960s, who ran it with love for three decades until their sad deaths in the late nineties. And although the network has changed hands several times in the decades since, it is very fitting that we are closing our beloved show's final chapter once again representing the true love and partnership that echoes the very people without whom, none of us would ever have had this wonderful show to cherish and enjoy for nearly half a century. And it goes without saying that tonight our special thoughts will also be with the other family who have brought the same care and love for the show as the original creators into our cast and crew's lives, albeit briefly in terms of their time here, led by the late Madeline Kane. Although sadly no longer with us, she will of course always be a part of our wonderful show's history. She's with us tonight, I have no doubt, in spirit.'

There was a pause at the mention of Madeline's name and as she finished her speech, a couple of younger vloggers that she'd taken extra time to be nice to on their way in started a round of applause. Candy knew the vloggers were the ones with the power these days and had to hold back the smug grin she wanted to break into, knowing that her impassioned speech, which she'd been practising all day and didn't really mean a word of, would probably be trending online for at least an hour before the show aired.

As she made her way back through the packed gantry and down the stairs, she gestured for the others to follow her towards the waiting buggies at the exit doors. They were outside the studio ready to take them on a tour of the exterior sets, as the final tech rehearsal needed absolute silence. As she looked at their faces, the absence of the odious Ross Owen was a welcome relief; he'd have made his presence well and truly known, trying to speak over her and hijack the event with his foul one-liners. He would probably have derailed at least half of her pieces to camera by now and was guaranteed to be the one most likely to ask awkward questions and cause the others to follow suit, just as he had done last Christmas Day. She did, however, think it was bizarre that he, Honey Hunter and Madeline Kane now made up a trio of people to have met horrible fates, which had many fan forums concluding the island was cursed. So, whilst she was relishing the power she'd been given today, she was also rather happy in the knowledge that after the way she'd handled TV's biggest farewell, she'd be leaving St Augustine's before anything bad could happen to her.

If there was a curse, not that she really believed in such things, then it was the perfect time to move on. She didn't like the way that press balcony had moved when they were on it. The last thing she wanted was to be in an accident that might scar her lovely looks, just as she was about to be plastered all over the media. As the gaggle of reporters followed as her six-inch hot pink heels clacked down the stairs, she made a mental note to call maintenance and have it checked before the show went live. She pulled open the door that led onto the gorgeous sand dunes of their beautiful beach, which she'd now be giving the journalists a tour of for the very last time.

Up in the director's box, Farrah was breathing deeply, just like they'd taught her in the Lamaze class she'd been attending online. She'd tried going to one of the group sessions at the local hospital, but she'd felt left out being not only the only single woman, but also the only black woman in the group. She didn't usually think about her race but she certainly felt out of place in the mummy mix. After that she had just logged on sporadically to learn the basics of what to expect.

Thank god she had at least learnt the breathing routine, she thought to herself. She tried to control the contractions that were making her want to rip her Versace leggings off and start the push that would introduce her to her baby, who was clearly more than ready to make his appearance at this very minute. She was banking on the only other thing she could remember from the classes being true, that labour could last several hours. They were due to go live in twenty minutes and would be off-air sixty minutes after that, and with the local hospital being less than thirty minutes away, she was cutting it fine, but she prayed that somehow she was going to be able to do this. As she looked at the monitors and zoomed in on an anxious-looking Catherine, resplendent in her stunning wedding dress, she knew she needed her.

The door swung open, and Amanda and Helen, both wearing bold-coloured dresses with matching high heels, appeared. Amanda took one look at Farrah and knew exactly what was happening.

'Oh my god,' she said, grabbing one of the walkie talkies that would connect her to the medical team downstairs. After last night's surprise dinner with the Kanes, she'd upgraded the team to have a midwife and ambulance on standby the whole day. Helen looked concerned but Farrah snatched the walkie talkie from Amanda's hand and sat back in the director's chair.

'I am not leaving until those credits roll,' she said between deep breaths. 'And I'm borrowing both those outfits when I get my figure back,' she puffed.

Amanda went over to her swivel chair and turned it round so they were face to face. 'Listen to me, that baby is coming whether you like it or not. I can take over the directing. No one even has to know you are not here. We can sneak you out the back and we'll never reveal you missed it,' she said, as calmly as she could whilst eyeing her friend's face. It was etched with an agony she knew only too well.

Farrah swung the chair back to face the monitors and picked up her headset, which would connect her to the camera crew all poised and ready to hear her run them through the last-minute tech check.

'I am not leaving,' Farrah said again between breaths.

'Farrah!' Helen echoed, as Amanda looked at her for help.

'If I have to have this baby on the floor in this room as those credits roll then that's what I will do. I will be damned if seventy minutes of agony is going to stop me directing the show that we all know is hanging by a wire thanks to the Kane family's sudden presence. I will not risk Catherine being further spooked into doing anything that could ruin our futures. Not now Candy has given us the surprise of knowing we're in the clear over the Ross Owen mess. We just can't risk it. Catherine needs to hear me in her ear, to know that I'm up here covering her back, that I'll get her and our show safely off-air. If that means that I have to suffer the feeling that a watermelon is trying to split me open for an extra hour before some doctor can inject me with the most amounts of drugs anyone is legally allowed to administer, then that is what I am going to do. End of conversation.'

Helen and Amanda looked at her face, which was deadly serious. Knowing her as they did, it was clear there was no way they were going to change her mind. Amanda walked over to her and hugged her; Helen did the same.

'It's only because we love you,' Amanda said, looking worried as Farrah gritted her teeth.

Farrah reached for the control desk and pulled up the various shots of the set, which was teeming with actors all ready to hear the word 'action' called for the very last time.

'And I love you, but I'm not budging, so get down there now and check on Catherine. Send one of the ambulance medics up here with me if it will put your mind at rest,' she said, trying to get a smile out of her pained face for Amanda. 'And Dustin can come up. He can handle some of the back-up shots. Will that make you happier?'

Amanda nodded. Then Farrah looked at the clock on the wall, which showed they were only nine minutes from beaming live. If the figures Candy had been tweeting were right, it showed an estimated 150 million viewers were tuning in, and nothing and no one, not even the baby she was so desperate

362

to meet, was going to make her miss this moment. She'd already emailed all the top production companies in America to say she was at the helm. A girl had to think about her future, after all.

Helen and Amanda could see there was no reasoning with her.

'Right, so send them up, and you both get out of here as I need to start!' Farrah said, then flicked on her mic system to talk to the team. 'Cameras at the ready. Give me the pan shot of the bay that will bring us to the pre-shots of Catherine and Lee, and let's get our final show on the road, you wonderful people. Here we go, one last time,' she said, without a hint of the pain she was in.

With nothing left to try to persuade her with, Helen and Amanda left the box and made their way down to the main studio, where they could see Sheena, looking fabulous in another of her silk animal-print catsuits and killer heels, smoking by an open fire door. Pushing their way through the packed crowd they finally reached her.

'How is she?' Sheena asked, raising her eyes towards the director's box whilst taking the last drag on her cigarette then stubbing it out on the studio door. She wouldn't usually have been so disrespectful but as this was the property of the Kane family, she'd have happily burnt it down if she could. The look on Helen and Amanda's faces told her all she needed to know before they could answer.

'That close, huh?'

They nodded.

'How about her?' Helen said, gesturing towards Catherine, who was being held tightly by Lee in the corner of the Cove Bar.

Brad from wardrobe was hovering just feet away from them with a handheld steamer. He was clearly beside himself with worry that the gown the legendary Vera Wang had donated for Catherine's big moment as she and Lucy got married was going to have more creases in it than Princess Diana's when she emerged from that car to walk up the aisle of St Paul's Cathedral. Even the designers of Diana's dress, the Emanuels, had told the world how horrified they were at the state of it, and he didn't want to get in Vera Wang's bad books, especially not when he was about to be unemployed. From the angsty look on his face, Helen could feel his professional pain, but the way Catherine looked right now was less important than her mental state. Sheena was about to fill them in on that, having been the one to visit her condo late last night with the shock news that it was very likely she'd come face to face with Chad Kane on set again tonight.

'She's bizarrely calm, almost too calm,' Sheena said, getting another cigarette out and lighting up. 'She must be back on the Xanax because she was hysterical when I arrived at hers last night to tell her they were both here – so much so Lee actually made me leave, saying only he knew how to calm her down. Whatever that means.'

Amanda and Helen's faces flashed with worry

'Oh yes, she's told him everything, and I mean everything,' Sheena said, taking a huge drag on the cigarette, then holding it in for a moment before she exhaled. 'So he knows exactly what we all did for her, which is a real fucking kick in the teeth after Candy saved our asses in the eleventh hour. We thought it was all over.'

Amanda looked like she was going to faint. Even the worry of Farrah giving birth in the director's box had been washed away by the knowledge that a man outside of their circle knew the secret that could ruin their whole lives. Helen's face wasn't looking too dissimilar to Amanda's either. Her mind was flashing with the idea of losing the one man, the only man, she'd finally decided she wanted to spend her life with; maybe he'd even be the one to arrest her. Her mind was descending into a spiralling pit of worry when Sheena dropped her cigarette on the floor and stubbed it out with her bright red Jimmy Choos, which were the only pop of colour on her with her zebra-print jumpsuit. She pulled them both towards her.

'Look, I can't use the word relax, because obviously we are minutes away from a live broadcast and there's no time to tell you the full saga of how last night went down right now.' She gestured to the clock, which showed they now had only three minutes before Farrah, who they could all see was breathing heavily through the glass window high up in the director's booth, would soon be calling action. 'But I can tell you this, he's not going to derail the ceremony that is going to see him entitled to half of her assets. Did I mention she hasn't signed a pre-nup?'

The women looked aghast but urged Sheena to continue.

'He's not going to be revealing anything during this show. What we have to worry about is him down the line – if they break up, it's a different matter. Judging by the cut I've got of him now, he's more likely to blackmail us into finding him work than with threats to the police. But of course, now he knows, he's as much an accessory to what she did as we are for covering for her. Plus, there's no evidence, as Candy confirmed. Amanda did an excellent job on deleting that underwater footage, so it would be a scorned actor's word against ours. Not great odds for him. So, although here we are once again in yet another hellish situation, I think if we all stay calm we can get through tonight, I really do. We can deal with any other issues her big mouth might have caused us later.'

Helen and Amanda still looked worried but less panicked. Sheena was always blunt and although the news wasn't good it was certainly a lot better than it could have been.

Amanda looked over to Catherine again, who was finally allowing Brad to steam her dress but still had one hand held in Lee's.

'Did she say whether she felt she could hold herself together if Chad comes to talk to her?'

'As you can imagine, she admitted she was terrified of not being able to hold it in, and I'm not exactly wanting to give Lee any credit here, as he's clearly in it for money more than the motives of true love. But before he made me leave, Lee made her a drink and calmed her down, persuading her that their future was more important than the past. He made her swear to put them first and said that a confession would only tear them apart. He told me later by phone that after a few glasses and more tears, she'd promised she would hold it together.' Sheena lit yet another cigarette, knowing that this would be the last one she'd manage to have before all the studio doors were bolted and the red lights would flick on announcing the set was about to go live.

'Will she get through the episode if you think she's back on Xanax? She's got so many massive pieces of dialogue,' Amanda said, her head back in producer mode, hoping Lee's intervention might just have done the trick.

'Look, she's in an understandably emotional state, but she wants to give Lucy Dean the happy ending that the world's been hoping for for nearly half a century.' Sheena paused a for an eye-roll and drag on her cigarette. 'If I was a betting woman, which I am, I'd say forty years of acting enabled her to do the tech run earlier, as if nothing in the world could distract her from those final scenes or her future away from here. I'm confident she's going to pull this off as long as she avoids Chad. Thank god he hasn't been to see her in her dressing room, or on set, hence me hovering here watching like a hawk from the sidelines. So, if we can get her off the island the moment we are off-air and into the car waiting outside, I think we'll be OK.'

Ever quick-thinking, Helen's brain whirled back into work mode. 'I'll tell Candy they're doing no press as they're starting their honeymoon immediately, and you tell them they can't give any comments, or it will damage the mega-bucks wedding deal you've set up.'

'Already done it,' Sheena said with a wink. 'She's pretty hot, Candy. Do you know if she swings my way?'

Amanda was just about to manage a faint smile at Sheena's inappropriate time to be looking for a hook up, when the studio lights flashed, signalling the rollercoaster ride they were all about to go on for the next sixty minutes was about to begin.

Minutes to airing, Melissa and Chad Kane entered the set, taking seats in the chairs laid out for senior producers to watch the filming directly under Farrah's directing box. Before she could comment, the door on the other side of the studio swung open and Jake appeared.

'What the hell?' Amanda said. 'He's been nowhere near this set since that day in the office. I can't believe he's here.'

Jake, wearing his usual skin-tight black jeans, tight T-shirt and leather jacket, strolled through the crowded set high-fiving old crew members he'd known years and shaking hands with male actors he had a history with. It was obvious by the female reaction on the floor that his presence was much less welcome to them. As he reached Melissa and Chad, he took the seat next to them and they briefly exchanged words before he turned his gaze to Sheena, Amanda and Helen, who were still on the edge of the set. He dramatically pointed to the studio clock, which showed twenty seconds until the opening credits would roll.

Amanda eyed the trio curiously, as Jake's directed his words to them.

'Ladies, I may not have organised our show's farewell, but I'm pretty certain that unless there's been even more casting changes since my departure, I don't believe you hags are due to be on screen? So I suggest you move your fat asses off Lucy Dean's Cove set before you ruin the pan shot.' His voice rang out loudly across the set. The women looked to Chad, who they knew to have the most chivalrous approach to women, expecting to see him chide Jake for his disgusting language, but his face remained unmoved. Melissa was the one that spoke.

'Ladies, please,' she said.

Then Farrah's voice boomed out of the speakers, calling, 'Places everyone.'

With no choice, the three women had to exit through the fire door, which would mean they'd have to run round the whole block of sets to get back to the studio floor. As the door closed behind them, Sheena just managed to catch Catherine's eye and mouthed, 'Good luck.' A hazy-eyed Catherine smiled back at her before the door closed, and just as it did Chad got back out of his seat and started making his way towards the director's box.

Chapter 35

Falcon Bay Episode 3025 – The Live Farewell Episode

The first thirty minutes of the show had gone without a hitch. Several build-up scenes had been filmed where characters old and new appeared to tie up old storylines, which would leave *Falcon Bay*'s audiences happy that no one would be left without resolution.

When she'd crafted the script, Farrah had kept in mind the disastrous balcony scene from *Dynasty*. It was how the legendary Aaron Spelling had allowed the original *Dynasty* to come to its end. Its star Dame Joan Collins's character, the scheming Alexis Carrington, had fallen off a balcony, leaving its loyal audience never knowing what had become of a woman they'd loved to hate for so long. Having been an actress before she'd turned to scriptwriting and eventually directing, Farrah had always promised herself she'd never leave an audience hanging like that if a show she was at the helm of was to come to an end.

If she wasn't wrong, she could feel what she remembered the online midwife describing as what must be the baby's head pushing its way downwards, desperately wanting to emerge from her body. Even though she was in absolute agony, and in severe denial, as the scenes played out perfectly one by one, she'd managed to keep her breathing under control, knowing she'd very nearly made it. Even under the added pressure of Chad Kane sitting right beside her, studying the monitors and watching every scene as it went out, she hadn't lost her extremely determined cool.

Chad had been strangely silent throughout, which had only added to the bizarreness of the situation, but with the pain she was in, not having to talk to him had been a blessing. They were coming into what would be their second-to-last ad break and setting up for Lydia's big scene with Lucy Dean, before part four, where the wedding would take place. Suddenly, she felt a flood drench her legs and a pain that made all the other pains she'd been experiencing up until now seem like pinpricks. She screamed out as Dustin rushed over to her, grabbing the walkie talkie. Chad watched silently.

'That's it,' Dustin said, turning to the midwife who, over-awed at the showbiz world she'd never seen, wasn't really paying attention to Farrah's plight despite the fact that she'd been waiting on-hand all day, ready for this moment.

'Get her down those stairs now before it's too late,' Dustin said in a panicked tone that made his voice rise several octaves.

The midwife rushed over, just as Farrah pushed her chair back and slipped down onto the floor, throwing him her headset.

'It's too late,' the midwife managed, finally realising she'd lost her focus. 'Lie on your back and just start pushing,' she said. Farrah, already feeling the desperate urge to push, didn't need telling twice.

'Dustin, this baby is coming now, call down to the team, and take over, quick,' Farrah barked.

Even in her agonised state Farrah could still see they were ninety seconds from being back on air and Dustin was going to have to bring this home. She turned to look at Chad, who looked back at her but again didn't speak.

'Hurry up,' she screamed back at Dustin. He'd made the call down into the set's earpieces and was now in Farrah's director seat, cueing in from the ad break.

'And we're live in twenty seconds, guys.' Dustin tried to remain calm.

Catherine suddenly felt spooked that Farrah's voice was no longer in her ear, but Lee, sensing her mood, was quick to reassure her.

'It will be the baby,' he said, and squeezed her hand.

She took a deep breath and managed a smile, imagining that maybe before she and Lee left for their honeymoon she might get a chance for a quick cuddle with Farrah's new arrival. She was just hoping it didn't look like Jake when Dustin's voice took over her wandering mind.

'We're back on-air and live, people. Three, two, one – action!' he called out.

He studied the monitors showing close-ups of Lucy Dean in her wedding dress, taking one last look at The Cove Bar, when Lydia's character Claudia appeared for one final show-down. After that, Lucy would make the short walk to the boardwalk set where Lee and the rest of the show's characters were set up for the wedding scene. That would take them into the marriage and into Lucy's farewell scene, which would cue the credits rolling.

'Close up on three,' Dustin said.

Two more female medics entered the director's box and got down on the floor with Farrah, who was now biting a towel to stop her screams being heard outside the booth. Chad moved into the seat next to Dustin and watched as Lydia, dressed to kill in a pillar-box red silk dress, which floated as she walked, hit her mark, then the camera went in close and her beautiful face filled the screen.

CLAUDIA RAYMOND

Don't worry, Lucy, I'll take good care of St Augustine's. After all, it's all mine now, so it's in my best interest to make it the best that it can be.

Catherine took in Lydia's outfit, which was clearly designed to take attention away from her own wedding dress, and paused as Lydia delivered her second line.

CLAUDIA RAYMOND

Obviously, I'll be changing the name. The Cove Bar seems so dated, but then again, I guess it is.

She hissed as she came in closer to the cameras that now had the two women in full length, with the stunning backdrop of St Augustine's and The Cove's terrace overlooking the sea behind them. Catherine's 'Lucy Dean' looked sanguine and stayed silent as Lydia's character continued.

CLAUDIA RAYMOND

I've decided to knock the old place down and totally rebuild it. After all it's going to be a new era now that I own everything, so it makes sense to give it a fresh look, something that befits my style. Do you want me to take a photo of it for you now before I demolish it? I understand, what with you being here so long, that these tired old surroundings must be full of memories, so no doubt you'll want a memento of your life on the island that now belongs to me. You can take the Cove sign if you like, it's only going to be firewood anyway.

Sheena watched from the back of the studio. It was sad knowing Catherine was leaving but she couldn't help but feel a thrill from seeing Lydia practically sizzling on screen. She was sure they had a great future working together again. You could see Lydia's hunger for the spotlight from a mile off. As an actress she was right up there with the best of them and Sheena was pleased that now Lydia was back on the McQueen Agency books, although this would be her final appearance on *Falcon Bay*, Sheena would be making sure Lydia Chambers never left the screens again.

Back up in the director's box, Farrah couldn't hold back her screams or her desire to push any longer. With one of the medical team holding her hand and the midwife urging her to follow nature's instructions, with what felt like a sword cutting her in two, suddenly she felt the baby exit her body and fall into the hands of the other nurse who was at her feet.

Dustin, who was queasy at the best of times, fought back the gagging in his throat as he desperately tried to concentrate on bringing the scenes in on time, knowing as they were live, every second was vital. The Lydia and Catherine showdown had taken them to the final ad break. Being so close to the sweeping finale and with no on-screen disasters or missed lines so far, he was confident that even with the chaos going on around him, he could bring this to a close.

Chad, who was still silently watching next to him, hadn't even looked back to see Farrah deliver the baby. One thing

373

that was unsettling Dustin more than being in control of a live show going out to millions was the fact that he couldn't hear Farrah's baby crying. He'd done enough scripts to know that was not a good sign and as a father himself it sent a chill down his spine so cold he didn't dare turn round. Instead, he focused on his earpiece and tried to block out the fear that things may not have gone as they should on the floor behind him.

He cued in Catherine for her big reaction to Lydia's scathing 'winner takes all' speech they'd gone into the advert break on. Hearing 'action' in her ears, Catherine, who always knew how to find the exact light that would illuminate her perfect skin, turned away from The Cove Bar, where she'd spent the last forty years in the viewers' lives, and looked Lydia's character directly in the eye.

LUCY DEAN

I don't need a photo or a sign made of wood, Claudia.

Catherine turned slightly to survey the island she'd called home for four decades, then cast her eyes back to Lydia.

LUCY DEAN

I have a lifetime of memories of my time here. They will be etched in my heart forever. Not you, nor your snide words, can ever take those away from me, so burn the place down if you like. I'll even strike the match for you, because *my Falcon Bay* will always be there in spirit, now and forever.

She delivered the line with a calmness that suggested Lucy really was ready to move on.

374

LUCY DEAN

You know, there was a time when I'd have fought a vengeful, power-mad woman like you to keep hold of all this, Claudia . . .

She gestured around the terrace and the land that came with The Cove Bar.

LUCY DEAN

But those days are over. I'm leaving here with a man who loves me and for a future where I won't have to spend my days facing bitter, jealous bitches like you, who can only find enjoyment in causing misery in other people's lives. So, enjoy everything St Augustine's has to offer you. I just pray that one day you find happiness and not just money here, because I'll tell you one thing: bricks, mortar, sand, sea and all the power you can wield over this island are nothing compared to being with a man you know wants to hold your hand to the end.

The two women faced off as Lydia's character appeared surprised by Lucy's words.

LUCY DEAN

And it seems to me that all you have to keep you warm at night is the temperature around here, but as you're new here, Claudia, you'll find out, it can get cold on *Falcon Bay*, especially when you're all alone.

375

Catherine leaned forward and kissed Lydia on the cheek, leaving a bright pink lipstick mark on her face, which camera four zoomed in on. Then she turned to begin her walk to where Lee and all the wedding guests were positioned on the boardwalk set at the end of the stage by the sea, with the actor playing the marriage celebrant smiling in her direction.

With one last glance, Lucy Dean delivered her final parting shot to Claudia . . .

LUCY DEAN

See, there's a whole crowd of friends and family waiting for me, so I need to be going. I wish you good luck here, Claudia, I've a feeling you're going to need it.

Catherine exits with a smile. Close-up on Claudia's face shows she feels burnt by Lucy's words. Camera 3 focuses on a tight shot of Lucy, genuinely happy to be walking towards her future and away from her past.

Dustin just managed to call 'Cut' in the transition when an almighty cry erupted from behind him. Catherine heard this down her earpiece and her face, which was already beaming, broke into an even more joyous expression knowing a new life was here. Dustin's heartbeat quickened as he spun his chair round to see a tearful Farrah cradling a beautiful baby boy, who was now absolutely making his presence known with what was clearly a powerful set of lungs.

'Oh thank god,' Farrah kept saying over and over again.

The wait whilst the medical team had cleared the baby's throat when he'd stayed silent had felt like hours not moments, and she'd never heard anything so beautiful as the horrendously loud roar he'd finally made when he appeared to spring to life. As she held him close to her skin, she was almost unaware of where she was. The bond she'd heard about, the one Amanda had told her would wash over her the moment she met her baby, was something she'd never really believed, but was a million times more powerful than even that first big kick. She took in his perfect features. He had her colouring but definitely Jake's nose. The rush of love hit her like a force-ten gale. Nothing in the world would make her want to part from him; she was a mother now and suddenly that seemed the most important thing in her life.

Chapter 36

Tabitha Tate was back in the still blood-stained crime scene in upscale Brentwood, Los Angeles, where Dr Durand had held Honey Hunter captive for the last few weeks of his life. She was filming promos for her appearance on an Oprah Winfrey special to coincide with the release of the book, which Mickey had rushed into production with a speed she'd not even known was possible.

She was surprised that the place hadn't been cleaned but it turned out that as Durand had no relatives, the house had been acquired directly by a crime fanatics' organisation. One of the more ghoulish practices in Hollywood was tours of murder houses, so she realised that the evidence of the horror that had gone on in this room was now going to stay this way, at the very least until interest and visitors waned. Then it would be sold to a developer who would do a rebuild that would probably feature on *Million Dollar Listing*. Honey's distress milked for all it was worth by reality TV production companies. But who was she to judge?

She'd had her hair coiffed and make-up done ready for her close-ups in the very bathroom Honey had probably screamed

378

for her life in. She hadn't realised it at the time but Nicole Brown, the wife of O. J. Simpson, had been slain in a home half a mile from here. Also in a quaint little house up in the hills was the place where Marilyn Monroe had taken her own life, nearly sixty years ago. Perhaps Murder Valley was a more appropriate title than Brentwood, she mused, as she touched up her lipstick and re-pencilled her eyebrows. She was definitely not going to be spending any of her book money, which had already run into the millions with advances from foreign sales, buying a place near here, that was for sure.

She'd requested a break during the taping so she could go and watch the live episode of *Falcon Bay* in one of the other rooms in the creepy house. She'd found audio tapes Dr Durant had made of his time spent with Honey, which were almost as chilling as what he'd done to her physically. Mickey assured her Honey was already on the road to recovery, having had reconstructive surgery to undo the damage that had been done to her, but whilst Tabitha had no doubt that LA's finest doctors could restore her beauty, she wondered how on earth she'd be able to recover from what was one of the most chilling and traumatic stories Tabitha had covered in her whole career.

She studied *Falcon Bay* on an old TV screen, watching Catherine Belle walk up St Augustine's beach in the wedding scene. But she couldn't concentrate. She just kept wishing, praying, she could go back in time and had never been so greedy as to tell Mickey that Vlad had found Honey. If only she had given the police her whereabouts instead, Honey might have stood a chance of some privacy. Tabitha was so ill at ease at the way Mickey had been leaking headlines on the flight over of what Honey had been through, without even asking for her consent. She'd tried to reason with herself that she hadn't realised what sort of man Mickey was until it was too late. She felt overwhelmed by guilt that a woman's brutalisation was being capitalised on. She also felt guilty about abandoning Candy. In time she'd like to make that up to her but it would have to wait until the media storm was over, and she was not even fully in its hurricane yet.

'Ten minutes please, Ms Tate.' The director's voice rang out down the hall.

She took one last look at Catherine Belle smiling in her wedding dress. She said to herself that at least one woman was getting a happy ending, then, smoothing down her blue YSL jacket and skinny jeans, checked her make-up in the mirror. She switched the TV off and walked back to film her next interview.

Chapter 37

Back in the director's box, Dustin was looking rather pale as he took in the floor where Farrah lay, which resembled a scene from a horror film. He tried to keep his eyes on Farrah's face, as the sight of blood always made him faint, but it was no good. Once his eyes had taken in the fluids that surrounded her splayed legs, still lying on the floor, he collapsed in his chair and was out cold. The reality of the fact there was no one directing the show suddenly pulled Farrah from her motherly haze and as one of the medics went to attend to Dustin she called out to Chad, who still had his back to her.

'Chad! Signal for Amanda to come up to the box. We're live in two minutes,' she said, gesturing towards the control panel whilst also trying to lean over and grab a walkie talkie from the floor without dropping the baby. Still Chad didn't turn round, but Farrah watched in confusion as he pulled Dustin's headset off his still unconscious head and put it on himself.

'Call Amanda!' Farrah urged as her fingers finally reached the walkie talkie, but he ignored her.

'You don't know what you're doing. We're live in sixty

seconds,' she said frantically. The professional in her was back in the room. She was still cradling the baby as the medic wrapped a blanket around her body to cover her up. Suddenly Chad turned around to face her. His eyes appeared black, like she'd never seem them before; he reached forward and grabbed the handset off her, then leaned back towards the monitors.

'Oh, I know exactly what I'm doing, Farrah. I've waited long enough for this moment,' he said, with his back to her once again as Dustin began to come round. Farrah suddenly felt a terrible foreboding wash the joy of childbirth away from her. As Dustin began to wake up and his eyes focused, she tried to catch his attention but Chad was on him immediately.

'Get this back on and cue the final scene,' Chad barked, thrusting the headset back towards him. He stood up from his seat to move behind Dustin, who did as he was told, although he still felt faint. He clicked the connect button to the cast and began what would be the final set of cues to start the cameras rolling on *Falcon Bay*'s last ever scene.

Down on the set, Amanda was seated next to Jake and Melissa in the viewing row; none of them had spoken a word as the show had so far gone to plan. She'd held back several tears knowing such a huge chapter in her life was minutes from being over, but one look at Dan, who'd been standing in the corner of the studio with a sleeping Olivia in his arms to give her moral support from afar, had helped keep her from breaking down. The thought of getting in the car with them later that evening and driving away from all this stress and into their new lives was what had kept her calm. When she'd heard Dustin's voice take over from Farrah in her earpiece, and later the definite first screams of a gorgeous infant's arrival, she'd actually felt relieved and knew that the moment the credits rolled she'd rush right upstairs to meet Olivia's half-brother and see how Farrah was.

As they sat just inches apart, she thought about how her and Jake's lives had played out on this island. It hadn't all been bad, and despite Jake's vile comments when he'd made his arrival earlier, she knew how much pride he'd taken in the show. It would be eating him up knowing his time here was up and they were just minutes from being off-air forever. So she resisted the urge to dig back at him.

On the other side of the studio, watching from the wings, she could see Helen with Matt's arms around her waist. Sheena stood with them all, getting ready to witness their friend Catherine say 'I do', on screen as well as in real life. The women all caught each other's eyes and smiled. It was nearly over and they'd made it. Together. Their friendship had survived to the bittersweet end.

The cast took their places on the beautifully decorated board-walk. Another lump appeared in her throat when she realised that with all the drama that had been going on since the last-minute arrival of the Kanes, she'd almost forgotten that, along with the world, she and her friends were about to see their beloved friend get married. Despite the madness of it all, it suddenly struck her that this was a very special moment indeed. She looked down at her engagement ring and imagined saying 'I do' to Dan as soon as the divorce from Jake was finalised and suddenly, she couldn't stop smiling. Jake watched her out of the corner of his eye, then flicked his gaze away. Aware she had perhaps been a bit insensitive, she decided to speak to Melissa as the sounds of the final advert played out – before the red lights would appear on the cameras beaming them live to the world for their grand finale.

'It's gone so well, hasn't it? I'm so glad we're going out on a happy ending,' she whispered.

Melissa, who hadn't spoken the whole way though the show, slowly turned towards her. 'It isn't over yet,' she said in her deep Louisiana drawl.

Assuming she was worried that something could still go wrong, like a glitch, Amanda leaned in to reassure her. 'Oh, we'll be fine, if anything technical was going to go wrong it would have happened by now,' she said with a smile.

Melissa stared her darkly in the face. 'That's not what I meant,' she said, then turned back towards the stage where Catherine was set to make her entrance and walk towards Lee for the exchange of vows.

There was no time for Amanda to push Melissa further. But as Dustin's countdown filled her ears, the feeling of joy she'd had moments before was suddenly replaced with a nervousness at Melissa's strange tone. She turned to look to at Jake for a reaction but he was staring at Catherine, and with Dustin's voice once again in her ear calling action, all she could do was do the same.

Falcon Bay Scene 19, the final scene, exterior Cove

Lucy Dean walks down the stunningly decorated boardwalk towards where Marcus Lane, along with the registrar and all of their friends and family, are standing together waiting for her inside the wedding chapel set.

In Catherine's head, all she could think about was how handsome Lee looked. She had to carefully navigate the gaps in the boardwalk in Lucy Dean's wedding shoes, which were taking her and the character she'd played for all these years to their happy-every-afters. On a huge screen above the wedding booth, a montage of Lucy's life on the show was intermixed with pictures of her and Lee from when they first played a couple over twenty years ago. It was so beautifully done, it made tears want to well up in her eyes. But Brad, whom she could see crying in the wings, had made her swear that she wouldn't let her make-up run, so she swallowed down hard and blinked them away.

She was so happy, even with the upset of knowing the Kanes were on set watching. She hadn't been able to quash the feeling of freedom she felt knowing that in just a few minutes' time she'd be Mrs Lee Landers and the wonderful Lucy would be Mrs Lane. They'd both leave the island and all its good and bad memories behind for a new life. It just felt so right.

She barely allowed herself to think of the horrible events that had happened in this very spot the Christmas before, when she'd believed that fighting to the death to stay on this show was worth it. She now knew it wasn't. With the knowledge from the girls that the Ross Owen incident was never going to be raised again, she really did feel free, confident that nothing from her past could now ruin her future. As Dustin called 'action' in her ear, she was truly ready to give the performance of her life, for the very last time.

'Pan shot wide on the bay.' Dustin's voice filled the earpieces, and then 'Close-up on Catherine and Lee' was all she heard before she could see the studio manager's arm cueing her to speak.

She manged one sneaky look towards where she knew her best friends were in the studio – after all, this was a special moment. After catching their faces for the briefest of looks, she switched into full Lucy Dean mode and let her eyes fall upon Lee, who looked ravishingly handsome in his white linen suit. He was stood by the wedding bower.

REGISTRAR

Welcome everyone. We are here today, in this special place, to celebrate the union of two people who lost each other once but are now firmly reunited and have chosen to spend the rest of their lives together.

As the cameras captured the expressions on the cast's faces, tears streamed all over the world from viewers who'd been waiting a lifetime for Lucy to get her happy ending. Households had held viewing parties. Those who had dressed as Catherine in wedding dresses were sobbing in bars where they'd congregated to watch the grand finale. Even in old people's homes, communal television rooms were packed with residents who'd grown old watching the show, all tuned in to watch the soap stars who felt like members of their real family. Fans all over the world were on the edge of their seats, ready to cheer with sheer joy for a character they'd emotionally invested so much of their lives in as she finally sailed off into the sunset with a man who loved her. Though they'd miss the show being part of their lives, they found comfort in knowing that Catherine had found true love in her real life, and although she'd be gone from their screens, like a relative they'd miss, they knew she was going to be in good hands.

The press den above the stage, filled with the hardest of hacks, was also a surprisingly emotional place. Even Candy was feeling tearful as she watched their eyes, transfixed, on the upcoming moment where forty-one years of TV history were about to come to an end. Online was awash with love for the episode with critics already calling it 'the perfect ending'. She smiled as she sat back along with the press team to see the last moments where Lucy would finally say farewell.

'Camera three on a close-up of the registrar.' Dustin's voice filled Amanda's ear as she watched on, still feeling uneasy about Melissa's strange comment, but determined not to let her worry infect the big finale. After all, there were just minutes till one of her best friends was about to say 'I do'.

Here we go, she thought as she and the girls exchanged excited looks again.

REGISTRAR
Before we begin the vows that our beloved couple have written themselves, is there anyone here who objects? Please speak now or forever hold your peace.

In the script, the local handyman Adam Roscoe was supposed to cough, provoking a ripple of laughter amongst the residents of St Augustine's before the registrar would call for Lucy to begin her vows first, in a break from tradition and a nod to female empowerment thanks to Farrah's fabulous script. But just as Adam, who as ever liked to milk his part, leaned towards camera three, which he knew was the best angled profile shot, a loud crackling sound rang out of the studio's speaker systems.

'Shit!' Amanda said, knowing it was so loud it would have been broadcast.

She turned to Jake and then Melissa for a reaction, but neither looked back at her. On set, Adam looked thrown and Catherine and Lee, both determined a technical fault wasn't going to ruin their big moment, geared up to carry on. But before Catherine, who had turned to hold Lee's hand as the cameras zoomed in on them, could speak, Chad Kane's familiar Louisianan tones echoed over the studio floor, out of every speaker on set.

'I know a reason why this ceremony will not be taking place.' His familiar voice boomed out as his face suddenly

387

appeared via a web camera in the director's box projected onto the screen above the wedding booth, which had been displaying the Lucy and Lee montage. Chad's handsome face was now on camera and in view of the audience alongside the cast, being beamed live to television screens around the world.

Amanda felt the breath leave her body as the confusion of what was happening started to turn to stomach-churning nausea as Jake and Melissa turned towards her with broad smiles.

'I told you it wasn't over,' Melissa hissed with menace.

Jake leaned in towards Amanda. 'I just want you to know, oh wifey dear,' he sneered, with a massive grin spreading across his villainous face, 'you brought all of this on yourselves.'

Still breathless, Amanda remained silent with shock as he snatched her studio headset roughly from her head then strode off with Melissa towards the edge of the stage, just off camera. The whole of the cast and studio floor crew looked panicked and unclear as to what to do with what looked like an imminent stage invasion. Up in the press pen, everyone's eyes were on stalks. Sheena, who'd been at the back of the studio, could be seen running towards the set, where Catherine was physically shaking in her wedding gown, looking terrified on the stage. But Sheena couldn't reach her. Thanks to a signal by Jake, she was held back by two security guards who'd grabbed her roughly.

Helen's face turned white, and her mouth went dry as she witnessed what was happening. Matt, whom she'd invited to watch the grand finale, whispered in her ear, asking her what was going on. Next to them, Dan was desperately signalling towards Amanda, trying to catch her attention, but her focus was fully on the still trembling Catherine Belle.

Twitter, which was projected onto a huge screen in the press pit, exploded with #WTF hashtags and shark emojis. Candy and the press team scanned it before returning their open-mouthed gaze back to the stage to witness Lee desperately trying to push the service part of the show on, determined to get the ceremony validated.

'We want to be married, just say we are married,' he said, using his own accent, forgetting the one he used for his character Marcus. The registrar looked around, waiting for a signal as to what to do, but all eyes were now on Chad on the screen above them.

'Say we are married!' Lee shouted, forcing the ring onto Catherine's shaking hand. 'Look, we do, we do!'

'There'll be no wedding here today for Catherine Belle, and no happy ever after,' Chad said from the screen, his eyes burning black as coals.

The cast and crew looked around again; everyone was confused as Catherine began to cry.

Lee, realising that the secret Catherine had confided in him months earlier was about to come back and bite her as hard as the shark that had snapped Madeline Kane in two, knew that it was now or never to be legally entitled to half of her estate in the divorce that would inevitably follow tonight's disaster.

'Just say I do before it's too late,' he said frantically, jostling her body towards the panic-stricken registrar.

Catherine's face paled at the mercenary expression on his face as Lee gestured to the registrar again. 'We do, right? We do! Have you got that? Write it down and just say we are married,' he barked in a frenzy, looking deranged.

Brad watched in horror from across the stage as realisation dawned on Catherine's face. Her heart looked as though it was breaking.

On the screen above them, Chad continued.

'Nine months ago, in this very place, Catherine Belle killed my wife.' His voice was full of rage, but his tone remained controlled.

Gasps rang out amongst the crew, in the studio and in living rooms all over the world. Dan rushed over to Amanda's side as more hell broke loose in the press gallery, with journalists and bloggers live streaming from the balcony – which Candy had made clear was strictly prohibited. Clearly, all rules were off tonight.

'It wasn't like that!' Catherine screamed down on the stage, her face contorted in tears as she looked around, trapped, to find all eyes on her. The cameras zoomed closer from every direction.

Jake was smirking at the side of the stage, with a triumphant-looking Melissa stood next to him.

'But she wasn't alone in what she did,' Chad continued as an audible gasp filled the room. 'In this studio right now are four other women, just as guilty as she is – guilty of helping her hide the fact that she'd taken my wife's life. Madeline was the most loving and caring woman in the world and tonight I am here to get justice for her. What happened wasn't a tragic accident – it was murder.'

Helen felt bile rise in her throat as she let go of Matt's hand. Up in the director's box, Farrah, still on the floor, was clinging to her baby, just feet away from Chad, but unable to do anything other than watch helplessly as he instructed a white-as-a-sheet Dustin to roll what looked like some sort of night vision security camera video of Catherine and Sheena into the edit suite.

Silence filled the studio as footage of the Kane mansion's vast terrace began to roll. Footage of a hysterical Catherine, screaming about killing Madeline, and of Sheena shaking her, stating that if she confessed, she'd be taking Farrah, Amanda, Helen and herself down with her for helping to cover it up.

As Sheena and Catherine's crystal-clear voices in the grainy scenes were beamed live across the world, faces in living rooms dropped. Silence even fell on social media platforms too as people stopped posting, needing to focus instead on the carnage unfolding in front of them.

By the time the CCTV footage ended and the screen above the wedding party went blank, Chad had made his way down to the studio floor, to the sound of Jake doing a slow clap, which echoed in the sudden silence. Jake only stopped once Chad had reached Catherine on set. She was sobbing alone at the altar, as everyone, even Lee, had now stepped away from her.

Chad's handsome face and impressive frame joined Catherine on the screen. Dustin, whom Chad had threatened he would ruin if he dared take them off-air, had no choice but to move to a wide shot, which took in the full horror of Catherine's expression as she threw herself down at Chad's feet, splitting the material on her beautiful dress, and looked up at him, mascara-streaked tears streaming down her face.

'I wanted to tell you. I tried to tell you so many times at the funeral, that's why I came,' she began, her body racked with sobs and her words tumbling out.

With a swift back of her heel into the balls of the security guard who was holding her, Sheena managed to break free. As he yelped with pain, she ran across the studio floor onto the stage and got between Catherine and Chad. Dustin panicked and switched cameras, as Sheena's presence now needed a three shot.

'Listen, I know it looks bad,' Sheena began, 'but what you saw on that tape isn't what it sounds like. She was out of her mind on drugs, she still is, I was just saying that to . . .'

Chad cut her off before she could finish.

'Save your lies for the courtroom.'

'They are not lies,' Sheena shouted at the top of her voice in frustration. Aware she wasn't winning, she decided to change tack. 'Chad, you don't know what Madeline was trying to do to Catherine, I doubt you even knew what your wife was really like at all, she wasn't the innocent party here!'

Chad eyeballed her with pure hatred.

'Well, she's the only one of this party who is dead, I know that!' he roared. 'And you know she's dead because of her,' he snarled in Catherine's direction. 'All of you played a part in it,' he said, his eyes scanning around the room. He'd briefed the security guards he'd flown in from New Orleans, moments before he'd set his plan in action, so they were ready when he called out his instructions.

'Bring the others out here.'

Helen, Amanda – holding Olivia – and Farrah, who, when Sheena had appeared on the stage, had struggled down the stairs from the director's box clutching her baby, were all escorted onto the stage by Chad's team, straight into the world's media glare.

Catherine's sobs turned into screams as the reality of how her actions were about to affect her friends' lives sunk in, but Sheena's face filled was filled with rage as Chad's minions closed in on her once more.

'She's dead because your wife was a fucking evil bitch who brought everything she got on herself!' she shouted, then looked for and found the camera that she knew would capture the best shot of her. Even thirty years since she'd last been on TV screens as an actress herself, she still knew exactly how to land a line down the lens and into millions of homes around the world with a sniper's precision. 'Viewers, don't believe what you've seen tonight, there's so much more to this than it seems . . .' she began as Chad's face flushed with colour, enraged by her attempts to control the situation.

Sensing she had only moments before she'd be cut off, Sheena chose her words carefully.

'Madeline wasn't who you all think she was. She came here last year with one mission – revenge on Catherine – and it went horribly wrong – for her. That's how she ended up dead. The rest we can explain, but there is much more to this story than you can ever imagine.'

The security men began to drag her away from the cameras, but Sheena fought back and continued, this time looking at Chad.

'And if you're so sure of what you're saying, Chad, why have you waited all this time to accuse us, and why do it like this?' She gestured with her one free arm around the stage.

There was a beat of silence. All eyes were on the two of them now – Sheena's tone had ended with an authoritarian touch to it, which had been her exact intention. Despite the footage, which she knew looked damning, she was already trying to work out how to justify it in her head. This was a desperate attempt make Chad look insane; she knew only too well the power of spin, and at this moment in time, a moment she'd been dreading since they'd gone to that damn funeral, anything was worth a shot. She'd swear on a Bible that she'd been dubbed if it saved her from a prison sentence.

Chad wasn't falling for it though. He dropped his tone to match hers and addressed the same camera she'd used.

'Oh, I could have done it sooner, but I asked myself, how would Madeline do it, how would she like her justice to be served? And that's when I knew that this was it – on live TV, just like when you killed her! Now the whole wide world knows what vile, monstrous women you are, and there nowhere left to hide.'

Cameras whizzed around; everything was still being broadcast.

'But now my wait is over. It's time for you to pay for what you've done, all of you,' Chad said as the rest of the women, still being held back, looked at each other, horrified at just how bad the situation they were in was.

Still in her beautiful costume, Lydia Chambers was watching from the wings, a single tear dripping down her perfectly made-up face. It wasn't because of what had happened to Madeline. Seeing Sheena, her only true hope of a future beyond Falcon Bay, still wrestling with the burly guards, and knowing she was now alone and on the outside once more, was what had caused her to cry.

Above Lydia, Candy took a deep breath, smoothed down her bright pink suit and steadied herself in the press pit. The full enormity of what had just unfolded – which she'd be dealing with – had finally hit her. These were not women she wanted to be associated with, that was for sure. Her mind flashed back to when she'd told Helen she hadn't kept copies of what was on Ross's phone, which of course she had. The first thing she was going to do when she got home was move it to a safer location and in the meanwhile pray that none of them brought his death into this mess. Like Sheena, she was not designed for prison. With a real-life plot twist like this, all bets were off.

But there was no time to let her mind wander as to what she might or might not do with that footage in the future, as her eyes were drawn back to Chad. It appeared tonight's car crash wasn't fully over, as he took a step towards one of the cameras.

'Viewers, my wife loved this show and wanted to save it for you, so I am sorry you've had to find all this out this way.' Chad thought back to the night of the horrendous dinner party with his father. He'd never had any reason to thank him for anything in his life before now, but had his vile behaviour not prompted Chad to storm out onto the terrace to grieve alone on the night of Madeline's funeral in Louisiana, he would never have overheard what had really happened to the woman he'd have crawled across hot coals to protect. Once he knew not only that her death was no accident but also what the women had used to control Madeline, he knew the time for him to finally share his truth had also come.

'Although I will never get my wife back, I hope she would approve of the way I have done things tonight. There is more left to say about why they did what they did to her,' he said, looking up at Madeline's photo, which Dustin, again under strict instruction from Chad, had projected onto the screens above the stage. 'To get true justice for her I must share it all,' he said, still intently addressing viewers worldwide who were watching the biggest car crash of TV history.

Melissa, who was now directing Dustin via the headset Jake had snatched from Amanda, told him to switch to a mix of wide and close up shots to make sure all the women's faces were on screen as Chad cleared his throat to speak once more. Now he'd had had his moment of retribution, with the women's fates now seemingly sealed, despite his huge frame and anger- filled face, he seemed broken. Seeing Chad's eyes were full of tears, Jake gestured for one of the crew to wave and make it clear that camera two was the one on him. Chad paused for a moment, trying to regain his composure. He looked back at Madeline's photo one last time, took a deep breath, then turned back to the lens.

'I was always proud of my wife,' he said heavily, 'but she had a secret that she wasn't proud of, though she should have been. These women used that secret against her. The truth is, they killed her because she was different . . .'

An irate Sheena knew exactly what was coming, and how damning the repercussions of it on their reputations would be. Whatever might happen in a legal system she could possibly quash, but the court of global cancellation would be even harder to survive than nylon sheets and porridge.

She thrashed in the security guard's hold, shouting out in pure anger, but all mics on her side of the stage were turned off, meaning no one could hear her protesting as Chad's tear-filled eyes continued to stare out to the audience as he damned them to the world.

'So I'm no longer going to hide her past from you, because to do that would mean that I was ashamed to love her, and I wasn't. I was lucky to love her. They discovered she wasn't born into the woman's body I married her in.'

Another deafening silence filled the studio as Chad's words sunk in. Even Jake's smirk, which had been in place from the moment it had all kicked off, quickly now turned to shock. Candy watched the hacks and bloggers salivate as their posts, mixed with the public's comments, sent social media ablaze. Within seconds, Sheena's fears of what Chad's revelations and accusations could do to them were trending all around the world.

'I want it to be known,' Chad continued, 'that my wife, Madeline Kane, was more of a lady than any one of the monsters who blackmailed her with her past and ended her life. Now, the truth of how incredible she was, and what she and others like her have to go through just to be themselves, is out there. I want the whole world to know not only how brave she was and they are, but also just how evil her killers are.'

A sob rose up in Chad's throat, and just as he finished, police descended on the set and began taking over from the security guards. Quick as a flash, as two armed officers marched Catherine and Sheena towards the others, Jake strode across the stage and snatched the baby from Farrah's arms and Olivia from Amanda's exactly as the police reached the women. Farrah's screams were muffled as she and the others were handcuffed and led away. Helen looked back at Matt, who was staring at her in disbelief. Dan was looking at Amanda with tears in his eyes. Within seconds the women were out of view, leaving Jake and Chad centre stage amongst a cast who didn't know where to look and cameramen who were on autopilot, as if filming amongst the wreckage of a plane crash. That wasn't far off what they and the world had witnessed tonight.

Jake held both the children close to him and smiled. He knew this was a TV-gold moment. He was also revelling in the knowledge of finally knowing what the bitches used to make Madeline fire him with. Whilst he'd certainly never imagined it was anything this dramatic, and he would never in a million years have believed she hadn't always been a woman, he didn't really care about that – he just felt smug knowing she hadn't wanted to fire him after all. It was something that had never sat well with him, as they had always got on, and even knowing what he'd found out tonight, if she was still alive, and if she'd have finally given in to his advances, he'd have fucked her in a heartbeat.

Dragging his mind back from the dead Madeline Kane's sexy body, and reminding himself they were still live on air, he quickly realised that the revelation about her past meant she would soon be connected to the gender wars, one of, if not the hottest topics trending globally right now. So many celebrities and TV network controllers had waded into the argument and been cancelled for saying the wrong thing – Jake often couldn't really see what the big deal was himself, but he knew what an opportunity this was for him to seize, and couldn't resist a line down the barrel of the camera whilst Chad, clearly emotional at the success of his plan coming together, had gone quiet.

He cast his eyes towards ashen-faced Duncan up in the director's galley and signalled to him to keep rolling, then found his camera.

'Dear viewers,' he began calmly, his tone sombre and serious, with as much sincerity as he could muster. 'I truly don't know what to say to all of you who have witnessed the shocking scenes from this evening. They have of course affected us all deeply, and we must go off-air immediately to deal with the true casualties of these terrible revelations. I of course had no knowledge that my former wife, or any of her colleagues, including the star of our show, a woman we all thought we knew, Catherine Belle, were involved in the tragic death of our network owner and Falcon Bay's newest star, Madeline.

'I had the great privilege to know her, and the hugest respect for her while she was alive. I already knew she was truly a remarkable lady, but now, so much more so than any of us realised. As everyone knows, diversity is paramount in CITV's foundations, so to have heard the horror of what happened to this magnificent woman, my heart truly breaks for anyone, anywhere in the world, who has been persecuted just for being different. Obviously, there will be a trial and the truth of what really happened that tragic night last Christmas will finally come to light, and so I pledge to you, our wonderful viewers, that we as a team will do everything we can to assist in justice being done.'

The cameras kept rolling as Jake paused to readjust his grip on the children, turning them towards the lens. 'Please rest assured,' he continued, 'that we will take care of everyone here, on screen and off. Helplines will be made available for those of you who need to talk about what you've witnessed tonight, and it goes without saying that I will take custody of both my children whilst their wicked mothers are punished for their crimes.'

Dustin could tell when the end of one of Jake's speeches was coming from a mile off, and on his last word, he switched the stage shot to Falcon Bay's now infamous logo, and flicked the switches that would take them off-air.

6 months later . . .

The pavement that led to the Royal Court in the heart of St Helier, Jersey's oldest courthouse, was packed. Five police wagons arrived, and officers formed a chain to hold back the jeering crowds, made up of rival groups, who were being held apart to stop the tensions from boiling over. On one side, activists held up signs that read 'stop killing trans women'. Others held up pictures of Madeline with a halo superimposed above her head. On the other side, rival campaigners waved placards reading 'only real women bleed' and 'trans women are men'.

The noise from the crowds of onlookers was thunderous. In front of them, lapping up the circus, were a gaggle of photographers, die-hard fans of Falcon Bay wearing T-shirts with slogans including 'Catherine Belle is innocent', as well as a huge press pack. Ahead of about a dozen reporters, all doing pieces to the camera, stood Tabitha Tate, dressed in a smart black Gucci trouser suit. She was reporting live for the American network where, ever since her book on Honey Hunter had been a New York Times bestseller, she was now based, anchoring their top-rated weekly crime investigation show.

As the doors of the wagons opened, Helen, Catherine, Sheena, Farrah and Amanda emerged. Flash bulbs went off, blinding them as the crowd shouted vile slurs, mixed in with cheers. The world's press documented every moment of the madness. The build-up to today's first appearance, which even the international broadsheets were calling the trial of the

399

century, had been the story of the year from coast to coast and country to country.

The women were led separately down the long walk towards the court, each handcuffed to a female officer. They saw each other for the first time since they'd been arrested in front of the world, and as their eyes met, each had a look of terror. The noise of the crowd was deafening, and reporters shouted questions in their direction. Catherine was almost grateful that the press helicopters hovering overhead were so loud they were almost cancelling out the angry chants, but she could make out enough words to know that they were bad.

Moments later, finally in courtroom number one, they were placed side by side in the dock, so close they could touch. Their handcuffs had been removed, but under the watchful eye of the court's security, all they could do was look ahead as Judge Walker entered the courtroom with his usual arrogance. He'd been shipped in from the mainland as this was a high-profile trial and his demeanour showed that he was going to enjoy every moment of it.

The bailiff solemnly said, 'All rise.'

There was shuffling from the public gallery as people jostled for position for the best view of the five women.

'Catherine Belle, you are charged with the manslaughter of Madeline Kane,' the judge said, looking at Catherine. Devoid of any make-up, she looked like a shell of the woman who'd been on the front cover of every paper for the last six months. He then looked along the line and continued, 'Helen Gold, Amanda King, Farrah Adams and Sheena McQueen, you are all charged with perverting the course of justice. How do you all plead?'

The women finally turned to each other and held hands as they prepared to deliver their answers – answers that would determine the destiny of the rest of their lives . . .

Acknowledgements

In my own career in the television and agenting industry, I've been up close and personal with some of the biggest stars who appear on your screens nightly, and behind the scenes of most of your favourite long-running dramas that you've been watching for decades . . . so when they say write about what you know, let me tell you, in *Guilty Women* and its prequel *Ruthless Women*, I really have . . .

On a legal note, I'm duty bound to tell you that my books are entirely fictional (and whilst my own artists were mainly delightful, and many of their bosses have become friends for life, believe me when I say the 'Jake Monroes' of this world exist, as do the fabulously feisty women who fight back against them, and of course the odd sassy female showbiz agent or two . . .) What you read in my books truly is a peek behind that camera lens, dressing room, studio or even bedroom door where some of the real drama from your favourite soap operas is really going down . . . I'll let you guess who might have inspired me the most, but if you ever spot me in a bar, come over and say hello, and after a cocktail or two I may just tell you! Until then, keep reading, and keep wondering . . .

Firstly, I would like to thank my agents, Jason Bartholomew and Joanna Kaliszewska at the BKS Agency for constantly believing in me and fighting my corner back in the days when no one else would. It often takes many years to become an 'overnight bestselling success,' and a bit like an iceberg, most people only ever see the tip of the work that goes into keeping 'The Melanie Blake Ship Afloat' so hats off to both of you, and to the ever-fabulous Tory Lynn-Pirkis who always believed I could re-invent 'the blockbuster' – Tory, you rock.

Second on the honours list are Laura Palmer, Dan Groenewald and their team at Head of Zeus who published my previous book *Ruthless Women* in hardback and gave me my dream, my first *Sunday Times* bestseller. Without your hard work, *Guilty Women* would not exist. Thank you for everything, we shall be forever friends and always 'Ruthlessly related!'

As you'll have read in my novels, my leading ladies are not afraid to 'reinvent their wheels' (or faces, ha ha) so that brings me to my wonderful new team at HarperCollins, who, steered by the fabulously talented Phoebe Morgan and her wonderful colleagues Elizabeth Burrell, Emma Pickard, Amy Winchester, Isobel Coburn, Sarah Munro, Amber Ivatt and Holly MacDonald are steering me and *Guilty Women* into new uncharted territories! Phoebe, thank you for not only your skill and patience but also believing in my ability to tell a bigger story than perhaps I dared to believe I could. I've learnt so much from you, and will forever appreciate you pushing me to, I hope, achieve my finest work so far. I'm so proud of the book we've created. I hope everyone loves it as much as we do!

Without the support of some fabulous people in the media, yet again I wouldn't be in the position I am. I am living my dream of having you read my work because you might have seen me in one of their publications or platforms where they've supported me through thick and thin, giving my books 'air time' in a world where often so many 'literary' doors are closed for the likes of a working class author like me. So, in no particular order . . . Thank you to Caroline Waterstone, Gemma Aldridge, Alison Phillips, Gary Jones, Karen Cross, Lisa Jarvis, Emma Jones, Dermot McNamara, Michelle Darlow, Claire O' Boyle, Julia Davis, Sally Morgan, Carl Greenwood, Duncan Lindsay, Jack White, Charlotte Seligman, Emma Morris, Zoe West, Claire O'Boyle, Becky Want, Nicola Jeal and the gorgeous Rylan Clark. I'll be forever grateful for your support and friendship.

We must now raise the curtain for the wonderful actresses who put their faith in me to guide their careers and lives, on and off screen, to take a bow. I would never have been in this position of knowledge to be able to 'craft these tales' without them, so ladies, even a dozen standing ovations could never be enough . . . Thank you Claire King, Beverley Callard, Stephanie Beacham, Gaynor Faye, Sherrie Hewson, Patsy Kensit, Adele Silva, Amanda Barrie, Stephanie Waring, Jennie McAlpine, Danniella Westbrook, Samantha Giles, Claire Sweeney, Carol Harrison, Gillian Taylforth and Emily Lloyd.

Some were only in my life a short time, for others we are still together twenty-five years later, and some I've not listed at all...Either way, every one of them helped make me the woman I am today, and gave me the insight to take you, my dear readers, behind that barbed wire covered velvet rope . . .

I'd also like to thank all the book bloggers and book club hosts who have been so supportive; I really love how often you take the time to let me know what you think of my novels!

To my forever friends, without you, I'm nothing. My double A team – Amanda Beckman and Angela Squire, you two are simply irreplaceable. ❤

And finally, to my much loved crew, Coleen Nolan, Nicky Johnston, Matthew Tortolano, Carl Stanley, Sally O'Neil,

Daniel Cocklin, Elaine Stoddart, Sally Lindsay, Lesley Reynolds, Aamer Khan, Moiya Saint, Amanda Bragnoli, Cindy Weinert, Chantelle Sheehan, Claire Richards and Reece Hill, Sharon Marshall, Saira Khan, Caroline and David, Jon McEwan, Nick Patrick, Kate and Michelle Brookes and everyone else who wishes to remain unnamed – thank you!

So that's it for now, just one request from me if I may . . . if you've enjoyed *Guilty Women*, please tell your friends about it (no spoilers!) as it's those bestseller flags that keep these books being commissioned, so if you want to know what happens next, spread the *Ruthless* and *Guilty Women* word!

And I love to hear from you, so come and find me on social media: I'm on Twitter @MelanieBlakeUK, Instagram @melanieblakeuk or over on my website www.melanieblake online.com – please do say hello! Thanks again, and lots of love from Melanie Blake xxx